W9-BVW-750
DARK
MESSIAH

MARTIN CAIDIN

BAEN
BOOKS

DARK MESSIAH

This is a work of fiction. All the characters and events portrayed in this book are fictional, and any resemblance to real people or incidents is purely coincidental.

A Baen Books Original

Baen Publishing Enterprises
P.O. Box 1403
Riverdale, N.Y. 10471

ISBN: 0-671-72022-8

Cover art by Ken Kelly

First printing, November 1990

Distributed by
SIMON & SCHUSTER
1230 Avenue of the Americas
New York, N.Y. 10020

Printed in the United States of America

This book is for
Vicki Oloffson

TO LIVE YOU ONLY HAVE TO DIE

"A hundred years ago you would have been a witch," Stavers said.

"I'm a witch *now*. The uniform is different and the knife is antiseptic," Rebecca Weinstein answered.

"And you've got all that good machinery, monitors, lasers—"

"And knowledge," she broke in. "Along with experience."

"Can you kill a man on your operating table?"

"*Could* I do that? Why on earth would I—"

"No questions for answers. An answer, please."

"If I *had* to, but—" She sensed a change in mood, a hard and serious vein behind his easy flow of words. This man by her side; a professional killer all his life. She was in the midst of casual death. She laughed to herself. *And I thought I was the tough cookie in the operating room!*

She took a deep breath. "Yes. Yes, I could."

"You're learning fast. You didn't give me a vacuous explanation to go along with your answer. I like that."

She made a swift stab to trap him. "Do you have someone in mind you want me to, ah, terminate on the table?"

"Yes."

The single word came so softly, velvety sibilant.

"But—*why!*"

"So this man can know death. And then be brought back to life with that knowledge. It's critical for him to do so."

She studied this strange, frightening, charismatic man. "You have somebody in mind for this, ah, experiment?"

"It's not an experiment. It's life-*and*-death. You will never for an instant forget that I said *and*, not, *or*."

"I'll remember." *Goddamn him. I'll play his game*— "Who do you have in mind?"

"Why," he smiled, "me, of course."

Novels by MARTIN CAIDIN

Dark Messiah
Beamriders
Prison Ship
The God Machine
Four Came Back
Manfac
Three Corners to Nowhere
Exit Earth
Zoboa
The Messiah Stone
Killer Station
Marooned
No Man's World
The Cape
Starbright
Jericho 52
Aquarius Mission
Cyborg
Operation Nuke
High Crystal
Devil Take All
The Last Dogfight
Anytime, Anywhere
Whip
The Last Fathom
The Mendelov Conspiracy
Almost Midnight
Maryjane Tonight at Angels 12
Wingborn
The Final Countdown
Deathmate
The Long Night
Cyborg IV

Part One

Chapter 1

He spoke to her silently. Not so much as a grunt or any sound of verbalization. His eyes spoke for him, commanding, piercing as cold steel in soft mental flesh. His eyes and the look of his face, the communication that flashed between animals, four-footed or bipedal. Doug Stavers looked at the woman in spiked heels and patterned seamed stockings, the mockery of a skirt, full breasts squeezed and pushed to pink globes. Yet her entire presence changed from the neck up. Whore and prostitute and anything else she might be, her face told a thousand unwritten and unspoken tales of some other time past. A touch of quality showed, the eyes not entirely dimmed by indeterminate and senseless and countless fucking and unmeasured quantities of drugs swallowed, inhaled and needled directly into what had been a body young and nubile and owned with pride. For this timeless moment the whore, rocking back and forth on her spiked heels, her voice the bare whisper of a crooning moan, knew the veil had been penetrated, that this strange man before her saw through the makeup and the whoring and the drugs and time itself. For this moment, only this moment, she felt the *clean* with which she had once clothed herself. Her eyes seemed to brighten a hint as she took, in more months than she could recall, a serious look at this john before— *No; he's no ordinary john. This is something special. This is . . . God, it's so hard to think. What's so different about this one?* A smile hazed about the corners of her mouth. *Everything about this one is different. I want to please this one. Love him.* A snort of self-derision came unbidden from her throat. *Love? I'm a fuck machine. A suck machine. What the hell is love? I don't know anymore, but . . .* She edged toward the unmoving, stolid man, staring at her with eyes burning into her.

I love him. I . . . I adore him. I want to worship him, please him. Oh, God, let me suck his cock, lick it, please him, bring him to ecstasy. I'll do anything. He doesn't move or speak. He doesn't have to. This is . . . I don't know what this is. He's . . . shit, he's like a god. I don't understand this feeling . . .

She had been too far gone, for too long a time, to do more than feel and sense and respond to the power aura flowing from Doug Stavers. Her mind, sodden with drugs and with alcohol and unknown diseases dancing through her system, functioned at barely half its former capacity. What she experienced as a total sense of awe might in earlier days have been recognized as a very real, powerful aura emanating from this man, unquestionably devastating in its effect, but still recognizable. Not now. At this moment the sex machine moved almost as an automaton. Fuck for the cash, suck for the glittering dust, do anything for the transport to the higher somewhere absent of pain and longing and where she curled wonderfully, protectively, so safely within the arms of her—mother? Father? Lover? No time to waste on questions; enjoy. Bliss, wonder, safety, warmth through and through, floating and dreaming and—

The needs that lived on her shoulder with bared fangs nudged her. It was coming on again, the gnawing hunger, the crawling pain, the jibbering and screeching still only the faintest hoarse whispering of sometime ago. But it would accelerate, it would grow like the true nightmare it was and it would try to consume her. *Don't let this one get away. There's something so special here. Blow him. Lick his ass. This one's a god. Do it NOW.*

Some other time, some other place, she might have seen the real Doug Stavers, and had her senses and true fears still served her, she would have known a terrible rupturing of desire and fear, and she might have fled for her very life. Either capitulated totally and freely and with adoration, or sensed an—evil? Do the gods bring *evil* with them? No matter. Not now. Her true senses, her strong family upbringing, the sturdy morality, the dedication to the future; that all belonged to some strange woman in some faraway and strange land served only by memory blurred with shards of broken promises.

She never tried to see beyond the heavy leather jacket, the woolen cap, the strong trousers and massive buckle, or the steel-tipped boots and the beautiful gloves that gave not a hint of the knuckle-molded steel within. The woman moved forward, her hands reaching down for the full groin, shaking as they sought cloth and zipper and the bulging firmness within.

The man did not move.

Why, he mused silently, *do we gods always walk through garbage?*

Three men watched the tableau of the stranger and the whore moving closer with hands reaching for his groin. They clustered at the far end of the alley off Eighth Avenue, three blocks from the huge bus station of downtown Manhattan. Three blocks is a relative distance. On a sunny tree-lined residential street it is a delightful walk, a view of snug homes and green lawns and driveways bustling with children at play. But that is another planet.

Three blocks from the Manhattan bus station is a plunge into dank, fetid scumminess. The three men were longtime residents of the city's alley slime. A burly figure in western garb, as outlandish as the stubble-faced brute with blackened teeth and the smell of a dead wet goat, nudged a friend. "What the fuck's the matter with the bitch?" he complained. "Just look at Rita. She swooning or sumpin'?"

"Ahh, she's on the shit again."

"I'll kill the cunt. I *told* her she don't get juiced until *after* we hit the mark."

The third man, tall and lanky and cadaverous, his

face a lunar map of pits and craters, gestured instinctively. "Better take care of that guy first."

Two men turned as one to look at Preacher. "What makes you say that? He's just one more fuckin' idiot. Anybody comes into an alley around here for ass is just a crazy fucker. Using his dick for brains."

"Yeah," grunted their companion.

"Shut the fuck up, Scumbag. Nobody asked *you*."

"Hey, I just—"

"Zip it, Scumbag."

Scumbag took no offense at the name. That *was* his name. Virtually toothless, skin a greasy sheen with all the look of old latex that had earned him his name, and a raging homosexual, he had only one saving grace. He wielded a straight razor with the finesse of a surgeon. Or a swinging butcher. That was his mark. No simple stab of a shiv for him. No blade in the ribs or the heart. Scumbag left his trademark on these brainless dicks who penetrated his territory. He made hamburger out of people. For the moment, Scumbag lapsed into silence. Preacher and Hog were his only real friends in the whole world. Besides, Scumbag was getting mad now. He planned to do a *real* number on that prick with Rita.

For an instant time froze. *The same scene revisited once more*. Deep in the jungle of concrete and alleys and garbage strewn before the storm of daily hustling life. A slab-walled jungle; four of its feral creatures gathered in this alley of greasy underfooting, of overflowing garbage cans and dead rats and bustling rats, of roaches and broken hypodermics, of crushed bags once holding sweet and deadly powder, empty boxes and tins once filled with pills and tablets and capsules. Dried blood, spittle and vomit and old beer and the stink of urine and feces hanging everywhere in its familiar cloying mist. Four predators. Rita, once beautiful, long dead in her brain from the tumbling flow of drugs into her body. Rita with the willing lips and flashing tongue and silicon-swollen globes and the vagina with its pustules and red slashes hidden from view. Rita, the decoy for the dicks-for-brains.

Scumbag, licking his lips, the straight razor for this moment within its scabbard within his pocket, caressed by his hands, eager and jaggedly waiting for its fleshy target. Hog, big and brutal and wholly amoral, trembling with the excitement of bones breaking beneath his great cement-like fists and his adrenalin rush of smashing and *hurting*. And, Preacher. Different from the others. Intelligent, swift of mind, a derelict fleeing from a church school in Kansas where he had succumbed to the lure of pink little boys and had committed sinful, lust-driven crimes against their bodies. Preacher, who fled into oblivion, who brought with him dim memories of other times when he had been a soldier and a biker, a man superbly drilled in swift and professional killing. Preacher, within whose old leather jacket lay snugged a long-barreled .38 Smith and Wesson, who wore around his waist a deadly chain for flailing, with knives sheathed in the small of his back, in each old engineering boot; Preacher with a dozen killing implements about his body. Preacher, who paid his penance every day and every night with self-imprisonment in this filthy rotten jungle.

Preacher, who despite the rotgut whiskey and the occasional plunge into a drug-crazy world, still answered to instinct.

Preacher looked down the alley at the man, before whom Rita slowly sank to her knees, ready to release his great member and bring it fully within her mouth. Somehow, Preacher knew that would not happen.

Preacher felt the cold wind blow through his leather jacket and laugh along his suddenly icy skin. And Preacher was afraid in a way and with a fear he had never before known.

Time remained frozen . . .

Doug Stavers felt the steelmesh container lashed by flat steel cabling to his chest, snugged tight, impossible to remove without powerful cable cutters. The cables ran about his chest and across his back and over his shoulders and finally about his waist, as much a part of his rugged body as his own sinew and muscles and flesh. Within the steelmesh rested the great yellow diamond, the huge flawless stone that had raged and ripped and torn and killed through more than two thousand years of riotous history. The Stone of God. The Rock of the Lord. *The Messiah Stone.* For a fleeting moment Doug Stavers, his weight resting on muscles coiled like great springs, thought of the African tribe that had worshipped this very stone that fell from the heavens. And had died for that stone when a great winged machine landed in their midst and the men in the huge airplane struck the tribe with machine guns and poison gas and terrible explosions. The stone that had been cut by a genius into its present shape. The stone with the aura that overwhelmed human senses, that magnified the mental and emotional and instinctual strengths of a man.

The Messiah Stone. Tens of thousands of human beings had died for and because of it, and most of them had died at the hands of this man who now wore the great yellow diamond within its steelmesh, so tightly wrapped about his body. Doug Stavers looked at the diseased eyes and face and body before him and again he had that sorrowful thought. *Why do we gods always walk through garbage?*

He had a phantom look at a face raced by his memory. Adolf Hitler had murdered uncounted thousands to gain and to wear this very diamond. With its powers Hitler had almost—

Stavers pushed away the thoughts. *Stay with it. Stay sharp. It's coming down to the wire now. They'll move in. They're like a pack of wild dogs.* He thrilled to the thought of the struggle he knew must take place within moments. He knew no fear, hosted no concern. Three two-legged dogs against *him*? They were vastly outnumbered.

He could feel time pulsing about him. These moments came more and more frequently to him. The longer he wore the great yellow diamond, the greater his ability to seem removed from everything about him, to leave it all in stasis while his thoughts raced with superhuman speed through his mind. All about him whatever was happening moved with incredible slow-motion. And he accepted the thoughts in his tremendous acceleration of time for himself, knowing the world and its inhabitants about him dragged so slowly they seemed frozen in sludge.

He knew what The Organization had said about him less than a year before. A time when he did *not* have the Messiah Stone. A time when he lacked knowledge of its existence. A man named Gibraldi had spoken to his associates. Gibraldi and his group, ah, *they knew* of the mysterious great diamond with its fabled powers. And they hired the professional mercenary, Doug Stavers, to get it for them. At any cost. For any price in money or lives. None of that mattered.

Gibraldi had spoken almost in awe of Doug Stavers. "Even in the Legion we knew of him," he had told his group. "He is a mercenary and yet he is more than that. He is a soldier of fortune but on the highest levels. He deals with governments. He has an uncanny ability to lead men, to bring men to follow him without reason, with blind faith." Gibraldi paused with his thoughts of Doug Stavers, and he smiled humorlessly. "He is more than a killer. He is a devil. I've never known a man like him. Death is his friend. It never touches him. He has a reputation of never having failed to get what he wants."

Gibraldi's partner, one of The Six, felt his eyes widen. Kovanowicz's world was the global underworld of spies and espionage. He joined then in memories with Gibraldi. "If he is the same one, then he is the man who killed the KGB's entire assassination team in Berlin." He laughed harshly. "He was wounded, again and again, but he refused to die. He seemed to gather strength from those wounds. A modern Rasputin. A killing machine without peer."

Gibraldi and Kovanowicz, and the rest of their group, hired Doug Stavers. They paid him millions. He fulfilled his contract. He left a swath of death about half the planet and he returned to Nevada with the great gleaming, flashing yellow diamond. He killed Gibraldi and Kovanowicz and their partners, because now Doug

Stavers knew how much more powerful he was than any such group.

Before he held the magnificent stone of the gods in his hands he had been as close to invincible as any mortal might ever be.

That was then. This was *now*. And everything he had been before was infinitely stronger.

He felt that silent, almost indefinable *click* in his mind. Time picked up its metronome beat.

Rita's fingers brushed tremulously against the fabric of his trousers. Her tongue wet her lips. An instant later her tongue shredded into pulped red meat, a moment before her teeth tore from their sockets and stabbed in a shriek of pain into her windpipe.

Preacher gasped. He'd never seen the stranger move. One instant he stood rocklike before Rita grasping forward and before Preacher could even blink his eyes the right knee of the mysterious one seemed to be smashing through the face of the hapless woman. No; *not* seemed to be. It was happening faster than he ever dreamed possible. Preacher knew the signs. The painted face dissolving into gory hues, pink and red and white teeth flipping to the sides of her mouth and a tiny flash of white bone where her cheeks had been smashed outward, sideways, through her skin. *He must have a fucking steel leg. Who the hell is he?* Preacher felt the ice heavier than before in his bones and he knew he hadn't asked himself the right question. *What is he?*

It was happening in realtime and in slow motion. Rita's head snapped back violently and as her body lifted and flew away from the terrible impact of Stavers' knee her head snapped forward, and in that single glance Preacher knew the girl was dead, her neck broken, her upper spine a broken shambles. Her chin and cheeks and mouth and teeth and nose had been rammed into her skull as if struck with an enormous battering ram. Then Preacher saw the signs he feared the most. The stranger turned to look at Preacher and Hog and Scumbag. He turned and he stood silently. And his eyes invited them to come forward to kill him. He seemed to smile as if all that was happening was barely a touch beyond boredom.

His eyes tore into Preacher's mind and Preacher felt himself moving forward, his feet bending and lifting beneath his legs, all his movement unbidden by conscious thought. *Someone's pulling my strings.* The thought made him want to giggle, but his throat sucked in air desperately, to meet the demands of a suddenly pounding heart and a heaving chest. Preacher saw a vision. Real or his own mind yielding to this fear expanding outward like an explosion. Hooves and horns and a demonic smile. *Come, come . . .*

Hog rushed forward. Brutish, moronic, his reactions wholly linear. Kill this fucker. Tear his head off. Hog burst ahead, leaning into his rush as he had done so many years earlier as a football tackle, the professional boring ahead to hammer down the opposition. His eyes narrowed to a snakelike fixation. Instinct and a thousand battles behind him led him to look for the swing, the sidestep, whatever maneuver this stranger would make to meet Hog's rush.

The stranger didn't move. He waited. Time was his friend, his weapon. Time and above all, *timing.* At precisely the exact instant Stavers' right foot went forward, the steel-toed boot positioned perfectly, and it crashed with mind-gibbering impact into Hog's chest, the clothing offering no more resistance than air. Bones snapped, flesh yielded as the boot ripped *into* Hog's chest and destroyed his heart. Hog never uttered a sound, so much warm dead meat as he fell forward through the space where the stranger had stood, and, almost as if to avoid an annoying fly, had sidestepped easily and gracefully. And paid not another moment's attention to Hog thudding against the alley slime and skidding lifelessly into a heap of fetid garbage.

Scumbag and Preacher came forward as a well-oiled machine, following their practices of old. The straight-edged razor was already in Scumbag's hand, for an instant reflecting some unseen light source and starting down to slash into the neck of the stranger. Doug Stavers smiled. They were so clumsy, so easy.

Stavers stepped inside the descending blade, glanced at the man's other hand for a possible second knife, saw none, and then Stavers' left hand lashed forward, uncoiling with the faster-than-the-eye-can-follow speed of a striking rattler. The hand that had killed a hundred, perhaps several hundred men, reached Scumbag's wrist, closed tightly and then twisted with terrible speed. Twist left, pressure up and back and the alley echoed with the *crack!* of the bones breaking. Not a bone; *all* the wrist bones in that terrible move. The move continued. Contemptuously, Stavers half-turned, moving the wrist as if it had no more weight than a lily, maneuvering with ease, and Scumbag's razor sliced deeply into the side of his own neck. Before the blood could fountain outward, Stavers' hand jerked sideways and brought the blade completely through the forward neck and the jugular of Scumbag. The latter tried desperately to scream and produced only a pathetic gurgle as he bounced and jerked on the ground, a chicken with its throat slashed gory-open, a humping animal in its mindless final throes.

Stavers half-turned again to face the one remaining life form in the alley with him. Preacher stood perhaps six feet distant. The professional distance. Close enough never to miss with the heavy revolver in his hand, hammer cocked, yet not so close that a blindingfast movement of this incredible stranger could outspeed the clenching of a finger on the trigger. *I've got the motherfucker now*, Preacher shouted to himself.

His own voice in his mind mocked him. *No, you don't. You can't pull the trigger.*

"The hell I can't!" Preacher shouted wildly. His body shook with tormenting emotional conflict. He *wanted* to jerk the trigger, he *wanted* to shoot, he *wanted* to . . .

"You can't do it." Stavers' voice rolled gently over Preacher. The man's eyes seemed bottomless. Preacher felt as if he were being lifted weightlessly and he was falling down an abyss into those eyes. His muscles seemed to melt, the gun began to sag of its own weight in his powerless arm. His mouth opened, he felt his lower lip tremble, the saliva beading and trickling along his chin.

"N-no . . . c-can't do it," Preacher intoned. He felt icy cold and broiled in terrible heat at the same time. His mind spun, his senses turned to jello.

Stavers never took his eyes away. *He's within that circle of twenty feet*, Stavers mused. *The magic twenty feet. Where the diamond is strongest. Where I, me, and the diamond, are strongest. Ah, but I like this. The perfect test. This soulless piece of human shit, this killer, this creature of murder. Let us see where his own mind now takes him . . .*

"You *want* to kill me," Stavers said gently.

"N-no," Preacher forced out. "Terrible . . . no, no."

"You waited to kill me." Stavers didn't bother to even glance at the crumpled doll form that had been Rita, its body fluids still gurgling softly into the cesspool about them. "When she would bring her disease to me."

"Y-yes. I did."

"You have the gun. Go ahead."

"I can't . . . I mean, I—"

"Tell me what is in your heart." Stavers smiled.

"I . . . I . . . love you." The words came forth attached with strings of misery and pain and worship from Preacher.

"You love me," Stavers said, his tone flat, unemotional. Statement; not a question.

"I love you. I . . . I can't help it." Preacher sank slowly to his knees before Stavers, his arms at his sides, the heavy gun resting on the filth beneath him.

Stavers painted a scene in his mind. His thoughts drew masterful strokes. He wondered if the visualization reached into this dungheap's mind.

Preacher's hand tightened about the weapon.

I do believe it's working, Stavers thought with sudden mirth.

"I adore you," Preacher moaned, face twisted, spittle drooling in a stringy mess from his face.

"You want to meet God, don't you," Stavers said, again without query in his inflection.

"Y-yes."

"Then you must show me how much you love me. How much you adore me. How badly you wish to see your Father."

"Yes, yes, *I do.*"

He's disgusting, this miserable cretin. I've had enough.

"Do it, you filth!" Stavers' voice rolled forth with a thunder answering in Preacher's mind.

"*Yes!* Oh, yes!" he shrieked. "I will! *I will!*" He jammed the barrel into his ear and jerked hard against the trigger.

The thunder still rolled back and forth through the alley as Preacher's brains and blood and bones oozed down the nearby alley wall.

Unimpressed, already disinterested, Doug Stavers turned toward the street side of the alley. Beyond that squared space hugged between high walls existed yet another world of massive indifference to whatever might go on within these walls, or any walls like them. What you do not see in the bowels of Manhattan does not exist. It is that simple. The three monkeys that could not see, hear or speak any evil could take lessons from the street people of this slagheap city, Stavers knew. Even that booming roar of a shot had created no more disturbance than an idly turned head. Stavers walked toward the street scene of people and traffic flowing noisily in the usual cacaphony of the worst parts of midtown Manhattan.

I need a shower, he thought idly. *A shower to scrub myself clean. And a good steak and brandy.* As he walked he reached idly into his leather jacket inside pocket for a cigar handmade personally for him; a cigar that cost the equal of a full day's pay for a working man. He stopped for a moment, bit off the end and spat away the tobacco. He lit up, completely at ease, the perfect killing animal triumphant in yet another jungle.

He looked up at the sudden shadow. A giant stood wide-legged before him, heavy boots planted like tree trunks against the concrete. "You're out of your fucking mind, you know that?!" he shouted.

Stavers stopped before the giant. Skip Marden was as

much a killing machine as was Stavers; perhaps more because of his single-minded, selfless dedication to specifically that task. In an all-out, no-holds-barred, kill-or-be-killed conflict, Stavers would not have chosen to be Marden's opponent.

Marden was a breed different from any other man Stavers had ever encountered or known. He was also the only man surviving from Stavers' own violent and turbulent past whom Stavers trusted. And trusted absolutely, as he had done so many times with his life. He was the perfect companion-servant-human pit bull for Stavers; skilled in close combat, an expert with weapons, an absolute lover of battle, and with a disdain for personal injury and pain that at times made him seem more machine than man.

Stavers grinned at Marden, occupied for the moment with his own thoughts of this killing machine. Marden was a lover of battle even more than of whoring, at which he had established an unsavory, yet enviable reputation. He had been known to rip and tear his way through a dozen women during a single night of totally uninhibited ramming and thrusting—like a monster bullock of limitless energy and seminal discharge.

He towered six feet seven inches tall; his shoulders spread out to each side of a thickly corded neck like massive boards. Big as he was he did not easily reveal his weight of 305 pounds because he was knotted sinew and muscle. His hands spanned the size of a baseball catcher's mitt and he had many times used an open-handed slap with fury sufficient to split open another man's face and skull.

All this served to conceal the "other side" of the man that was to be measured in keen intelligence, a multiplicity of technical skills and ability, and a dedication to whatever might be demanded of him from his pursuits in life. He seemed too huge and thickhewn to use his hands and fingers for more than bludgeons, yet those same massive hands and sausage-like fingers enabled him to fly as the best pilot Stavers had ever known. Behind that granite jaw and battered visage lay a mind of unprecedented abilities. Skip Marden flew everything from skittish helicopters to swift and dangerous fighters with his own consummate skill, and just as easily slipped behind the controls of an airliner and flew that machine with babyskin gentleness. It didn't matter what the machine was. If it had wings or rotors and the bloody thing could become airborne then Marden flew it like a demon or an angel as the moment dictated. He was lethal in a manner that scorned death and dismemberment with equal contempt. Not that he emerged unscathed from his lunging brushes with weapons and forces aimed in his direction. Like Doug Stavers, and their close companions who by now were only memories to them, he'd been bombed, burned, slashed, stabbed, torn, battered, buried alive and nearly drowned. Almost every type of weapon used by other men had left its mark on him. He took great joy in having numbers tattoed by his scars. He liked that. He was past eighty-one by now and he wondered if he would run out of numbers or years before the game came to its finale.

Yet all this was distant background at this moment in the lip of the alley reaching back to Manhattan's Eighth Avenue. No other man alive spoke to Doug Stavers with the unbridled fury he now took from Skip Marden; or more accurately, they did not remain alive for long. Marden harbored no fears. He was totally and absolutely loyal to Stavers. He had saved Doug's life more times than they bothered to count and the favor had been returned.

For the past year he had only one goal in life. To protect and to serve Stavers. *Before* Stavers had brought within his grasp the incredible yellow diamond that twisted the senses and emotions of other men. Marden's anger now was because he had failed to be present when Stavers so openly invited disaster in this rectangular box of filth and murder.

"You are one dumb son of a bitch," Marden continued, his voice now gentled to a bullish crescendo.

Stavers looked behind him at four broken, bleeding and dead bodies. "How so?" he asked quietly.

Marden brushed aside Stavers' victims with a diffident wave of his hand. "That shit don't impress me and you know it," he growled. "But one of them crazy fuckers one day is going to open up on you from a distance. Or they'll drop a garbage can full of bricks from the rooftop on you. *It's just not worth this crazy shit for you to have your fucking jollies!*" He sucked in air, his great chest heaving with controlled fury. And fear that he might have failed Stavers in an instance of peril.

"I didn't kill that one," Stavers pointed. "He was a test."

Marden blinked. "You're not really playing that game in *this* shithouse. Jesus Christ," he groaned.

Stavers didn't smile. "No game. I said he was a test."

"You didn't do him?"

"Uh uh." Stavers smiled; peace and contentment and death warmly embraced in one. "He loves me."

"Past tense," Marden rebuked gently.

"He blew out his own brains, my friend."

Marden took a longer look at the shattered skull of Preacher. "He had dead aim on you. I saw it. I was afraid to move. Anything could have twitched his finger on that trigger."

"Anything but love. He wanted very badly to see God," Stavers countered. "I let him have his way."

"I can't picture God wanting to see *him*."

Stavers shrugged. "I'm tired of this. Let's go."

Marden stepped aside. "Name it."

"We'll hit the Marine Terminal at LaGuardia."

Their jet was tucked away securely in a locked and guarded hangar at the executive terminal.

Marden gestured. "Got a limo waiting."

Stavers raised an eyebrow. "Limo? What are we doing? Advertising?"

Marden chuckled. "It don't *look* like no limo, Doug. But it's bulletproof and it's got a powerhouse under the hood, and the driver has a big sieve for a skull. He knows nothing, says nothing, remembers nothing." Marden led the way to the dark grey Lincoln with shielded windows. Stavers caught a glimpse through the side mirror of eyes watching them. Just as they reached the limo the door close to them sprang open. Stavers nodded approvingly and started inside. An enormous hand held him back. The move was automatic. Marden leaned inside to check out the interior *and* to be certain the same driver was behind the wheel. He stepped back and nodded. "Okay."

"Mother's little helper," Stavers remarked as he settled back in his seat. "How come this is waiting like this?"

"The way you play alley pool, Doug," Marden said, "I figured we might need to take a very quick powder."

Stavers closed his eyes. "Wake me up when we hit the terminal."

Marden nodded to the driver. "LaGuardia Marine," he said. "Use the Customs gate. And call ahead."

"Yes, sir."

Damned good man. Marden sat erect in his seat alongside Doug Stavers. His eyes missed nothing, scanning the roads before them, behind them, the cars and trucks on each side as they passed other vehicles or were passed.

Occasionally he looked directly at Doug Stavers. *I know how that man in the alley felt before he blew himself to Kingdom Come. I know only too well how he felt. I just don't know how to tell Doug I love him too. More than life itself. He doesn't know I'd die for him.*

He was wrong. Stavers knew.

Chapter 2

"Remove your clothes, please."

The woman who spoke these words so casually to Doug Stavers leaned back in her executive chair, perfect legs crossed perfectly. For the moment he studied her. What a goddamned combination she made. She was about as perfect a woman—physically—as he'd ever known, and in his time Doug Stavers had been blessed with a profusion of beauties of a dozen races and nationalities. His long studied sweep of Dr. Rebecca Weinstein only reinforced his judgment of her physical attributes. Beauty, as Stavers knew from deep intimacy to philosophical judgment, came in many forms and sizes. There didn't exist and there had never existed *the* most beautiful woman. The concept was ridiculous and Stavers silently thanked the gods who decreed that beauty came light and dark and a dozen shapes in between, that breasts and legs and pubis and neckline and nose and the whole damned package went sour almost instantly when the rich or pliant voice was lacking, when the smile proved lackluster or revealing of a dim and shadowy wallow behind the pearly teeth. And eyes; ah, the woman without eyes alive and daring and challenging and mysterious, well, forget her, because something very special was left out of the package if the eyes could not speak for the mind. You didn't need words to communicate; you could just about verbalize with eyes and looks and a tug at the corner of the mouth.

Rebecca Weinstein was almost a twin sister—facially and physically—to a Hollywood actress who often graced both theater screens and the electronic box at home with looks that nailed male viewers to their seats. Kelly LeBrock was the actress, and no small part of her dazzling attraction was voice and accent. Rebecca Weinstein had everything that made LeBrock a global male fantasy, *and more*. Dr. Weinstein spoke with that crisp and beautiful annunciation of the British. There wasn't much doubt, however, that the subjects *she* spoke of were very different.

Rebecca Weinstein was a gifted and utterly brilliant medical doctor and surgeon. Thirty-two years old, she looked the perfect twenty-six years of age. Stavers once again swept his eyes across her stunning figure, all the more provocative as her full breasts pushed hard against the crisp white uniform. She was *his* doctor. He chewed on that a moment as he began to undress. *His* doctor. *His doctor*.

But not his woman. He offered himself the relief of a momentary grimace; from the sudden change in look on her face he knew she had caught the facial expression. Physically she didn't move. Her eyes darted about his body like a scalpel, an extension of her visual observation that held a tantalizing almost-physical sensation to her optical survey of himself.

If nothing else, Doug Stavers was blessed with animal instincts of survival. A lifetime of surviving lethal situations had honed this *feeling* within him to obsidian-bladed sharpness. He felt a slight prickling of the hairs along the base of his neck. *She* did this to him. This stunning woman, this doctor, without even being aware of what was happening, was able to look directly at him as if sizing up a great slab of frozen meat swinging from a butcher's hook. It brought him almost to the point of being unnerved by the sensation. He had the feeling that beneath all her obvious physical and cerebral abilities, staggering enough by themselves, lay another source of strength, or power. He didn't know, and—

She cut short his introspection as her eyes continued their search for physical injury. When she failed to discern visible damage, she voiced normal concern in her typical, direct, clipped fashion.

"Did you sustain injury?" she asked. Her words were so clinical they smelled hospital.

He stopped, awkward, his trousers half removed. "Do you mean was I hurt?" He grinned crookedly. "Like stabbed, punched, kicked, shot?"

He *never* reached her.

"Yes."

He shook his head. "Not *from* them. *To* them." He shrugged, draping his pants across a chair and starting to remove his shorts.

"Them," she repeated. "Whoever they are."

"*What*ever is more like it," he countered. "Scum. Unimportant."

"You had physical contact?"

"Yes."

"You were alley-catting?"

"How the hell did you know?"

"You were alley-catting," she said to confirm aloud her judgment. "In that filth beyond filth. A jungle epidemic couldn't touch this sleaze."

"Jesus, woman, I didn't wallow in it."

"But you touched, breathed, inhaled, carried it on your shoes, your clothes, your . . . your skin."

"But—"

"You smell," she went on relentlessly, and he knew she also enjoyed his discomfiture. "You reek; you—" she took a shuddering breath "—stink of a thousand foul odors."

"All that?" he mocked her, smiling.

She remained unfazed. "You've been exposed to bacterial and viral assaults that medical science can't even identify," she reeled off. "You've permitted a scrape on the side of your right hand—"

He lifted his hand, astonished to see how accurate her penetrating glance had been.

"—to expose you, as well," she drilled at him, "to herpes, syphilis, unidentified venereal rot, pneumonic and tuberculosic infection, AIDS—"

"You forgot the clap."

"That was coming," she snapped.

"Goddamnit, Weinstein!" he shouted. "I didn't fuck anybody!"

"Please," she protested in gentle rebuke, a smile tugging at the corner of her mouth, reminding him again of those beautiful lips. "Even I would not even consider such idiotic self-abuse on your part. Besides, you're fully aware of everything I've said. And more," she added tartly.

He stood naked before her, not fully aware of the staggering effect he produced within Dr. Rebecca Weinstein. Impassive to his masculinity, adhering rigidly to her position as his doctor—ah, how well she concealed her own reactions to this magnificent male creature. She could, and she did, but it required no more than a long moment, her study masked clinically, her memory serving her as well, to capture in her mind the entire package of this man. Hers was a demanding dichotomy of observation. She saw Doug Stavers as a medical doctor and she saw Doug Stavers as an individual and she longed for him as a man, and would have bitten through her tongue before admitting to the almost lustful yearning for him. First and foremost and last she was and *must* be what he needed from her: her medical observations, treatment, anticipation of problems, and as swiftly as possible a cure or fix for whatever failed this man.

Rebecca Weinstein was a surgeon. Observing the naked male body, moving of its own volition or stilled forever without life, studying it in its entirety or examining various dissected parts; all was professional to her. There was no nudity or nakedness on the surgeon's table or even in the privacy of an examining room, and so Rebecca Weinstein found all the more baffling and frustrating her division of professional and a woman who would willingly act in wild sin, if only she could achieve the latter without compromising the former. Which she couldn't do, and she clung grimly to her professional objectivity, no matter how painful the lie.

But there was an objective study to fascinate her when Doug Stavers eased into her care. Standing before her, she could accept him in physical bulk for what he was: thick-hewn and yet with long, flowing and powerful musculature. She knew the signs of the perfectly honed human machine and Doug Stavers was one of its finest examples. He was a cerebral wonder and a vicious killer in the animal world, especially since that time when she had come to embrace *his* definition of bipedal human beings as prey equal to any four-footed creature.

Her gaze passed with clinical measure across his muscle-ribbed stomach, scarred and browned, flowing into thick pubic hair and a heavy, pendulous penis. No more than a fleeting instant of pause would she permit herself unless medical care demanded further attention; her eyes flicked from one wrist to the other. The first time she saw the blue tint to his wrists had been perplexing to her, and then she remembered. The masters of the martial arts. The best of the men who waged hand-to-hand combat. The blue wrists of metal-hard bone and tendon and sinew and muscle, all to transform the sides of his hands into rock-hard boards. A blow from his hand could crack a man's skull as easily as he might smash his hand into a melon.

He had no upper stomach to speak of. Ribbed and patterned muscle as if carved from dark autumn marble. *The Greeks and the Romans built statues to men like this*, she mused. *This man would rule the gladiators. Only he's deadlier. He's the true predator.* She took a deep breath. *So why am I not fearful of him?* No answer met her unspoken question.

Stavers lifted his arms and held them high to each side and began a slow turn, unbidden, but anticipating her request. Muscled ribs, buttocks like a water buffalo, a back of piano-wire strung tightly in bunched mass. A neck of corded muscle. He moved as if to music. *He flowed.* She forced herself back to reality, to those first moments when she met in private with Skip Marden so that Marden might reveal to her whatever she might require to best serve Doug Stavers.

Marden held a bottle of vodka in a hand so huge the bottle seemed a toy. She knew Marden's appetite for alcohol and his strange resistance to its effect. He could drink pure ethyl alcohol and with sudden concentration dismiss its effects from his mind and body and function as if he'd never taken a drink in his life. Yet the tales of his great drunken bouts in the bars of Arizona and back Indian country were as legendary as anything befitting Paul Bunyan.

"I don't like talking about *him*," he told Dr. Weinstein.

"Why?" she asked delicately.

"Lot of women ask questions about that man."

"I'm not here as a woman."

"You sure as hell *are* a lot of woman!"

"I repeat, I'm here as—"

"I know, I know," he interrupted, gesturing with the bottle, taking a huge swallow before continuing. "You're his sawbones. The medical wonder. Hell, Doc, I know your dossier backwards and forwards."

Her eyes seemed to laugh. "Then why don't you trust me?" she queried.

"Stay a doctor," he rebuked her. "*Don't* be an asshole."

"I don't understand," she chided him, smiling.

"Lady, just do *not* bullshit me. Not now, not ever," he warned. His eyes went dark. Eyes buried in the skull of a great coiled python. "And *don't* patronize me. You know goddamned well we trust you. If I didn't trust you, you'd have been dogmeat—*literally*—long before now." His eyes stripped her. "And that would have been a shame."

She shifted uncomfortably. "Then I apologize. I did not intend to act, as you say, like an asshole or to bullshit you. I need information—data—on Mr. Stavers, and my questions are intended to permit me to function in the best manner possible for his well-being."

"Apology accepted. That's also a hell of a speech."

"Then speak up!" she snapped.

"You do have fangs," he said in appreciation, rising respect clear in his face. "Itty-bitty fangs, but," he shrugged, "you got to start somewhere."

"Jesus Christ," she said, exasperated, "I'd been told you were a man of a few words."

"You turn me on, Doc."

"Then turn off your seminal flow, *Mister* Marden."

He laughed, a deep throaty shout that rocked the

room. "Not in the way you took that. You turn me on as a real people."

She blushed. She was stunned with her reaction. "Please," she said weakly, grasping for a clue, a start. "His attitude; tell me about his attitude toward life. I know much of his background. I mean, the records are there. He's fought in wars, large and small, through half the world. He has a reputation as a destroyer, a man who always gets what he wants. I don't understand that strange harness he wears. It's a taboo subject. No one will talk about it." She saw the eyes darken again and she held up a hand to stop any angry reaction from Marden. "I'm *not* asking you about that. I'll ask *him*. But what makes him so deadly? So special?"

Marden smiled, a thin slash across his powerful, battered face. "Contempt," he said, and as he became serious about Doug Stavers, his tone, his entire demeanor changed, as if he were talking about someone beyond normal, almost supernatural.

"Contempt?" she echoed. She paused only a moment. "For what?"

"Everything." Marden put aside the bottle. Rebecca Weinstein knew she'd been right in her assessment of this man. He had become *very* serious. A sudden thought chilled her. "Mr. Marden, if I—"

"Skip," he slid easily between her words. "You and I, Doc, we're gonna be just like Siamese twins where Doug Stavers is concerned, so let's cut out all the in-betweens. You just accept that I'm part of you and you're part of me and that we are going to be the best damned gestalt there ever was."

Marden bedeviled her. Massive brute and killer that he was, openly contemptuous himself of women, or just about anything else, she had quickly discerned, he still thought with a brain of great and diverse capability. Not that he'd simply uttered *gestalt*; the phrase held deep and long-standing meaning to him, and he'd accepted that *she* also would catch all its implications. That took swift and multiple channel reasoning and *that* arose only from long-standing and accomplished discipline. She cautioned herself not to even remotely judge this towering book before her by its drastically misleading cover. Then she forced all thoughts of Marden from her mind to concentrate on her purpose for this exchange.

"You said contempt, um, about everything, made him deadly," she went on, returning the subject to Stavers. "How do you mean that?"

His laugh was more deep chuckle now and he shook his head in a visible derision of her attempt to probe. "Don't go Freud on me, Doc. Remember? We're a team? Ask your questions straight out or," he paused that briefest of time clicks, barely perceptible but heavy with meaning, "you go straight out of here."

"Sorry," she murmured, lowering her eyes.

"Sure you are," he said easily. "No fish likes the hook."

She looked up sharply. *Who the hell is the doctor here?* she wondered. *He's playing with me, damnit! And he's right. Stay straight with the questions, Doc,* she added as a final silent admonition.

"He reminds me of a cat," she said suddenly. "Feral, deadly, but not like a tiger." She reflected a moment, called up a mental picture. "A sabertooth. Shorter, more muscle-coupled in body—"

"Excellent," Marden told her with evident pleasure. "Sabertooth. Yeah. Very good."

"This is *not* a leading question. It is—I'm—serious. If he is without weapons, the so-called great claws and fangs of the cat and any variety of weapons in the man, *what then* separates him from the pack? How does the contempt fit in as an advantage?"

"Well, consider how the big cats function," Marden said thoughtfully, and Rebecca Weinstein knew he spoke as much from experience as contemplation. "A jaguar's a good example. When he gets into a scrape, every thought is dedicated to the kill, *or*, to his own self-preservation. It's all instinct tempered with experience, but I can't see how there's deliberate thought to it. Instinct, reaction, slavish to needs, and in an animal like that, desire and need are the same."

Marden put aside the bottle and took the moment to light a cigar. His booted feet crashed down on a low table before him. "Doug does what the cat can't do. First, he can select any cerebral level he wants for any particular situation. He can sidestep instinct, he plans his moves, and he takes instant advantage of any opportunity that comes to him. Do you see what I'm getting at? He's like a super computer that's also the jaguar. He gets into the scrape with absolute killing efficiency, but a part of him is constantly, in realtime, updating what's going on. I said he was contemptuous and when he's in the thick of it he's also contemptuous of his own life."

Marden smiled with a swift passage of memory. "That's the greatest of all the weapons. There's an old saying that all creatures always choose the least difficult of two pathways. Exclude Doug from that. He's totally objective when his life is on the line. He doesn't worry about being killed. You take time out for that and you've given away the initiative."

Her brow creased with the words. "But the instinct for self-preservation," she offered in mild protest. "If he gives that away, doesn't he make himself *more* vulnerable?"

"In a fight to the death, lady, that figures *only* if you stop to figure it."

"That's a neat little catch 22," she said.

"I guess so. You see, Doc, you're asking for rationalization. You start doing that in a brawl and likely you're dead before you can reach any conclusions." He laughed loudly with his own words. "Shit, I like that," he murmured. "Never thought of it that way, but that's the way it works."

"You're saying, then, and I'm trying to get this correctly," she added quickly, "that if he has all those other attributes of fighting, or killing, or whatever, then never questioning that he'll win becomes its own weapon?"

"Beautiful," he said with admiration. "You've cut through the thickets, Doc."

"I don't think it's contempt, Skip." His facial reaction told her she'd sliced neatly with a verbal blade.

"It may be contempt for the opposition," she went on, "but *not* for himself. He's deeper than that."

"You're the doctor. You tell me, then."

"He's *free* of the restrictions and the inhibitions that affect just about all of us in our lives." Rebecca Weinstein smiled. "Even this little exchange has emphasized to me, *through you*, that we all lie a little every day to protect ourselves. You caught me playing a word game with you and you came at me with almost physical force. I hadn't intended to play the game, yet," she brought herself up a bit straighter in her seat, "there I was at the old word tricks." She made a steeple of her fingers and peered at Marden.

"It's not simply indifference," she repeated. "He's *aloof*. He's beyond indifference or contempt."

"The word," Marden said with a sly smile, the mind once again emerging above the brute, "is committed. That's the word, Doc. You see, Doug is a man of incredible logic. His mind's more than a computer. It's a whole goddamned bank of computers. But he lives in the real world. You know the real world? There's no Easter Bunny. And the whole world is a rotten neighborhood at three o'clock in the morning. So when hit comes to shove, and your ass and life are on the line, and anything logic can do has been done, *then* you shift those gears between your ears and in your gut to the survival mode. Then logic is for diddly-shit and physical action is what keeps you alive. That's when killing, destroying, eliminating the opposition, whatever you want to call it, *is the only logic*."

Marden studied her for a long moment, appreciated her silence, and went on. "You were almost right when you said he wasn't really indifferent. Almost, Doc. You just got to change the words a little. Unconsidered indifference to the lives and affairs of anybody, to any person, who's not important to Doug Stavers. There's the keyhole, baby. He is totally uninterested in anything else. Your life touches his, he accepts you, but only under his own rules, and he *never* considers the rules of anyone else."

"And he gets away with it?" she asked, knowing it was true even as she indicated a tinge of disbelief in her words.

"Gets away with it?" Marden chuckled again. "He *is* it."

"And it carries across the physical line," she murmured.

"What?"

"I said it carries across the physical line. Into the rest of his life. His business activities, and I have only a hazy glimpse of what he does. International affairs, political, military," she paused and went on almost at once, "his personal lifestyle, his women—"

"Back off, Doc." She didn't mistake the real warning in his tone. "There's quicksand out there and you're headed straight for it. You ever see him buckass naked?"

The question hit her with sudden surprise. "W-why, yes, of course, I mean, I'm his doctor, and—"

"Why are you so flustered?" Marden sat straight now, feet planted solidly on the floor, eyes boring into hers. "I didn't ask you if you were a doctor, so why tell me what I already know? You ever see the man swinging-dick naked, damnit!"

She had control again. "Yes," she said firmly.

"Then *that's* what you think about," Marden snapped. "The physical man. Well-being. Health. Strength. All those good things. Stay out of where you don't belong."

"I didn't mean—" Her hand was half-raised in protest.

"The fuck you didn't," he said heavily. He got up and left her staring at an empty doorway.

She gaped at what a moment before had been empty space. Marden was back, his great bulk looming in the space, filling the doorway, one hand on each side as if he were holding up the building. He had a look of stone about his face, unreadable, a cover of great emotion roiling his mind.

"You haven't met the real Stavers yet, have you?" He didn't ask the question but hurled it at her like a javelin.

Something brought her to her feet, a sense of a terribly critical moment at hand. "The *real* Stavers?" she echoed. "I don't understand—"

"You will when you do." He shook his head with the sound of his own inadequate words. "I meant to say, you'll understand what I mean when you meet the real Stavers. The one that's down, real-deepdown. The one that people are coming to worship."

This is crazy. What does he mean about people coming to—

"You ever meet a god, Doc?"

She had a firm grip on herself. "You sound as if you've lost your mind, Skip." She *almost* laughed aloud.

"Oh, thanks for the tip. But I haven't. Lost my mind, that is." He laughed softly, a breeze of sound from his great bulk. "But when you meet the one I'm talking about, you'd better hang on to yours."

That was days ago. Now, here and *now*, was the second floor of Vulcan Flight Operations, a massive two-story structure in the heart of the Marine Terminal of LaGuardia Airport in the borough of Queens in New York City. Like almost everything else associated with Doug Stavers, only part of the Vulcan facility could be seen by the eye. The entire perimeter of the second floor held a row of offices that girdled the building. Deep inside the structure, surrounded by those offices, was the private domain of Doug Stavers who, through an intricate web of corporate stepdown holdings, was the true owner of *all* of Vulcan Flight, one of the largest and most successful jet charter and sales operations in the world.

To the men and women who staffed Vulcan Flight, this inner sanctum, to which admittance was granted to an intensely screened and investigated few, was known simply as the Anechoic Chamber. The room of no echoes. The chamber of silence. No one discussed the structure, its inhabitants or visitors. You did not talk about it. *Period.* Any such conversation resulted in instant dismissal. Any conversation made for the specific benefit of anyone with too many questions in mind about Vulcan or Stavers often resulted in an obituary within several days of the fatal indiscretion.

The Chamber had nothing to do with the flying, sales or operational affairs of Vulcan Flight. It was but one of a dozen similar facilities maintained throughout the country. A magnificent collection of apartments, hot baths, medical facilities, superb communications systems and a private restaurant in each. It provided the full comfort, services and security desired by Doug Stavers when and where he wanted.

And where he now turned slowly, stark naked, before the sharp eyes of Dr. Rebecca Weinstein. She recalled her conversations with Skip Marden about Stavers; once again she experienced the strange sensation of surprise at always seeming to discover something different about this man that she had missed before. She knew the human body in the most exquisite detail and once again, as always, she reflected with no small wonder as his muscles rippled with that marvelous combination of hardness and flex. She had examined Stavers in detail, had kneaded those muscles and discovered the broken bones in his wrists and arms and legs. The X-ray file told its own grim story of past terrible damage, and it took only the naked eye to see the scars of bullet punctures, the thin and often jagged white lines of steel slicing his flesh. She shuddered at the sight of whip burns laced into his back and buttocks and legs. She shuddered not only because of the wounds and rips and tears but because Stavers had a marvelous skin structure, like prime leather well kneaded. She looked for and found the deep scar along the third finger of his left hand. This mark needed no explanation; Skip Marden had told her about it.

"It came from a gold ring. Not the ring itself but because it was there," he related. "I watched the whole thing. Angola. I tried to get to him but a concussion grenade had knocked me into never-never land and my legs wouldn't work. Doug had been blasted by the same shock wave and I saw him face down in muck, trying to turn over to breathe. A native soldier, crazy bastard, pulled a knife. Tried to cut off his finger to get the ring."

"From the looks of that scar . . . he didn't get it, did he?" she asked.

Marden shook his head. "Doug got his fingers into the bastard's eyes. Then he got him by the throat. It saved his life. The native pulled back and Doug held on and that goddamned black just pulled Doug out of the buffalo shit or whatever it was. Doug never let go. He crushed that bastard's jugular. I mean, pulped it like it was a rotten grapefruit. Then he dragged me the hell out of there." Marden shook his head. "I was supposed to watch *his* back and there he was saving *my* life."

"Where are you, Doc?"

Stavers' voice pushed aside the strange flow in her mind from past to present. She came to with a sudden start, flustered. "I—I'm sorry," she said quickly. "I was thinking, remembering—"

"About what?"

He stood before her, splendidly nude, completely oblivious to their physical proximity. She fought for clarity in her thoughts.

"About you," she forced out. "Scars, burns, bones. I told you. You were crazy to do what you did."

"Yes. You told me."

She reached for his hand, turned it to expose the raw scrape of skin. She reached behind her to a cabinet, withdrew a bottle of clear iodine. "This may hurt." Her words sounded lame even as she spoke them but there was no way to recall what must have been an insipid remark to him. Angrily she poured iodine freely on the scrape. A white froth rose on his skin. No flinch; no reaction.

"That's it?" he asked. His voice seemed to ring a bell of humor.

"Yes. Will you shower now, please? And really scrub in that special soap." She sighed. "I meant what I said before. About what you were exposed to."

"You should go to Calcutta. Or Cairo. Someplace like that," he said matter-of-factly. "Eighth Avenue's antiseptic by comparison."

She gestured to the harness snugged tightly about his chest and back. "Aren't you going to remove that strapping first?"

His eyes became a dark fire. "No," he said, his voice barely audible. "Don't ask about it again. Don't refer to it in any way unless I bring it up first. And do *not*, please, minimize what I've just said to you. Your life could depend on it. Is that clear to you?"

She met his gaze. It took all her strength. The intensity of his eyes robbed her of physical strength. "Yes," she said finally, her voice almost a croak.

"Good. Get the dogs in here." He walked into the shower room. She paused only a moment, turned to a wall phone, picked it up, tapped in the number four, three times. "Templin here."

"The dogs, now," she spoke into the phone. She was a quick learner. One of the first things she'd learned was that when an order was being given you didn't use many words and you *never* gave explanations. Almost immediately a side door opened. Al Templin, ebony dark with glistening bald head, *two* revolvers in underarm holsters, held open the door. He looked down and to the side. "Guard," he commanded.

Two large dogs came quickly into the room. Luger trotted to the entryway of the shower room, turned to face her, and sat stolidly. One hundred and twenty-five pounds looked at her, unblinking. Nothing would get past him to that shower now until Stavers released the great Bernese Mountain Dog from his guard station. The second animal, almost as large, trotted to her and lay down at her feet. Rebel was of the same breed. They were gorgeous dogs, black and rust and white. Before she came to work for Doug Stavers she'd never seen one of the powerful mountain breeds that originated in ancient Rome. The original fighting dogs of the Roman Empire, trained to protect the families of the senators and high officials of that empire. These were their direct descendants.

Dr. Rebecca Weinstein sighed. She leaned back in her chair and closed her eyes. What a hell of a group. Stavers, Luger and Rebel. And the most dangerous of the three was standing on two legs in the shower.

She opened her eyes slowly. A smile tugged at one corner of her mouth. *They're so primitive. They are themselves what they term aborigine in others. But I must never forget the first rule. I walk through* their *jungle and I must bide my time.*

Chapter 3

Lew Morgan and John Garber stretched a lift cable across the rooftop of the Vulcan Flight hangar at the Marine Terminal of LaGuardia Airport. They wore the familiar blue jumpsuits of Vulcan, the words SERVICE CREW embroidered front and back of the jumpsuits, and each man wore about his neck a slim steel cable with his sealed identity card. The cards showed color photographs of their named owners, fingerprints, and were printed, embossed and sealed with magnetic data almost impossible to counterfeit. Which didn't matter very much, anyway, since the cards could be interpreted only by computer.

Morgan and Garber seemed almost to be cut from the same mold; each man stood six feet tall, showed broad shoulders and an athletic build. Morgan had ash-blond hair and Garber dark hair, neither man spoke much and both were exceedingly alert to their surroundings. They had other things in common. Each man was a Mormon and totally dedicated to his responsibilities, which were, directly or ultimately, to preserve the well-being and health of one Douglas Stavers, and any of his group, and anything that was his building or property. Morgan and Garber were but two of twenty-six powerful young men who worked for Stavers, either at Vulcan Flight or any other facility connected with Doug Stavers.

Stavers, in turn, had adopted the security rule of a man who had through much of his life desperately needed the absolute loyalty of his security people: Howard Hughes. Wisely, knowing the system, he had approached directly the officials of the Mormon Church in Salt Lake City, Utah, for the purpose of retaining eight bodyguards to accompany him at any time, on any trip, and, when not traveling, to attend to security functions for his home or any workplace.

None of the bodyguards carried weapons. When hired by Hughes, their select number of eight was in itself a weapon. Revolvers packed six rounds. Semiautomatic pistols usually six, sometimes seven rounds of ammunition. Hughes' Mormon guards were sworn to protect him at any cost. An individual facing the group of eight, holding a weapon on the *unarmed* Mormons, was given a most disquieting message.

"You're not going to be able to kill all of us. When you pull that trigger some of us likely will die. It doesn't matter. What does matter is that you also will die. After, of course, we squeeze whatever information we want from you." There was always a brief pause. "Drop the weapon and you leave here unharmed. You have our word."

There existed no doubt the Mormon guards meant what they said. And in all the time they did their duty for Howard Hughes, no one *ever* fired a weapon at them.

Doug Stavers' group didn't have as spotless a record. Neither did his men make speeches. They were instructed to *perform*. They did as they were instructed and with the full blessings of the church, which found its coffers increased each year by a contribution from Vulcan Flight of three million dollars. The men also were paid well, held the respect of others who worked for Doug Stavers, no small reason being that they never discussed their duties with anyone save Doug Stavers, Skip Marden, or Al Templin, the security chief for Stavers. During the past six months, Al Templin had personally attended the funeral rites of nine Mormon guards. He always left a blank envelope with the elders in Salt Lake City. Every death was worth a cool hundred thousand.

* * *

Morgan and Garber had raised one particular antenna on the roof of the Vulcan hangar at least a hundred times. The antenna was a decoy. It justified their attention, and the crews who replaced them on round-the-clock shifts. Vulcan Flight was famous for its constant modernization program of electronics.

Each man wore an engraved necklace with Vulcan pilot wings. Each set of wings contained an exquisitely microprocessed microphone and transmitter; its wearer needed only to talk in a loud whisper for the supersensitive mike to pick up his words. He could receive return signals from a microreceiver embedded tightly against an earbone. Nothing was visible in the way of powerful communications equipment.

Lew Morgan heard the alert signal in his earpiece. "Vulcan Six, this is Landscape. You copy?"

Morgan looked to Garber; he'd heard and acknowledged with a curt nod. "Go ahead, Landscape," Morgan said to empty air. Landscape was their man in the LaGuardia Tower. There was always at least one man in that tower working for Vulcan. And nothing moved in the airport without observation from the tower.

"Ah, you've got a seven-thirty-seven on a ten-mile final. We have a signal on this bird. Departure originally from Sardinia. It's got long-range tanks and it staged through Africa to Brazil and then north."

"Identify," Morgan said curtly.

"Red and white. Blue swan on the tail. Turkish registration. It's three-dollar-bill time. Oh, they cleared Customs in Miami. Only eight souls aboard."

"Vulcan Seven here," Garber broke in. He had more than a hunch on this iron bird. A Boeing 737 doesn't make a flight from Sardinia, which he knew could not be its *original* departure point. People who make those kind of long-distance flights use long-distance airplanes and the 737 was *not*.

"Yo, Seven," Landscape replied.

"Tell me about their antenna," Garber said quickly.

"Yeah, it's weird. They got some crazy stuff on that machine. Identical LORAN systems on each wingtip, the vertical fin and along the belly."

"That isn't LORAN," Gerber said quietly. "Landscape, stand by. And keep everybody else clear of that aircraft."

"Roger, Seven."

Garber switched frequencies to the scrambled in-house transceivers. "Security, you copy Six and Seven with Landscape?"

"Affirmative, Seven. We've got a scope on him now. Those LORANs are receivers for an external signal."

"They're loaded," Garber said.

"Just what we figure. Maybe a ton or two of high-energy stuff scattered through the bird."

"When they roll off the runway they'll come straight here," Garber warned.

"We agree. Are you ready?"

"Seven is ready." Garber looked to Morgan who was tracking the descending Boeing with a long helical antenna.

"When you see the tires hit, do it," Security said.

"That's affirm," Garber replied quickly.

He switched back to the private line with the tower. "Landscape, how far out is our company?"

"Ah, Seven, three miles. Nobody within five miles in the air and we just turned off an Airbus. He's clear."

"Don't wait for tire smoke, Landscape."

"Jesus Christ, you're going to do it *now*?"

"Seven out," Garber said, ignoring any further calls from Landscape.

"I've got him clean," Morgan said, holding powerful binoculars tight on the jetliner.

"Keep him there," Garber said brusquely. "Give me the call and then drop."

Al Templin spoke with deceptive calm into his microphone. He sat before a wide wall display of eighteen video monitors and a single larger, central video screen showing great detail that he could call up from any of the security cameras scattered through the area.

"It looks like a double hit," he said into the mike. "We can expect at least one or two trucks, probably delivery or service vehicles. They'll make their move when their chopper transmits the boom button." Templin might have been transmitting a business message. He was a cadaverous man, flesh drawn tightly over his bones, his cheeks hollow and his face as close as a man might get to a skull and still be alive. Years of jungle warfare and strange diseases that wracked his body brought him to this physical state, but it denied him nothing with his sixth sense of danger and extraordinary skills in running a security operation.

At least thirty men and women listened to his words. Templin spoke with the quiet, unquestioned authority of Doug Stavers. To the security chief, he was, if not the actual person of Doug Stavers, his alter ego in every sense, including life-or-death. Templin's disease-wracked body, his ghoulish appearance, had closed doors to him almost everywhere in industry and absolutely in government. Doug Stavers, who more than once had encountered Templin in various international capers, and fully cognizant of his talents, snatched Templin from his quiet near-despair of being left on the rocks of *persona non grata*.

"You'll work for me. Security chief. Absolute authority second to me," Stavers told him in their first official interview. "But you've got to do more than *work* for me. You become my shadow. You become, you *are* me, when I'm not around. In matters of security the only person other than myself to whom you'll answer is Skip Marden. No one else. Absolutely no one else. You interested?"

"Yes," Templin said. No need to waste words.

"It's more than that," Stavers said, weighing the man and the critical points about his past performance and future potential. "If I tell you to kill someone, you kill him. Can you anticipate that situation?"

"Yes."

"And if you need to kill more than one?"

Templin gave himself the latitude of a cold smile. "There are no restrictions. I'm also aware that being in the position you'll place me, and with access to information about you I would never otherwise have, I will be terminated instantly if I fail you. And by failure I don't mean performance; I mean trust."

Stavers chuckled. "Why did you use terminated rather than killed?"

"I prefer the luxurious term in reference to my imminent demise."

Stavers leaned forward. "You're it, then. From this moment on you sever *every* connection with *every* person you have ever known in your life. No exceptions."

Templin barely nodded. "Done."

"How much do you want?" Stavers asked.

"Unimportant," Templin said instantly.

And the money didn't matter. Purpose in life mattered. Doug Stavers had offered him that purpose, and Al Templin returned that offer with absolute loyalty and performance.

As he was doing at this moment within the electronic control center of Vulcan Flight at LaGuardia's Marine Terminal.

"Launch the robot chopper," he commanded quietly, in his familiar choked hoarse voice. "Get behind their helicopter, lock on, and be ready for immediate collision on my call."

A male voice responded through Templin's earpiece and through a wall speaker. "Roger on the robot. Launching now. We will have video, radar lock and infrared lock. We'll hold position two hundred yards directly astern their chopper."

"You're on track-and-lock?" Templin queried.

"Yes, sir. They're using a JetRanger. Port Authority numbers and call signs."

Templin pressed a button to his right. "Swat Two, you ready to roll?"

Another earpiece and speaker callback came immediately. "Swat Two affirm. Two fire trucks with us."

Templin almost laughed aloud. Give those crazy security teams the first edge of freedom and immediately they wax creative. But it was a damned good idea. Fred Kasner ran the mobile security force and he knew this damned city inside out and how its people acted and reacted and if he had fire trucks ready to roll he also knew they'd be the most effective force on the scene.

"All right, Swat Two," Templin answered, almost laconic in his speech. "I want all engines running and the feet ready to take the pedal to the metal."

"You're on, Number One."

Skip Marden's face snapped into view on the top security videoline. "You set, Al?"

"We're covered. Air and ground." Templin hesitated a bare moment. "I don't like this, Skip. More than meets the eye. Put up *all* the blast shields."

"They're up. Hangar, office; the works."

"Confirm Herbie."

Who would ever guess Herbie was their code name for Doug Stavers? But it worked. People react to semantics input. Herbie was the perfect name for the typical nerd. There was an automatic cerebral cutoff to connect Herbie with anything even remotely resembling Doug Stavers.

"Shower. Med room."

"Shields up?"

"Confirm."

"What about the lady doc?"

"In the med room waiting for him."

"Seal them off," Templin ordered. "All halon systems ready for high-pressure spray."

Marden seemed a touch annoyed. "It's all been done."

Al Templin ignored everything except the business at hand. He glanced at the main video screen, tapped in another camera position and the Boeing 737 appeared in brilliant color, enlarging swiftly as it cleared the dike preceding the touchdown area of the runway for a landing to the west.

"Party time, Skip. Maybe ten seconds."

"Yeah."

They could only wait these few moments until rubber whipped against the runway at 130 miles an hour. When the tires hit ground at that speed, they'd burn off an outer layer of their surface. That kind of friction always threw off a telltale flash of white smoke.

Marden's voice was a sudden interruption. "Got any ideas about who's coming to dinner, Al?"

Templin didn't bother trying to answer. In the first place, he'd never have used *this* kind of line for *that* kind of information, and in the second place, there wasn't any time to answer. Templin glanced at the screen showing Lew Morgan and John Garber on the Vulcan roof. Morgan had been waiting with his transmitter on the same frequency that their "visitors" had set up to detonate the Boeing's on-board charges. By his side, Garber still had his binoculars glued to the jetliner about to touch down.

It didn't take a genius, being aware of how many people were trying desperately to capture or to kill Doug Stavers, to know that *this* airplane, allegedly from Turkey or Sardinia or wherever, was on a suicide mission. And that it had areas within its wings and fuselage crammed with extremely powerful high explosives. And possibly, deadly nerve gas as well, their canisters to be blown open in the scheduled explosion to permeate the target area. Which, unquestionably, was Vulcan Flight. They would never have bothered to go after Vulcan *unless they knew* it would most likely be occupied at this time by Doug Stavers. If Stavers were absent the plane would have landed, carried on "normal business activity" and then departed.

Not now. With confirmation (somehow) that Stavers was in Vulcan, the planned events were painfully obvious. The 737 would land normally. The pilots would call for the fast exit ramp from the runway so they could take it at high speed. Once they'd made that turn it was a straight shot to the Vulcan hangar, and with the way clear the pilots would ram the throttles forward to full takeoff power and go straight for Vulcan.

The rest of the plan was utter simplicity. The heavy Boeing would rip through the hangar doors. As the nose of the plane entered with the body guaranteed to follow out of sheer inertia, someone in that aircraft would set off the detonator signal. Several tons of high explosive would go off with terrible force. The fuel aboard the 737 would also erupt and the explosion would produce a fireball great enough to engulf the disintegrating structure of Vulcan and everyone within.

If anyone *did* survive the explosion there would still be that nerve gas, most likely Tabun or Sarin, the old German agents from the second world war. Nasty stuff; one good lungful and you were paralyzed and dying within seconds. No reprieve once it hit the alveoli structure of the lungs.

Templin brought in his high-powered zoom lens. The tires were about to touch. He glanced at the screen showing the JetRanger from the video view of their remote helicopter killer. Then the thought struck him. *The gas! We haven't—* He didn't bother completing the thought. His right hand shot out and banged down on a large round pad. As fast as his hand closed the electrical circuit, blast doors and panels slammed shut throughout the hangar, sealing off all air intakes and switching the entire structure to internal systems. He—

"*Smoke!*" Garber's voice burst from the speakers.

All hell broke loose at LaGuardia Airport.

With the cry of "*Smoke!*" Lew Morgan pressed his detonator switch. The radio signal received within the Boeing set off the explosive charges. At 130 miles an hour the 737 changed instantly into a huge mushrooming ball of dazzling flame. The explosion blew out through the wings and the fuselage and as the still-rupturing machine hurled itself along the runway, the shattered fuel tanks exposed their jet fuel to the blast and ignited. A great horizontal mushroom of writhing flame, twisted and roiling with shock waves and smoke, erupted along the runway. The horrific scene bore a shocking resemblance to a mass drop of napalm tanks, all of which exploded violently with unerring precision and timing. Everyone aboard the Boeing died instantly.

The runway remained free of innocent targets; Landscape in the tower had made certain of that as he moved airplanes on the ground and ordered long separations from the jetliners driving down the long incline through the sky to the runway. But there's little escape from so devastating a blast. The shock wave tore outward from the savage explosion. The curving front of the steel-hard shock wave ripped into the control tower and exploded the thick glass of the tower control deck with the ease of puncturing cellophane. Great chunks of jagged glass whirled crazily and also punched backward with the force of the shock wave. Ironically, unexpectedly, Landscape was the first to die as a great jagged chunk of glass sliced sideways into his chest, immediately below his neck, and separated the upper part of his chest, neck, shoulders and head from the torso below. The halved lower body stood rockstill for a moment, blood spurting upward in its own garish fountains, and then the legs collapsed. The upper remains of Landscape, along with the dismembered parts and spray of blood and flesh from other tower operators, scattered for another hundred yards beyond the tower.

A Fokker F-28 jetliner had been taxiing in the direction opposite to the landing path of the mystery 737. The Fokker was just distant enough and heavy enough to recoil with the force of the shock wave; the airplane rocked wildly on the landing gear farthest from the source of the blast. The shock wave forced the tail around and collapsed one main gear; the nose swung upward and the jetliner bounced like a toy with the howling wind. The broken gear came up through the wing to sever hydraulic and fuel lines. What could have been only an incident transformed into a shattering explosion as flames from the runway, carried by wreckage twisting through the air, touched spraying fluids from the Fokker. Fire raced along the ground, danced upward along the pouring fuel and the right wing of the airliner disappeared in a massive crunching explosion. The machine fell heavily to its side, nose stabbing upward at a crazy angle, and continuing blasts shook the airliner like a plastic toy in a windstorm.

Along the main runway, what remained of the Boeing tumbled and bounced wildly. What resembled blackened human forms bounced horribly on the runway surface just before the jagged wreckage sliced and chopped charred flesh and bone. For fully two-thirds of the runway it appeared that war had come to visit LaGuardia.

The Vulcan Flight hangar remained untouched, trembling from the shock waves but without damage.

Sensors along the exterior of the building caught the faintest wisps of nerve gas. None entered the structure; every opening and gap had been sealed when Al Templin's hand banged down on the emergency button. *But the nerve gas had been released.* Invisible, odorless, tasteless, mixing with smoke from the shattered remains of the Boeing, it drifted back down the runway and across the runway from the quartering wind.

Aboard a number of jetliners, along the flight lines and the passenger loading ramps, sucked into the terminal itself by great air-conditioning systems, the remnants of the nerve gas struck with devastating effect. Within seconds of inhaling the gas, pilots, crews, passengers, baggage handlers, mechanics and service crews were choking violently, clutching throats, staring with bulging eyes as flames seemed to explode within their throats and chests. Nerves jerked like piano wire struck sledgehammer blows. Hundreds of hapless human beings snapped and twitched violently, their nerve systems savaged by the gas. They would have screamed except for the paralyzing effect of the gas on their vocal cords; instead, they choked and gagged, uttering hoarse animal gurgles, throwing themselves about in a frenzy of death.

That was center stage at LaGuardia.

There were other acts to play through.

The Bell JetRanger, painted with exacting thoroughness in the colors and with the identifying numbers of the Port Authority of New York, had positioned itself to dive swiftly for the rooftop of Vulcan Flight if the Boeing 737 immolation failed. Obviously, something had gone terribly wrong, a fact all the more dramatized by the blazing charnel scene along the runway. In the helicopter, Mummar Garang pounded his pilot on the shoulder. "Get down *now!*" he screamed. "Now, *NOW!* Land on the roof—" He interrupted himself to haul a heavy leather case from the seat behind him. Forty pounds of plastique would shatter the rooftop and drive a shaped charge of another ten pounds deep within the building. Only ten pounds of the RD9 plastique was enough to shatter every wall and office in the upper floor of the Vulcan hangar. Mummar Garang hauled back on the sliding panel beneath his feet. He spread his legs wide as wind howled up at him with the roar of the helicopter engine. The Vulcan hangar tilted at a crazy angle as the pilot began a dizzying curving drop into the wind to land on the rooftop.

That was the last thing Mummar Garang ever saw in this life. Al Templin had "released" the robot helicopter, locked onto the JetRanger with three separate tracking systems, and activated the "Ram" signal to the robot's computer. A solid rocket motor hurled the unmanned helicopter forward and in its own downward curve. Seven seconds after "release" the robot ripped into the JetRanger and detonated its own explosive charge. Again the sequence of events flame-rippled with terrifying speed. The robot exploded, the JetRanger blew apart and its own fuel lines and tanks tore away in a mushrooming ball of flame.

The blazing wreckage, flames and bodies tumbled to earth, a shocking sputum of destroyed machinery and dismembered humans. This time no victims on the ground would be counted; the blazing mass spewed into a parking lot and ignited a dozen vehicles. It was an impressive and frightening sight, but those who would die from this crash were already dead.

The last act was already under way, as if a murderous three-ring circus was in full flaming flower on and adjacent to LaGuardia.

Whoever—what organization, what group, what persons—had orchestrated what had become shocking horror at LaGuardia had also backed up everything they arranged with alternate plans for getting within Vulcan Flight. They cared nothing for the structure or its aircraft or even any of its personnel. They not only did not care if Doug Stavers died in the multiple strike against Vulcan; quite the opposite. They all had the same orders from "the highest headquarters."

"Do whatever is necessary to reach Stavers. If he is alive and resists, overpower him. Kill anyone, *everyone*, who survives our attack. Do not kill Stavers at once. If he is already dead, be ready to cut open his body. Start with his neck and down his chest, tear away his rib cage, push your hands into his stomach, throw his intestines from his body. *You must reach the diamond. You must gain the holy stone. You must bring it back here, to us. You are commanded, you are blessed by the All High. Heaven awaits your success and if you return here with what we seek, you will find Heaven in this life as well as the next.*"

"If he lives and we cannot find the stone you wish us to return to you, what are your orders?"

They all turned to Richard Boesch, bull-necked, shaven-skulled, powerful, scarred and weathered. A special agent of the secret Brigade of the Fourth Reich, a deeply concealed movement to regain military prowess to a Germany slowly coming together again, squeezing the Berlin Wall to a transparency that would finally vanish altogether and begin the torturous road back. The Movement, the only name Boesch knew, paid *his* Secret Brigade astonishing sums for special services. Boesch would lead the ground assault to penetrate the remains of Vulcan Flight after it had been crushed and torn open by the Boeing 737. If that failed, then the JetRanger would plunge like a great golden eagle to its target. And if *that* failed, then Boesch would lead his strike team with armor-penetrating weapons directly into Vulcan Flight and go after the elusive and dangerous Doug Stavers.

"If this American lackey is still alive," Boesch told his men, "then I will attend to him. If I am killed, any or all of you who still live must reach him physically. Overpower him but do not kill him." Boesch held up a small vial with its top tightly screwed down. "In here is a powder. It is from the legs of a centipede. The Great Tropical Scolopendra from the deep jungles of the Amazon. The powder causes a pain so excruciating that having a live wire shoved up your ass with over a hundred volts is like a woman's gentle caress. You need only spread it on Stavers' body, *anywhere*, and he will feel as if he were burning alive, on fire from head to foot. He will beg to die to be released from this pain.

There is no defense against it. I do not care if he lives or dies. I care only for what we are charged. To find this strange diamond he is reported to carry on his person or within his body and return it here. Nothing else, from this moment on, matters."

Boesch and his group planned well. Once in New York, they gathered in Astoria in the borough of Queens. They rolled two heavy fire trucks into a warehouse only three blocks from the Marine Terminal of LaGuardia Airport. They timed everything down to the last second. When the Boeing 737, broadcasting its secret signal on a discrete frequency, was within thirty seconds of touchdown, the fire trucks with Boesch and his teams would rush from the warehouse, lights flashing and sirens screaming. Even as they rolled they knew the explosions and flames would dominate everything at LaGuardia Terminal. No one would question the sight of fire trucks shrieking their way toward the obvious disaster at the airport.

The fire truck hoses concealed rocket launchers within. The smoke masks carried by every man, and their impermeable rubber suits, would protect them against the nerve gas of the Boeing, as well as the vomiting gas they planned to pour into the Vulcan hangar wreckage. If *all* the plans failed, then *they* must smash their way through. They carried explosive charges, gas, incendiary bombs, rockets and automatic weapons.

Nothing could stop them.

Flame and smoke shot skyward from the airport. Boesch knew the layout by heart and knew something was very wrong. There should have been no eruption of smoke and flame from the runway. And over there; smoke boiling upward from the parking lot. The helicopter! He cursed angrily. The explosives could have gone off prematurely. Or somehow Stavers' men had penetrated Boesch's plans and were successful in blunting the attack. No matter! Boesch was grimly satisfied with his own abilities. All else had failed, but *he* would succeed. He would become a great force within the Fourth Brigade secreted within the Bavarian Alps.

He counted on it.

* * *

Steve Cordas drove the first fire truck with the large green lettering on its sides that read LAGUARDIA FIRE STATION ONE. Boesch had no idea that what made sense to him might also fit neatly into the mobile defensive perimeter of Vulcan Flight so carefully established by the cadaverous Al Templin. And compared to Templin, with experience in all his many wars, Boesch was a thick-lipped lout with a thick brain to match.

The truck Cordas drove contained two massive engines in its body, one under the front hood and the other in the belly of the machine to drive the rear wheels. The entire vehicle was fashioned of thick armor, and the forefront of the vehicle was a carefully manufactured ramming system. This particular fire truck, its driver and assistant sealed within a massive armor-shielded cab, could drive through any ordinary building with all the punch of a great armored tank.

Cordas rolled with high speed from the Vulcan service building behind the hangar. Every move he made was choreographed by Templin in master control within the hangar. Templin enjoyed the vantage of glancing at the video screens that fed images from all streets and roads leading to the Marine Terminal.

"They're two blocks away coming down the main boulevard right in front of you," he radioed to Steve Cordas. "Doing, ah, just about forty-five. I've got both of you on a single screen, so you can floor it, ah, *now*."

"Balls to the wall," Cordas grunted into the microphone about his neck. He slammed the pedal down, a huge turbocharger howled into demon sound and the massive "fire truck" burned rubber down the street as it accelerated to the right-angled rendezvous with the unsuspecting Boesch and his crew.

"You take the lead vehicle," Templin added. "When you plow them under, if your truck is still able to roll, get the hell out of there. Take Ambrose Boulevard south to the number three warehouse and disappear."

Cordas chuckled at the suggestion that his massive armored vehicle might not be "able to roll." But he had a fast question. "What about their followup?" he asked, in reference to the second fire truck bearing down on Vulcan Flight.

"Andy Wynn and his boys have that one," Templin chided.

"Got it," Cordas said. Siren howling, traffic horn blasting, the turbocharged engines thundering, he barreled down the street and caught sight of the fire truck with Boesch and his group inside. They hammered down the two traffic lanes of a wide street.

Beautiful! Cordas shouted to himself. *They're locked in with the traffic dividers in road center and the parked cars to their right. They've got to continue just the way they are—*

He hit the control button to shut off all air intakes to their driving cab, snugged tighter the lap and shoulder harnesses, flexed his toes within his metal-tipped boots in their braces against the foot controls. As a final safety measure, Cordas' assistant pulled an asbestos hood and a mouth oxygen clamp over his head, then did the same for himself. Outside of direct blows against their bodies, the two men could withstand virtually any impact or violence they were about to initiate.

It all came together with blinding speed. Cordas watched the other fire truck race into the edge of the intersection; he was perhaps two seconds behind for a perfect collision of the front of each vehicle. Yet his own timing was perfect. The driver's cab of Boesch's vehicle blurred past him and then the entire world filled with the enlarging bulk of the fire truck as his own vehicle tore with locomotive force into the midsection of his target—its weakest point. The effect was much the same as a bull charging and smashing into a thin wooden fence. The sheer plunging mass of Cordas' heavy vehicle was that of a monster piston—unstoppable, fury-driven. It tore through running board, sideboards, hoses and equipment, punctured, cut and shattered fuel lines, electrical circuits, and hydraulic lines, and slashed the heavy steel frame of the truck as if it were so much cardboard. It continued through the middle of the truck to its other side, literally tearing Boesch's vehicle in two, flinging the front and aft sections wildly into the air. The hapless human forms were sent violently tumbling, spinning and hurling to inevitable impact, severe injury and inescapable death.

Cordas felt his body jerk with impact, then laughed aloud with the magnificent feel of the monster piston hurled forward—the unstoppable force mashing, crushing, destroying whatever stood before it. His armored vehicle ripped through the Boesch truck and as the wreckage scraped and tumbled and showered sparks and debris all about the boulevard, Cordas kept driving straight ahead through the intersection. Moments later he was just one more fire truck speeding through the airport section of Queens, where the howl of sirens and klaxon horns could already be heard in a rising crescendo.

Al Templin allowed himself the luxury of a brief smile as he witnessed on his large video screen the flaming carnage of Cordas' plunge through the Boesch fire truck. He flicked his gaze to the second truck driven by Andy Wynn and his crew. On the screen, the crushed burning wreckage and bodies from Boesch's vehicle filled the roadway directly before the backup truck to Boesch's attack.

"Andy, you're coming up for your move," Templin spoke into his mike.

"Yeah. Man, he's going crazy trying to slow down," Wynn answered in a cowpoke drawl. Driving a truck or riding a quarter horse was all the same to him. "I mean, he's skidding something awful out there."

"Expect him to try to punch through that concrete median," Temple warned. "He can't go straight ahead. Too much wreckage and fire. If I guess right, he'll lock all his tires, plow through the median and he should end up hitting that abutment and light pole at the corner."

"Sounds right to me, and— Whoops! There he goes, right through the concrete. Thought it would flip him for a—"

"Zip it, Andy. Make your move. He'll be locked in for you. *We don't want anyone getting out of that thing alive.*"

"Gotcha, boss," Wynn cracked and then devoted his full attention to his prey. Chunks of concrete bounced and skidded along the roadway from where the fire truck, exactly as Templin had predicted, had punched through the traffic median. Cars and trucks on the roadway scattered like quail, skidding and veering wildly to avoid collisions. Wynn ignored them all as the truck slammed into the concrete abutment at the intersection and hurled the light pole away with an audible *Crack!* of metal breaking away from its supports. The truck rocked and shook wildly for a moment, then stopped. Wynn saw figures moving in the cab and starting to leap from the back steps.

Wynn pressed the intercom button on his steering wheel. "This is it," he told his crew. "Hit them with everything." He brought his truck to a stop broadside to their target. The men on the crashed truck looked at them, puzzled but not yet alarmed.

To onlookers everything went as it should. Powerful nozzles on Wynn's trucks aimed at the other vehicle and a huge spray of foam gushed forth from three hoses under great pressure. In moments the white foam inundated the target. Onlookers nodded in appreciation. Any danger of fire from leaking fuel or oil lines or tanks was now suppressed by the familiar fire-dousing foam.

Appreciation was short-lived. The foam contained a gel mixture of aerated napalm and jet fuel. Normally it was harmless because of its high flash point. A match thrown into the foam would have been extinguished immediately. But a fire sourcepoint of extremely high temperature was enough to *detonate* the foam. Wynn was already accelerating his own vehicle as a fourth nozzle spewed a tight beam of powdered aluminum and crystal chlorine under great pressure into the quivering mass of foam to their side. A moment later an igniter in Wynn's truck transformed the almost solid lance of material into an intense jet of flame.

Instantly the foam flowered into a soft explosion, a mushrooming ball of flame that rose upward like a huge burning evil eye. Beneath the surging balloon-like fireball the fire truck burned through every inch of its exterior and internal surfaces, setting aflame anything that could ignite. Burning foam was sucked into mouths, noses and lungs of the men within and aboard the truck; most lacked the last surges of energy to scream as their lungs first exploded and then imploded from the lack of pressure that had ripped out of their bodies.

By the time anyone could even start to believe the unbelievable, Wynn's truck was already several blocks distant and racing toward another warehouse where it would drive down a ramp to an underground garage and be sealed from sight.

The attack was over, stillborn by flame and fury.

Al Templin took several moments to lean back in his chair, scanning all his video scenes, checking every camera and surveillance device. Nothing else was coming in toward them. Outside the building, LaGuardia Airport was a blazing, screaming madhouse.

Templin sighed. Doug Stavers had planned to depart LaGuardia in their Skua jet. That was now out of the question. Nothing would move on a runway or taxiway for hours, perhaps days. A horde of investigators would swarm over the airport. Vulcan Flight must be ready to open its doors and invite them in, must make available anything they wished to examine. Everything must be, *would be*, in order.

But Doug Stavers could not remain here. And he must leave without being seen. Templin had no doubts other eyes were trained on Vulcan Flight. It was time for their twisted play on the Trojan Horse.

He leaned forward to isolate his communications circuit to Skip Marden. "It's time to roll," he told Marden.

Marden's face showed a flash of disbelief. "Nothing flies out of here now, Al."

"Right," Templin confirmed. "Let's do the burn unit thing."

Marden scowled. "The man won't like it. He goes *to* trouble, not away from it."

Templin didn't smile. "Mister, I do my job. I do it in his best interests. You tell him he can kill me, but he can't fire me."

Marden laughed. "That's pretty good." His expression sobered. "I'm on my way. You got the equipment ready?"

Templin appreciated a swift mind. Skip Marden had already judged all the aspects and consequences of the events that had savaged the airport and its environs. Departing LaGuardia, any part of the field, by helicopter was simply too dangerous. They could not be certain of who might be keeping them under surveillance. Even the local and federal authorities could not help but take sharp notice of a helicopter rising from the field without tower clearance, and the tower was a twisted and bloody shambles at this moment. They had to disappear, literally become invisible. Melt into the swirling mass of confusion and fear all about them.

Sometimes the best way to be invisible was to blaze with flashing lights, dazzling strobes, a brilliant paint scheme and a screaming siren.

Chapter 4

The blast doors to the medical quarters opened with a hard thudding sound and a burst of compressed air. *It sounds like a giant snake.* Dr. Rebecca Weinstein stared in near-disbelief at the armored plates sliding apart and into recessed panels in the walls. *I feel like I'm in some crazy Star Trek movie. . . .*

Skip Marden burst into the room with all the grace of a charging water buffalo. One glance told him that in his brief absence Doug Stavers had felt the mushrooming shock wave from the exploding Boeing strike the Vulcan structure. He'd come out of his shower soaking wet and slipped into boots and jeans. Marden looked at the Ruger P.85 automatic in Stavers' hand. "You won't need that now," he barked to Stavers as he crossed the room and hit the switch to open the blast shields before the windows. *Here we go again,* Weinstein mused, bewildered but fully observant. Obviously something of catastrophic proportions had happened and the two men with her were charged to hair-trigger alertness.

Stavers moved to the thick armored-glass windows. He beckoned to Weinstein. She joined him and as she caught a full view of the airport she felt the gasp leave her lips. She didn't say a word. Questions at this moment would be awfully stupid; she also realized immediately that anything they told her wouldn't meet *their* immediate needs. Along the main runway she saw smashed and burning chunks of wreckage. The tail of a jetliner, scorched and torn, stood out amidst spattering flames. Where the airplane had crashed (*accept it crashed; for now,* she told herself) the runway was a great blackened area. Then she saw flames leaping higher from an airliner on the taxiway. Dozens of emergency vehicles with flashing lights and strobes sparkled and shone everywhere. Another column of thick black smoke rose into the air to the side of the terminal building.

"They get close to us?" Stavers queried Marden.

Marden shook his head. "We got the word about a Boeing coming in from Europe—"

"We get his frequency?" Stavers was anticipating every possible situation and coming up with his own swift conclusions. Rebecca Weinstein became ever more fascinated and impressed.

"You got it, Doug—"

"So you timed it for the frequency," Stavers judged correctly. He glanced across the airport at the blazing wreckage of the Fokker jetliner. "They got in the way," he said quietly. He didn't turn to face Marden. "They must have had at least two backups."

"They did," Marden answered immediately. "Chopper in the air and in a holding pattern. We took it out with one of the robots."

"Wipe everybody?"

"From what we can tell there wasn't anything left to breathe."

"And on the ground?"

"Templin was right on top of it. Two firetrucks. I watched it on the remotes. From the looks of it they were really carrying heavy stuff."

"Anything special?"

"From what we can tell so far, nerve gas."

That piqued Stavers' interest. He turned back to Marden, smiling. Weinstein stared from one man to the other. They might have been holding a business meeting for all the excitement they expressed.

"Who'd they use?"

Marden shrugged. "No way for me to tell from where I was. But whoever set it up was a pro. Our boy in ATC reported the Boeing had started from Sardinia." He grinned. "Top Wop Airlines."

Stavers lifted an eyebrow. "A seven-thirty-seven? That

was stupid. They might as well have sent us an engraved invitation."

Marden grinned. "They did. We went to their party. Lots of fireworks and nobody's partying."

Al Templin's voice burst from the wall speakers. "Marden, will you stop the shit and get with it? Move it, you asshole."

Marden jerked a thumb at the speaker. "Templin's in a sweat. He wants you the hell out of here before the feds and the locals come charging up on their white horses."

"He sounds pretty upset," Stavers acknowledged.

"Stavers, if you can hear me, goddamnit," Templin's voice burst forth again, "and I know you can, stop jawing and get going! We're running out of time."

Rebecca Weinstein knew her eyes had widened. She'd never heard *anyone* speak in that tone or use that manner with Stavers. The word was out from her first day with this mob of thugs and maniacs that to do so was an invitation to meet your Maker. But Stavers didn't show any sign of upset.

Marden laughed. "He told me to tell you that you can kill him but you can't fire him, and man, he is really pissed."

"He's right on both counts," Stavers said, becoming a touch more serious. He looked through the window again. "But I hate to leave right now. You're wrong, Skip. This party isn't over."

"That's what Al said," Marden agreed. "However," he shrugged again, "he feels that if you stay here you get in the web of the closedown and investigation and you become vulnerable."

"That's true. Give me the cut-and-run, *tight*."

"We leave here on four wheels, hit the Bronx Whitestone Bridge, north on Henry Hudson Parkway, double back on TreeTop Road into Westchester County. The crew will have the Skua there ready to power up and go." He scratched his chin. "On second thought, we can have the engines running just before we get there."

"Do that," Stavers said. "We go out of here in the

white-and-orange." He nodded to himself. "That's the best shot." He sighed as he looked at Weinstein.

"Doc, you're now a burn victim. You and me."

For the first time she found her tongue. "I'm a *what*?"

"Move it, *move it!*" Templin shouted through the speakers. "They're coming into all hangars and buildings, starting from the west and coming this way. Goddamnit, we're running out of time!"

Stavers nodded to Marden, who answered the speaker box. "We're on the way, Al. Have the motor running."

Stavers grasped Weinstein's arm. "On the double, Doc." He started out fast, catching her by surprise, and she was jerked cruelly along, his fingers, immensely strong, stabbing pain through her arm. She cried out in the sudden pain. "Sorry, Doc. *Move it, damnit.*" She tried to wrench her arm free. "I don't need to be dragged, damn you," she retorted angrily. "I'll keep up with you."

He didn't comment. In moments Stavers and Marden, running from the medical center, were dashing down a hallway with Weinstein in hot pursuit. They held a heavy door open for her, and the threesome rushed down a flight of stairs to the ground floor. Before her, gleaming and huge, loomed the winged shape of the Skua jet. She had expected to be leaving LaGuardia in this very machine. She forced herself to hurry after the two men. They ran beneath the airplane's tail, turned a corner to a loading ramp. She stumbled as she stopped, staring at a white-and-orange ambulance, white and red lights and flashers blazing in the confined space. As she caught up with the others, Marden turned to her. "Get your blouse off, Doc."

She knew her mouth had formed a stupid O. Finally she stammered a pathetic, "W-what?"

"Your blouse!" he snarled. "Take off your fucking blouse!"

Instinctively she stepped back, her arms covering her breasts, and just as quickly as she saw the anger in Marden's eyes she knew she was being both slow *and* stupid. Before she could move to comply, Marden's arm flashed to her neck, a steel talon gripped silk, and he tore the blouse into shreds and hurled it aside. He gestured to the back of the ambulance. "Move it! Over there!" he shouted, trying to goad her into proper response without hauling her there physically.

One arm still foolishly before her cleavage in her bra she moved hesitantly toward the ambulance. Several men were swathing Doug Stavers in heavy white bandages. He grinned at Weinstein as two technicians moved to either side of her body, bandage rolls in their hands.

"Raise your arms," one man told her. She was still slow in response and again, before she knew the physical act was going to take place, her arms were jerked up and outward. She rallied her wits about her. "This is a strange moment to be carried on a crucifix," she said, more timidly than she liked. But her words had their effect.

"You're not being crucified," one man joshed her. "Just burned at the stake."

She blinked. "What?"

"You're a burn victim, ma'am. Badly burned over most of your body." White bandages swirled about her in steady wrapping as the men moved briskly at their task. She stared at Stavers. He grinned at her a moment before his face and head disappeared beneath two halves of head bandages. They joined neatly from front to back. His eyes peered out at her from the white mass and he winked. "Neat stuff. Self-adhering. You can breathe easily," he said in a slightly muffled voice, "and talk well enough. And you can pull the headgear off if that's necessary. But in the meantime," he paused to chuckle, "you think and act as if you were burned. You're on your way to a burn unit hospital. You're in pain and drugged so you can moan all you want. Just do *not* react to any orders or requests or conversations unless it comes from us. Got it?"

"Uh, yes, of course, but—"

A powerful arm out of her peripheral sight yanked her from her feet to haul her like a rag doll into the ambulance. She caught a glimpse of Stavers' bandaged form easing onto a stretcher. A white-suited paramedic strapped him down. She still couldn't think quickly enough to get with the action. Her feet were whisked out beneath her, she felt herself falling and strong hands gentled her to the stretcher. Straps pinned her down. Skip Marden looked down at her. "It's moaning time, babe," he chuckled. She saw his hand gesture, bodies moved barely within her view of the immediate world as seen through bandage slits, doors slammed close and the ambulance started off with a surge of power and squealing tires. A siren howled like a wounded dog as they plunged into traffic.

For the first time in many long hours she had time to *think*. She'd sweated out Stavers' stupid jaunt into the city to test his—well, it wasn't any of this macho crap because he was far beyond that. He'd been testing something else that called for a horribly asinine exposure to danger. She had studied the body signals of Stavers and Marden; the marks on Stavers' body told her much and the horrific stink of the back alleys told her even more. She had refused to ask *what* had happened, but there had been the aura and stench of blood and death, surrounding and following Doug Stavers like an animated fog. Death, fury, danger; all those elements that had always heightened the senses of anyone she had ever known. Wide eyes, flared nostrils, quickened pulse, higher blood pressure, adrenalin shooting through the system like water through a hose and *none* of these signs had been evident in any form from these two men. Could killing actually, literally, be so casual? Were Marden's words—she recalled indifferent, aloof; ah, yes, but to that could she also add callous? Or, amoral? It wasn't immoral, not from Stavers' point of view, anyway, and he didn't care what might be the viewpoint of anyone else. There lay the rub.

Doug Stavers might as well have announced, *This is my world, my life, my existence, my universe, my reality; you're part of me and what I know and recognize and that's all there is to it, so jump to it or unexist. Un*exist? She'd never even imagined such a word and now it had meaning to her!

She became aware through the rocking motions of the ambulance plunging through traffic, siren howling, that the sounds within the vehicle had eased to a deceptive and professional calm. No one spoke in a raised voice; commentary was terse and easy, inflection was as close as she dared compare it to skilled boredom. Through the slits of the facial bandages she saw Doug Stavers raise himself to a sitting position. He removed his head bandage; she almost laughed aloud at the sight. Doug looked, for all the world, like a living body within Egyptian mummy wrappings. He slipped a headset over his ears and began a conversation by radio with some unknown, to her, anyway, contact. He was so calm, so detached, *so like an android*, that it struck her that Stavers had come to some critical crossroad in his mind. For several moments she raised herself to her elbows, studying the man for whom she was medically responsible. *And psychologically as well*, she told herself. She didn't listen or even attempt to hear *what* he said into the lip mike. It was the growing, almost alarming intensity emanating from the man, bringing the others in the ambulance to an irritating alertness.

With a start she realized that whatever power, whatever aura roiled from Stavers, it had become almost a direct and visible force. The whole idea surprised and fascinated her. She could only liken the effect to identifiable phenomena; Stavers could have been beaming out, in all directions, a screeching but soundless ultrasonic howl. You can't hear it but it sets your teeth on edge and irritates and brings the ears to fearsome itching, and your stomach feels raspy and you tighten your sphincter muscle because every fiber of your mind and body is screaming a warning that something is very wrong, very deadly, and you cannot come to grips with it.

I don't have to fight it, she warned herself. *Something's about to change with this madhouse. All this time Stavers has been moving at what is to him a slow, casual, idling speed. They're getting revved up. The boom's about to fall. Why am I shoving all these stupid homilies through my mind? I don't know what's happening but I'm a part of it. If I try to not be a part of it my life's not worth a nickel. How do I know that?*

The voice seemed to come from everywhere about her, to penetrate her skull bones as well as her hearing mechanism. *This is what it must feel like to know the wrath of God . . . and he's not even angry.* The beat held her thoughts and the clincher came with a single word.

Yet.

She thought of the bizarre body harness snugged so tightly about that muscular chest. She'd heard strange references to a godstone. Something messianic. God-power. It made little sense. There had been snatches of words pregnant with meaning you needed to reach out to grasp. A fire of ice. Yellow. Gleaming, magnificent yellow. Strange powers.

Metaphysical? She almost laughed aloud. *This bunch? Metaphysical?* They'd be hysterical to know she'd considered that thought even for an instant. These were the most *un*metaphysical human beings she'd ever encountered in her life. They gave pragmatism a meaning beyond any boundaries she'd ever known. *They're not just a killing machine. My God, they'd scare the shit out of Genghis Khan!*

Something terribly important was not only *going* to happen. It had begun. She didn't know how or what or why, only that she *knew* it was happening and she was a passenger, or perhaps a crew member, being swept along at the head of the enormous surge of power hammering her body and mind.

Stop it! she commanded herself. *You'll go crazy like this. Push it away. Put yourself to sleep, Rebecca. You need the protection of a sharp and alert mind against this force.*

She had trained herself as masterfully *inward* as she had as a physician to those for whom she cared. Moments later she slipped into deep sleep, unaware and uncaring as the ambulance sped along the riverfront highway, up and along the high bridge ramparts and well into Westchester County before swinging wide to approach the airport from the north. From a direction opposite to that of an ambulance arriving from the holocaust at LaGuardia Airport.

* * *

They moved with the speed, precision and unerring confidence of men with machine-like power. Rebecca Weinstein awoke as the ambulance turned into the entryway of Westchester County Airport. She lifted herself on her elbows just long enough for a powerful hand to reach out from beyond her bandage-slitted vision and press her back down. The ambulance rolled through a series of turns, sunlight and shadow mottling her cramped view of the outside world. Then she had a glimpse of a large steel structure, felt the tires bump over the rails—*the rails?* Of course. The rails along which slid the doors to the huge hangar of Vulcan Flight. She waited patiently, knowing now what to expect. The ambulance interior darkened as she heard and felt the rumble of huge doors closing. A final thud; sudden new light as overhead floods came on. With the light came a friendly hand to remove the head bandages, release the body straps and ease her to her feet. A medic held out a white jacket to cover her near-nakedness and she slipped into the garment.

They gave her not a moment to think. "Move it, Doc," Skip Marden urged, leading the way from the ambulance. She walked to the front of the vehicle and almost stumbled as she looked up. It wasn't possible. The same Skua jet they'd left in LaGuardia loomed high over her. That couldn't be and—

She skewered herself mentally for retarded thinking. *There's more than one Skua painted in the same colors and the same numbers, you idiot,* she chided herself, and again commanded her thoughts to the immediate moment and surroundings. A crewman stood by the airstair door and she hurried into the aircraft. Marden gestured to a leather-covered oval table and deep leather armchairs lined about the table. "Seat number four, Doc," he told her.

She'd never been able to accept easily the incredible luxury of this machine. Leather, suede, thick pile carpeting, cushioned walls and ceiling. Room for sixteen people in almost sinful comfort in a cabin that could hold sixty. Several bathrooms, a full kitchen (or was it galley?), dressing rooms, clothing changes, a shower (!), and—she pushed it aside. It didn't matter. About her the crew moved with drill-team efficiency. Doug Stavers started into the cockpit, stopped suddenly and she watched him staring at Marden. "You take it, Skip." He didn't explain his sudden decision not to fly the Skua out himself or why he'd ordered Marden into the left seat, especially when every one of the five crew members of this Skua, right on down to the cabin attendant, was fully qualified to fly the machine. Stavers came back to take the seat across from her. Somewhere between the ambulance and boarding the Skua he'd changed into a leather jerkin, a snatched-out-of-time garment that would have been found in some ancient medieval castle. Another twist in personality and presence.

The seat belt chime sounded and the warning lights came on. The view of the hangar through her oval window brightened as great doors to the front and aft of the Skua slid aside. Before the airplane would move from the hangar its engines would be running fully and its early checklists completed. She recognized their routine; by the time they rolled from the taxiway onto the active runway they'd be rolling for takeoff. Not a second wasted between one surface and the other.

"Your belt," Stavers said. No concern or care in his voice. A statement flat-toned, indifferent; *part of the mental checklist.*

She felt stupid again as she brought together the two ends of the belt and tightened the strap across her thighs. He looked at her as if waiting patiently for a child to recognize the obvious; she felt the blush coming, could not for her life understand *why.* His eyes stabbed into her skull. Why did she feel this way? He showed no expression in his face, no narrowing of eyes, not the slightest tenseness of lips, and yet—

She understood as he reached up behind him and brought forward the double shoulder harness. He remained silent as he brought the straps down across his chest and hooked into the circular lock. Why hadn't she recognized what was so obvious? What she'd done before a dozen times! She secured the shoulder harness, the straps sliding outward of each full breast. She expected him to smile with the sight. He wasn't even looking at her. The airplane was rolling; she'd never noticed the slight rise of sound that told of increased thrust from the two main engines. God, she was weary of dragging a few seconds behind the rest of the world! She turned her seat so that she faced forward, tapped the locking button to hold the seat in place as bright sunlight streamed through the windows.

They taxied with a solid feel, a thudding of great weight and enormous power through the machine. Well ahead of them the cockpit doors remained locked wide open and she could see into the flight deck and through the windshield beyond, catching fleeting glimpses of other planes about the wide expanse of the airport. For a moment she shifted forward as Marden applied brakes. Before them, from a taxiway to their right, another Skua rolled swiftly and turned directly before them. The two Skuas taxied one behind the other. Voices crackled from the cabin speakers dialed into the pilots' radio frequencies. On a panel facing her, directly aft of the flight deck, a battery of gauges and digital readouts told a knowing observer (which she was *not*) everything the pilots judged in the cockpit.

Then they were turning. A blowtorch cry howled at them from the lead Skua as it throttled up to full power, rolling swiftly. A final turning movement, she saw the runway extending far ahead of them, the shape of the other Skua bursting upward from the ground, and an invisible hand shoved her hard back into her seat. Thunder boomed through the machine as Marden's right hand on the throttles went full forward; a second hand rested on his to assure the throttles stayed there and they rushed down white concrete. In moments she felt the nose lift, the horizon fell before them, and she looked into the rich blue of the sky above. They climbed at a frightening angle; she felt as if they must fall backwards, all lifting energy torn from them by their ridiculously steep incline. Her fears, she knew even as she hosted them briefly, were meaningless. The Skua tore into the sky with its usual furious pace.

Doug Stavers turned his seat. He set his gaze directly upon her and that familiar unease rippled through her. He sighed finally. "Release your shoulder harness, Rebecca."

Rebecca? He'd never before used her first name. Quickly she loosened and released the harness. She waited. He gave no signal but an attendant was by his side almost before he saw the man appear. Stavers spoke briefly; the man was gone. Stavers turned to her. "He's bringing food. We've all been burning energy like it's going out of style."

She tried to think of something meaningful to say, knew small talk would only bring a look of contempt, and said simply, "Thank you." She didn't have anything else to say.

But he did.

"You're a brilliant surgeon," he stated matter-of-factly.

He was in her territory now. Confidence rushed back into her like a frightened tide. "Yes."

"You've done transplants." Statement; not question. He was after something.

She nodded. "Yes," she repeated. "Heart, lungs, liver—most organs," she concluded quickly.

"Bionic systems?" he asked.

She hesitated but an instant, needing only that time fully to interpret his question. "Pacemakers, silicote membranes for acoustic rebuild, hip joints, chronate elbow, microdiam optic fibers—" She stopped herself in midsentence. Quickly enough, at least, to interfere with his game. "You have my complete dossier," she added.

"You comfortable when you're deep inside?" The question almost threw her.

"Yes. As a surgeon I'm a priest within the body temple."

"Neat turn of words," he offered, bringing her almost to flush with a compliment so rare he might have shouted the words. He thought heavily. A strange description but fitting for this man.

"Ever lose anyone on the table? Under your knife?"

"On my table," she told him at once, "but never under my knife."

"You weren't top dog at that time?"

"No. More than one surgeon under whom I trained was an incompetent fool."

"Harsh words."

"Stupid, insensitive, money-grubbing—"

"I get your message."

"As trite as the words seem," she added quickly, "truth is truth."

He seemed to ignore her remark as he pushed his own message. "You ever operate on a dead man?"

"You could mean that several ways." She knew he expected the query to throw her. *If he only knew!*

"Such as?"

"Cadavers. Slicing, probing, dissecting, learning—"

"No," he broke in. "Not classroom crap. Your patient on the table under your knife and he dies."

"Yes." She hesitated a moment. "Sometimes, in emergency, you get bodies too broken to heal. Hearts already damaged, brains devoid of oxygen, organs ruptured; one and a hundred things. They're the living dead. They were dying before we got them. We go through the routine." She shrugged. "Most of them are better off dead. By that I mean total cessation of all body and brain function."

"Someone else stabs 'em and you slab 'em."

"Crude but accurate," she returned, her expression blank.

"You ever bring a dead man back to life? Someone who was worth saving?"

She started to speak, ran memories swiftly through her mind. "Yes. They *were* dead. We pulled off medical miracles."

"How do you mean, dead?"

"Complete cessation of brain function. EEG's a straight line. Bingo time."

He chuckled with her last remark. "How does it feel to play God?"

Her answers came swift and sure. "We weren't playing. Never."

"A hundred years ago you would have been a witch."

"I'm a witch *now.* The uniform is different and the knife is antiseptic."

"And you've got all that good machinery, monitors, lasers—"

"And knowledge," she broke in. "Along with experience. The old saw, Mr. Stavers—"

"From now on it's Doug. You've been baptized."

"Thank you. How'd I do on the test?"

"Seven out of ten. But you're a fast learner. You were saying?"

"Yes; the old saw. Our feet on the shoulders of giants."

"Can you kill a man on your operating table?"

"*Could* I do that? Why on earth would I—"

"No questions for answers. An answer, please."

"If I *had* to, but—" She sensed a change in mood, a hard and serious vein behind his easy flow of words. She looked about the aircraft cabin. This man by her side; a professional killer all his life. Skip Marden; on the edge of mass homicide *all* the time. She didn't want to know about the others. She was in the midst of casual death. She laughed to herself. *And I thought I was the tough cookie in the operating room!*

She took a deep breath. "Yes. Yes, I could."

"You're learning fast. You didn't give me a vacuous explanation to go along with your answer. I like that."

She made a swift stab to trap him. "Do you have someone in mind you want me to, ah, terminate on the table?"

"Yes."

The single word came so softly, so velvety sibilant, it startled her. He smiled at her discomfiture.

"You terminate him. Complete EEG straightline, as you put it. The brain is dead. All electrical activity ceases. A machine keeps the heart pumping, the juices flowing, the air sucking in and out—"

"But—*why!*"

"So this man can know death. And then be brought

back to life with that knowledge. It's critical for him to do so."

She studied this strange, frightening, charismatic man. "You have somebody in mind for this, ah, experiment?"

"It's not an experiment. It's life-*and*-death. You will never for an instant forget that I said *and*, not, *or*."

"I'll remember." *Goddamn him. I'll play his game—* "Who do you have in mind?"

"Why," he smiled, "me, of course."

She started to reply. Her lips moved, her mouth opened, but no sound emerged. Suddenly a crewman was by Stavers' side. "Sir, up front, please."

Stavers' raised an eyebrow. "Mr. Marden, sir. He says it's fun and games time."

Stavers was on his feet immediately, starting forward in the cabin. He stopped, turned, smiled at Rebecca Weinstein, and patted her hand as a wise man might soothe a child. Then he was gone.

She took the moment of being alone to review swiftly what he had asked her, what he was even specifying. The idea fascinated her. He had no idea how easily life could be withdrawn from a man or even how easily it could be *replaced*. Or, as needed, how it could be modified so that the man's body, and his mind, could serve needs *these* men never dreamed of.

Chapter 5

"Holy shit!"

The cry burst from Skip Marden unbidden, explosively. Doug Stavers leaned forward to view a broader expanse of sky. Higher than even the accompanying Skua, a thin trail of smoke etched across the sky, a tiny blossom of flame leading the smoke.

"The fuckers!" Marden yelled again. "Heat seekers! They're way up there!" Stavers caught a glimpse of sun-reflecting metal. Big bastard. That meant a shitload of missiles. *This was trouble.* He banged a hand on the copilot's shoulder. "Bill, out," he snapped. Immediately the copilot unstrapped and climbed from his seat, sidestepping out of the way. Stavers stepped onto the seat and dropped down. In a moment he was hooked into his harness. This could get pretty wild. He saw Marden's hand move in a blur. Pressure masks dropped before both pilots. They had no need for words. They were level at 57,000 feet and if they lost cabin pressure they'd be out cold in seconds without those masks.

Marden worked the controls and the Skua's nose came up and banked right to give them a clear view of the attack against their lead plane. The Skua spouted flames. For an instant Stavers judged his other aircraft to have been struck with a missile; but, no. Those guys were good. Wilkinson flew the other ship and he had over a thousand missions in jet fighters in both public and private wars. And the Skuas were all outfitted against just the kind of killer moves being made against them now. Small rockets tore upwards from the Skua.

Magnesium-colindrite alloy flares burn with a devastating temperature and they'll attract *any* heat-seeker for miles around. Sure enough; even as they watched, the long thin streak of smoke belching downward from its parent aircraft bent in its path and went hellbent for leather after a decoy flare. A mushrooming burst of flame and smoke marked detonation against the decoy.

Then another missile arrowed downward and another. "You know what they got up there?" Marden yelled to Stavers. "It's a fucking Bear. One of them Russian turboprops. Bigger than a goddamn—"

"I know what it is," Stavers said icily. "That means they've got a freightcar-load of missiles and they can sit up there for an hour and lob shit down on us." He cursed beneath his breath as he thought swiftly. "And it's not your ordinary Bear. Turboprops can't keep up with us at this altitude. Son of a bitch," he exclaimed within his own remarks. "Someone bought that thing and added a bunch of big jets to it and they've got damned good altitude capability." He glanced at Marden. "They're tougher than I thought. There's either big money or big government behind all this."

"Tell me later!" Marden burst out, racking the Skua over in a hard climb. Stavers caught the glistening starburst as a whole *cluster* of missiles showered toward them.

Stavers' first instinct was to shout orders to the electronics specialist in his sealed cubicle behind them. "Baxter, you got that cluster coming down?"

Baxter's voice crackled through the flight deck speakers. "Got them," he said with unnerving calm, his voice as soothing as if he were running through a simulation on the ground. "I'm releasing the MACflares now." They felt the dull thud beneath them as a weapons-bay door opened in the belly of the Skua. A moment later they winced as a dozen long, thin rockets sliced heavenward, trailing flame and burning with dazzling light and heat from their magnesium-colindrite. The sight brought them a sense of fighting back; as quickly as the rocket flares sped from the Skua, arcing up and outward in a bursting pattern, the missiles from above bent in their own flight to chase hungrily after the intense heat patterns.

Baxter gave them no time to enjoy the moment of escape. "Sir, you'd better go balls to the wall. I'm picking up another pattern on my systems. From the looks of it they're going for a visually-directed missile strike. It's old-fashioned, but it works."

Stavers knew Baxter's voice should also have carried to the lead Skua flown by Wilkinson. "Gumdrop," Stavers called, "you read that last comm?"

They watched the Skua go through a wide barrel roll in the sky, slipping over and around a brace of heat-seekers snaking toward them. "Gotcha, Boss," Wilkinson came back, and Stavers knew he was grinning with the heady adrenalin of the unexpected fight. "I'm gonna give those boys a taste of their own medicine." They heard his orders to his own crew. "Let 'em have four skin-trackers," Wilkinson ordered. "One-second intervals. Just like a fucking submarine. Fire!"

The Skua was rolling out of a wild curve when flame and smoke flared beneath the jet, falling swiftly behind. Four dark shapes shot ahead of the Skua, weaving slightly as they accelerated toward the Bear still high above them.

"Whoever's in that 'bar up thar," Wilkinson drawled, "he's *very good.*"

"I can tell," Stavers said, sour-voiced. That 'bar' in the huge aircraft was an old hand at missile infighting. He had his own missile under visual control. As the radar systems of his weapon responded to the electronic signals from the skin-trackers fired from Wilkinson's Skua, the unknown enemy worked small flight control systems in the mother plane. In effect, he eyeballed the decoys and overcontrolled his own missile to speed downward.

Baxter fired a brace of decoys to thwart the downcoming visual strike. His ECM decoys broadcast a wide spectrum of electromagnetic signals and even sent out a signal that made each decoy to be the size—electronically, at least—of a huge jetliner.

"It ain't gonna wash," Marden snapped angrily. "Baxter, you got anything else in your bag of tricks?"

They could feel the tense stricture of Baxter's voice. "No, sir, and I'd sure appreciate it if you'd do *something* about that pigsticker on its way down. He's going to hit us, unless—"

That's all they needed to hear in the cockpit. Time to quit the fun-and-games routine and go to the all-out survival mode. "Wilkinson!" Stavers shouted into his radio. "Dump everything you've got at that guy. *Everything! Now!*"

His words were barely received in the upper Skua when smoke and flame shrouded the jet; an instant later the airplane emerged from its own blast as two dozen missiles of various sizes and missions tore away from the airplane and headed for the Bear.

But that was another man, another airplane, and Stavers and Marden had their own moves to make. The Skua was more than a minor modification of the Canadair Challenger with the three huge engines, two podded to the aft fuselage sides and one through the bottom of and forming the keel for the vertical fin. That engine was a dupe. It looked like a jet, and it was, but in the sense of a distant, highly advanced cousin. It was a ramjet that operated at speeds only in excess of 400 miles an hour. It also had a hundred thousand pounds of thrust, burning a hydrogen-laced fuel of enormous energy. At full power the engine exhausted its fuel in precisely seven minutes. But in those seven minutes it transformed the Skua jet into its equal as a giant rocket.

Now they'd need everything they had. The big missile gained speed with tremendous acceleration, a rocket-driven pigsticker with an explosive snout plunging down the gravity well at them. Stavers snapped away the safety cover on the ramjet and hit the igniter. The engine had only two working speeds. None at all, and, full blast. They felt and heard the tremendous eruption of flame in the long tailpipe above and behind them as the ramjet lit. Everything happened with punishing speed and force. Invisible hands slammed Marden and Stavers back into their seats. In the ECM cubicle Baxter's head cracked against a sidewall, missing the padded headrest behind him. Groggy, he fumbled at his controls, but he was clumsy and helpless at the moment.

Not so the Skua as it leaped forward, a great rocket spearing upward in an almost vertical climb. Stavers half-rolled the thundering machine onto its back to keep the oncoming missile in sight. The controller in the Bear was doing everything possible to change the downward rush of the missile, but now the tremendous speed and plunge of the missile worked against him. With all the missile controls trying for a maximum shift in course the systems overloaded, the missile tumbled violently, shedding its wings and arcing downward in a whirling spiral of flame. In a last-ditch maneuver the missile controller detonated the warhead, hoping to snare the wildly accelerating Skua in a desperation embrace of shock wave. Flame snapped into existence, a fireball blossoming outward in the thin air, casting its steelhard shockwave before its own appearance.

Too late and not enough punch. Stavers rode the Skua through the shock wave with a rumble of turbulence and then he kept the Skua coming over even more on her back, a maneuver of madness at their height, but made possible by the thundering thrust of the ramjet. He came up and over in a wide-soaring loop.

"Oh, Jesus . . ."

He saw it himself even as he heard Marden's whispered call of death. The other Skua, Wilkinson, all his crew. Despite their own desperate salvo of all their remaining missiles, the Bear had launched its own ring of death, a great circle of missiles catching the Skua like a great steel trap snapping closed about it. Four missiles sped harmlessly by the other plane; two did not. One missile tore into the tail section, another ripped away part of the left wing.

"And we're out of missiles," Stavers said very quietly, a sense of helplessness in his voice to aid his own men. He rolled the Skua again to bring the airplane right side up, preparing to race away from the great Bear in the sky, faster than another onslaught of missiles might pursue and chew them into tangled metal.

"We won't need them," Marden broke into his thoughts. "Holy shit, look at Wilkinson *fly* that thing!"

The other Skua was doomed, its pilots and crew guaranteed dead even if they still breathed and fought their shattered machine. With part of their tail crushed to battered metal, part of a wing gone, the machine sluggish to its aerodynamic controls, Wilkinson chose to die fighting. Flame lanced back from his ramjet engine. A simple but tricky equation in the cruelly thin air at their height. What was uncontrollable became barely controllable with that monster thrust spearing the airplane. He couldn't sustain controlled flight but Wilkinson now had the battering-ram thrust of energy that permitted him to *aim* his disintegrating aircraft.

His voice came into their headsets, a voice tight with straining muscles, with death sucking into his nostrils. "You copy, Boss-man?"

Stavers pushed his words into his lip mike. "We copy you, Gumdrop."

Stavers could hear the bubbling of blood in the voice from the other machine. "Break a leg, guys. So lon—"

He never finished his farewell. The flaming, splintered Skua tore with accelerating fury into the huge Bear. Soundlessly to those watching from Stavers' plane, the two machines locked in ultimate embrace mingled, twisting one within the other, and then the great fuel tanks and blazing fire of both machines joined in the savage final chorus of detonation. First the flash, then the twisting eruption, the shock wave crunching metal and squeezing bodies lifeless before they could char in that hellish furnace.

Gravity provides a great swooping descent for such moments. Black smoke poured forth and instantly shredded in the tremendous winds of their high-altitude flight. Only a swiftly-fading smudge, thinning and dissipating, marked where there had been the explosion. Along the downward arc fell pieces large and small, shiny, blackened, some still burning, twisting and shredding in the final descent, and mixed within that flaming mess were smaller objects with arms and legs akimbo, lifeless flopping of once-alive limbs.

Stavers brought the Skua about in a wide circle, holding a dangerously steep angle at their height, only the furious thrust of the ramjet carrying them through a turn nibbling at high-speed stall. At such moments men like Stavers and Marden were of a single-minded thought, requiring no verbal utterance of sharing. Each man followed for a moment the now-distant twinkling and sparkling metal reflecting sunlight, for all air disasters are only for the moment and fade away into history with shocking suddenness. Both men looked down, both men without a driven, deliberate thought brought up their right hands in a crisp, snapped salute, their final homage to friends newly gone from life.

Then Stavers was again all business. He rolled the Skua out of its perilous steep bank, felt the sudden "comfort" of the machine as its wings tightened their grip on the sky. A red light blinked on the panel and a chime sounded in their headsets. "Thirty seconds to ram bingo," Marden spoke calmly, as much all-business as the man to his side.

"Kill it," Stavers replied. Marden snapped back the lever that shut down fuel flow to the ramjet; the engine had less than thirty seconds of its howling life remaining. Instantly the sudden sharp deceleration threw them forward against their harness; they bobbed forward, then backward. "You've got it," Stavers said to Marden. Marden nodded as he took the controls.

"Baxter?" Stavers spoke into his mike.

His electronics specialist replied immediately, if not a bit groggily, from his cubicle. "Baxter here, sir."

"You got any more company on your erector set back there?"

Baxter offered a chuckle. "Nothing, sir. No; belay that, Mr. Stavers. We've got four Eagles climbing up to—"

"F-fifteens?"

"Yes, sir. Sorry. Four F-fifteens on intercept. I've been talking with them. You should see them any moment now. They're climbing on full afterburner."

And they can climb at forty thousand feet a minute, Stavers thought. Four of the big F-15E fighters. NORAD obviously scrambled them when ground radar began to show the mess in the sky. Hell, there was enough fire going on for even a few satellites to start screaming electronic warnings. He had barely completed his thought when the big fighters eased into view, sailing upward on magic invisible strings, slowing down from supersonic flight to take up escort positions.

"Ah, Vulcan," came the voice in his headset. "This is Eagle Leader. Acknowledge, please. Use homeopath freq, Vulcan."

"*Oho!*" Stavers exclaimed, not intending to speak aloud for a moment. Those few words from the F-15E flight leader told him everything. Requesting contact on "homeopath freq" meant a highly-guarded special frequency. So the Pentagon was escorting them, *protecting* them. No bullshit here as to what was going on. They already knew a great deal and what they didn't know they'd find out with full cooperation from Stavers.

He punched in the sequenced numbers on his UHF system. "Eagle, Vulcan here. Nice to have you along."

A gloved hand raised in an easy salute to a helmet visor. "Yes, sir. We're to stay with you to home plate. We're fuel fat for the whole run."

"Sounds good, Eagle."

"It looked pretty nasty back there for a while, Vulcan. What's your status?"

"We're okay, Eagle. We're pretty light now and we'll stay at fifty-seven grand until starting descent. That okay with you guys?"

"That's affirm, sir. We'll take care of ATC." The F-15E pilot laughed easily. "Just leave the driving to us, Vulcan."

"You got it, friend," Stavers told the other man sitting fifty feet away from him, across bitter cold thin air and cruising at a leisurely (for the Eagle) six hundred miles an hour. Then suddenly, with that snap-abruptness Marden had come to know so well for so long, Stavers had enough of the cockpit. He hit the harness releases, shoved his oxygen mask out of the way, unhooked his last connections and climbed out of his seat. Without another word to Marden he walked back into the cabin. He didn't see the other man move but he knew his copilot was already in the right seat. Stavers had already dismissed the details of the flight from his mind as his eyes caught the gaze of Rebecca Weinstein.

He stood for several moments before her. Her eyes still held the pinkish glaze of someone who's been through fierce gravity loads, and she'd been through plenty as they'd thrown the Skua about so violently. She looked up at him, not speaking, all their communication through eyes and facial expressions. The steward approached and waited without speaking.

"Straight vodka for me," he told him, not turning his head. "Rebecca?"

Her voice came through, strained, husky-sounding. "The same."

"Bring water and tissues," Stavers added. Then he gestured to the woman. "Don't talk. Not yet." The steward returned, opened a table tray, placed their glasses before them. Stavers took the tissues and the water. He wet an edge of the tissue. "Hold still," he told Weinstein. Gently, he wiped away the blood that had slipped from her nose across her upper lip.

She stared at the red-stained tissue. "I didn't know—"

He handed her the vodka. "Drink."

He took his own in a long, steady swallow, grateful for the burning sensation down his throat and into his gut. She sipped more slowly. Again without taking his eyes from her he gestured with a hand. The steward was there almost immediately with two more drinks. Stavers waited until they were on the tray and waved him away.

"That helps," she said with a shuddering, deep breath. He nodded. She looked at him with both knowledge and curiosity. "We lost the other plane, didn't we." It was a statement; no question there, seeking confirmation. Stavers nodded.

"I didn't see all of it. It was crazy back here. I could feel my insides sloshing back and forth like liquid metal." She paused only a moment. "It hurt."

"It does that." He leaned back in his seat, sucking vodka. "Yes; we lost them. Wilkinson was a damned good man. Now he's dead. Maybe it's why we're alive."

She glanced through her window. Two huge fighters held perfect formation on her side of the Skua. "Nice escort."

"The best."

"Obviously, you rate," she said. For a moment he wondered if her words contained a touch of acid, then accepted they didn't.

"We work with them, they work with us. I'm much more valuable to the Pentagon alive than dead."

"As the old saying goes," she said quickly, "dead men tell no tales."

"And?"

"And live men have no end of tales to tell."

"Neat. Where'd you learn all that?"

"Among other things, Father was a philosopher."

"Tell me more."

"A question."

"Shoot."

"Where could that Bear have come from?"

A warning bell began to sound in the back of his head. He gave no sign of his heightened alertness to her.

"Bear, Backfire, Vulcan; whatever. You got money, you got connections. You got money and connections, you got what you want."

"Crude but direct," she smiled. Again there was that brief pause by the good woman doctor. "Isn't that airplane far beyond its range? I mean, this deep in the United States?"

"Uh uh. Not when you have aerial refueling any time you want." He didn't say anything about the jet pods on the Bear, wondering if she'd bring it up. She didn't.

But she knew it was a Bear. She knew the NATO code name for that goddamn thing. And there's nothing we found in her background that shows experience in this field, or even any real interest. And according to her records, she's not a pilot. How the hell did she know precisely what that ship was?

He decided to put it aside for the moment. There'd be plenty of time and plenty of people to start peeling away whatever cover this woman had wrapped so invisibly— *and so effectively!*—he thought with admiration—about herself. He shifted comfortably in his seat, toying with his drink. Abruptly he put it onto the tray and reached for a slim cigar. For a moment he permitted himself the luxury of non-thinking; yet, that was impossible for him and more than shutting off that incessant thought flow, he had simply gone blank facially.

Or so he had always believed himself capable of doing. Rebecca Weinstein was a medical doctor. She was also sensitive beyond feminine intuition or long training. She needed only a glance in those black, contracted pupils of the man beside her to detect that somewhere, somehow, she had committed a breach. Perhaps no more than the tiniest sliver in her armor, yet to this man, who seemed to sense deep inside anyone close to him, that tiniest sliver in an otherwise unmarred surface became a gaping abyss within which he saw what was denied to all other men. The cold chill she had known before swept through her, and she shuddered, not so much from that sudden icy grasp within body and psyche, but also the turbulent clash of the cold sensation and the almost desperate urge to clutch that magnificent man and hold his head firmly and tightly against her full breasts.

The aroma of Jamaican tobacco drifted past her, startlingly pleasant and toasted; she had always disliked cigar smoke and was continually surprised to find it so welcoming. The cigar or the man? A combination of both? He had that astonishing, unsettling ability to constantly stab his mind deep into hers. A touch of a frown crossed her forehead. How amazing. She had just been through a wild, raging to-the-death swirl miles above the earth and emerged with twisted insides and blood on her face, but her inner self, her mind, was so completely composed it amazed her. And now it took only these very few, these barely identifiable signs of this man to rattle her cage.

Could he possibly realize, or even suspect, what I

really know? She pushed aside the thought as they both accepted the uneasy, unbidden standoff, which to Stavers was far more remarkable than it was to Rebecca Weinstein. As she pondered what only she knew between them, he was disturbed with thoughts he hadn't embraced for many long months.

She's getting to me. Goddamnit, I don't believe this! Somehow she's under my skin and she's getting to me, and it's a hell of a lot more than her being just a splendid female. Jesus . . . I'd hate to kill her because of what I don't *know . . .*

One thing is certain, mused Dr. Rebecca Weinstein, turning the vodka glass slowly within her fingers, *my identifying that Russian bomber has him on hair-trigger alert. What he doesn't know is that I know more about that thing he's wearing against his body than he does . . .*

Chapter 6

"Full ski gear. Thermals underneath, good boots, gloves. Consider in the windchill factor." Doug Stavers scratched his left earlobe, an unrecognized habit refecting easy thinking. "Use a backpack for coffee."

"*Ski* gear?" Rebecca Weinstein hated her own echoed remarks. It sounded simpering but he'd caught her unawares. "There's no snow out—"

"I didn't say skiing. I said ski gear. Goddamnit, Weinstein, call it whatever you want. Just get with it, Doc. Be ready in twenty minutes."

"Yes*sir*," she rattled in an unavoidable flippant tone. "Any other special orders, *sir*?"

"Yes. Can the shit."

She caught the slight tug at the corner of his mouth, recognizing the smile that lurked beneath. She offered her own smile in response. "Got it," she said. "You, me, who else?"

"You, me, Skip," he grunted. "Besides, you're wrong about the snow."

She thought of the barren Arizona desert stretching away from Indian's Bluff. Not more than an hour ago she'd been topside in the town, well above this sprawling underground complex concealed from the world. No snow. No clouds. You didn't need to be a genius to figure out the rest. No snow *here*. By helicopter to the mountains and you had snow. She knew better than to prattle with unnecessary conversation. If it didn't serve a purpose, keep your mouth shut. She smiled to herself. Her father had taught that to her as a young girl.

"Know what you're going to say and let people *think* that you're an idiot. That's better than shooting off your mouth and *proving* you're a fool." *Great, Dad,* she mused, *if only I could stick to that rule. Sometimes my mouth thinks on its own—*

She cut off the meandering within her head. "Twenty minutes," she tossed over her shoulder as she left for her quarters.

"Nineteen, *now,*" he threw back.

She offered a theatrical wince. "Ouch," she murmured, and left. The airtight door closed with a hiss behind her as she walked along the corridor of the East Wing. *Jesus, it's like being in Star Trek. Doors opening and closing by themselves. Microphones and receivers built into our clothes or worn on a necklace. Instant communications all the time and anywhere.* She shook her head with the simplistic marvels of the city beneath the town.

I like that, she thought idly, walking along the carpeted corridor that reduced her footfalls to soft muffled sound. *The city beneath the town.* The locals had their own, *very* private joke about the two communities. The Indian's Bluff that the outside world knew, and Staversville, the invisible city that nobody ever saw from above. It was true enough. Eons ago underground rivers had carved enormous channels and caves fifty feet below the desert floor. Stavers' engineers tracked down old rumors and proved their truth. Old mines once scratched and pawed at for silver and gold abounded in the region. The perfect cover. Stavers' bought out the mines and renewed digging for gold. That *proved* to the locals he was mad. *Loco.*

"Ate one tumbleweed too many," they said. But they didn't say it loud enough to be overheard because soon all of them worked for Stavers Mining and Engineering. Then they discovered Stavers' had bought them as well. Bought up their homes and stores and gas stations at prices they could never turn down. Bought the banks and the realty companies (which hadn't done much business for years, anyway). Then he bought the town. Bought it lock, stock, and barrel. Stavers, through his assigned people, *was* Indian's Bluff. He had it all: police, security, fire, the courts. Nobody argued. They'd never seen so much money in their lives. They also signed contracts that guaranteed their silence about what was going on beneath their feet, where Stavers Mining and Engineering transformed the ancient riverbeds and caves into a sprawling underground city of steel and glass, electronics and generators, computers and weapons arsenals, huge kitchen and medical facilities, living quarters, and the kind of communications that kept Stavers and his teams in realtime contact with anywhere in the world.

Dr. Rebecca Weinstein had been through the entire complex. Stavers ordered that tour. She marveled at the films of a giant Ariane rocket launching from the eastern coast of South America; Stavers made it financially worthwhile for the French to put up his own communications satellite. It sat out in space more than twenty-two thousand miles high in geosynchronous orbit and he had twelve hundred channels to say what he wanted and to hear what he demanded.

If you could think of it, and it had a worthwhile purpose, you could find it in the underground marvel Stavers created about his needs and wants. Machine shops, nuclear-generated power, huge underground hangars for more than thirty aircraft from small jet fighters to international transports. It was all there. And that arsenal. That one was more a closed than an opened door. Oh, she knew about the rifles, machine guns, assault weapons, chemical agents; the deadly toys grown men loved so much. But she knew only rumors about the bigger stuff. Hints of nuclear weapons. She'd asked Stavers directly about *that* matter. Just the idea of being buried beneath the desert with nukes chilled her to the bone.

"I've heard you have atomic bombs down here," she confronted him. "Maybe even bigger stuff." She paused. Cold steel eyes looked back at her. Not a flicker of emotion. She shifted uncomfortably, the cold trickling down her back with tiny sounds of cracking ice. "I'm not pushing," she added hastily. She sought frantically for the right words. "You told me to learn absolutely everything about you I could learn. You're looking at me like a pit viper about to strike a rabbit. Damnit, frankly, you're scaring the hell out of me!"

The deep fire she'd seen beyond his eyes dimmed slowly but purposefully and she felt a bit more alive than the moment before. *Now I know what it's like to be on the razor's edge*, she thought wildly.

"I didn't hear your question," he said after his own thoughtful pause.

"I—"

"And I don't want to hear it," he added, very softly.

Those were the moments when she thought the real world had evaporated. That she existed in some monumental facade. And it was true enough. This division between the crackerbox town with nine out of every ten people being of Indian blood, and this sprawling underground complex— *I have my own name for this place. And it's not Staversville. This is a real Potemkin Village, but the czar is Doug Stavers and he built it this way to fool the whole outside world.*

She pushed aside as much of the emotional and intellectual conflict as she could. *Stick to what he hired you to do*, she reminded herself. *Attend his health and well-being and mind your own damned business. Don't let him probe too deeply into what you really are.*

And that was excellent advice. It was pure twenty-four-karat, great, sensational advice. The security system run by Al Templin was ruthless and permanent. Anyone who babbled about Indian's Bluff—which in its own way *was* the Potemkin Village for the underground complex—broke his or her unbreakable contract. That contradiction in terms was completed by eradication of the errant parties. Not only those who talked too much *but those who had queried, or, simply listened.*

They *all* came down with fatal illness, disease or suffered the most incredible accidents. But they were *always* accidents. Al Templin wouldn't talk about his security system, but Skip Marden held few reservations where Rebecca Weinstein was concerned.

"Look, Doc," he said in his usual grating manner that

seemed to attack rather than discuss verbally, "it works this way. Doug's seen fit to put his life in your hands, see? That means he's also put *your* life in *my* hands. Something goes real bad with Doug, then you dance on the grill."

"I don't like that," she said, surprised with her suddenly vehement tone. She had all the effect of a fly hitting a mountain.

"What's there to like?" He grinned as he shrugged. "That's the way it works. You knew that when you made the inside team. Doug trusts you. So do I. That's why you're still breathing, and—"

"Shove your threats up your ass," she snapped, in a fashion most uncharacteristic for herself. She felt as if she were battling phantoms made of stone.

He sighed with forced patience. "When will you understand, Doc? *We don't threaten.* That's dumb. We make simple statements."

She sought desperately to shift his emphasis. "You were telling me about people who talk too much and—"

"Yeah, so I was," and he renewed the grin. He was into a subject dear to his heart. "They talk too much and we cancel their contract. You ever hear of the Great Tropical Scolopendra, Doc?"

She shook her head.

"Centipede. Big sucker from South America. It's got long hairs and they've got a powder on them that causes the goddamndest pain you could ever imagine. Let one of those things walk across the arm of a sleeping man and he wakes up like his whole arm's been dipped in molten iron. He'll scream until his vocal cords don't work any more and his arm is as dead as a block of wood. He can't stay still, he can't lie down, he's mad with the pain. He runs around like a chicken with its head cut off, howling the whole time like a mad dog." He thought about past incidents. "Come to think of it, they also froth at the mouth. Like a damn dog with rabies. The whole point is that they'll do *anything* to get away from that pain. They'll run in front of a speeding truck. Throw themselves out of windows. If they can get a gun they'll shoot themselves. If they can get a knife, well, we had one guy who stabbed himself over a hundred times before he bled to death. Kept jamming that knife again and again into himself—"

"Spare me, Marden."

A smiling death's head looked back at her. "No," he said softly. "You asked, I answer. But I'll wrap it up for you. We had a whore drop some of that powder on a guy's dick. He went mad in seconds. He grabbed a knife and cut off his own prick, and he killed the whore, and he ran down the hall in the cathouse, blood pumping from what was left of his dick like a fountain and he killed three more before he shoved the knife into his own heart."

Silence hung heavily between them.

"You're the doctor," he went on finally. "You get, say, a case like that for an autopsy. By the time you get the body the powder is so much dust like anything else. Not a trace of it. And there's nothing in the blood, nothing internal. So it goes down on the record books that the dude flipped out, went bananas, or maybe a poison spider or a scorpion got his ass. The point is the whole thing gets buried and forgotten." He chuckled. "There's more—"

"I don't need—I don't *want* to hear any more," she said coldly.

"You're a doctor. You cut up bodies. Slice them open, pull out organs and bones, right? You cut up cadavers for practice. You do stuff for a living that would make most people puke out their guts. And now you've got the willies because of what a little powder can do."

"The difference is that I try to *save* lives," she said angrily.

"Little lady," Marden replied, leaning forward, "if you ever get a taste of that dust you'll never even try to save your *own* life. Got it?" He laughed again. "Then, of course, there's traffic accidents. We burn 'em, crush, mangle, decapitate, you know, Doc."

She knew. She'd worked emergency rooms, she'd been on the road as a paramedic; she knew. The crazy thing about all this was that *without* this so-called Stavers' brand of contract termination, thousands of people tore themselves to bloody shards every day of the week in the normal, prosaic, "decent" world. She hated her own self-rationalization. Nothing performed by this group in its enforced silence and isolation, in the total number of people it affected, could hold a candle to the drunks and the addicts ripping apart lives in normal life.

She forced a switch in their conversation. "Mind another question?" she asked, more hopefully this time.

"Anything, babe."

He talks like an old movie, for God's sake! "All this," she gestured to take in the great underground complex, "has a purpose. I know that Stavers has airlines, shipping companies—"

"Steel mills, electronics plants, aircraft factories, shipyards, export-import, plantations, oil fields, mining, architecture and engineering," he added to her list.

"And that's just touching the surface, isn't it?"

"Uh huh. You could add casinos in Vegas and Atlantic City, mercenary forces for hire, and very legit. He buys and sells weapons all over the world. You want the stuff to fight a war? Come to Stavers Industries. You got enough bread and we'll fight the war for you." He laughed at her expression of astonishment. "Hey, it's all business, Doc. How the hell do you think the world is run, anyway?"

"But . . . but what does he do *here*? I mean," she faltered, "I know he's got this incredible empire, but what does he *want*?"

Marden's expression was blank. "Anything. Everything." He paused a heartbeat. "Sometimes, nothing." He grew serious and it was the first time he'd shown a serious side without malevolence stirring within his words. "Christ, Weinstein, think of it. He owns medical research centers and hospitals. Half the damned cosmetics industry in the country. Supermarkets. Churches and—"

"*Churches*?"

"Why not?" He was honestly puzzled. "God's a hell of a business. Just ask the Vatican."

He rose to his feet and stretched. "Later, Doc. And close your mouth. You'll start catching flies like that."

And now they were going to take a walk in the high snow of Arizona.

It wasn't *that* simple. The snow Stavers sought was sixty miles away across rugged country in even more rugged mountains. Clad in the cold-weather gear Stavers had urged, she returned to the operations room to meet Stavers and Marden. Stavers had dressed in what she recognized as military mountain gear; plain, rugged and effective, a drab contrast to her own brightly-colored outer clothing. Marden stood silently to the side; it was impossible not to notice the heavy pack strapped about his shoulders or the weapons slung about his body. Her first impulse was to smirk at the lethal "toys." As quickly as she entertained that thought she dismissed it as stupid. How could she have forgotten their flight west in the Skua with a modified Russian bomber—*not* crewed by Russians—doing its very best to kill them all? Stavers' world was another planet.

She watched as he studied an electronic situation map and a live television broadcast from some sort of aircraft. "You're clear for the area," Templin said in his brisk manner of speaking. "Anything that's flying is either very high and traversing the area on a flight plan, or it's got feathers."

Marden moved forward. "Give me the IR plot," he ordered.

Templin worked the electronic control console and the situation map flickered to a different readout. "Infrared shows only scattered life forms," Templin told him. "We've got high resolution on each target. Whatever you see moving out there has four legs and a tail." Templin turned to Stavers. "You'll have your usual chase chopper, of course."

Stavers nodded. "When we put down I want both choppers to fly out."

"But we can't cover you if—"

"And they come back here *and they land,*" Stavers added quietly.

"Damnit, Doug, I can't—"

"Yes, you can," Stavers told him, still quiet and businesslike. "Can and will. Don't break my orders."

Templin clenched his teeth. "Yes, sir." He swung about in his chair. "But I am *not* shutting down high surveillance."

Stavers didn't bother to answer. He was already walking toward the exit to the main vehicle roadway of the underground complex. Marden waited for Weinstein to follow and then brought up the rear. Through the doors that opened and closed with that unreal sound and movement of a spaceship they found a military-type vehicle waiting, engine running and a driver at the wheel. "Let's roll," Stavers told the driver as they took their seats. "Heliport Three."

Everything moved with a strange, futuristic, almost robotic sense of unreality, as if she were *in* some futuristic film. They left the vehicle (she'd never seen one like it before) and entered a jet helicopter. Two pilots were at the controls, and this was strange enough to merit heavy thinking. Neither Stavers nor Marden showed any indication of flying the machine themselves. Questions bunched in her mind, but Rebecca Weinstein knew that when other people were within earshot you did not ask questions. Period.

A hydraulic ramp lifted them upward as large horizontal doors slid away above them. Moments later they rested on desert floor and the twin jet engines of the chopper moaned into life and quickly changed their tone to screeching jet blasts and howling rotors. Weinstein watched in silence. Everything happened crisply, smoothly, without wasted motion. The lead pilot glanced back to Stavers, who nodded, and the earth fell away as the helicopter rose and banked into a climbing turn. They never rose more than a few hundred feet above the ground, but climbing steadily as the barren earth rose in its upslope beneath them. The ground features changed; gorges and huge boulders appeared in greater numbers, rugged crags passed beside and beneath them and then they climbed more steeply as patches of snow appeared. Suddenly everything was either fresh snow or barren rock.

Stavers pointed to a large flat area in the midst of angry rock formations. "Land there."

They settled down in a miniature snowstorm hurled about by the rotors. Stavers climbed out, guiding Weinstein through the eye-stinging snow. She caught a glimpse of Marden behind them as they cleared the worst of the howling wind. Stavers gestured, the jet engines screamed with added power, and in a whirlwind of its own making the machine was gone.

This is great. Just great. I'm in the middle of nowhere with snow up to my ass with two professional killers and I haven't the faintest idea why I'm here.

The ear-ringing sound of whining jet engines faded into the presence of winds surging along the snow, bursting suddenly in gusts about tumbled boulders. Then those sounds, too, began to fade beneath the painfully bright and clear blue sky. Rebecca Weinstein turned slowly to absorb the full view; she could see mountains more than a hundred miles distant, thin lines cresting the visual edge of the world. *We could be in Antarctica.* The thought comparison surprised her. She forced herself back to her earlier thorny query. *I'm* still *in the middle of nowhere with two professional killers and I haven't the faintest idea why I'm here.* She stopped the turn of her gaze to rest her eyes on Doug Stavers. He stood motionless, his eyes unreadable to her, and she knew something was *wrong*. Then Stavers spoke, his words easy and comfortable, and any question of danger instantly became fact.

He's the very big, very dangerous cat, and I'm one lousy, fragile mouse. A smile came unbidden to her lips as she thought of her father, that brilliant philosopher-scientist-warrior who had so long ago prepared her for this moment, without ever knowing when and how the moment would come.

"When that time is with you, Rebecca, you will know it. Death will be scarcely more than a heartbeat away.

You will know the scent of flowers, no matter where you are or what you're doing. That is the time you must be willing, almost but not quite eager, to embrace death. Because he will be ready to gather you into his bony arms."

I smell roses. That's bad. That's the smell of death. A rose has no fragrance until it begins to die.

"Do you know where you are, Rebecca?"

Even with her tremendous self-control, she was almost startled with the question and its verbalization in a soft, easy tone. She locked eyes with Stavers before she answered, needing that brief moment to gather herself into a tight, armored *persona.*

She gestured offhandedly. "It could be Antarctica, but I know it's Arizona." She hesitated only a moment, deciding in that interval not to remain the fragile mouse. "That's a strange question from you, Doug, seeing that you know that I know where we are."

"I wasn't referring to a physical location," he answered easily.

"When did we become metaphysical?" she countered quickly and smoothly.

He offered a barely visible curl at the side of his mouth. The Doug Stavers' admission of riposte from a worthwhile opponent. The smile vanished as quickly as it appeared.

"Metaphysical," he repeated. "You're closer than you think to the truth." He gestured, half-turning to take in the bleak, snow-streaked vastlands. "A long time ago, Rebecca—"

I hate his calling me that. The way he uses my name. There's something very wrong here—

"—the great shamans of the Indian tribes came here, walked these same hills, stood right where we are now," Stavers went on. "They came here to talk with their gods. Not talk *to.* They could do that anywhere, in their teepee or hut or cave. But when they sought answers from their gods, the medicine men walked out among these hills. Because here they were close to the two most important things in their lives. Their gods." He paused, his eyes seeming to flash suddenly. "And, truth."

She kept her silence. Stavers sighed, the visible sign of a man whose patience trickled away from him like sand between a man's fingers.

"You're betwixt and between, Rebecca. You're closer to whatever gods you worship, and—"

She'd had enough of the waiting. "And the truth, or whatever it is *you* call the truth," she finished for him, anger sharpening her tone.

"Yes," he nodded. Marden was a huge spectre well behind and to his side, stoic, human granite, part of the scenery instead of part of them. "And anything less than the truth, from this moment on, means you will be with your gods."

She held his eyes and she was grateful she never dropped her gaze. "You'd kill me?" she said, amazed at the strong tone of her voice, feeling none of the shakes she thought might betray her self-control.

Stavers laughed. "Of course." The laugh died away to a deep rumble from his chest.

"Now, I ask, you answer." He sighed again. "What a damned shame. I was honestly becoming quite fond of you."

She nailed him. "I know," she said, again with that amazing calm. "Go ahead. But keep one thing in mind, Stavers." She enjoyed this use of his name at this moment. "Even the leaders of the Inquisition didn't kill their own victims. They had executioners." She pointed with open disdain to Skip Marden.

"I see you're no different. You had to bring along your bully boy to do your dirty work."

She had never before seen Doug Stavers' jaw drop.

She took the moment to think furiously. For Rebecca Weinstein this was no simple human task. She had been trained and practiced in the technique developed generations ago with her people to shut off every part of her mind except what was needed to meet the immediate threat. It wasn't a matter of winning, or, simply surviving. It was emerging from the trap closing in on her in such a way she would turn this man's own strength against him. To Stavers, caught off balance at this moment, it might be reduced simply to Beauty and the Beast. Or Beauty *vs.* the Beast.

But as good as this man was, she was better. Faster, trickier, vastly more experienced, and in her own way a survivor for more years than he could ever believe possible.

Chapter 7

"You're pressing me," Stavers said finally. Weinstein's words struck a note of confusion in him. Not simply the words but the manner in which she'd accepted his virtual promise of her demise. Fear *should* have been apparent to him; it wasn't there for him to see. In this sudden standoff, Rebecca Weinstein knew that without a stunning impact on the psyche of Doug Stavers, by her words, actions, *and attitude*, she would never leave this mountain fastness alive. Well, that was the game, she thought wryly, but she was a top player and Stavers was just beginning to suspect that was the case.

"Yes," she told him, aware the cat-and-mouse parrying now tilted slightly in her favor. She tried but failed to keep a smile from her face. *And he's got much more to learn.*

"You're not afraid to die." He spoke the words as a statement, not a question. His eyes widened as he realized the truth of his own words. He'd only known two women in his life who equaled the strength of this woman standing in the bitter cold of a desert winter. *And they're dead. Does this one have to go the same way?*

"I'm quite prepared to die," she said easily, and again she knew she'd struck a sensitive nerve. "I have been for a very long time." Strength flowed from her body into her words. "My training was very good, Doug. I need but to will to end and it . . ." she faltered, searching for the right words but accepting the clumsy repetition, "and it *will* end."

His eyes darkened as she studied him. He shook his head. "My people are too good to let someone slip through," he said, as much to himself as to her. "Much too good for any organization to get this close to—"

"No organization," she broke in.

"Tough to believe, Weinstein."

"The truth."

"There are all kinds of truth. Spoken and unspoken."

She smiled. "I realized my mistake even when I spoke those few words on the flight here."

An eyebrow rose. What he had started as an inquisition had become an all-too-rare contest. "Tell me."

"The Tupolev."

He nodded. "There's no reason why you should have known the NATO code name for the Bear. You said volumes when you did that."

She shrugged. "And that was enough to let the cat out of the bag?"

"You're slick," he said, strangely relaxed despite the killing physical posture he'd adopted by instinct. "Very slick. Neat way for *me* to tell *you* things."

"You're wrong. What would be my purpose in that? If you believe I'm part of any organization trying to infiltrate, to get close to you, for whatever reasons you believe, this is my last day in this life. This isn't some stupid Hollywood script!"

"Yet," he spoke slowly, "you *did* get closer to me than . . . well, than . . ."

"Than Rasputin, there," she said as she pointed to Marden.

"He has no part in this," Stavers snapped. "Different categories."

"All right," she said.

"You *are* a doctor." He threw out the statement to elicit a response he wanted in his own fashion.

"A *surgeon*," she offered in mild correction. "All my skills, all my credentials, are real."

"You've been close enough so that not even Marden could have stopped you from—"

"From *what*?" she said harshly. "From hurting you?

From *killing* you? *Don't you even realize the flaw in all your thinking?*"

"I have. It bothers me."

"It damned well should."

"Why doesn't the diamond work on you, Weinstein?"

"I think now I prefer Rebecca."

"Fuck what you *think*. Tell me what you *know*."

She shook her head. "No. Not yet."

"That means something else lies ahead."

"True."

"I won't let Marden kill you," he said calmly. "I'm beginning to think I'll do it myself."

"Only if you're stupid. You're *not* stupid. You won't kill me."

"Goddamned sure of yourself, Doc."

"I'm scared shitless, Stavers."

"You're very, *very* good, then."

"Yes."

"Why doesn't the diamond work on you, Weinstein?" he finally repeated.

"I told you. I can't tell you *yet*."

"Tell me *why*."

"We need to be closer. You. Me. A single entity. Total, absolute trust." She took a deep breath. "Damnit, Doug, I had a dozen chances, a *hundred* chances, to do you in. A scalpel, a needle, any one of fifty poisons, bacterial, viral. I know more ways to quietly, to secretly kill a man than your gorilla over there with all that hardware he's carrying."

"You want a *partnership?*" He was incredulous.

"Nothing so *basic*. The answer to that is *no*. Partnership implies ownership, business, possessions, money. I don't have interest in *that*."

"In what, then?"

She gestured clumsily. "I haven't even formed the words. A *different* excitement. Challenge. Accomplishment. Many of the same things you want. Goals beyond your, mine, *our* reach. King of the hill; maybe that's a clumsy way to say it. But you're the one to be king. Not me. You have the aura. What you're wearing in that steel harness is powerful medicine. But you have your own power without it. It shows up every now and then in history. Atilla, the Khans, Stalin, Mussolini, Hitler, Christ, dozens of men who *could* have been kings and rulers but for their own reasons chose not to be."

He laughed. "That the kicker for a Shakespearean quote?"

She fought off the tendency to fall into easy banter. "To be or not to be is for you to say. Neither Hamlet nor myself," she said with deceptive calm.

He had the uncanny ability to switch from one extreme to another in their exchange. "How'd you come to know Russian bombers?"

"I studied them," she answered smoothly. "I can tell you the Russian designation and the NATO code names of every major Soviet fighter, bomber, transport, *and* missile, *and* missile-firing surface ships and submarines."

Stavers almost blinked; almost, but not quite. "What else?"

"The standing military forces of every major and secondary power in the world." The words rolled easily, with confidence, from her.

"Why?" he asked; demanded.

"For this moment," she said and, as she intended, it forced him into deeper consideration of the word clash between them.

"How did you know about the diamond?" Reflex brought up his hand to brush fleetingly across his chest where the magnificent yellow diamond lay captured in the steelmesh harness.

"It's—" She stopped herself as she began her reply.

"*Don't arrange your answers, goddamnit!*" he shouted suddenly, brutally.

But she had caught the lapse before it escaped her; they both knew it and Stavers could not pursue the issue. *Not yet*, he swore, *but later*—

"I've known of it before you sought it out for that group in Las Vegas."

"I fucking don't believe her." The words rumbled heavily from Marden. For the first time he intruded into their exchange. "Kill her," he added.

The face of granite showed clouds of doubt, anger,

confusion; a chink in the Marden armor appeared. As much as he fathomed what he heard, he had also never heard anyone speak in this manner to the man he worshipped. It was . . . it was sacrilegious, damnit.

A brief gesture started from Stavers for Marden to hold his words; as quickly as his hand moved, however, Rebecca Weinstein fixed him with a sharp look of utter disdain. "What *you* believe is immaterial. What *I know* is everything. But to satisfy your loutish curiosity, *Mister* Marden," she added with enough scorn in her voice to twist the knife with skill, "need I describe to you the Board of Directors? And their virtual fortress atop El Cid in Vegas? Oh, you show doubt on your face, Marden!" She sighed, allowing one shoulder to slump *just* enough to add to the contempt. She began ticking off names on her gloved fingers. "Benito Gibraldi. Harold Metzbaum. Alberto Grazzi. Vernon Kovanowicz. That beauty, the black widow, Concetta de Luca. And, of course, their security man, Monte Hinyub." She smiled, tight-lipped and humorless. "You arranged for them all to leave this world. Permanently."

Stavers was both openly surprised and bemused. "You're better than I thought," he admitted with open admiration. "How'd you know all this?" His brow knitted. "And you know my, ah, relationship with them?"

"Metzbaum," she answered smoothly. "More than four hundred pounds. Gross, corpulent, *and* a cancerous prostate. I did the surgery to keep him alive."

Stavers grinned. "Perfect," he congratulated her. "Spinal tap, right?" She nodded. "And while he's opened up like a fat worm he hurts just enough to need a shot. He goes into a spin, he shoots off his mouth, and he remembers nothing except that the surgery was successful, *and* that he's going to live a while longer."

"An excellent summation."

"And you learned—?"

"One name should do." She paused a moment. "No. You deserve more than that." She paused but a moment, making some inner decision before plunging on. "You questioned Kurt Mueller in Berlin. He knew Hitler *very* well. You paid the old man but he paid in higher coin. The Russians butchered him when they discovered your session with him."

"You know a hell of a lot of names," Stavers said heavily.

"It's but the beginning. *You*, Mr. Stavers, have been the focal point of most of my adult life. The planning all led to this moment."

"If you didn't have those names I'd have killed you by now."

She laughed, a burst of hilarity that came from deep within her, laughter honest and true and the mirth unbidden. "What regression!" she taunted him. "Could you honestly stop me *now?* What vast mystery lies behind what I know, how exquisitely the preparations for this meeting! You'd kill *anyone else* who interfered with what I yet have to say to you."

He glowered. "Go on," he said, menacing, but as put out with himself as with this woman who had such devastating intimate knowledge of a past he had been convinced, until this moment, lay shrouded in the darkest, tightest secrecy.

"Prince Antoine Bibesco. The Roumanian who flew that three-engined German machine to Africa, the same man who slaughtered most of a peaceful tribe, who brought back," she paused, smiling with the strength of her knowledge, "the great yellow fire of ice. Mueller, Bibesco, Joachim Fest; and, then, Colonel-General von Greim. The final hours in the bunker in Berlin. Hanna Reitsch, von Greim, that sergeant pilot in another big transport all braving the Russian anti-aircraft and their fighters to fly from the Victory Column, to break free of Berlin before the Russians swallowed it whole." Weinstein shook her head. "I speak of too many names. They—"

"The Roumanians," Stavers pressed.

Weinstein gestured, an offhanded manner that made little of her extraordinary information. "Oh, you met with Yevdokia Budilova. He was utterly devoted to the old woman, Simeon Tuleca, well, she had the historical details you wanted. A truly remarkable woman. Now dead," she appended. The news of this death had no visible effect on Stavers. Weinstein felt the cold thin air starting to reach her skin. She shivered, a motion Stavers couldn't miss. He ignored her discomfort.

"And, Africa?" he pushed her.

"The Manturu tribe. But don't forget Andre Gardescu of the Roumanian secret police. *He* tried very hard to kill you." She took a deep breath, let it out suddenly, watching the moistness of her breath condense into a frosty cloud immediately swept away by the biting wind. "Shall I get to what you wear in that harness, Doug?"

"Keep it tight, Rebecca."

She studied him. His expression, the manner in which he'd relaxed his physical stance told her everything. He had no intention of seeing her dead *by anybody*. All this was too carefully done, there was too much information she had. *And there's a lot more, my bucko*, she smiled to herself, *and you're going to be the most attentive listener on this planet.*

"The world's first radiant cut. The records are still in secret vault files at Three, quai du Mont Blanc in Geneva. After it was cut—and the man who cut it was killed so he could never talk about what he'd done—the Roumanians had what is known in the trade as a cushion octagon modified brilliant. I *will* keep this to specifics because I'm freezing my ass off, and—"

He motioned her impatiently to go on without verbal sidebars. She smiled quickly at him. "All right. It came in at two-eight point six-five by two-two point two-seven millimeters." She ticked off the numbers on gloved fingers. "Add the third side at one-five point eight-zero millimeters. And absolutely flawless at eighty-one point one-two carats. I'll wrap it up, Doug. Depth perception seventy point nine percent, table diameter percentage sixty percent, girdle thickness medium, and official rarity grade flawless. In the books it goes under the description of fancy yellow, natural color, and under ultraviolet light it emits a faint yellow glow."

She deliberately went silent, letting it all sink in. Even Skip Marden stared at her with a changing perception. She wasn't explaining anything to Doug Stavers—*she was telling him.* He knew when someone might bargain for their life. This woman wasn't having any of that. He was astonished to find his admiration for Rebecca Weinstein growing in leaps and bounds, although he'd still kill her with no more signal than a finger twitch by Stavers. Somehow he knew that wouldn't happen; in these few moments he knew his own world was turning upside down, and from now on he must protect Weinstein with the same slavish dedication he had always given to Stavers. He felt befuddled, at a loss; he could not yet fully grasp this situation, and his only hard grip on his own senses was that Doug Stavers seemed almost as much at a loss as he'd found himself.

"And that is what I have in this harness?" Stavers asked after the long mutual pause.

"Yes." She shivered from a cutting knife of wind. "But you do not wear it properly."

He was so startled his body jerked, a muscular reflex action. She could have struck him and achieved less physical reaction than he showed. She saw the other signs as well. The suddenly flared nostrils, the hardness settling in his eyes, the subtle shift of his body as he resumed his fighting stance. All of it, she recognized also, reflex, and she also knew what he recognized, that the mystery thrust upon him on this desolate mesa was *not* going to be solved by his physical prowess or skills as a killing machine.

Finally he found his voice again. "What the hell do you mean by that?" he rasped.

"It belongs *in* your body. *Within*. Inside. And it needs a precise emplacement."

"How could you—?" He stopped, again caught off balance. He showed a flicker of a smile. "You missed on that one, Doctor. It *was*—"

"For Christ's sake, Stavers, that's when you *swallowed* it!" She allowed exasperation and impatience to hover between them. "When you were in that temple in India. You'd just done in Patschke after chasing him around half the planet and you yanked the diamond from him, or her, depending upon how you judge male-female before and after surgery, and then you swallowed it. *I know about it, Stavers*. Including when you went through surgery to remove it from your stomach, and then everybody in that medical clinic died when the whole damned place exploded."

"And you say it's got to go back inside me."

"Yes."

"I don't want to miss a single nuance of this, Weinstein. Precise emplacement, you said."

"Yes," she repeated.

"And if I figure you right, *you're* going to do it."

"You figure right."

"Why you?"

"Because I know things about that diamond *you don't know*, and because I'm the only surgeon in the world you can trust completely, and because—"

He'd made a very dangerous decision and once again, knew Rebecca Weinstein was balancing her life against this headache she'd brought to him. "I'm going to ask you one more time, Doc. Why doesn't the diamond have the same effect on you as it does on others?"

"It does."

"*What?*"

"I said, it does," she repeated emphatically.

"You damned well don't show it," he said, a touch of heat in his voice.

"You damned well don't know how to *look* for it," she countered immediately. "You think that between your own psyche, and it is *very* real, *and* the diamond strapped to your body, everyone within close reach of you responds slavishly. Adoration, awe, impressiveness, love, worship; all that guck. What you have *not* considered, very obviously, is that you can be loyal, devoted, honest, dedicated, whatever words you wish to use, and not be a fawning, foppish ass-kisser."

"And that's you?" He'd bent his head slightly to one side, intrigue immediately replacing the anger he'd felt.

"Absolutely," she said.

"Why do you have these feelings? Oh, I don't mean aura or personality *or* the diamond. I mean, *you*," he emphasized.

"You are the only man I have ever met, or know of, or hope ever to meet," she said slowly, "who is worthy of me, and my absolute loyalty and devotion to him."

"Jesus Christ," Marden said.

"He's dead. He doesn't count," she offered in riposte.

"You don't know that much about me," Stavers said to Weinstein, ignoring the brief exchange between her and Marden. "Or," he added quickly, "perhaps you do."

"I do," she said without hesitation.

"Maybe you don't fit *my* bill," he said.

"Your sarcasm is what doesn't fit," she snapped. "You, of all people, Doug Stavers, do not need to bandy words."

"I will admit you've put me back on my heels a few times."

"Yes, I have."

"I think you've got an ego greater than mine."

She smiled. "I won't fall into your snare of snappy word exchanges, Doug. And my ego needs no assistance from you or anybody else."

He sighed. "All right, lady. Time to get to the nitty-gritty. What's behind all this?"

"You and me, Stavers," she said softly, "you and me."

"And then what?"

"Solving the problem that's driving you mad."

He didn't answer her for a while. It had become colder, the wind stronger. She was freezing, yet she was thrilled to the bones within her. *It was working. It was happening. All these years of preparation. The gambles, the risks. It was actually happening!* "Tell me the problem, Weinstein."

She laughed, the mirth bubbling over him with his surprise at its sudden appearance. "You're bored out of your skull, Douglas Stavers. Bored to madness. You're not king of the hill. You're the big ant in a whole mess of antpiles. To put it in your own manner of expression, it all comes to a big fucking nothing deal."

His voice came back at her, sibilant, a huge python weighing life and death. "And what do I want, Weinstein?"

"The world."

"The world," he echoed.

"Yes, the world. The whole damned planet."

"Why?"

"Nothing else is worth the game. Nothing less, for sure."

"You know too much. You know too many things about me."

Here it comes, she thought, gripping herself from within.

"You're too dangerous to go on living."

"Oh, really?" It took all her self-control to manage the lightness in her voice. The coils of the death python were tightening about her. "Bullshit, Stavers. *You need me.*"

"You better have one hell of an answer. *Why* do I need you?"

"Because," she said slowly, holding his eyes tightly, "I'm the only person alive on this planet who knows that the diamond you're wearing . . ." she took a deep breath, "*isn't a diamond.*"

I've got him now. There's no question. I've sliced through his mind like a laser beam through fat. Nothing could have hit him harder. His eyes tell it all. Will these people never learn? Will they ever discover how to control the expansion and contraction of their pupils? It tells everything! A doorway to the inner mind. Stavers came here to threaten or to frighten me, or even to kill me, but he did that out of frustration. Now I've replaced frustration with his fascination, his determination to know so much more.

She took a deep breath and sighed, nothing in her facial expression revealing the enormous strength behind that facade. *How I hate playing the game out this way. Cat-and-mouse, and he's the unknowing mouse. But my master is Time. I've got to go through the whole slow, sorry mess these people consider the acme of their science. And there's no changing that.*

She smiled to herself. *It's so strange. As animals go, he would make a marvelous pet. A trained, healthy animal made for breeding. Well, my fine friend, you're going to be the king whether you like it or not.*

The smile turned to inner ice. *I wonder what Marden would do if he knew I could kill him from right where I stand, without moving a muscle. One day I might even do that just to find out how it feels.*

Chapter 8

The questions he had ready to hurl back at Dr. Rebecca Weinstein were so immediate, so bloody *obvious* that he hesitated giving them voice. Never in his entire life had he felt so manipulated as he was right now. Weinstein held the strings in the manner of the master puppeteer and he was jerking back and forth to every twitch and snap of her fingers. Of course he must ask her all the questions that leaped into being. But if he spoke quickly he would be reversing their roles; he would be openly dependent upon her. On her answers. *And I must know what she knows.* He accepted without reservation that she spoke the absolute, literal truth. No word games. That would have served no purpose. She played her game in a different way than he'd ever encountered before. Oh, she could have sat with him in privacy, told him straight out without all this dizzying probing and dodging, but somehow it wouldn't have carried the impact it presented *because this was his setup.*

He felt jumpy. Being startled like one gunshot after another wasn't his way of doing things. And this woman had nailed him again and again. *The NATO code name for that Russian bomber . . . goddamnit, now I'd bet my last dollar she never slipped at all! That everything she said was deliberate, that she laid out the bait for me to bite. And it worked . . .*

There was something else. It *had* to be. Rebecca Weinstein hadn't become what she was, hadn't traveled this far, hadn't gained so much knowledge, *without an organization.* Weinstein. Jewish; it might be Austrian or German but that didn't matter. She had the touch of the Mediterranean in her. *No; not Jewish. Not unless you're thinking of the warriors of Saul and David, or . . . or, the Sabra.*

He lifted his head suddenly. "Your organization. What was it called?"

"You used the past tense," she fended away the question. "Why?"

Goddamnit, but she's fast. And slippery. "Just answer me, Doc."

"It had no name. A number, that's all. A number picked at random so it didn't mean anything and it could never mean anything. Triple Five."

"Neat," he acknowledged. "The numeral prefix used in all Hollywood movies because the five-five-five isn't used *anywhere.*" He had a sudden hunch. "You're trained in weapons, aren't you?"

"Yes."

"I'm getting the strangest feeling your past is somehow interconnected with mine."

She waited. He was moving perfectly. Precisely the way her father had predicted.

"Well, you're not volunteering much. Then give me just one name that fits, Weinstein, and I'll do the rest."

"Call for the chopper, Stavers," she said, shivering anew. "I'm *not* joking. I don't know how you two lunatics handle all this cold but I'm starting to get into serious trouble just standing here."

He turned to Marden and nodded. Marden pressed a button on a belt transmitter. A yellow light glowed. "They've got it."

Stavers had already dismissed the helicopter that in moments would be on its way to pick them up. He studied Weinstein anew. "The name, Doc."

"You're not going to like it, Doug."

"Why?"

"Memories. Knife to the heart. That sort of thing."

A premonition swept through him. He pushed it aside. "The name."

"Stan Horvath."

He swore softly to himself. A flood of emotions raced and pounded across his face. She saw surprise, the rush of memory, *and* pain.

"I'm sorry," she said quietly.

"What the hell for?" he half-shouted. "Stan Horvath was a professional killer. Like myself, like Skip. So what?"

"He trained me."

"So he trained you. So fucking *what*?"

"I hate this," she murmured.

"Why?" he demanded.

"You sent Jack North to Israel to meet with Stan Horvath." She saw his eyes widen and she knew Stavers was anticipating, even dreading, what she *knew*. Worse, what she might *say*. "You wanted Horvath to lead you and your group to Patschke in the high Ecuador country. Not to lead you there personally, but to pinpoint the mountain fortress of Patschke."

"A lot of people know that, Weinstein," he said, glowering, his eyes like red coals.

"Jack North was Tracy's father." She took a deep breath, hoping the old and terrible wound had been healed enough for Stavers to keep a tight grip on himself.

"You loved Tracy. She loved you. Total, complete, perfect love. She burned to death on an airport runway in Philadelphia. You were the only survivor of the crash. Part of you died in that fire."

Marden knew of the pain Doug Stavers had gone through for so long. He knew how much Stavers had loved Tracy, and—

"Let me kill the bitch," Marden snarled. He could think only of the pain she had brought to Stavers. *Kill the bitch and I end all this shit.*

"Shut the hell up," Stavers said through gritted teeth to Marden, then turned back to Weinstein. For a long and anguished moment he studied this incredible woman, shivering in the cold, master of more knowledge of Doug Stavers than any other person in the world. She knew *inside* him.

"I've got a thousand questions for you, Doc."

"I know that."

"You'll answer them."

"I'll even tell you the questions you won't think to ask."

"Do you love me, Weinstein?"

"Do I answer in triplicate? Press hard with the pen to make clean copies?"

"I'm serious."

"So am I," she retorted.

"Answer me, straight. Do you love me?"

"Yes."

"*Why?*"

"I was trained, psychologically prepared, emotionally controlled to love you. What you are, *and* that damned stone you wear, *and* what we've already been through, the jaws of death and all that, yes, I love you."

He smiled; his teeth barely showed. "Do I love you, Weinstein?"

"No."

The smile became a grin. She shut it off with an almost audible bang.

"But you will," she added.

He started to laugh, shut it off as quickly as the unbidden mirth started. She was crazy! And yet . . .

"You have always believed you would never love anyone, again, after Tracy," Rebecca Weinstein told him slowly, carefully. "Even when that splendid, superb woman got to you."

He felt a chill run through him; not a sliver of the cold about them, but an icicle from the past. "You know?"

"She did everything she could to kill you. That was her sole purpose in life. She was of the holy of the holies. One of the Six Hundred. The blessed of the Vatican. She tried to kill you again and again, she caused the death of Tracy North, and she came to you as a virgin. Rosa Montini of the family of the popes. A direct family member of Joseph Montini. *Pope Pius*. And his brother, Senato Lodovici Montini, a great and wonderful senator of Rome. Rosa Montini, deadly, beautiful, magnificent, virginal. Yet she gave herself to you. You overcame the blessings of God Himself. You overcame her sworn duty in life. You made love to her." Weinstein skipped a heartbeat. "Did you know her body lies in holy state in the catacombs of the Vatican? Of course, they did great plastic surgery on her face after," another heartbeat pause, "she was hurled from that helicopter in India."

"Good God, what the hell *don't* you know!"

"It's not that difficult, Doug. My father was a close friend of Cardinal Butto Giovanni, and *he* was chosen by the Pope to create and to guide the Six Hundred in their search for the object you now wear." She showed a brief, wan smile as she brought up old memories. "But not even *they* knew what it truly was. *Is*," she ammended. She sighed. "To the Vatican, what you wear was the *adamas*, the holiest of holies. To the Vatican, the stone appeared two thousand years ago, simultaneously with the birth of Christ. They called it the Star of Bethlehem." She shook her head. "But that's a mix, confused and fantasizing; it had nothing to do with Bethlehem, which in itself is an allegory."

She looked back in the direction of Indian's Bluff, shuffling from one foot to the other, wrapping her arms about herself to stave off the cold. "Where the hell is that chopper?" she hissed.

"It's on the way," Stavers said unnecessarily. "The cold getting to your brain, Weinstein?"

"Oh, God. Up yours," she threw back at him, pleased with her sudden descent to gutter wording. "No; it's just going into deep freeze." She flashed a shivering smile. "But don't count me out yet, Stavers. All right; I'll give this thing a quick wrap. The Vatican believed, *believes*, the stone is a diamond. Born in the fires of atmospheric entry to the earth. Fifty to eighty thousand miles an hour. That's enough heat and pressure to create a diamond from meteoric material. It doesn't matter," she waved a hand to dismiss that issue. "What *does* matter is what they believe, and the fact that the stone, or diamond, or whatever they wish to call it, *does* have an incredible effect on people, even animals, within the effective reach, the range of field, of the object. Put simply, and you already know this, the Manturu tribe, in the midst of savage tribal wars, raids and jealousies, lived without war for some two thousand years. That is powerful medicine, my friend. So powerful the Vatican would do just about *anything* to get that object."

She laughed, another sudden quiet offering of inner mirth. "But why am I telling you what you already know? You fought the Israelis, *and* the Americans, *and* the Vatican, *and* the Russians, from Berlin to South America and India and—" She shook her head and lapsed into silence, an unspoken passing of the exchange to Stavers.

He walked closer to her, so close they stood face to face, the condensation vapor from their breath mingling in a single cloud. "You know all these things," he said, quietly and directly, "yet you tease me."

"I am *not* teasing," she answered immediately.

"Then you are so clever as to be phenomenal," he countered.

"True; I am," she told him, without a trace of ego. "But you already know that."

"You said you were trained for," he smiled, "this moment."

"Yes."

"By whom?"

"My father, or, by people under his supervision."

She could also feel his mind speeding into new thoughts, wheeling freely to concepts he'd let lie for too long. The questions came faster, sharper-edged.

"How many languages do you speak, Weinstein?"

"Twenty-four."

Stavers blinked; that for him, in this context, was a monumental expression, a startling reaction to what he'd heard. He nodded slightly to his own thoughts.

"Religions; how well do you know them?"

She smiled, only a quirky lifting of one corner of her mouth. The expression hurt her teeth from the cold. "I could be a priest in almost any of the major religions, and ten times as many in the minor leagues."

"To say nothing of the weirdos," he appended.

"They are *all* weirdos," she said to refine their mutual definition.

"Who's your father, Weinstein?"

"Take away the W in the family name," she said, ever so softly.

"*Abraham* Einstein?"

"You'll never know how desperately I wanted you to say that name without my verbalizing it first."

"Direct cousins," he added, his acknowledgement of the family of pure genius unhidden in his expression.

"It's starting to come together, Rebecca. Piece by little piece. You play a mean jigsaw puzzle, lady."

"God, *don't stop now*," she almost begged him.

"Your father trained you *for* me?"

She shook her head. "No. For what you wear on your body. For what must be placed surgically *within* you. For what was so incredibly beyond any monetary or other value that tens of thousands of people have already died for it. My father said—we'll call it the stone for the moment—that it would finally become the possession of a single individual who would rise through, let me use his own words, a torment of combat, terror, horror, death and emotional pain. *That* is where I've been directed almost all my life."

"Why?"

"Because my father, and myself, are the only two persons who have ever known what you have in that harness, Doug. And my father is dead."

"I have a hunch it wasn't of natural causes."

"The Vatican."

"I thought he was friends with the big-cheese cardinal?"

"Friendship has nothing to do with the higher aims of the church."

She heard the distant chopping sounds of helicopter blades.

"You're convinced, strangely so, that I'll submit to this surgery you keep going back to. The stone, uh, the diamond, inside me."

"Yes. Yes, you will do just that."

"After you tell me why?"

"I'll never *tell* you. I'll *show* you. Then you'll understand."

"When? Where?"

"Soon." The helicopter glinted in the low sun as it approached, the blades flat-blatting in the heavy cold air.

"Weinstein, I have another question for you."

"One of many," she smiled.

"This one stands alone," he told her, and she waited for his words.

"Would you kill me if it were necessary? If you believed it were necessary?"

She held his eyes. "No."

"*Could—*" He stopped his words, eyes widening as the new thought came to him. "*Could you kill me?*"

Her smile was everything; warm, deep, honest, simple and vastly complex. "No, Doug," she said, touching his arm. "Don't you understand yet? The program. The way *I've* been programmed. If ever I tried to kill you I would suffer a lethal stroke immediately. Surgical implant. A truly brilliant accomplishment. The man who did the surgery believed the precaution was necessary."

"Damn, you're mixing me up again, Weinstein! *Who* did that kind of surgery!"

"Abraham Einstein."

"Your *father*?"

"Yes. Does that remove some of your concern?" *Go on, Doug. Swallow the lies, eat the fairy tales. One day you'll really know but not yet.*

He chuckled; a grisly and dangerous cousin to a laugh. "Only if all this wild stuff you've been telling me is true."

She watched the helicopter touch down and a door open. She started for the warmth of the cabin, then stopped. "It's not that complicated, Doug. If I *am* lying, then *you'll* kill *me*. And I have absolutely no fear of *that*." She motioned toward the waiting machine. "Now, can we *please* go? I'll need to thaw out before I'm ready."

They started together for the helicopter. Her words intrigued him. "Ready for what, Rebecca?"

She looked up at him as she placed her arm through his. "Sometimes, even the best and the brightest are very dumb," she said. "For you to make love to me, of course."

Chapter 9

Even the gladiators must practice. Not just *any* combatant for the arena. *All* of them. Keep the killing juices going. The muscles limber and snap-powerful. The bloodlust free and yet controlled.

And there are many, many different arenas, and they do not look the same, yet they all serve the same purpose.

For a man to test himself.

Doug Stavers left the helicopter on its landing platform beneath Indian's Bluff. The hydraulic piston lowered them slowly and the earth sealed above them and they were lost to the outside world. Marden eased his heavy bulk from the machine first; that was habit and practice. He stood to the side, first scanning everyone and everything about him. Stavers emerged, his face its usual unreadable granite. Rebecca Weinstein held out her hand, ready for Stavers to take it in his. She felt stupid as he walked away from the landing platform without a single word or even a glance in her direction.

They walked together down a long corridor, Stavers and Marden, the untouchables. Alone, and yet their movement monitored by the concealed television scanners of Templin's security system. Stavers kept his gaze directly before them as their boots thudded into the plastimetal beneath their stride. "Get the wolves. Two of them. Bay Six."

Marden nodded. "As you say. I'll be there with you."

"No weapons," Stavers instructed.

"Of course. No guns. Just the knife."

"*No* weapons. No knives." He offered a wan smile to Marden. "Just you. And," he said sharply, unusually so in speaking to Marden, "no interference."

Skip Marden had his answer ready for that, but he kept his silence. When Stavers was in this mood, and that bitch doctor had put him into one *hell* of a mood, you just did not mess with the man.

They separated as Stavers went into a locker room. He threw off his cold-weather garments, stripped himself naked. He looked toward the entrance to Bay Six, stopped and looked up to where he knew a scanner held him in view. "You on, Al?" he spoke to empty space.

"Yes, sir."

"Kill all other surveillance but your own unit. Here, and, Bay Six. No interference from you."

"Yes, sir." Templin's voice was flat, mechanical, obedient. It wasn't the first time he'd seen Doug Stavers naked except for the steel harness, and he wasn't being paid to ask questions when he knew the answers were none of his affair.

Stavers turned into the doorway to Bay Six, hesitated for the door to slide open, and walked inside. The door hissed closed behind him. The room was big. Big, and empty. A cork floor, cork walls, the illumination from overhead translucent panels. Nothing bright or protruding. A room of soft grey-blue empty.

A panel slid away from a far wall. He watched Marden enter, wearing military trousers and a tank top. No weapons; as Stavers had ordered. Marden showed the question in his face, Stavers nodded. Marden pressed a concealed button on the wall close to him and another panel whisked away.

Two great wolves moved cautiously into the bay. The panel closed behind them. The great feral creatures were hungry; they hadn't been fed for nearly a week. Hungry, angry, aggressive. They sniffed the air, focusing on the strange unfamiliar man-figure.

Food.

The wolves moved cautiously, every instinct screeching its silent warning. Everything was *wrong*. They had smelled the man-smell in their territory, heard the explosive sounds, felt pain as needles lanced them and, unknowing to the four-footed targets, became the victims of a powerful drug. Some unknown time later they regained their senses in a strange and frightening enclosure. The sharp odor of steel cages, straw beneath, more cold substance holding water. Days later, ferocious with hunger and snarling-mad with their strange confinement, they were fed. Barely enough to sustain them; instinct brought the bloody meat into their systems. Then the strange pains began. Their feet; sudden sharp pains brought them yelping and jumping. *Electric shocks.* As their keepers attested, "They are mean sons of bitches now."

The two biggest, most powerful of these animals circled slowly about and between the two man-figures. They knew their smell, and while familiar, it was somehow different. One stood far away, unmoving, his back to a rocklike wall. Not the other. The smell from him was powerful, menacing. Experience had taught these animals well. They sniffed and looked for the long sticks that hurled fire and thunder and pain. They looked for the shine of light from metal teeth that also could bring terrible pain and open bodies. The hands of the man-figure held nothing they could see. The lead animal growled deep and low, a feral snarl from his innards, an instinctive rumble signaling signs of his growing confidence. Quickly the second animal, less dominant than the accepted leader, echoed the throaty rumble. Hair erected; ruffs expanded, lips curled back. Shoulders rolled and muscle bunched and great teeth appeared. They moved closer, slowly but inexorably, to the man-figure standing alone.

The man-figure without the killing metal teeth, or the thundersticks that could be smelled across hills.

The lead wolf stopped, sniffing, curious, feeling strange sensations he had never before known. There was no fear-stink. This was a very dangerous animal. A drumroll of hunger growled in the wolf's stomach. Lips curled more, teeth flashed. The wolf prepared to spring. The throat; always cut at the throat. The second animal would move swiftly, also. They had hunted before. The first attack to the throat, the second at the feet to topple the prey or directly at the mating appendages to render the animal helpless. Teeth through throat, springing blood; instincts met. Food.

The wolf backed slightly. Without conscious thought his legs moved him backward. The man-animal was advancing against him. The wolf stared, then blinked, strange forces swirling through his brain, tying his instincts into knots. He struggled within, prepared to leap and throat-slash with his terrible teeth, but he could no longer move.

The huge animal whined. He had not summoned the sound, but his brain ordered the submission sound. Surprised, uncomprehending, he heard his own keening yield to the man-animal.

Emotions swirled. Fear of the man-animal, savage hunger, feral instinct, and . . . writhing from the brain-twist of himself, the man-animal seemed to bend and swirl, to embrace itself within a changing-shape-fog, and without the clear picture of understanding, without the shape of the wolf, the great animal saw and smelled and *knew* that before him was the pack leader, the ultimate of his kind. Whatever is love, devotion, loyalty, protection; whatever are these feelings in the animal, they thrummed and beat madly in the chest of the wolf. The sensations and the feelings burst upward, enveloped the animal and it no longer followed its earlier powerful emotions. Whining, tail drooping, the great wolf sidled close to Stavers, rubbed warmly, wildly, hysterical with joy, against his thigh. The wolf reveled in the kinesthetic sensing, in the scent of Stavers, in recognition of this creature as the absolute lobo.

Marden leaned forward, his own instincts ready to launch him against that huge animal, those powerful teeth and jaws now so close to Stavers. Even the power of that animal would not prevail against a killing animal like Skip Marden. More than once, many times, indeed, he had been attacked by powerful animals. More than once he had gripped a Doberman or a rottweiler by its throat, held the animal out at arm's length and squeezed the life from its jugular. So not even this great killer of the forests held fear for him. His only fear was for Stavers, and then he saw the brief shake of the other man's head. Marden relaxed and watched in wonder at the marvelous scene.

Stavers projected his thoughts, sensations, his strength, his love, as powerfully as he could radiate the feelings he wanted to embrace and soak into the wolf by his side. He had no idea until this moment that his own personality, his own lack of fear for animals, no matter how wild and dangerous, could be so incredibly heightened. He wasn't the man-figure; he was the man-animal, the lord of the animal kingdom, and he felt an incredible kinship as the wolf offered its absolute submission and acceptance of everything Stavers wanted him to feel and *to know*.

Then he stood straight, body bristling, springsteel tightening in the power of the wolf body. Stavers looked not at the animal by his side but at the second wolf, trembling, frightened, confused. Stavers unleashed a torrent of hate at the second animal. The huge creature by his side looked up to Stavers, totally immersed in lupus loyalty, and Stavers growled deep in his own throat and pointed to the second wolf.

The speed and fury of the attack surprised even these two men. One hundred and thirty pounds of timber wolf hurtled at the other animal, jaws closing with a terrible ripping sound into the throat. A lupus scream of pain, spattering blood, snarling; it was over. One animal lay dead. The other stood silently, waiting.

Stavers gestured. "Throw the carcass into the cage. The other one will follow. Close it up and come back here." He started from the bay, stopped and half-turned. "I'll be back. Wait here for me." Stavers went to the locker, dressed and returned to the bay, letting the door thud tight behind him. Slowly, deliberately, not speaking, he withdrew a cigar from his shirt and lit up.

Marden studied him. A different Marden from everyday. A man whose usually granite expression displayed his mixture of emotion and wonder at what had happened. "That's the goddamndest shit I have *ever* seen," he exclaimed quietly to Stavers. "Man, I have been up against everything from pythons to tigers to water buffalo, *and* wolves, *and* hyenas—" He stopped to shake his head in another sign of wonder and awe at what he'd just witnessed. "You know what I saw?" he shot at Stavers.

Staves smiled. *He* knew. What Marden believed he himself knew would be interesting. The big son of a bitch was just as much jungle cat as he was human. "Tell me," Stavers said.

"That big timber came in here functioning on pure instinct," Marden replied. "I know those wolves. You watch their ruff, ears, their eyes; everything's a sign. And he was hungry. Shit, he was starving. And when a timber wolf gets to starving, he throws away all caution. In fact, you can be chased by a whole goddamn pack of them—I was, once, and without a damn gun to my name—and use them against themselves."

Stavers searched old memories; indistinct shapes and knowledge, but nothing he'd ever used himself. He was more than interested. He motioned for Marden to continue.

"We were part of a team checking out a Russian radar station in the middle of fucking nowhere," Marden said, reliving the experience. "Weren't supposed to be there, of course. Came in by parachute and we planned to go out with a C-130 scooping us up on a hung line. You know the system." Stavers nodded. "Anyway, to cut it to the hard nut, the Russians nailed us, and we took off for the deep woods. We got chopped up pretty bad. Most of our people killed right off and the others wounded or captured. I got away, in deep snow. I *thought* I'd got away, that is. The Russians must have been laughing like hell, because I was headed straight for some really heavy wolf country. And in that part of the world the clock stopped ticking a hundred years ago. Killer wolf packs were as common there as a poodle on Fifth Avenue here."

"You didn't go up a tree?"

"Uh uh," Marden said ruefully. "Wouldn't have helped. I'd have frozen to death by morning and the wolves would just have waited for me to fall out of the tree. I said I didn't have any guns, but I *did* have a whole passel of knives. Like I usually carry. Boots, belt; you know. When I could hear the wolves getting closer, I stopped long enough to cut a slice in my forearm. Bloodied up the blade real good and I jammed it butt down into the snow, and then I kept running like hell. We had left some cargo drops about ten miles away. If I got there I'd be okay. Weapons, food, barrel shelter; radio, the works."

He grinned with memories. "Anyway, the first wolf comes up and smells all that fresh blood on the knife. So, right off he licks the blood. That knife was razor sharp. Wolf sliced his tongue all to hamburger and *he* began to bleed. The more he bled the more he licked, he was so mad with hunger *and* bloodlust. Two more wolves came up, got the blood smell, saw the first wolf covered with blood and they tore into *him*. Killed him. Don't know if they were going to eat one of their own, but I didn't wait to find out. Kept running until I heard more of them getting closer. This time I smeared blood over *two* knives. That split 'em. Two animals cut their tongues to hot pastrami, and there was blood everywhere. I did that one more time and I was half-frozen and out of breath and got to that supply drop one jump ahead of the rest of the wolves."

"You didn't use any more knives," Stavers said quietly.

"Hell, no. Not with one of those auto magnums with the 200-round plasticlip. Shot the hell out of those critters. I must have killed twelve or fifteen of them. Got into heavy clothes, some good rations and whiskey, and *then* I climbed a tree. Had five clips by then. Just potshotted anything that moved. They got me out with a turbo. Pilatus job from Switzerland."

Stavers dragged deeply on his cigar. "What does all that, and whatever else you know about these animals, tell you about what happened here?"

"There wasn't any conflict with that wolf," Marden said, choosing his words carefully. "Inner conflict, I mean. Whatever you're sending out with that diamond—and as far as I'm concerned, Weinstein may be a great sawbones, but she don't know shit about the stone—along with whatever *you* are, it overwhelmed that animal. First look he had of you he was going to eat your ass from ears to toes. Then, a few moments of confusion, and all *that* was gone. Once you got between his ears, even his hunger got buried. You flat overwhelmed him. From that point on that animal never hesitated. He loved you, like that bitch back in that alley in New York. *Loved* you, man, however an animal loves, or whatever emotion is involved. His acceptance of you as the pack leader, the ultimate lupus, was absolute. I never saw anything like it."

Marden's face showed a grimace of struggle to refine his thoughts. "Then he attacked the other one. You did that, didn't you?"

Stavers nodded. "And when he returns to the pack, to the other wolves, he'll be the same to them, as I was to him." Stavers smiled, more from growing knowledge than humor. He flicked cigar ash to the floor. "He won't think because he *can't* think, in terms of higher reasoning. But his feelings, instincts, whatever they are, will be, are, absolute."

Stavers laughed, a harsh tone reflecting some inner turmoil of his own. "As close as those animals are to man, and our histories are intertwined, we're also as far apart as we can imagine. They're superb animals. It's their very instinct, historical instinct, call it genetic memory, whatever, that makes them so special. They're smarter than hell, and yet auto-instinct gives them the edge in a world where claw and fang and cunning are everything. You know something, Skip? I'll never again be a factor in that animal's life *unless* he comes in contact with me. Oh, sure, memory will alert him to me if sight or smell is involved, but what if I'm not wearing this diamond? What if it isn't adding to, accelerating, boosting, whatever the hell it does, this aura or power I'm generating? Will the wolf *know* that somehow I'm different than I was before?"

"He'll sense it," Marden said emphatically. "He'll sense it and he'll get the hell out of your way. Instinct, cunning, survival; all of it comes into play."

"But he won't *fear* me until he comes within the reach, the grasp of energy—I lack the right words for this—of the diamond. Maybe he'll run and maybe he won't, but it won't be because he reasons it out."

Marden shrugged. "You're using human logic with lupine intelligence. It's not just a matter of more or less, Doug. It's *alien*. That wolf, and you and me, we may have come from the same pool of genetic slime hundreds of millions of years ago, but we're *still* alien. Like as much, say, that a man and a scorpion are cut from the same cloth."

Stavers took a long drag on his cigar. He smiled. "Same cloth, different tailor." His facial expression changed; Marden knew the signs of Stavers shifting to a completely different plateau of thinking. "Let's go," he said sharply, his unbidden patience evident. "I'll meet you in the training room. You arm yourself to the teeth. Everything you'd pick for a hellfight, got it?"

"Yep. Got it. Any special instructions?"

"Be there in fifteen minutes. I'll follow you in. Just you and me," Stavers instructed. "And be ready for *anything*." Stavers went through the door, Marden following. In the corridor they split in different directions.

Stavers walked to the living quarters, stood before the entrance to Rebecca Weinstein's studio, a mixture of luxury apartment and very private medical facility. He pressed the announcer button. *She must have been waiting for me to show up*, he judged as the door opened only seconds later. Weinstein was stunning. And clever as hell. She wore a lounging shift of her own design. A mixture of ancient Greek or Roman with modern touches, revealing the deep hollow between her full breasts, yet something less than an open or brazen invitation.

"Come in," she said, studying his face. Stavers recognized the signs of a woman wanting to make love, to be loved fiercely, to abandon herself, and yet walking her own psychological tightrope. *This* lover was totally unpredictable. She wanted him, desperately so. She wanted even more for him to want, to *take* her, and yet she must remain at arm's length until the right moment—

But she didn't *know* the right moment. Not with this man, to whom she had already, in brief and unquestionable words, given her complete commitment.

Stavers shook his head. "No; I've got something to do. Down in the weapons bay with Marden. Give me thirty minutes, Rebecca, and meet me in the spa. The private one. We'll do the spa together." He turned and she stared at his back as he walked away as though he'd never even spoken to her.

Thirty minutes. God, is it really going to happen? Finally? Do we go through a mating ritual in that pool of bubbling water and fragrance? Music and champagne? And what's so important with Marden that we've got this waiting period?

She closed the door slowly, leaned back against it, startled with the sensations of her flaring nostrils, her pounding heart and shortness of breath. *I'm acting like a goddamned schoolgirl!* she berated herself. *Jesus, all I need to do is swallow water in that spa and choke in his face when he's ready for—* She thought of his pendulous organ, that heavy penis. How many times had she imagined Stavers hard and brutally sexual? She'd never seen him aroused. Not sexually. *Good grief, woman, slow down! You're going to hyperventilate!*

She forced her breathing deeper and slower. Dizziness abated. She smiled, then giggled aloud. *Just be the woman you are. You're dynamite in the sack. So this time it's a spa instead of a mattress. You know every trick there is in pleasing a man.* She stood before a full-length mirror, humming a tune to herself.

Doug Stavers was moving into *her* arena. She didn't need stiffened nipples or coyness. *His* stimulus lay much deeper. She fascinated him and even more important, he was still perplexed, still confused by what she knew and had told him, and even more to the point, what she still withheld *from* him.

It was going to be marvelous to yield to him physically, sexually. She glanced at a wall clock. *Only five minutes had passed so far!*

Chapter 10

Stavers entered the weapons bay quietly. Skip Marden stood in room center, a human killing arsenal. He'd followed Stavers' instructions to the letter. Hand weapons, laser sights, grenades, throwing knives, automatic weapons, even a riot gun slung from a side pouch. And those were only the weapons that were visible. Stavers grunted with satisfaction, turned and dropped a steel bar across the entryway. It would take a small bulldozer to get in now. He turned back to Marden. Without prelude or reminder he dropped back to their conversation in the bay with the wolves.

"That wolf," he said slowly, choosing his words deliberately, "is a killer." He pointed to Marden. "You're a killer. What's the difference between you and that animal?"

"I'm unpredictable," Marden answered quickly, easily. "That is, I have a virtually unlimited reach in what I can do as an aggressor or killing machine. I can modify my instincts across a tremendous range. The wolf can't do that. The animal has instinct and memory and the two operate on full automatic. Within his mental range the animal is completely predictable. But people work on a different plane altogether."

Stavers considered Marden's words; more specifically, he considered Marden as the *source* for these words. They were both killers, Stavers and Marden, and yet they could be and at times were vastly different in their calculated, even methodical savagery.

"Explain further what you just said," Stavers directed.

Skip Marden showed his surprise. "You're baiting me, aren't you?"

Stavers' showed contempt. "If I were, you wouldn't be *asking* me to confirm your little worries." His words had a nasty cutting edge to them and they only reinforced for Marden the belief that Stavers was moving through some intricate cerebral maze with him. He cut off that line of thinking almost at once. Matching wits with Doug Stavers was a hopeless task. He'd had plenty of proof in the past in *that* area.

"All right," Marden said after that brief pause of caution to himself. "I still say it's something you know better than I do. But," he shrugged, "let's say, and I'm very sure of this, I know people on a feral level. Raw gut instinct. Survival, killing—"

"Goddamnit, I know all that shit," Stavers said scathingly. "Now tell me what I don't know, or what you believe I've forgotten."

"*You're* the master with people," Marden went on, his surprise undiminished. "You read them like an open book. I *feel* them. I guess you do also but you *read* them. You get under a man's scalp and you go hunting for their thoughts. Invasive; that's the word. And somehow you know *what they remember*. Most people have memories that are poorly instinctive. They're highly trained, but a natural talent for really detailed memory is on the rare side. Those are the few people really worth a shit, anyway. Like, well, when that wolf returned to his pack, like you said, his memory functioning is automatic. While he's with the pack, nothing's changed. I mean, the goddamn animals don't compare notes. But people do just that; they take their mental notes and their recorded information with them wherever they go. So even if their instincts aren't worth diddly-shit, they've got the means to carry past lessons into the present moment."

Marden had a pained look on his face. "I still don't get this, Doug. Jesus, man, you're the brains here. Everything I'm saying I learned from watching you, listening to you, supporting you." He shook his head, his continuing discomfort a revelation to Stavers. Marden had saved his life more times than he could remember; in this respect he was an extension of Stavers' own survival instincts and abilities. And now he was floundering.

Good; just the way I want him to be. The more screwed up he gets in his head, the more he'll be like that damned wolf. Now; in deeper with the needle, Stavers judged.

"Spell it out," Stavers demanded. He kept pushing Marden because he'd never heard Marden express a depth of feeling as he'd just done. Was the aura, his own aura, so enormously energized and expanded by the great yellow diamond, having a *positive* effect on Marden? *What a hell of a concept! But that woman . . . Weinstein said it's not a diamond. I ought to kill her. She gives me one hell of a headache. I should kill her, but she knows I can't until I find out what's behind her words. Goddamnit it . . .*

He forced himself back to the bewildered giant before him. Marden was functioning as a mirror of Stavers' own thoughts. It was a viewpoint of observation he'd never before encountered. It was so surprising it stood apart as a commanding revelation. Marden had been with him through every kind of thick and thin. Battles about half the planet. Fighting everything from hired killers in dark alleys to savage firefights on a full war scale, against the massed firepower of the Blue Light killer chopper teams of the Americans, those wily and dedicated professional savages of the Israelis, the Allah-seeking Moslems, the fanatics of the Vatican's holy 600; natives, professionals, madmen, geniuses, even the terrible dominance of God-fever generated by Ernst Patschke in India *where Stavers had overcome the power of the diamond* and cut down Patschke like a great bag of blood.

Skip Marden had been through it all covering Stavers' back. Stavers was still alive because of this man, and here he was, tearing into Marden.

"I wish I knew what the hell you're after, Doug," Marden said finally. "Christ, man, I'm no genius but I'm also not just a dumb hired mercenary. You couldn't hire me to be what I am for you, Doug!" Pain creased that scarred face.

"I know that," Stavers said quietly, easing the pain but not releasing the hook.

"Then you know I've also *studied* my business," Marden said quickly. "Look," he said suddenly, almost pleading for Stavers' understanding, "I ain't no scholar and sure as hell I'm no egghead, but I deal in life and killing and surviving and controlling. I'm a hell of a lot closer to that wolf than I am to most *people*. I'm damned well familiar with some of the greatest leaders, *and* the warriors of history—and that includes the limpwrists, like Ghandi, who had to have more heart than a fucking lion to do what he did—and out of all of this, because I *know* these kind of people, *you*," he paused for a deep breath, never accustomed to the torrent of words now pouring from him, "and I mean this, you're among the best of them. The only reason you ain't never ruled an army or a country is because you never gave a shit about doing that. But you could. *You can. Now. Any time you want to go that route.*"

He shifted his feet and balance, as uneasy with his verbal onslaught as he would be against an enemy with unknown prowess. He had more to say, he *wanted* to say more, but with the unease bringing hackles to the back of his neck, he clamped down on his teeth and fell into silence.

Son of a bitch, thought Stavers. *He's right. And that's why I'm so fucked up between my ears. I've got the power and I forgot the power isn't worth piss without its catalyst.*

He laughed aloud, amusing himself with his own thoughts. *Run an army? Rule a country? That's piss-ant stuff! Fuck the armies and the countries! There's a whole goddamned world out there and I've got something that fell from heaven and it ruled warring tribes for a couple thousand years, and I'm screwing around in the mud!*

I'm bored. Holy Jesus Fucking Christ, I'm bored. Skip's got a part of it, but not all, because he's like the wolf and he can see only so far and no more.

I see it now. I'm like the professional gambler in the perfect casino with perfect women and perfect drinks and perfect food and I've got the ultimate streak of luck and I never, never lose at any gamble I take. I always win. Always. It takes a while for a gambler in that position to understand that perfection in gambling is the final of all curses, that you're in Hell. It is total and utter boredom. No risk, no challenge, no gamble. The man who can't lose has already lost everything because the one thing he doesn't have is challenge. Maybe risk is a better word. There's no penalty. So life becomes a matter of eating perfect food and dropping turds of pure gold but gold under these conditions isn't worth even shit. Like pissing in a gold urinal. Big fucking thrill!

I've got this power. But if I've destroyed so many power groups with all their global influence, what did I really accomplish? Why am I here?

Stavers stared at Skip Marden and perhaps for the first time he saw the dog-devotion, the shine of awe in the eyes of the other man, and it didn't mean anything any more.

I'm fucking bored! What's the purpose? Of anything? Did God give me this power? Is this all some sort of master plan? But that's bullshit. Einstein was wrong. God throws dice all the damned time. But right here, now, imprisoned on this one fucking planet, am I really the manGod that Marden sees in me? Is that crazy? Or is it purpose? Is this what Christ went through, trying to reach the idiot rabble all about him in his time? Am I like Christ when he was a kid, a real mean little sucker with telekinetic powers? Or God-given powers because God was bored and gave this kid the means to use his mind and kid's greed as a bludgeon? He had his priests then, too, just like Skip, here. And Christ would strike other kids dead, and then the older folks dead, and he blinded as many as he cured and all the priests about him would shit a brick and mutter to themselves about whether or not they had a messiah in their midst, or this kid was crazy and possessed by demons and he was going to shake up the whole world. But why did Christ do what he did?

He felt an explosion mushrooming silently in his head. *He did it because he was fucking bored! He was so bored he risked whatever the Romans might dump on him, and if he fucked up, and I guess he did because they nailed his ass to a hunk of wood and strung him up like beef jerky just like any other human mongrel in the eyes of the Romans. Was Christ laughing with the futility of it all? Or was the whole thing a big joke to him to get out of being bored? What's the use of being a king in a pigpen?*

So he took his shot and they strung his ass up on the hill. I'll bet he laughed at them. Laughed at the nails and laughed at the spear chunked into his side. I'll be a son of a bitch. He had the power. He could have thrown away the nails any time he wanted without ever touching them. But he was bored, bored, bored! He didn't just die. He took the only gamble left to him. And it was worth it.

The laughter rang loud and clarion clear and echoing in his mind. Stavers locked his eyes on Skip Marden. *You love me, you big son of a bitch,* he thought, concentrating hard. Marden blinked, rocked back on his heels as the aura of power swept over him and rushed silently through his mind.

He saw the smile on Stavers' face, saw the man lift his arms to each side, palms extended upward. Stavers thought fiercely at Marden.

Kill me.

Shock swept through the face of Marden.

You love me. Show me your love, you son of a bitch. Go on! Kill me!

Chapter 11

I can take him out with the star. Just snap my forearm straight and it will whip faster than a thrown blade into his throat. Right through the jugular and the other side of the windpipe and . . .

Skip Marden staggered backward as if struck a physical blow. He caught one boot against the other and swung out an arm for balance. A tiny wire seemed to pierce his brain, bringing with it a keening cry of pain. Why? What was happening? Did Doug—? No; the other man stood quietly, the trace of a smile on his lips, his body relaxed, both unafraid and unthreatening. *Then why do I want to hurt him? What the hell is happening to me?*

His imagination brought his fingers curling. Neatly, tightly, snugly about the grip of the P.85 in his belt. Fifteen rounds of nine millimeter. Jacketed slugs made to tear through a man's body and chop up skin and the subcutaneous layers, severing the lesser blood vessels and arteries and veins, chunking out organs and bone, tendons and sinew and muscle, and if you did it right, it would shatter a portion of the spinal cord and that slug, God, but it was so beautiful, would keep right on ripping through to burst outward from his innards, making a great big wonderful hole, flaying the skin apart in an explosive shredding, sending huge gobs of blood and pieces of flesh with it and—

The pain whipped about his forehead, an invisible wire snaking silently, invisibly against his skin, bringing on a ring of agony worse than any migraine he could imagine. His vision blurred as he tried to focus on Stavers. *I love him. Oh, God, how I love him. I love him so much, and an alumipower rocket would . . .*

He could almost see the short-barreled, big diameter rocket launcher unsnapping like a bungee stick to come together from pieces of metal folded, oh, so neatly and beautifully, and in that clanking and tinkle of metal he'd have the launcher in his hands, and you couldn't miss at this range with one of those suckers, a tiny warhead that could blow away the head and shoulders of a fucking water buffalo, and what it did to a man, oh, it was beautiful, it was just what Doug wanted, what Doug had told him to do, it was a message from God, yes, yes, that's what it was, just one small rocket projectile and it would blow that wonderful body in half, explode it from within so that the bottom torso would still be standing, gravity gluing it to the floor as the chest and the upper torso blew away in a great showering gout of bloody, strawberry, pinkshell spray, and before the man would have time to die, his body would be cut in half, whirling away, and he'd still be able to see, to feel, because it takes time, it takes a moment or two and that's forever when you realize you've been blown in half—

Bile rose in Marden's throat, spilled back down into his system, burning hot, steaming, bubbling. He staggered again. A knee began to buckle and he hung grimly to his balance.

The MAC Eleven. Yeah. That's a hell of a way to go. Doug would like that. I could get off six, maybe seven rounds with a good squeeze of that trigger and before Doug could move, we could blow his head apart like an overripe melon. Juice and seeds and gore and spaghetti of brains erupting, what a shower of dying! It would be all over the room, spraying wildly everywhere and even at this distance I'd feel it spray onto my face and skin, and I could lick my lips and taste his death and I could—

Marden wiped spittle with the back of his hand from his lips. He lurched forward, driven by this terrible compulsion to *obey.* His fingers curled, opening and closing spasmodically, claws and talons and steel strands, itching, burning to feel skin tearing and bone breaking in their grip. Another step forward. *Oh, God, it hurts. Where is this pain from? Pain . . . I am not obeying his command to kill him and I am being punished, and the demons run wild and mad through me, biting and tearing at me because I am bad, I do not obey—*

Gurgling sounds rose in his throat. One more step. Sweat bursting from his pores. Knees twisting in pain. His fingers on fire. Needles stabbing into his eyeballs. He bent over, gasping. *There's no one here and yet . . .* The vomit sprayed onto his clothes as he felt the terrible twisting pain in his testicles, the wet, hot helpless pain. He dropped to one knee, fought his way up, looked through a bloody film, loving Stavers and—

I know what's wrong. I'm bad. No weapons. You do not take godlife with steel and explosives. No, no, NO. I must embrace him, fold him in my arms, crack his bones with my own hands, squeeze his head so his eyes bulge and—

He staggered, but his hands moved, and they worked. The weapons fell from him. Automatic pistols, rocket launcher, throwing stars and knives, submachine gun. Killing implements rained down from Marden with clanking, metallic, echoing sounds. For the moment he felt better, he was free of that terrible weight, now he could use his hands, his feet and his teeth and *yes, YES! my fingers in his throat, tear out his windpipe, a thumb into each eye, twisting so the great white and purple grapes hang on thin stems of optic nerves, oh, yes, that is what he wants. But maybe he'll kill me. That could happen. But I love him so it doesn't matter. But I must obey, I must kill him. Why am I so confused? I'll fight him one on one. Why isn't he defending himself?*

He groped and stumbled forward, a disjointed human automaton in agony and seeking surcease through atonement of obedience. A lifetime of experience and natural instinct, and the blinding devotion for the manGod figure before him, kept Marden lurching ahead. He leaned into his movement, a precarious giant teetering on collapse, shifting his weight, shuffling, shoulder muscles bunched like bungee cords, leg muscles cramping as if blown by pumped bellows. Marden was unaware of his lips twisted in a cruel grimace, spittle forming on his lips and chin. From his chest and throat issued a deep throaty growl, as feral as any four-footed predator. Stumbling, jerking as if he were a robot ripped by short-circuiting systems, he moved inexorably towards Stavers. He no longer *thought.* All was instinct, reflex, utter obedience.

Stavers stood his ground. He stared unblinking at the killer rumbling towards him in obedience to the silent mental *howl.* Primal cry; naked compulsion. Not an order or a command, a sense rather than a thought, a compulsion from primitive times. The closer Marden came to Doug Stavers, the more powerful became the effect from the stone in its steelmesh container. The stone from before biblical times. His hands jerked forward, fingers clawed and locked into talons as he groped for the face of the manGod he loved so desperately. Stavers felt the heat from the other man's body, felt and smelled the animal breath, studied the clawed hands that could bend metal bars or crush a human skull like a hydraulic press.

Stavers smiled.

The sun exploded within Marden's brain. One instant he saw the manGod within reach of his hands, and felt the thrill and the wonder of absolute obedience as he reached for Stavers' throat and began to close his terrible fingers and then the sun exploded and savage light ripped through his eyeballs and seared every fold and tributary of his mind, and he roared, a primal bellow of pain and terror. "I can't see!" he howled. *"I'm blind!"* Pain and terror assailed him, as he spun about, a Frankensteinian monster unable to function, struck by unholy wrath. *"I'm blind!"* he howled again.

Stavers laughed. "Yes, you are." He chuckled. "And then again, you aren't." He studied the wildly-flailing blind man before him as Marden dropped to his knees, face uplifted, eyes unseeing, and Stavers imagined himself choking and in his mind he rammed that sensation to the stricken Marden.

Marden's hands grasped his throat as he coughed and hacked for air and then vomited wildly as breath refused to enter his lungs.

"Having fun?"

Stavers spun about, gaping at the sight of Dr. Rebecca Weinstein in a loose, revealing shift. She stood with her arms crossed, raising the globes of her breasts, studying the wild scene before her. She lifted a hand to point to Marden. "While you're looking at me," she said over the rasping death rattle of Marden, "*he's* dying."

Stavers turned. Marden had fallen forward, face down on the floor, blood and white foam issuing from his nostrils, his face twisted, clammy and grey. Stavers sucked in air, a deep and penetrating ingestion of oxygen, and he immersed Marden in that same thought. Marden's body jerked and spasmed as his lungs filled, and he coughed up blood, but his lungs labored and his chest pumped his body up and down.

"He'll live," Stavers snarled at Weinstein. "Where the hell did you come from?"

"The spa. That was a neat little reception you had for me there." She smiled at Stavers. "I didn't figure you for that touch. That was quite a lesson you were going to give me. Three nubile teenagers, naked, as hungry for sex with you as a flower casting out perfume. Very, *very* neat. What were you going to do? Wait for me to come into the spa and remove my clothes, and force me to watch you fucking those children?"

Something snapped in Stavers. He glanced at Marden, forced a sensation of muscle rigidity through the body, hurled the feeling of being frozen, unable to move from the floor. He spun about, took angry steps, almost an animal bounding motion to Weinstein. A powerful hand tore her shift away from her body, left her naked before him. She stood silent, eyes wide as he tore away his own clothes. Anger, hatred, fury, the man within, lust; whatever part or all of it, brought him erect, his penis jutting forth. Faster than she could follow he scooped her up into his arms, turned back to Marden and threw her down onto Marden's back.

He never heard his own bellow of raging lust as he dropped heavily onto her, throwing her legs apart and plunging violently within her. Rebecca stifled the scream of pain, biting her lip until she tasted her own blood from her teeth cutting into flesh. He pounded against her with mindless sexual fury, and through the pain she looked into his eyes, ignored the animal breath coming over her in waves.

"That's good," she forced the words at him. "You're too hung up to make love to me, but rape's the name of your game. Go ahead, fuck me, *rape me* if that's the best you can do!"

He pulled away from her, his face a twisted mask of rage and fury. "Oh, no! No, you don't!" she shrieked, nails grasping his ear, the other hand digging her nails into a buttock and forcing him back to her.

"Do it, you son of a bitch!" she screamed into his ear, thrusting upward to take all of him. "Do it—*if you can!*"

If you can!

Her words thundered in his head. *If you can!* What the hell did she mean by that? And why did she . . . This was crazy. He felt leaden in his belly. *Jesus Christ, I'm losing it! I don't believe this!*

"Is *this* how you rape a woman?"

Her words hit him like ice. She wasn't mocking him. Not even . . . laughing. He could have taken that, accepted it as a challenge. But he *felt* her thoughts. That was impossible, but it was happening. For the first time in his life he felt dismay in the act of loving a woman. Dismay, and he softened, lost the organ with which he had loved so powerfully.

He couldn't believe it. *She pities me. Good God, she's pitying me!*

Rage exploded within him, his hand drew back and his fist rushed at her head. A single blow could kill her; they both knew it.

"Go ahead, Doug. You can't fuck me, so why not kill me?"

Shock froze him, then he felt empty, hollowed out. His arm hesitated, then fell limply. *All* of him felt limp. He rolled away.

Without a word she rose to her feet, slipped into her robe and left the room.

In her apartment, she made certain not to laugh aloud. Not with the secret microphones that would pick up every sound. But she didn't need laughter. She had plunged the knife deep into him and twisted, her few words crumpling his proud erection, sapping his strength.

I wonder how many women, if they only knew, would wish to thank me . . .

Chapter 12

She slipped into a jumpsuit and surveyed herself in the mirror. Her reflection satisfied her. A high-necked silk sweater beneath the jumpsuit. Feminine but not provocative. The less skin she revealed in their next meeting—or, encounter—the better would be the moment. He wouldn't need any reminders of what had happened in that room. It wouldn't even do for her to joke that Marden's unconscious form made a really lousy mattress.

Doug Stavers had spent a lifetime doing his women. Somewhere in that turbulent past he had been gentle, even loving, but he more than made up for those rare moments by the very brutality he visited so callously on other people. Now he had become victim of a malady that crushed most men, robbed them of their masculinity. That would not happen with Stavers. There had been too many conquests in the past for him to question his own virility, and he had already been confounded repeatedly by her remarks and actions. They would let the incident slip into the past, unspoken and as far as the world knew, and as far as they would both ever speak, an incident that had never happened.

She knew surprise with her sense of triumph. A victory far removed from the sexual, or even man-woman confrontation. That was silly nonsense for minds that were immature or emotionally strung out. Her triumph went far deeper than that. *He had lost control.* She knew men. She knew Doug Stavers. He would find some other fulcrum about which to cross swords with her, a convenient spoke about which they would both turn.

He performed almost on schedule. Her room speaker rang softly and she pressed the open transceiver button. "Yes?"

He didn't bother to identify himself. "My apartment, Rebecca."

"Of course. When?"

The query of one word forced him to respond with unplanned irritation. "Now, for Christ's sake. You have something more pressing to do?"

"Never," she said warmly. "I'll be right there."

"The door's open. I'll be in the spa. I want you in there with me."

She switched off. A smile spread slowly across her face. Neutral ground, that spa! They would be nude, immersed in perfumed oils and swirling water, and there would be not even a hint of sex. Wonderful! In this manner, Stavers would return to intimacy and push aside less pleasant memories still burning within him.

Stavers eased his body to the left to catch the full thrust of water pummeling his groin from the spa thrusters. He rested both elbows behind him on the spa ledge to keep his chest above the swirling water. He reached to his side for his cognac and took a long drink, then lit a fresh cigar as Rebecca slipped from her clothes and eased into the swirling froth. He nodded to her right; her own cognac awaited her.

How romantic, she thought wryly, then told herself to shut it off and pay attention. She studied him. He *was* again in full control. He *had* put behind him what had happened earlier. That meant he was functioning again as the dangerous man she had come to know so well. *Take this carefully*, she warned herself. She bid for several additional moments by sipping slowly of her cognac.

Stavers wasn't even thinking of anything even remotely involving sex—past, present or future. His own instincts had come to the fore; the basic animal was once again in charge. For a period longer than he could recall, he had not considered the security of his person. But suddenly his defenses were down, banished. An event had taken place that both amazed and angered him. *Weinstein had entered a fully-secured room.*

"Rebecca."

The sound of her name brought her up from the water until her breasts swelled and bobbed gently before the rushing froth. She showed no emotion, no expression save that of waiting.

"You had me helpless," he said, a bit more acidly than he intended.

"Yes."

"How the hell did you get into that room? It's as secure as a fortress. I *know* I dropped that steel bar across the door. There's no way to open it from the outside short of blowing the whole place apart."

"Obviously, there is," she answered.

"We playing games? I have to push? Don't be so damned literal, Rebecca. If you can't read my lips then read my mind."

Laughter for the first time from her. "No; I can't do that. But I know what you mean. And," she added quickly, "obviously there was a way into that room, sans explosives, because I did get in and you never knew it."

"How?"

A shoulder lifted in a bare hint of a shrug. "Electromagnet. Outside the door. The door itself is nonmagnetic."

He nodded, remembering. That had been by his own orders. Even before she continued he'd figured it out. "Power electromagnet. Against the door. The field goes through, you move the magnet and it lifts the bar out of the way."

"If you'd used wood or brass, or even an aluminum bar, I couldn't have gotten inside. Don't you understand, Doug? Your own security system, that steel bar, was the weak link, the key I needed to open the door."

He scowled. "I damned well don't like that."

"Blame yourself. Blame Templin. Your whole security team." She raised herself higher, breasts above the water. "Every security system has its flaws, its loopholes. Especially against the amateur who doesn't know he, or," she smiled, "in this case, *she*, me, is supposed to know they can't get through."

"And we were in a room filled with weapons," he mused aloud. "Guns, knives; enough stuff there to kill a hundred men." He studied her carefully. No tenseness there. Calm, ease, confidence. "You could have done me in. I never saw you until . . ."

"Yes."

"I feel stupid," he said. "I haven't known that feeling for a very long time. One woman overcame everything and had me completely vulnerable."

"Would you be the ruler of this world if you were the only human alive on the planet?"

"What the hell kind of question is that?"

"Consider it, please."

He shook his head. "Of course I wouldn't be any kind of damned ruler. You don't rule when there's nobody else around."

"Do you question, in any way, that I intend you any harm?"

He took his time with the question. "Hell, *no*. I had doubts. Past tense. I don't have them any more. You may give me reason to change my mind, Rebecca, but until that happens, no."

"Do you trust me completely?"

"You do know how to push," he said, anger coming into his words with what was turning into an interrogation.

"I don't mean to. Do you? At least, as much as you know how to trust someone completely, without reservation?"

"I've only known one person in my life with whom I had no reservations. Of *any* kind," he told her, his words and tone flat.

She showed surprise in her reaction. "Then it's not someone with whom I'm familiar," she said quickly.

"What makes you say that?"

"You've eliminated *men* from the way you're talking. Even if they're totally loyal to you, they can be controlled. That leaves women. Tracy North was very special, and you loved her, but the times of your love were violent and tumultuous and there was no way for you to let go completely, even if you had wanted to."

"Go on," he said, his face clouded and unreadable, but his emotions clearly troubled beneath the granite visage.

"Rosa Montini. Wild, spectacular, utterly marvelous. A great lover—"

"Whose burning passion for the greater glory of God was to kill me," he finished for her.

"Then there's someone else." Her brow creased. "That means I've missed something." Her voice grew gentle. "Who was she?"

"My wife."

Weinstein's eyes widened and she reacted physically to his words. "Your *wife?*" She watched him nod. "But . . . there's no record. Not even a hint, and we knew everything about—"

"There wasn't any record. Helena was Swedish; tall, utterly beautiful. She might have stepped into my life from Viking history. We met in Switzerland. Mountain skiing." His eyes glazed slightly as he accepted the painful memories. "It was all magic. Ordained, we believed. But there was the real world. I used another name. Easy enough. She used her mother's maiden name. A priest married us in a remote lodge. No one else knew."

He refilled his glass, drank deeply in a long ingestion of alcohol. "Hell comes without knocking on your door. We had four months. We were in Nevada. Commercial flight." His words came in staccato, halting, painful chops. "We hit really bad weather. Embedded thunderstorm cells. We hit a mountain slope." His words reflected terrible scenes, like still pictures snapping into view on a screen. "Explosion. Fire. I got out. Fuselage busted wide open. Carried Helena in my arms. Knew we were lucky. Until I put her down gently. Then I found out she was dead from a broken neck."

He lapsed into a dark, sullen silence. "I saw the pilot. Busted arm. He had alcohol on his breath. He'd been flying drunk. He never flew again." Another pause, eyes squeezed tightly.

"You killed him," she said matter-of-factly.

"Of course." He released long-held breath. "I wanted to do it slowly. Break each and every bone in his body so carefully he wouldn't die until he was a bag of jelly. I didn't do that. I hit him so hard I cracked his skull and the son of a bitch just died." Stavers toyed with the bottle of Scotch, poured slowly, but did not pick up his glass to drink. His eyes glazed and she knew he was somewhere way back in time. *He's on that mountain with his dead wife.* Weinstein kept her silence.

"I carried her higher up the mountain. I buried her there. A deep grave, filled and covered with heavy stones."

He said no more. She made the move to bring him out of that grievous spell by sipping from her own glass. The motion jarred him from the memory mists. He gestured with his glass in a silent salute to the past and drank slowly.

"How alone are we in here?" she asked suddenly.

Her question brought him fully alert. "How do you mean alone?"

"Security."

"Better than that room with the steel bar," he said both ruefully and with a touch of humor.

"And what we say to each other?"

"We're being monitored. Oh, not eavesdropping, but for an emergency, something like that."

"Demonstrate, please."

Stavers lifted his view to where he knew the location of sensitive microphones. "Code Apple Turkey Six Two Niner," he said to thin air. "Station security report."

"Yes, sir," came the immediate response. She searched for the speaker, gave up the job as hopeless. The mikes and speakers were most likely microchips built into the structures all about them. Then she knew she was right as Stavers tilted his head slightly, better to hear a ceramic tile that was, in fact, a speaker. She pushed her way across the spa to his side to listen.

"Two low satellite passes in the last ninety-seven minutes. Both vehicles, scanning with multiple systems, KH-26 spysats with max detail cameras and realtime transmissions to NORAD. One sweep, ah, forty-one minutes ago by an SR-128 at one hundred thirty thousand. We were intended to detect that vehicle. Also, twenty-seven minutes past, a 747 pass at forty-one thousand feet. Bogus commercial."

"Same old story," Stavers said to Weinstein. "Sometime during the night we'll get a spamcan or two—"

"Spamcan?"

"Private aircraft. Could be anything from a single-engined job to an execjet. They're all big noses, eyes and ears." He grinned. "One of their best bets is a solar-powered robot. Whole thing is solar cells. Big goddamned span. Composites and mylar, three props, loafs along at a hundred and forty thousand. It flies at night from the power the cells have dumped into batteries during the day."

He turned to speak again to the air. "Surface intrusions?"

"None, sir."

"Cancel report."

"Security out."

"That's a pretty smug look you have on your face," Weinstein remarked.

"Not really," Stavers replied, shrugging off any criticism. "Our system is the best. Electronic, mechanical, computerized, *and* human. I forgot one. We also use animals. They can operate on sense frequencies we can't even begin to touch."

She gestured at their naked bodies. "Maybe this isn't the best time and place," she remarked, "*and* you'll pardon the pun, but you're all wet."

"You sure got a smart mouth for a beautiful lady." He added a touch of scorn to his tone. "When did you become the expert on defense systems?"

"You forget," she said, her easy tone more effective than any acidic comment. "I was with you at LaGuardia. I know what happened there, and I'm certain a lot more happened that I *don't* know. I was with you upstairs, remember? That Russian bomber, the other ship we lost, our survival by the skin of our teeth of *all* of us? Incredible flying, miss-or-hit factors of split-seconds?"

"What's your point?" he asked darkly.

"Your security is shit," she stated matter-of-factly.

"Shit, huh."

"Absolutely." She gestured to take in the underground complex all about them. "Coming *here* was a terrible mistake on your part. You have the idea that concrete and television and all your little goodies *really* protect you. I wonder just how many thousands of people who'd like to see you dead *know* where you are. There's an entire international network that follows you around, and every time you hunker down in this glorified pillbox of yours you leave yourself wide open to get smeared."

He stared at her in wonder. Once again a new identity had emerged before his eyes.

"Every goddamn time you start to talk like this, Rebecca, you bring up more questions than answers," he snapped.

"I didn't think the truth would piss you off," she threw back at him.

"Truth?"

"Oh, for Christ's sake, Doug! You're protecting yourself against amateurs *and* professionals. But all the stuff you have couldn't stop a well-financed, well-equipped international group with high-tech people who'd be willing to die for their greater glory of, of," she gestured in frustration, "*of* Allah, or Jehovah, or Christ, or whatever bogeyman they worship."

"Fast answer," he said angrily. "Example."

"Pilot in an F-104, as *one* example. Or an F-5. Or an F-4 or a MiG-21 or even a MiG-29. They're *all* available as you know. High supersonic. One nuclear weapon in one of those and they come over at forty or fifty or even sixty thousand feet and they push over on the stick and they come straight down at high supersonic and they dive right into the middle of this complex. Suicide! Modern kamikaze for the greater glory of whatever. And all about you, right in the belly of this stupid battleship that can't move an inch, we have the detonation of a hundred kiloton atomic bomb. It could be bigger, because you can get those bombs anywhere in the world, but you don't need one. It punches well below the surface, and what the fireball and the shock wave and the heat pulse and the radiation don't get, the earthquake effect will absolutely pulverize."

She snapped her fingers. "Bingo. One fighter plane, one bomb, one suicidal maniac, and *poof!* Doug Stavers and all of us are so much radioactive shit floating through the air." She held her glass and drained the Scotch, swallowed hard. "If you only knew on how many situation maps you can find the *exact* latitude, longitude, depth, cross-section and size of this complex we're in!"

"How the hell do you know so much?" he demanded.

She held up one finger. "One, your question is a dead giveaway you're upset and the truth just sat down in your gut and it tastes terrible." She smiled at him and held up a second finger. "Two, I have told you, or tried to tell you repeatedly, my entire life has been spent in training through my father to *join with you*, to become a part of you, to—"

"*Why?*" The question stabbed at her with almost-visible heat.

She was astonished and didn't try to hide her reaction. "You mean you *really don't know*?"

"I don't—" He stopped himself as he was barely started. "I have ideas," he said cautiously. "But they're *my* ideas. Concepts, wrestling with myself in my head. I have *never*, and I repeat, *never* spoken any of the words aloud. No one knows *what* this wrestling match is between my ears, and I'm not even sure what the devil it is I'm fighting."

"I do," she said quietly.

"You do *to what*?" he demanded.

"Everything you just said."

"Bullsh—" He stopped again. Anger rose like a dark cloud within him. Why did she throw him off so beautifully like this? He hadn't been in a situation where he didn't absolutely command everyone about him for . . . for longer than he bothered to recall. And this woman wasn't fighting him; he knew that. He didn't know what the hell she was after and she tantalized him by withholding information he knew was crucial to his entire being, and she maddened the frustration because he knew, deep within him, that nothing would *force* it from her. And she *was for him!* He'd never known another person like Rebecca Weinstein, let alone just a woman. She transcended every competitor he had ever encountered, and—goddamnit, she's not competing with me! *Or*, he mused, *if she is, she is the smartest, fastest bitch I have ever known.*

"We're getting out of this overgrown bathtub in a minute," he said, picking up his own conversation. Abruptly he shifted the subject. "You hungry?"

"Starved."

"Yeah. So let's get some clothes on and I'll have—what? Breakfast? Name your poison."

"Fried eggs, T-bone steak, home-fried potatoes and a gallon of dark, strong Colombian coffee. Oh, yes, French bread. I sop up my egg remnants."

He looked across the room. "Code Five Niner Niner."

A voice issued immediately from an invisible microphone chip. "Yes, sir?"

"Fire up the chow hall. Breakfast time." He glanced at her. "How much time?"

"Half-hour. I need to attend to Marden. Have some of the medics move him to the infirmary. He's going to need IV and some special attention. After you scrambled his brains tonight, he *could* die."

"Christ, I forgot completely about—" He shook his head. "I'll take care of it."

She started from the spa, but a steel band encircled her wrist. "Before we leave, what is it that everyone else seems to know that I don't know, but makes them try to kill me?"

She touched his fingers gently with her own. "That you intend to take over control, Doug."

"Of what?"

"The world, silly. The world."

What did she say? *"The world, silly. The world."*

What the hell *was* she that she talked to him now as if he were some backward child? And that name! *Silly.* She'd said it with warmth! No insult there—He relaxed his grip, and they climbed from the spa. For several moments, naked, dripping wet, they stood close together, staring into each other's eyes.

"Where do you fit into all this, Doc?"

"You can't do it without me," she said, a quiet and awesome power in her voice. "So we're going to do it together."

"You are very sure of yourself, lady."

She held up her right hand, forefinger and thumb closed together as if holding an object.

"You see what I have here?" she asked. He didn't answer and she didn't expect him to. "It's the key to what you want, Doug. The key to the world. Only it's invisible, and right now, *I'm* the only person in all this world who can see it."

She reached for a robe. "I'll meet you in the dining room. Thirty minutes. And would you please consider one aspect of our conversation?"

"Which is?"

"You haven't found fault with a single thing I've said to you tonight. It's worth thinking about, isn't it?"

She leaned forward to kiss him lightly on the cheek, turned, and was gone.

He felt as if a tree had fallen on him.

Chapter 13

He had no idea how incredibly hungry he'd become. He didn't wait for Rebecca Weinstein to join him. He slipped into the dining room. Barry Andrews, one-eyed and as scarred as an old dump truck, waited for him in the private kitchen. "Bring the coffee pot to the table," Stavers told the grizzled cook who'd been part of his team for more than eight years. Stavers grabbed a heavy mug and went to a table at the far side of the room, Andrews following with a large old-fashioned coffee pot and a slab of fresh bread with the butter still melting on top. Stavers made no comment; this man knew better than himself what he wanted to eat and at what time of the day or night. But he always asked the questions.

"T-bone, rare. Home fries, crisped up a bit. Four eggs over medium. You want this bread toasted? The lady doctor called and asked for French bread. I told her my sourdough was better."

Stavers sipped coffee, lowered the cup to the table. "I see you had the coffee she wanted."

"Yessir, the strong Colombian. The *real* stuff. Sir, you want to wait for her?"

Stavers shook his head. "Get started, Barry. Oh, yes, close off this room once the doctor gets here."

"Yessirree." The old man tossed a loose salute to Stavers and went back to his kitchen. Stavers was on his second cup when Rebecca Weinstein joined him.

* * *

She glanced in the direction of the kitchen. Andrews waved with a skillet. Ten minutes later her meal was delivered to her.

"Anything else, boss?" He directed the question to Stavers.

"No; that's it. Clear out. It's bedtime for you, you old bastard."

"I'll be in my quarters, but I won't be sleeping. You want anything else—"

"I know. Throw my coffee mug against the wall." The old man grinned and left.

Weinstein dug into her food. She glanced at Stavers. "Coffee mug against the wall?"

"Old inside joke. I used to get his attention by throwing the coffee mug at his head. He likes the wall better." Stavers turned to the rim of the table to his left and pressed a diamond design. Weinstein no longer had to ask the questions. She knew by now that this entire complex was equipped with communications systems invisible to the uninitiated.

"Yes, sir," a voice from the table answered his finger pressure.

"Stavers here."

"Yes, sir. Print confirmed."

Weinstein listened with appreciation. It wasn't enough for someone to depress that concealed button. And it wasn't just a button; it was an electronic matrix that not only sensed the inward pressure but also took an electronic scan of the fingerprint and fed it immediately to a computer, which in turn, and just as swiftly, transmitted the identity data to the security chief on duty.

"Lock up this place. Doors open only from the inside. Do it now."

She heard metallic clicks and thunks. *Bingo; it's done.*

"Music and ultrasonic in the Q band. Confirm video scan off until you have print confirmation and voice command from me. Do it now."

"Yes, sir." A brief pause. "Done. Anything else, sir?"

"Kill all contact into here. Be ready for my call to return systems to standard ops. Stavers out."

A needle stabbed lightly but unquestionably into her

left ear, then her right, and an easy pain washed against her head, followed by a sound she thought she'd heard the moment Stavers cut contact with security. Music; soft and gentle music, washed through with the sounds of surf. And birds. She showed her surprise.

"We can talk freely now," he said, no longer wolfing down his food. He gestured with a fork to her plate. "Eat, lady. It just gets cold when you stare at it."

She cut steak, paused. "Music? Is that what I'm hearing?"

"You eat, I'll talk," he told her, refilling his mug. "It's music and more. That needle you felt, or perhaps sensed, in your ears?"

"Ultrasonic," she managed through her steak.

"Very good," he told her. "Ultrasonic in the Q band. The music chops up our voices. It's a mixture with the sonics. Our voices are distinguishable only at this table. Three feet from us there isn't a microphone or system in the world that can listen to us or record what we're saying." He pushed his plate away and lit a cigar. "The video coverage is off. No lip-reading, either."

"Neat." She ate slowly, relishing her food. "I needed this."

"You haven't said anything about Skip," he broke into her thoughts.

"You nearly killed him." She studied Stavers' reaction. "I mean that. It's as if you got inside his head with a baseball bat. He's got a gorilla-sized migraine, he's blind in his left eye but," she added quickly, "that will pass in a few hours. But every muscle in his body has been twisted. Massive spasms, some convulsion. I've sedated him and," she shrugged, "I have full time watch on him with two doctors. He'll sleep maybe twelve, fourteen hours, then he'll be coming out of it."

She took a bite of bread, washed down her food with coffee, and leaned back in her seat. "You *did* get inside his head with that bat, didn't you?"

"Never meant it that way." He rested his chin on his fists, elbows on the table, remembering the scene where Skip Marden had writhed in some terrible inner pain. "I didn't know the effect could be that strong. The diamond, I mean. Oh, on the smallbrains it's like a command. Almost hypnotic. But Skip? He's as tough between his ears as he is with his muscles. You're sure he'll be okay?"

She nodded, smiling, pleased with this unexpected concern for another human being. She hadn't encountered this before.

He smiled at her. "I forgot. According to you," he touched his chest lightly, "this *isn't* a diamond."

"Right."

"It comes to a head tonight, Rebecca. I can't, I *won't*, take any more of your leading me around by the nose." He grimaced with distaste. "That's just what you've been doing."

"Partially," she admitted. "Because some of this must proceed in a specific, a very deliberate series of events."

"What's this crap about so many people being worried that I want to control the world?"

"Don't you?"

"Christ, but you're slick with answering questions with questions!"

"Sorry."

"The hell you are."

She gestured with a wide sweep of her arm. "They *are* out to kill you, Doug! Either get that diamond, or what they think is a diamond, and if they can't get it, then kill you and destroy the, uh, stone."

He held her in a cobra's stare. "You almost said something else."

"I will, soon. But, if nothing else, stay with my line of thought just a bit longer?"

"I've got all night, Rebecca. You may not have tomorrow."

She smiled, but a chill gripped her. Was she pushing him too far? "Threat?" she said as easily as she could.

It didn't work. "Promise," he told her, and she knew from his tone and expression, his body English, that—*Damn, he's committed himself. He really can't or won't take any more of my guiding him. The danger point is here. His frustration is greater than his curiosity, and he's really not accepting that the . . . crystal isn't a diamond.*

"All right," she said, the pleasantries of exchange dismissed. "It's time to get down to cases."

"By all means," he said scornfully.

"My strength with you is manifold," she said abruptly. "You know if I had been sent to kill you, or if I wanted to kill you, I could have done you in long before now. Any one of a dozen times. It's vital—it is critical—that you absolutely believe this, and accept that I am absolutely no threat, in any way, to your well-being. How do we stand on *that?*"

Power seemed to flow from him. *No,* she warned herself, *it doesn't* seem *to anything. That power is real. That's why that thing he wears has such tremendous power. It needs a catalyst and he isn't aware he's precisely that.*

"I've heard this little speech from you before," he countered. "Why do I hear it again?"

"Reaffirmation before plunging ahead," she snapped back.

"Okay. Granted, but with reservations," he said, more coldly than she liked. "Kill me? No. You have bigger plans than that. So let's say I'm convinced you don't want me dead. But I don't know the reasons yet. That means you're trying to run me like a railroad, and that's even less acceptable than turning off my lights."

"Granted," she said, and he detected a power from her he had never before encountered. *What the hell is this? A female Doug Stavers?*

"Will you accept I have your best interests at heart?"

He burst into laughter. "Hell, *no!* What are you, some sort of goody two-shoes shaking with joy to make me safe and happy?"

"Hardly," she answered, displeased with his unexpected response.

"Come off the bullshit trail, Doc. You said something about plunging ahead. It's like skydiving," he said, grinning. "Any time you jump you know this could be the last step of your life. You're on the edge. *Step off!*"

"What do you want, Doug?"

He blinked. "What?"

"There!" she said triumphantly. "The man who absolutely knows his own mind, the man with the awesome power, the infamous mercenary, the ruthless killer, the avenging dark angel! I give you Doug Stavers with a simple question and he says, *What?*"

"Weinstein, what the hell are you getting at?"

"You know damned well! *What do you want, Doug?*"

He drummed fingers against the table, flicked away a cigar ash, stalled for time. "How do you mean that question?" he asked finally.

"Any way you'd like it." She wasn't giving away any edge.

"I'll accept you're talking about the big picture."

"Sure. Why not?" she shrugged. "It can't be money. You've got more money right now than you can spend, and if you ever run out, there's always more coming in. But therein lies a flaw. You don't know what to *do* with your money. As leverage, that is. As a weapon. As a means to an end, *because you haven't defined that end.*"

"And you have?" he asked acidly.

"Yes."

"Then *you* tell *me.*"

"Uh uh. Not yet. Why not try to *answer* the question? And don't tell me you don't *have* to. I already know that and those words would be juvenile."

"You trying to insult me, Rebecca?"

"Absolutely not. You're beyond insult. That's not a negative statement, either. You're too self-assured, too strong, too much aware of who and what you are, to be insulted."

He thought heavily for several moments. "The answer isn't that difficult, I suppose," he said at last. His facial muscles tightened as he set his jaw. "But I'm lying," he said suddenly. "Oh, not lying in the sense of untruth . . ." He let his words trail away.

"Would self-deception fit better?" she asked, phrasing her words as gently as she could.

"I hate to admit something like that." He was almost surly now and she knew his gorge would be rising within him. Stavers was one of those people who could build a paranoid anger against himself, but he had a perfect way of dispelling his violent bile: he killed *other* people. It was a habit he'd exercised all his life and she knew it could spill out from him without warning. He was still as dangerous as liquid nitroglycerine; she had to settle him down to something safe. *Like dynamite*, she thought wryly.

"Then don't *admit* anything. That's doctor's advice. Not personal." She rested her hand on his; satin against thick hair and scars. "Look, the purpose behind this entire conversation is that people are deciding whether or not to throw everything they have at you. We're back to square one. They see the great yellow diamond, and we'll go with *their* perception for the moment, as something worth any number of lives. Millions. Even billions. To them the game is worth the candle. This is the Holy Grail of power. *You have it.* They're afraid of what you might do with it. Since you haven't done *anything*, then whatever you do or don't do is terribly suspect to them. Sooner or later, Doug, they're going to feel trapped and they *must* act."

She sat back and burst into laughter. "The parallel is incredible," she cried out.

"*What* parallel?" he asked, almost but not able to grasp her point.

"You and me," she said, breathing deeply, her laughter born more of dark humor than any true mirth. "You want desperately to know what I haven't told you because you've judged, for many good reasons, that it's terribly important to you, and yet, because your patience is strained to the limit, you're at the boiling point of deciding to hell with how important it is. So, you make a decision. Eliminate the good Doctor Weinstein and your poor little brain doesn't have to cope with that problem any more. In short, fuck it, and let's get on with the ball game, right?"

He stared at her, unmoving, unblinking.

"I take it, from your reaction, that we have a basic agreement on this matter," she went on, feeling incredibly free of danger from Stavers. Not because of what he might or might not do, but because she didn't give a damn any more. *I'm at the same breaking point!* she cried, laughing and yet deadly serious, to herself.

"So, to honor an old homily, it's time to fish or cut bait, shit or get off the pot, do or die," she went on, almost airily. "*Mister* Stavers might do me in for all the reasons so recently elucidated." She giggled. "Half the powers in the world out there," she waved a hand carelessly about her head, "are ready from their fears and frustrations to do in our same Mister Stavers. And why? *Why* do they want to do you in?"

She leaned forward, totally aggressive now towards Stavers, her own strength almost palpable in the air between them. "Because they want to run this goddamned planet *and you're in their way.* Just as important, even more so, you may literally hold the key—that thing about your neck—that could let them become world-dominant. It's an old story, my bizarre friend. If the dragon won't fly with or for you, slay the hissing son of a bitch." She almost giggled like a schoolgirl. "But you don't really *look* like a dragon."

"You do go on," he said, calmly, smoothly, still trying to feel her out.

"Oh, I haven't yet said a word about the real *you,*" she offered.

"Nitty-gritty time," he said, his smile thin and unfriendly.

She didn't answer immediately, but went to the kitchen with the coffee pot, returned to the table and filled their mugs. She took her seat, held the heavy mug in both hands before her face and peered over the stoneware rim at Stavers. "You want it straight? No sugar, no cream?"

"The clock's ticking, Rebecca."

So he has made up his mind. I'm too confusing to him, too mysterious, too much of the unknown, and the clock's ticking for me. Well, fuck you, Mister Stavers—

"The real you," she repeated softly, with an undercurrent of strength that comes only from the soul that knows it is going to die and doesn't really give a tinker's damn. It is an exhilarating rush, a fierce joy of freedom, and Rebecca Weinstein immersed herself in that freedom. "The real you, Mister Stavers, this professional mercenary and pitiless killer, this paragon of death and murder, the man whose very name strikes fear into hearts hither and yon, well, the real you behind all this reality, and it *is* real, and you *are* literally all these things, once meant everything, but no longer."

"You've lost your marbles, Rebecca," he said, almost sadly, gentle now because he'd decided her fate. "I knew you were too good to be—"

"Not even a fart in a windstorm," she smirked.

"What?"

"A quitter isn't worth a fart in a windstorm. You make as much noise in the real world, now, as two snowflakes kissing ass in the arctic night." She raised her brows in self-reflection. "That isn't half-bad," she complimented herself. She felt giddy with her sense of inner freedom. "Almost poetic, in fact," she added.

The needle *had* gone in. She saw it in his face, the sudden flicking back and forth of his eyes, and like the true sharp-fanged vixen, she darted into the soft underbelly of his ego.

"You're so fucking bored you no longer have any real goals," she said scornfully. "The man who *should* have it all has lost the ability to define the only challenge left to him. In short, Stavers, you're so damned bored because of that doodad hanging around your neck, because you believe you're all-powerful, some form of piss-ant deity, and you don't know what to do with yourself. All that talent! All those things that make *you* the exceptional man! Right down the damned toilet because you're bored with winning and you don't know where to go or really what to do with yourself."

She hurled her coffee mug from the table in sudden frustration. It clattered on the floor and bounced from the wall. They waited as the rattling noise subsided.

"Did you ever stop to think that your, call it psyche, all your power, and that glitter around your neck, *never warns you of any danger to you?* Ever think of *that?*" Sarcasm hung almost visibly between them. "It's really amazing, isn't it? If that diamond has all that incredible power, then why doesn't it sound an alarm, ring a bell, jump up and down and clap hands when someone's trying to kill you? It doesn't do that, does it? You asshole, you came through that crazy scene at LaGuardia and that fucked-up dogfight in the air because of preparation, skill, dedication, courage and all those things on your part and the same from your men. *That fancy glop on your chest didn't have a thing to do with your surviving all that.*" She took a deep breath as she ran on. "*You*, and your men, that was your strength." She smiled.

"Consider this, *Mister* Stavers. If you're out walking in those snowy hills of yours, a man concealed a mile away from you with a telescopic sight can blow out your brains and you'll never know what hit you. One finger squeeze and there goes good old Staver's brains and guts and glory messing up the snow."

She was on her feet now, hands balled into fists, knuckles hard against the table, leaning forward. "You're scared, Stavers! Scared silly! You're scared because you're forty-two years old and you don't have enough time left to do what you really want most of all. *To be worshipped.* You're watching the years pile up behind you and you'd like to be immortal *and you don't know how.* You poor dumb pimple on God's ass, do you think I don't know about the thirteen women you've made pregnant so you'll have *something* to leave after you're gone? There's Yvette and Ricki and Sarah and Alicia, and all the others, scattered in different countries around the world, all provided for and protected and all that bullshit, and it doesn't matter one little bit because they'll never really *know you* and so they don't matter one way or the other. Except maybe when you're lying to yourself about how important all that is. It's *not!* It just doesn't matter. What *does* matter is what you do. *What you do now.* And instead of doing, you spend all your time going through some twisted psychological thumb-sucking!"

She almost fell back into her chair, nearly breathless, perspiration beading her face, soaking her clothes. "You can be the richest, the most powerful man in the world, and it doesn't mean shit." She sighed. "It's incredible how long it takes men like you to understand that the kind of power they want is a prison. You're *always* a target. You're always the score for the professional killer, the hired hit man. *Always*. Day and night, no matter where you go, the world becomes a lethal video arcade and everybody's gunning for you. Suddenly the money isn't worth anything and you'd trade all your power to be just free enough to mix in openly with the rest of the world."

His face had turned almost a dark red. It was a miracle he hadn't yielded to his violent temper and primal instincts and killed her with a single blow to her skull with one of his rock-hard fists. She gambled that she was getting through, slicing somewhere into that jellied mass of the brain so that she could touch the mind within.

"You are alive," he said slowly, forcing the words through clenched teeth, "only because of one thing. No," he corrected himself. "Three things. Do you know what they are, Rebecca?"

"Yes, I do," she said, to his astonishment. "At least, I think I do."

"Tell me what they are, Rebecca."

She locked her gaze with his. "Up yours. It works only if *you* tell *me*."

"All right." He clenched his two hands together, fingers interlocked, resting on the table before him. "First, everything you say is true."

He studied her carefully. "Funny. I expected your jaw to drop. I expected surprise, amazement—"

"Try a deep inner joy, Stavers. God, don't stop *now!*"

"That's the first of the three. The second is that I know, now, that you're going to tell me the truth about this diamond. Or whatever you call it."

"Close," she said, her voice barely above a whisper. "Very close. I won't tell you. I intend to *show* you."

He nodded slowly.

"What's the third, Stavers?"

He smiled. And in that instant, as his facial muscles relaxed, as the tension went away as if a switch had been thrown, she knew she had never, not for an instant, been in any danger from this man. *Never*.

"Oh, that's easy, Rebecca. You see, I've known for some time that you are more than three hundred years old."

Part Two

Chapter 14

"Take off your hat," Stavers told Skip Marden. "And you will *always* remove everything from your head except your hair whenever you enter a church again."

Marden took Stavers' admonition with open disbelief. Clad in timber gear with a heavy lumberman's jacket, laced boots and heavy trousers tucked into his brogans he was almost a full-scale edition of the mythical Paul Bunyan. Beneath the huge jacket he carried his usual complement of weapons. He stopped at the steps to the church, one foot on the first step, and looked for help from Rebecca Weinstein.

"It's all right, Skip. Just stuff your hat into a pocket if you like," she told him.

"I don't get it, Doc." Marden gestured at the huge, old stone building, as grim and forbidding as any fortress. "So it's a church. So what? I mean, Doug *bought* the goddamned thing. It ain't just *any* church. It's *our* church!" He studied the huge building, the largest structure by far in Black Rock, sitting astride Highway 10 in Utah, a shitty town memorable only for the fact that to the west soared the Manti-La Sal National Forest. North on the battered highway you ran into the nothing town of Hiawatha, and if you went in the other direction you reached the non-thriving metropolis of somnolent Castle Dale. Head east and you had dirt and clay roads in barren country; bleak Tavaputs plateaus, the nasty heights of Roan Cliffs, and the abject lonely misery of appropriately named Desolation Canyon.

"Just go along with the script," Weinstein urged

Marden. They climbed the steps together. Another world awaited them as they entered the newly-named Church of the Ascension. The land outside was remote, rough-hewn, isolated, fringe communities far beyond the templed strongholds of Provos, Salt Lake City, Ogden, Brigham City and the other centers of Mormon country.

"Jesus," Marden said softly. Arches soared above him. Great sheets of stained glass showered multihued glows through the structure. Sunlight danced on dust in visible pillars, and from loudspeakers scattered through the building organ music flowed about them.

"An appropriate comment," Weinstein said, smiling. They walked to a side aisle, their presence noted briefly by worshippers scattered amidst the long rows of pews. A priest opened a door, beckoning them to hurry to join Doug Stavers. The door closed, but Marden refused to be hurried. An eyebrow raised slightly, the only visible sign that he had already judged the true fortress-like nature of this building. That door was wood only on its exterior; a sheet of armored steel lay sandwiched between the wood. The bolts to secure the door would stop anything short of a bulldozer. Marden's interest heightened and he began to smile. This was more like it!

The visits to seven other churches in the past few days had driven Marden almost to distraction. They were *all* named the Church of the Ascension. They were *all* in remote locations with each church scattered in a different state. And every one of them had a new landing strip, or, an old strip lengthened and hardpacked to accommodate the weight of a heavy jet like the Skua, or a big turboprop of the Beech Starship class. Therein lay another similarity that snagged Marden's basically suspicious nature.

Not a single airstrip was paved. That seemed stupid; why land these multimillion dollar machines on dirt or clay rather than macadam or concrete? Then he walked across the first "primitive strip" and he understood. The surface beneath him had been prepared by a genius. It bore the weight of any aircraft as well as a paved surface. But being of dirt, or clay, it reflected heat in the same manner as the countryside. At night, infrared scanning of the countryside by high-flying reconnaissance aircraft, and satellites, would fail to "see" an airstrip that offered no telltale thermal signature. At each strip the jet or turboprop disappeared within a large, ramshackle-appearing barn. Tractors and pickup trucks moved through the area, mixing with cropdusters and helicopters, the movement of all the vehicles and aircraft scrubbing away any signature of the powerful jet machines. It was the ultimate camouflage. You did everything right out in the open for all the world to see and what you saw was everyday ordinary. And the jets kept flying in and out whether or not Doug Stavers was aboard.

Skip Marden failed to understand the whirlwind tour they followed across the country. Nonstop travel by aircraft and helicopter and large vans. People whom Marden had never seen or knew about met in brief, taut sessions with Stavers and Weinstein, and then vanished on affairs to be pursued under Stavers' orders. What at first had piqued Marden's interest, and then baffled him to the point of surliness, was the commanding interest in the churches. It made no sense to him. Of course, he grumbled to himself, no one *had* to explain anything to him. He had one assignment only in the world.

Cover the back of Doug Stavers. Cover it with all his guile and cunning, courage and expertise with weapons, and above all his animal-like sensitivity to danger; the latter was as much experience and finely-honed observation as any sixth sense. But there was a difference now. The doctor. Rebecca Weinstein was with Stavers day and night. They were more than doctor-patient. They were far more than lovers. And if they wanted to hump each other day and night that was their own affair. Not that they had much time to perform acrobatics in the sack. Not the way they kept on the go, a hammering roller-coaster journey throughout the country.

Something was up. Something very *big* was up. Excitement trembled beneath the surface. For this, Marden felt a combination of enormous relief and no small pleasure. Ever since he'd come into possession of the fabled yellow diamond, Stavers' life had gone downhill. He dumped on himself with petty pleasures. Often he snarled like a wounded bear when there was no apparent reason for such antagonism. None of this affected Marden except for his total dedication to the well-being of one Doug Stavers. But you couldn't fight ghosts and surliness. A man with Stavers' incredible skills and talents, his relentless crush of any opposition to what he sought or wanted, needed more than stuffing his salami between the legs of a nonstop procession of young quiff. That grows old quickly. There'd got to be a challenge, and Doug Stavers didn't know what the hell to do with himself.

Until Rebecca Weinstein came on the scene. And even then her presence didn't bring Stavers back up to snuff. It didn't light his fire. He wasn't acting on his own; *he was reacting to an extraordinary wave of attempts against his life.* Marden regarded Weinstein as a magnet for lethal trouble. It seemed to home in on her like a controlled missile. Missile, hell; it was a complete barrage! That attack at Butler Terminal in New York. Shit, that would never have happened unless Boesch, who ran the whole operation, hadn't felt both the pressures of time and a squeeze from the people who financed his worldwide terror attacks. You pay the piper when he plays a tune on his flute, and it wasn't too tough to figure that Boesch was a direct line down from the old guard of Nazi leaders who had tucked neatly in bed with a power group inside the Vatican, a rotten love affair stemming from the rare opportunities offered by a Europe festooned in the madness of the second world war. They'd been after Doug Stavers for a long time but it had always been little more than a casual affair. Doug was a thorn in their side but little more. Doug didn't care what they did with one another or what global racketeering they commanded, just so long as they didn't mess with him. All that changed when Doug went after the great yellow diamond in a world-spanning hysteria of intrigue, murder and bloody combat.

Even after Doug had what they referred to almost in hoarse whispers as The Messiah Stone, or simply the Godstone, the pressure increased, but not to any extent they couldn't handle.

Then Rebecca Weinstein came on stage. From the first moment he saw her, moved close to her, Marden knew they'd opened a Pandora's Box. It was a gut feeling as subtle as a kick to the nuts; cerebral comprehension didn't have shit to do with it. Marden recognized the honed killing instinct of *any* animal. This woman—and Marden wasn't surprised when he learned she was a medical doctor; a surgeon—had all that sleek power beneath her beauty. Her voice; Jesus, but she could do incredible things with her voice! That British accent, the crisp cool, the breath of a breeze blowing downwind of an iceberg. She could cut through surrounding bedlam with that voice. Especially to Marden with his recognition of that mysterious strength of hers behind her words.

The longer she remained as part of the elite inner circle of Doug Stavers—ostensibly as a medical watchdog for all of Stavers Industries—the more frequent and determined the attacks against Doug. Boesch's assault at LaGuardia was the most dangerous because Boesch had violated a cardinal rule in gunning down his prey by exposing his forces in the *multiplicity* of attack. He had thrown everything he had at Stavers; the Boeing, the helicopters and the missiles, and then that Keystone Kops routine with the fire engines. Keystone it might have been; lethal it was unquestioned. It might have worked against any other target, but even Boesch realized he was up against something that bordered on the supernatural. Or was regarded that way by a frightened clique within the Vatican. So they backed up their bets with that strike from the huge Russian bomber and again they almost succeeded.

Almost ain't good enough, Marden grunted to himself. And he knew that long before this moment Boesch had joined the ranks of the permanently departed. His fuckup was of monstrous proportions. He might have gotten away with his dramatic scenes in New York, but you don't have a huge Russian turboprop bomber falling out of the sky over the United States without the top people getting involved.

So they—either Moscow or the Vatican or hired guns—had by now disposed of Boesch. And for a while there had been a strange surcease of further assault, either blatantly open *or* covert. In the world he occupied that was *not* the norm for Doug Stavers. That goddamned rock hanging around his neck had no price in money, lives or anything else save *possession.* And they were coming for it. Jesus, you could taste it in the air. At least Skip Marden. All his animal instincts had been running at max sensitivity for weeks. The quiet was wrong. It was *dead.*

By now, mused Marden, Doctor Rebecca Weinstein should also have been dead. She had stomped and knifed and spat and clawed at Doug Stavers so many times she might as well have dug her own grave and climbed in. But that didn't happen. She got tighter and tighter with Doug. Marden would have given ten years of his life to know what happened after that episode with Doug in Indian Springs. That scene with the wolves. And then his own maddening, crazy urge to kill Doug, and the thousand devils running wild inside Marden, pulling and savaging and clawing him to bloody shreds, and jamming knives and picks and acid through his brain. He'd hurt for days afterward, as though they'd injected acid into every muscle and tendon of his body when he collapsed unconscious in his miserable struggle to obey that insane command within his mind to kill Doug.

It was like waking up in a world that had changed completely. No longer was there a danger that Weinstein would meet harm or more than harm at the hands or command of Doug Stavers. Exactly the opposite had happened! Even he, Marden, had been told beyond any question that he was to place the value of Weinstein's health and life on the same level as that of Doug Stavers.

It didn't fit!

Well, Marden had admitted grudgingly to himself, there *was* a positive side to all this. More and more the old Doug Stavers was back on the scene. Marden didn't know the game plan, but *something* was up. Something very big, maybe bigger than anything they'd ever done before. Doug had a purpose, a powerful drive again, and even if he did it in concert with Weinstein, as if they were two functioning as one (*they are, you asshole,* he snarled to himself; *admit it!*), they were on the move.

Then, the churches. Now, *that* just about blew away one Skip Marden. Churches! And he was buying them up like a starved kid set loose in a candy store! It didn't make any sense. None! Of course, maybe it wasn't supposed to make any sense. Doug had done crazy things before that in the end turned out to be some pretty damned brilliant strokes.

Like that medical center he'd bought through one of the distant corporations. There must have been a hundred of those in stock firms and, shit, he never understood that much about it, but Doug could own a hundred factories and other places and you couldn't find a direct connection between those facilities and Doug Stavers if you tried for a hundred years. The legal thickets grown by his staff of lawyers—and he had a whole office building filled with those snakes—put up barriers that *were* impenetrable. Doug needed his own medical facilities that couldn't be recognized as especially for him. Oh, there'd been that private sanitarium in Arizona, but when Doug finished with that place he'd given the job to Marden, and the whole clinic, including all the people within, had vanished in a roaring explosion that was heard a hundred miles away. Even the rubble had been ground down to nothing larger than the size of a man's fist.

The new clinic in Salt Lake City was a beaut. Especially the deep underground facility, now closed off to anyone not connected directly with one Doug Stavers. Above ground, the place was a medical marvel, run straight and clean by the Mormon Church and considered one of the world's finest. It already had a clientele stemming from the most influential and powerful people in the world who needed something more than could be acquired simply by signing a check. You needed a special touch to get into that place—Sigma Genetics, that's what they called it—and the "touch" was Stavers.

No; that was wrong. Stavers *or* Weinstein.

Skip Marden was still mostly in the dark during their whirlwind tour, and walking through this eye-stunning Church of the Ascension in Black Rock hadn't made him any the wiser. Well, he smiled to himself, *almost* none the wiser. That door. Ah, the door of wood exterior with its heavy steel interlining. *It was made to hold off armed intruders.* Even if he didn't understand *why*, just knowing they were thinking in that direction eased greatly this headache dogging Marden.

Then the headache got worse.

Not in Black Rock. Marden waited outside the sealed room where Stavers and Weinstein met with people Marden had never before seen. The meeting didn't last long. A half hour after they went in, Stavers and Weinstein came out.

"Let's do it," Stavers said to Marden, offering no other explanations. "We're flying out. The Skua. You go ahead."

Marden shook his head. "No. I'm sticking with you."

Weinstein raised an eyebrow. No other sign of surprise at Marden's unexpected refusal to obey Stavers. But not unexpected to Stavers, she realized. The three of them stood apart from the others, Weinstein keeping her silence, Stavers studying Marden.

"Explain," he said quickly to the big man.

"Something's different," Marden said quietly. Weinstein marveled at the sight of him. Muscles tightened, eyes narrowed, hair jutting outward from his body; he didn't know he was even sniffing the air for the smell of danger. He was more animal than human at this moment. "Something's . . . *wrong*," Marden added after a troubled pause.

Stavers nodded slowly, the thinnest wisp of a smile on his face. That disturbed Marden. It pissed him off highly. What kind of fucking game was going on here!

"Skip, you ever go to church?" Stavers asked suddenly.

"I'm in a fucking church *now*," Marden said, more

beset than ever with phantom warnings that could in an instant turn real.

"I mean, on your own."

"Sure," Marden answered, surly and mean as he looked about him. "To get out of the rain a couple of times. A couple more times I went inside to kill some people."

"You, ah, never attended a sermon?"

Marden stared in disbelief at Stavers. Was he mocking him? Why would Doug do this? Why—

"I want you to listen to *this* sermon," Stavers said, still quiet, but with a sudden new force to his voice. He gestured to the far end of the church where a priest ascended a podium and then stood beneath a huge cross. "I want you to listen to *him*," Stavers added.

"Doug, have you gone fucking crazy?" Marden asked, his tone plaintive, confused.

"Listen, that's all," Stavers said almost in a hush. "Listen, *and look*." He chuckled. "And do *not* comment about what you see and hear. Not now."

Marden turned about fully. He looked down the distance above the aisles and the pews, and the priest lifted both arms in a supplication to fucking something, it didn't matter what, and his voice rang out, and a silent explosion rocked Marden's brain, a pounding from side to side as reality fought with stark disbelief.

He watched, and he listened, to Doug Stavers preaching from that podium. Reflex brought him moving forward several feet, straining the better to see, to confirm, what his eyes and ears told him, and his brain skittered and rebelled against believing. He stumbled to a halt, still staring, then jerked about wildly as a hand dropped heavily on his shoulder.

Doug Stavers' hand. *But that was impossible!*

Stavers grinned at him. "Pretty neat, I'd say."

Marden jerked his view from Stavers resting a hand on his shoulder to look at Stavers hammering the word of God from the other end of the church.

"I, uh, I—" Skip Marden could not speak.

"Hey, easy; *easy*," Stavers said softly. "You're not

going crazy. I could have told you this before, Skip, but then I could never have gotten your reaction."

"How the fuck—"

"Let's go. We'll talk when we're outside."

Stavers led the way, Marden at his side, from the church. They had a ten-minute walk to the hangar where the Skua waited. Stavers waved away a van moving slowly towards them.

"Who'd you see on that pulpit, Skip?"

"You." Marden gritted his teeth. "But I know that's not true. *You're here.*"

"If I hadn't been next to you, if the only man you saw was that priest in the church, who would you have seen?"

"Doug Stavers." Marden's lips were pressed so tightly they were white.

"No question?"

"Jesus; *no.*"

"That's good, then. That's *very* good."

"I don't ask questions of you very much, Doug, but—"

"Ask."

"*Why?!*"

Stavers' voice was almost sing-song, laughing. "I got religion, man," he said in a sudden falsetto. He raised his arms to the heavens. "Religion! I got it *good!*"

Marden stopped. "You gone crazy, Doug? You don't make any sense, damnit!"

"*Who'd you see preaching in that fucking church, you big dummy?*" The words came from Stavers with a snarl. "*Tell me his name!*"

"I saw *you!* Doug Stavers!"

Stavers draped an arm about Marden's shoulders and nudged him to continue walking. "It's this way, Skip. You saw Doug Stavers. The man's got religion. He'll preach here every so often. But at the same time he preaches *here*, he'll be preaching in *every* Church of the Ascension. Got it?"

Marden looked aghast. "There's more of you?"

"Shit, yes. At least two dozen. Some of them will be on television. Big goddamned sermons. Some others will preach from different countries. Big religious revival. It's the Second Coming, Skip. The Second Coming, and it's going to be the biggest goddamned deal in two thousand years."

"*Who's* coming?"

"Why, the old boy himself. Jehoshua. Jesus, baby. The carpenter's little baby. Buddy-buddy of Lazarus, and Peter, and the whole watering-hole gang from Jerusalem. The messiah, gone and flown the coop all these centuries. *He's* coming. *I'm* going to bring him back. But first we got to get out the message." Stavers was laughing with his own feelings of delight. "That's why we got so many of me. Some really neat-o plastic surgery. Voice training. Studying films of me. Listening to tapes. And the new copies practicing over and over and over." Stavers motioned to Weinstein who walked on his opposite side. "Tell him, Doc."

"It's been a long program, Skip. Very secret."

"Secret? It's been *invisible*. I never knew the first thing about it."

"After we train these men, we do holographic computer runs on them. The holograms are matched against holos of Doug. When the holos match within ninety-nine percent in motions, actions, voice, gestures—within one percent of the real article walking right now between you and me—they go to a church or on revival tour."

"And just think," Stavers laughed aloud again. "Where's the *real* Doug Stavers? How do they tell who's who? What if they knock off a Doug Stavers? No matter what they do, there'll be another Stavers preaching, calling out the gospel, getting the sheep ready for the great second coming." He looked hard into Marden's eyes. "But *you'll* always know the *real* me, won't you, Skip?"

"Yes. Sure; of course I will!" Marden said in a shout of protest that there might even be a question of that issue.

"How, Skip? *How* will you know the real me?" Stavers pressed.

"That's easy."

"*How?*"

"What you look like don't matter, Doug. You're *inside* my head. There's no ever mistaking *that!*"

"Right," Stavers said to end the questions on that subject. He stopped short of the hangar. "We're going on a trip. So you'll know the routine, we fly from here to Canada. We'll have clothing, whatever we need waiting for us. We leave the Skua there and we'll fly as passengers on a Swedish commercial job to Stockholm."

Marden blinked. "Sweden? Stockholm?"

"Uh huh."

"That's just a stopover, of course," Rebecca Weinstein added.

Marden looked at them both. He hated this secretive shit, their doling out information to him in short gasps. He saw quickly that Stavers perceived his discomfort. Doug took his arm. "Don't sweat it, Skip. I'll fill you in when we're upstairs."

Skip Marden took the interval gratefully. His head pounded, a steady jungle banging of clubs on hollow logs. It was all too fucking much at one time. Nothing that Doug might do ever really surprised him (*at least not after that initial kick in your nuts*, he admonished himself with the truth) once he had a chance to think it through. Even the manufactured line of Doug Stavers. That didn't take too much grey matter to figure out. The old camouflage routine. Do your song and dance right out in front of everybody. Doug didn't give a shit about religion except where somebody else's beliefs, convictions, practices, or whatever, met his needs. They'd had enough evidence of that in the past several months.

Rosa Montini, darling of the Vatican's secret killer force, cameo beauty and jungle cat inside, and not even everything Doug had going for him, *even after he had the diamond!* The thought brought Marden up with a physical shock. Rosa the *Catholic* had remained in control over everything Doug Stavers could and did offer Rosa the *woman*, and then she whipped cold steel into his rib cage in a desperate attempt to kill him. The Israelis down in South America; hell, they didn't care why the Americans or anybody else was down there trying to rip apart a mountain. They were also on a crusade. The Godstone to them. The Messiah Stone to others. And then, Marden mused, their trip to India. Religion came out of the fucking ground, it floated in the trees, it drifted on the stink of sewage and garbage, it was a choking miasma from cooking pots and incense, and it flourished in starvation and holy worship and open sores on children and the streams along the roadsides where pilgrims trod in nonstop procession choked with human turds. But that religion was hot, and Patschke was on his way to spreading his faith and absolute worship to hundreds of millions of the devout. Until Doug Stavers tore the life out of that old but dangerous body.

Marden recalled that even Rosa Montini had flinched before, recoiled from the power of the faithful as she moved with Stavers into the frantic masses of India. So the church had reasons other than the Godstone to be concerned. Patschke's religion was spreading through the Asian subcontinent in the form of an unstoppable fire; Christian and Muslim alike showed their concern in secret gangs of killers.

Doug Stavers had The Messiah Stone. The Catholic Church was convinced, absolutely, it was the diamond of the Messiah, a fiery lance to match the presence of Jesus on the earth. It *must* be brought to the seat of power. But Rosa Montini was dead and her band of trained killers mostly dead and the rest scattered like wheat before a howling gale.

Marden thought of Doug Stavers preaching in the Church of the Ascension. He thought of Doug Stavers and his enormous personal aura reaching out to the masses hungry for salvation. He'd do Patschke better by a hundredfold. Marden knew the enormity of money and power that Doug controlled. He'd be a terrible new religious force. And what would the seers in the Vatican see?

Doug Stavers had The Messiah Stone. *The Godstone.*

Doug Stavers was assuming the mantle of the New Messiah. People were falling in adoration at his feet, already flocking to the churches, glued to their television sets, attending mass revivals.

This blasphemer must be stopped. So they'd send out their assassins. You can't always protect someone. Not *always*. If you're *really* good and you *really* want bad enough to kill someone, then you're going to get through.

The faithful of the Vatican, or of Islam, would go after Doug Stavers. They couldn't miss him, with his sermons in church and from the television sets and—hell, it didn't matter. They'd get through and they'd kill Doug Stavers.

They would know exultation and trepidation. Exulting that this blasphemous murderer was dead; fearful that the Godstone might be destroyed or lost. And while they mixed their celebrations with watching and waiting for news on the great yellow diamond, the ice of fire, the fire of ice, the dragon's teeth would be rising. Marden chuckled aloud.

"Of course!" he shouted aloud, not aware he had verbalized his own thought. They would kill Doug Stavers, but like the dragon's teeth rising from the ground, just like in the ancient myths and fables, a new Doug Stavers would arise from Death and cry forth his message to the faithful, ever more awed and stunned and believing, because if the church made the mistake of killing Doug while he was on live television, *they'd see him die and they'd see him rise from the dead.*

That would bring on some great head-fucking in the Vatican!

As quickly as he enjoyed these thoughts, Marden's frown reflected new inner doubts. He watched Stavers and Weinstein sitting at a table in the center of the Skua, deep in discussion. Obviously planning. But *what?* All this had to lead to *somewhere*. When they had pursued the elusive Messiah Stone they had *that* goal in mind. But now Marden felt himself adrift, confused, left out. For a moment he felt anger rising at the very sight of Rebecca Weinstein. As quickly as he felt the heat he dismissed the thought as both stupid and unworthy of him. That woman had brought a new steel to

Doug, had awakened whatever had been dormant in this man. Some new purpose was *alive*. Marden sighed. He'd find out soon enough, and—

He saw Doug motion for him to come forward to join the twosome. Marden glanced at the cabin instrument panel that told Skua passengers the essentials of their flight. Cruising at sixty-two thousand, heading zero five two degrees, right on up toward eastern Canada.

Marden slipped into a contoured and padded seat, notched the seat belt against his waist. Even this high you could hit a sudden finger of a jetstream. More than once, cruising in perfectly still air, they had seemed to smash into a wall of violent turbulence. There'd been no warning. His wearing a seat belt was automatic.

On the table were maps of Europe. Marden needed only a glance to recognize northern Europe. Norway, Sweden, Finland, the encroaching territory of western Russia; south of Norway and Sweden, Germany and the low countries. Doug placed the map of Sweden atop the others. For the moment he made no reference to the map. A cabin attendant moved to Marden's side, offering cognac and Jamaican cigars. Marden was grateful for both. He took a healthy slug of the cognac and felt the heat wash down his system. Then he lit up, savoring the fine tobacco. And waited.

"We're going here," Doug said finally, tapping the map of Sweden. Well, he'd already said that before. Now Marden might learn details and he leaned forward. Doug's finger traced positions on the map, moving into northern and inland Sweden.

"We take our first landing in Stockholm, here, in the south," Doug explained, his hand sweeping in an oval movement down the map and then starting back up again. "When we land, we'll be at a cargo terminal. No passengers, no customs, no nonsense."

Marden nodded. It usually went that way. "There'll be a British 146 waiting for us, and we'll take that ship north to the town of Kiruna, here." His finger pointed to the map. "Now, directly west of Kiruna, and this is rough country, we go to a military installation you won't find on any map or chart. The nearest map reference is this mountain, called Kebnekaise. It's seven thousand feet. And the exact position," Doug paused to mark the map, "you'll see, is just below sixty-eight degrees north latitude and twenty degrees north longitude."

"Above the Arctic Circle," Marden said, speaking for the first time.

"Right."

"What's there?" Marden asked, finishing off the cognac.

"We go inside the mountain. The three of us. You, me, and the lady. Nobody else. Several people will meet us inside the mountain."

Marden controlled impatience and questions and kept matters deliberate and professional. "How close is the strip for the One Forty Six to where we're going?"

"Twenty-seven miles. We make the lift by chopper. Alouette with turbines."

"The Swedes. Who are they?" Marden's questions weren't idle curiosity. He always sought all the information he could get on any situation.

"Their names don't matter. They're strictly caretakers and guides. They've been briefed by the proper authorities. They'll take us to where we need to go, well inside that mountain, to meet someone."

"Who?"

Dr. Rebecca Weinstein smiled. Doug Stavers looked about him, casually, but with the moves of the professional. No one was within hearing distance. Then Stavers turned back to Marden. He leaned back in his seat, toying with his cognac glass.

"Adolf Hitler," he said.

Chapter 15

"This is our first meeting as a complete working group, an entity that transcends the perception of corporate structure and function. This will also be our *only* gathering where we have the opportunity to study one another on the basis of one-on-one. Look at each person in this room. Study them. Note their characteristics. Make any conclusions you wish. Be as generous or as bigoted as you like. But whatever you do," the speaker's voice changed from silky-smooth to a no-nonsense permanence, "you will never permit personal feelings or prejudice, for *any* reason, ever to conflict with your responsibilities now and in the future."

Roberto Diaz leaned back in the high leather swivel chair at the head of the spacious oval conference table. Every other chair was of the same supple and luxurious deep red leather. Every chair had before it a lined pad and a single pen, an ashtray, a pitcher of water and another of coffee, a glass and a coffee mug. In the sumptuous surroundings of the sweeping conference room the items placed neatly before each occupant were spartan. In this same room of leather-lined walls, deep rich mahogany and Brazilian rosewood, plush carpeting, triple-thick armorglass windows to the outside world, the minimal arrangements seemed even tacky. Roberto Diaz had selected these items personally, had rejected all suggestions of gold pens and leathered portfolios and other such nonsense. Had he followed his own wishes, he would have held this conference in an old garage in a nondescript desert or farming community.

That, however, would have denied him the ability to acoustically and electronically isolate this very same room from the attentions of any observers of either casual or desperate interest in the words being spoken by Diaz and the seven other corporate officials of Satterhill Home Construction & Financing Corporation. Satterhill had been in the home construction business for thirty-two years. It reached out into banks and finance and mortgage firms through the length and breadth of the country. It controlled and owned banks. It wheeled and dealt virtually as it pleased. It moved through the nation on the wheels of its own trucks, rumbled through fields on its own bulldozers and construction vehicles. It dealt in electrical power, natural gas, oil pipelines, automobile maintenance, home appliances, supplies and equipment of every possible description. More than a million Americans lived in Satterhill homes. Millions more spent fortunes in Satterhill service companies; bathroom supplies, lawn maintenance, household upkeep, cleaning services, repairs and modifications. You didn't just buy a Satterhill home; you married the company and all its diverse tentacles of financing and servicing.

The eight officers and directors of Satterhill now present on the ninety-second floor of the Thompson, Thompson and Nelder building in downtown Kansas City, Kansas, home of the giant stock, money market and other financial dealings of American commerce, had absolutely nothing to do with the Satterhill Home Construction & Financing Corporation. Their presence there was a carefully orchestrated facade of corporate structure and murkiness, behind which their true purpose to assemble was obscured, even invisible, to the outside world. Even with the elaborate, complex and intricate security measures taken, there was still that chance that somehow, in some way, there existed a tiny sliver, a barely discernible crack through which an interloper might electronically penetrate the systematic isolation of these eight men and women.

Roberto Diaz sighed. He reached within an inside pocket of his janitor's overalls for a long, thin, expensive and wonderful cigar. He knew they were made especially in Jamaica but that their manufacture was never connected with the name of the man who had presented these cigars to Diaz. No one ever connected the name of Douglas Stavers with *anything* unless that was the express desire or command of Stavers. Like these cigars. They were the world's finest, but the paper band about the slim, tight wand of tobacco bore the name of a cheap brand that could be bought in almost any drugstore in the country. It would never do for a janitor to be arrested, or incapacitated, for *any* reason, and have suspicions raised because a man who earned less than eight dollars an hour was smoking cigars that cost fourteen dollars; *each*.

Roberto Diaz smiled; the others had been shocked to discover a *peon* janitor in soiled overalls at the head of the conference table. They were shocked; no one outside the room would pay attention to the man who cleared up stoppages in the toilets or made mundane, dirty but necessary maintenance repairs to the hundreds of offices (and toilets). So Diaz, slicked and greasy hair and soiled overalls and old sneakers came and went, about as invisible as a man might become when he is in full view every day, for months on end, of the same people.

No one in the conference room, shuddering at the smell of the greasy pomade in Diaz's kinky hair, would have dreamt this man was the director of Stavers Industries. No one *knew* who that person, man or woman, might be. It didn't take the others long to discover that while they didn't *know* the exact title or position of this Hispanic stinkpot, there remained absolutely no question of his authority within minutes of Diaz taking control of the meeting. Authority emanated in an almost visible glow from the man. Slumped shoulders and stooped posture gave way to an obviously fit and powerful body beneath the crumpled clothing. The singsong and toothy accented voice vanished as perfect articulation and an obviously intimate relationship with the English language sounded in the room.

"Does anybody in this room know me?" he began his infiltration of their senses.

No one spoke. Diaz expected that. Of course they didn't know him. They *might* have recognized him several weeks before as a powerful German industrialist, for Roberto Diaz was a master at disguise and a perfectionist in eight languages. But this pig who cleaned shit from clogged toilet bowls? Never!

"I am Roberto Diaz. That is the only name you need to remember. It is the only name by which you will address me. *Mister* Diaz. You may question my authority but that would be a terrible mistake. If you question it publicly or in such a manner that you draw undue attention to me, to *anyone* in this organization, you will pay for it with your life."

He held up his hand to close off the sudden murmuring and shifting of body positions. "Do not even *start* with me," he said curtly, with overwhelming confidence. "You will soon discover, as we continue, that I know more about each of you than your closest family, or your friends, *or* even the IRS. And it will be obvious to each of you that unless I were in the position of authority with whom you will concern yourselves, and from whom you will receive your orders, I would not be here and I would not, *could* not, relate to you what you will hear." He paused to light a cigar and pour his own coffee; he had forbidden any personal servicing of *anyone*.

He turned to the man at his right. "Al Templin. In charge of security for all systems, all organizations. The security man closest to our, ah, vice president." No one at these meetings ever used the name of Douglas Stavers; he was *always* the vice president. The man charged with the disbursement of student scholarships. The legends about this man transcended fiction, which was precisely their purpose.

Ed Carson raised his hand; no schoolroom interjection, a motion made with the elbow resting on the table. Diaz encouraged immediate interruptions so long as a query, never an objection, was the issue. Almost all profited from accurate response to a question; objections were bullshit ego posturing. Heads turned to Carson, took note of the stocky build, the massive chest and gut and thick neck that went along with the five o'clock shadow. Carson was a giant fireplug. His name should have been Dicarlo or Bonano or Testa or some good Italian monicker, but not Carson. That was too anglicized, too smooth for an unsmooth man. Diaz nodded to him.

"I don't mean to break in—"

He got no further for the moment. "Don't waste words," Diaz reprimanded lightly. "You *did* break in." Abruptly Diaz's words came heavily singsong slurred with a thick Hispanic accent. "You talk, man, okay?" It was an inside joke between the two men. Carson *was* Italian. His mother was named DiAngelo but she had married into the Carson name. She could still barely speak English. But her son spoke a multitude of languages and was highly skilled in the profanity of them all. When you're a steelworker, dockworker, miner, truck driver, wildcatter and lumberjack as your trade through life, you must speak all these languages and dialects to communicate with the spreading variety of nationalities. Carson was that marvelous cross of brilliant mind with blatant coarseness, the perfect man to be Director of Field Operations for the construction company (or wherever he was needed).

"We need a name," Carson said abruptly. "No name is bullshit. It attracts attention like flies. Mr. X is bullshit, but that's what we're going to start calling him. It's almost as bad as Batman."

Roberto Diaz agreed completely, but he turned and nodded the question to Al Templin. "Since he's an Irish drunk," Templin said slowly, "we'll use his real name. Angus McIver."

A hand rose over the seat of Roger Sabbai, the tall, asthetic, almost cadaverous figure in dark suit and white shirt and string bowtie of the Church Coordinator of their group. Religion was an important issue for the giant Satterhill firm. After all, they built the churches for the new communities, and they were famed for buying and then restoring old churches and donating them to whatever religion stood dominant in particular neighborhoods. It mattered little, or not at all, to this group, that Sabbai, a dark mixture of Burmese and Romanian, was absolutely a master of knowledge of world religions, and steeped deeply in the lore of the devout wriggling on their knees or bellies to the plenitude of gods found across the planet. Diaz nodded to Sabbai.

"An interesting name," he said in a voice echoing from deep within a stone cave; his own chest. "I will not be the only one to notice that Angus is Scotch rather than Irish."

Diaz kept his face straight. "I have it on good word, Reverend, that his mother was known to run rather freely among her choice of lovers." Without a moment's hesitation, Diaz turned back to Al Templin and wordlessly returned the baton to the security man.

"You will not have any need to speak with, to meet, or to have *any* contact with Mr. McIver," Templin said, his voice soft and yet strangely compelling. Only he and Diaz had ever met with and knew the identity of Douglas Stavers. "This is my purpose here today. To reinforce that rule with you all. You do not *need*. Therefore, you do not and you will not know anything further in the execution of your duties. Any attempt on your part, individually or collectively, to penetrate beyond the name of Angus McIver will bring on, immediately, your termination with this group."

Mark Baxter's verbal reaction without a physical gesture came from complete surprise. Baxter didn't understand *people*. He didn't like people. He was pure mathematical genius and singularly brilliant in his functioning as a part of a vast computer and electronics industry closely "allied with Satterhill Industries." He had without intent even adopted the cold and colorless dress of his machines; his physical actions and his speech were almost robotic in many ways. His world was vision through electronic blinders; a giant horse pounding through the nonsensical flotsam of everyday piddling by the masses. He was, in short, an unmitigated ass, but would never have understood such an unkind description. He rarely left the electromagnetic boundaries of his own beloved nonhumans.

"You would terminate us for so innocent an action?" he asked of Templin's reference to never attempting to ascertain the true name of "Angus McIver." "You'd fire us?"

"I said nothing about firing anyone," Templin told him quickly, adding a thin smile to his words.

"But I distinctly heard you say—"

"The word, Baxter, was *terminate*."

Baxter pulled back in his seat. Humans were crazy. "You mean you'd—"

Templin didn't want him to finish the issue as a question, and he broke in at once. "Precisely. Terminate. Eliminate. Dispatch. End of human program. The simple word, I believe, is death." He nodded to Diaz. "That's it. I've said my piece."

Roberto Diaz slid smoothly again into leading the group. His words came in a strange mixture of the Hispanic janitor and the wielder of secret, terrible power. "You all have private fortunes because of your association here. Each of you has a million dollars, plus, in your possession, legal, taxes prepaid. Your families are protected and their futures secured. *Only* if you keep in mind what you just heard. We will not review this matter. You already know it. Enough," he said finally, steel adding harshness to his closing the subject. He turned back to Templin.

"You're not quite through. The security program, please."

Al Templin nodded. "Let us cut through all this conversation and get to the hard nut. While it is not street knowledge, it is well accepted on Wall Street, the Pentagon and certain other circles not easily accessible to the public, that behind all the many companies, firms, factories and operations of Satterhill, and a hundred other business entities, there is the ultimate control of Stavers Industries. I had not intended to bring up this issue," he added, noticing the raised brow of Roberto Diaz, "but in some way that connection was made on a computer review seeking out data on Angus

McIver. Again, in some way yet not known to us, but identified by Mr. Baxter, here, those two names—McIver and Stavers—appeared in the same computer database program. It is no more important than my making the point that you do not know anything about the relationship between these two gentlemen. Angus McIver is all you need to know. The name of Douglas Stavers is well-known in the circles I have described. Mr. Stavers is an extremely wealthy and powerful man, but some time ago he abandoned control of all his industrial and business holdings to Mr. McIver, and Mr. Stavers has also been for some time the Reverend Douglas Stavers. *That* is his burning interest in life, to bring together the great religions into a single cohesive force. He is convinced that between the greenhouse effect, the continuing destruction of the ozone layer, the proliferation of nuclear and toxic wastes, acid rain, deforestation, the slaughter of many animal species, the unbridled explosion of population, and other elements, the future of this planet and the continued existence of the human race is in doubt. He intends to do everything he can to end this rape of our world. He believes powerful religious movements, combining the emotional and the psychic strength of billions of people, is our only salvation."

Al Templin went silent for the moment, astonished at his own fervor of presentation. *I'm starting to believe this shit myself,* he thought. *Careful, careful; don't overdo it.* "One second point," he went on smoothly. "The Reverend Stavers is no sissypants. He was for many years an international soldier of fortune. He served in the armed forces of our country. He is a combat veteran of many wars, known and unknown. In short, he is of tremendous pragmatic temperament. He is aware that no single movement will accomplish what he wishes to see emerge from his efforts. So there is a second movement that operates concurrently with his evangelical call to arms."

He poured a glass of water and drank slowly, then replaced the glass on the table. "This second activity is where you will direct your efforts. Reverend Stavers knows the world must have an outthrusting of its energy. He is aware, he believes implicitly, that mankind's ventures away from the earth, into space, are more of a genetic and religious response to the basic drive of our race for survival. We must reach other worlds. We must improve our ability to move through space. We need propulsion means far superior to the clumsy chemical rockets we are using. This will require the expenditure of several hundred billion dollars."

Templin again went silent to let that number sink in. "Reverend Stavers has the capacity to raise that level of funding, but it will require dedicated and loyal and skilled people like yourselves to bring all this to pass. From this moment on this will be your only goal in life. I am overstepping the boundaries of my responsibilities, and I hope Mr. Diaz will forgive this transgression into his territory."

Diaz nodded, gesturing for Templin to go on; his reaction precisely as they had planned well before this meeting.

"My position as the head of Security for our activities is less in terms of physical security—such things as guards, warning systems, all the bells and whistles of personal protection—than it is to assure that all this activity shall proceed smoothly, efficiently, entirely within the law, and without interference. The Internal Revenue Service is a good leading example. You will *never* provide the IRS the slightest opportunity to find fault with your tax returns. This has far greater importance than any of you may realize. If your personal lifestyle produces a shortfall you will come to Mr. Diaz to correct the matter. If he is unavailable, you will come to me. But you will never fudge on *anything*. We expect absolute loyalty from you and we will answer in kind, as well as support. People at times go overboard. You may do the same. Operate under the cloak of our protection. We will always have it for you and your families. Use your own CPA services. Do not have them involved with or connected with us in any manner."

Al Templin went through a list of another dozen items, all detailed matters that would be presented to each person at the meeting in the form of a transcript for them to study. They could have planned for those papers to self-destruct, but nothing was said at this meeting that could adversely affect—He stopped his talk and his thought patterns. No; he and Diaz were wrong. *No copies of anything*. No records. That system had hung many a Nazi officer who might have gotten off scot-free of war crimes except for that German penchant for elaborate record-keeping. And any lawyer worth his salt could always make something out of nothing. Templin made a mental note that before these people left the floor of this building, they would be strip-searched and their clothing shredded to individual fibers for any wires or electronic devices.

He turned the meeting back over to Roberto Diaz. The janitorial figure sipped coffee and turned to Ed Carson. "From here on I wish you to keep everything short, tight, succinct, condensed as to your *goals*. Not your responsibilities. It is your *goals* that I want. When you complete your presentations, all of which shall be mercifully brief, I will then listen to your needs if you have any beyond the authority already in your hands. Mr. Carson," he nodded to the beefy man at the table, "your subject is Field Operations." Diaz made a steeple of his fingers, slumped in his seat and studied Carson. "If you please, sir."

"Let me explain first what I do *not* do," Carson answered immediately. "I let my subordinates handle the everyday operations of all our industries and business. They're the best. They deliver, so that I can attend to what is my *real* job. Working with other officials of this organization, we are moving to take over control of the aerospace, electronic and related industries that make up the launch capabilities of just about every country firing heavy payloads into space. Note my emphasis on the term of heavy payloads. The Italians have launched small satellites. So has India, and Israel. That's kid stuff. I'm talking about the people who right now can launch the really big loads, or who will have that capability in the future, especially if we assist them with knowledge, manpower, resources and technology.

The big boys right now are obviously the United States and Russia. Our shuttles, the Energia boosters, the new Neptune cargo booster developed from the shuttle system, the oncoming Nova booster series. This is the real stuff. Even our old equipment got us to the moon back in the Apollo days. The new boosters will make the Saturn Fives and the shuttle rockets look like toys. It's a huge job and a bitch of a job, but we want launch capacity in places other than the U.S. and Russia. The French have some big stuff now. The Chinese have some monsters coming on line. The British are getting into the act with direct runway takeoff-to-orbit systems. That's what we're talking about. In short, we are to create and to control the ability of our organization to launch the materials to establish a manned moon base, and, concurrently with that effort, to get ships ready for manned flights to and exploration of the surface of the planet Mars."

Carson ended his briefing with a dead stop. Not another word of explanation or even a telltale expression on his face to reflect further information. Not to say that silence reigned among the group. There was plenty of self-murmuring and glances of surprise between them. Carson's face was frozen. Templin showed a thin and cold smile as if pitying the inability of even these selected people to handle what they'd just heard. Roberto Diaz smiled broadly, his golden tooth in the forefront of his mouth reflecting overhead lights with a garish sheen.

"Doctor Hammad Al-Binn," Diaz said suddenly, his calling out the name a direct order for the doctor to report. Al-Binn, a fierce and brilliant mixture of Arab, Hindu and Canadian who had practiced and researched medicine the world over, and then had been carefully directed to his present position, nodded slowly. But he failed to speak as Diaz desired. "It is appropriate to ask questions of what we have just heard?" he queried Diaz.

The shine faded from the gold tooth as Diaz leaned forward. Gone was the smile or any trace of pleasantry. "It is *not* appropriate," he said with deliberate distaste and an abrasive tone to his voice and demeanor. "Goddamnit, stick to what you're supposed to do, *Doctor*."

"I apologize," Al-Binn replied smoothly, unfazed by Diaz, for the doctor was as much psychologist as he was a medical doctor. He recognized double-teaming when he saw it and he knew to question the need for this behavior by the team of Diaz and Templin (they were *so* obvious!) would be a major error on his part.

"My task is simple," he said slowly, in a honeyed voice long ago smoothed by his own personal ventures into the forbidden and mostly forgotten medical practices of almost-vanished cultures about the world. "We are to assume control of the great pharmaceutical firms of the world. That, in a nutshell, so to speak, is our task. By control is meant we will control the voting stock of the corporations. This will be done under various companies and also individuals, all of whom you may correctly assume are under the control of Satterhill and Stavers. I personally know little of the mechanisms for accomplishing all this. My responsibility is to select the firms, evaluate their products, extrapolate their future needs, and then recommend what facilities we should also purchase outright or control. I speak of international conduct. It is obvious to anyone within this field that whoever controls pharmaceuticals controls much of the world. Ours is a planet with billions of people devouring *trillions* of capsules, pills, liquids and other means of ingesting drugs. Control their production and distribution and you control the people."

Dr. Hammad Al-Binn toyed with his pencil. "We go far beyond this, of course," he added finally. "We shall gain a controlling interest in the major genetic research firms and facilities of the world. We do not need to control agriculture, but we have need to control the chemicals and genetic substances on which they depend to continue their food production. In this manner, the group we represent will actually control much of what the world does every day. Man must eat; we control his source of supply. Man must have drugs to alleviate pain, control his ailments, improve and extend his life. We will also control this area."

A hand went up and Diaz nodded to the Reverend Roger Sabbai. The stringy cadaver leaned forward, his eyes ablaze with interest. "Question, not comment," he began by way of holding off any objection from Diaz. "Do you include in this compendium you have just described the illicit drugs of the world?"

Al-Binn didn't hide his sudden annoyance. "I find generic references a waste of time and words. I will respond to a specific query, if you please."

The reverend smiled. "Of course. Those who deal in narcotics of all kinds usually find disfavor in words that penetrate, and—"

"Sabbai, goddamnit," Diaz broke in, "knock off the editorial crap. If you can't bottom-line your questions, shut up."

Sabbai nodded. "Do we take over the international sale and distribution of drugs such as cocaine, heroin, marijuana—the whole litany of addictive materials, to further our needs? I ask the question because we are referring to an industry that earns some hundreds of billions of dollars a year."

Dr. Al-Binn offered a sly smile in response. "No. Our interest in the illicit narcotics trade will be to learn their contacts, routes and operations. Then, once I have ascertained the main flow, I turn my information over to Mr. Diaz."

"Two points," Diaz said brusquely. "We will go after the major drug dealers. We will, through forces *not* allied with us, strike at their funds and sources of funds. That is all you need to know on this subject, except to stress that we will *not* sell or disperse drugs that stupefy minds or create addicts. We want control of functioning minds and bodies." Diaz nodded to Al-Binn. "You may discuss, very briefly, your other main line, Doctor."

Al-Binn showed his surprise at being instructed to describe openly what was until this very moment a heavily guarded secret of his work. "We intend to replace most of the heroin and cocaine. The United States is our main area of research and testing. At this moment it is the United States that has five percent of the world population and consumes more than fifty percent of all these drugs consumed on this planet, or some seven hundred tons every year. Let me add a point I hope Mr. Diaz will not interrupt."

"Be specific, Doctor," Diaz said, gesturing for him to continue.

"We work with hard basics," Al-Binn said in a lecture tone, convinced his immediate audience knew little of the true psychological and physiological facts of life. "Man functions by responding to the overwhelming commands of his system and his survival. His single most overriding need is to eat, so, at the head of our list is hunger. It is simple. Eat or die. Second to food, almost a parallel, is the need for water. Thirst commands us. Food and drink. The moment a belly is full, sex assumes the dominant position. Sex with mankind transcends procreative needs. It is intoxicatingly satisfying. And there is the key to the fourth basic need for mankind. *Intoxication.* Every society, every culture in the history of the human race follows this pattern."

Al-Binn took a deep breath. "We intend to meet this fourth drive by producing and distributing, worldwide, a new addictive drug that is safe to consume, with which to intoxicate, but which will not have deleterious effects upon the human system. In street words, it does not hurt the body, but it will expand, it will almost explode, other sensations so incredibly that people will fight for and risk death for this drug. We have already produced this chemical."

He glanced at Diaz. "Do I identify?"

Diaz nodded and Al-Binn went on. "It is known by its code name of 4K dash S. It is a chemical-molecular quantum leap into the future. It turns sexual gratification into magnificent pleasure and obsession, yet does not harm the body or the mind. It makes food taste as if it were prepared for the gods. It increases tremendously the pleasure of working and creating. And it enormously expands the desired traits of loyalty, fealty and faith to whatever group supplies this drug." He took another deep breath. "That is my function and my report."

Diaz stretched his arms above his head, brought down his hands and cracked his knuckles. He wanted this speeded up. He nodded to the next chair and its occupant. "Dwight Grayson. Keep it tight."

Grayson could have stepped forward from an advertisement in *Forbes* or the *Wall Street Journal*. Attired impeccably, silver-grey hair "just so," moustache perfectly trimmed, long-perfected modulation to soothe and impress, he sat ramrod straight, yet relaxed. "My field is cosmetics and gambling." He smiled with the facial signs showing the startled response to unexpected words. He always enjoyed mashing down the inferiors about him with his superior intellect, and the record spoke for itself.

"Cosmetics and gambling," he repeated. "In some ways I disagree with the good doctor who preceded me. Gambling is as powerful a drive as intoxication. It *is* intoxicating. In today's world, and it will increase in the future, gambling as it *truly* exists is the perfect machinery with which to create, foster, perpetuate and enlarge upon mass hysteria. This has long been the goal of governments through legalized gambling and the huge payoffs of lotteries. The ultimate, sinful, wonderful, Cinderella reward. Pennsylvania paid one man the sum of three hundred and thirty million dollars in a lottery. So far, thirty-nine states have lotteries and they increase by leaps and bounds. We shall, through our government contacts, create the first lottery prize of one *billion* dollars. It is already underway. When we embark upon such a venture we will likely sell on the order of more than one hundred thousand tickets *every minute* throughout the country and likely five times that number throughout the world."

Grayson bestowed his most beatific smile upon the lowlifes about him. *His* was the business of true population control, as he would in a moment drop upon them with all the subtlety of an anvil.

"Gambling is more addictive than drugs. It meets all dreams, all wonder, and it makes illusion into reality, which drugs cannot do. Gambling is debasement, but then, so the human race, is debased, and it is this pairing of factuality we shall weld even tighter. You see, people are essentially fatalistic and we all wait for the wand of the sorcerer to wave over us and sprinkle us with dreams come true. Cinderella, indeed, for all of those who gamble! We offer wonders; we offer good fortune, blessings, luck, riches from randomness, miracles from bias, power from chance. The fall of dice, the slap of cards, the races; none of these can touch a lottery with a reward exceeding the power of kings and despots. And," he added with a courtly flourish, "we do all this through good citizenship. We are loyal and patriotic. We shall disperse to our government *all* the profits from such lotteries so that we may rectify the staggering, crushing burden of federal deficit. We shall—"

"Holy Jesus Shit Christ, man, get to it," Diaz growled.

"Sorry," Grayson said, not hiding his displeasure.

"Fuck your sorry," Diaz snapped, choosing his words deliberately to bring this pompous (but brilliant) asshole down to the level of the conference table. "Cut the bullshit, man. *Spell it out.*"

Grayson nodded. He knew the real power of the greasy man in the overalls and he knew absolutely he must never get on his wrong side. Diaz was performing; so be it.

"Every lottery ticket in this country for the national contests," Grayson went on, "and every lottery ticket to be sold throughout the world, will be printed by our companies. Every ticket will have a chemical composition that will rub off on fingers and hands and be absorbed by the body. The printers, distributors, store salespeople, the buyers and their families; each and every one of these people, hundreds of millions of them, even billions of people, will be absorbing 4K dash S. The chemical will be impregnated in every ticket, in every sales brochure. Along with this effort will be subliminal advertising extolling the virtues of the Reverend Douglas Stavers and the Church of the Ascension. The feelings toward this man and this church will be holy, God-gratifying, ultimate enrichment and a guaranteed trip to whatever heaven is popular at the moment. It will be a most carefully orchestrated effort, and we shall through two other means assure the connection."

He turned to the head of the table. "Mr. Diaz, I impinge upon the authority of Miss Maxine Stark, here at my left," he gestured to the heavyset, powerful woman with daggers for eyes, "who is charged with basic research for our, ah, group leaders."

Maxine Stark nodded slowly. She did not smile. She hadn't smiled for years. She didn't care for smiles except in the models she used for the worldwide cosmetics sales and advertising she ran for Stavers Industries, for the chemical products pouring into Satterhill homes and thousands of others. She made her decision to remain as silent as possible. She wanted great heights through Satterhill and Stavers, and she didn't need to mouth off to achieve that goal.

"You're doing fine, Mr. Grayson," she said, then looked to Diaz. "He speaks well for me."

Diaz nodded. "Stay with it, Grayson."

"This is where cosmetics come in. We already have the controlling interest in every major cosmetics firm in this country as well as seventy percent of those in other countries. They will carry our advertising on radio, on television, in all matter of publications. Every product, from lipstick to hairspray to aftershave lotion, will carry 4K dash S. The advertising is critical to making the subliminal connection between what effects this drug will produce and the goals of the Church of the Ascension.

"Now we attend to a major point. We are behind the vast mergers in global media. Well hidden from even the most astute financiers, we now have the majority control of Sony, Bertelsmann AG, the Australian News Corporation, Hachette of France, Maxwell of England as well as Pearson of England, and we are maneuvering into a control position of Turner out of Atlanta, as well as the three major television networks in this country. We'll attend to the smaller syndicators later. We will have the concealed but controlling interest in audio tapes, discs, and home videos. This will accomplish what I have already described."

He looked at each person in turn. "The sum total of all this is to bring the world, as individuals and power groups, to support the Reverend Stavers, and the Church of the Ascension in their goal. And that goal is to return man to the moon and send him on his way to the planet Mars."

Dwight Grayson had intended to add one more point to his briefing. But he noted that Dr. Hammad Al-Binn had stayed religiously away from the subject, that gaunt Sabbai had said not a word about it, and he judged he was being tested to see if he could decide on his own when to keep his mouth shut. If Douglas Stavers (and he knew the true identity of this man), or Angus McIver, as they chose to refer to him, wanted nothing said about the chemical substance a thousand times more effective than 4K dash S, then most certainly *he* wouldn't say a word. But he couldn't instantly dismiss the Etorphin Mark Six they had produced under a secrecy so tight that even mention of the chemical could result in punishment by execution. They simply called it Goddess, an innocuous brand of perfume they had kept active as a cover name.

Goddess—or Etorphin Mark Six—was the most potent mind-altering, *mind-controlling*, substance ever created. As a pain-killer it was on the order of twenty thousand times as effective as pure morphine. Which meant it was the most powerful control of *other* men ever devised, greater than any religious faith or fanaticism.

Loaded into the frangible tip of a narcotic dart and tested under every condition imaginable it had proven devastating. A single dart fired into the skin of a charging African elephant killed the beast before it lost its footing. It "froze" crocodiles to utter stupefaction so that they sank to the bottom of a river and drowned because they never came up for air. The test against a great blue whale ninety feet long startled the test crew. They fired one dart from a helicopter into that massive hide and sent the greatest creature on the planet into throes of ecstasy and drowning as it sank heedlessly into the depths. It turned a great white shark into an idiotic animal with its killer senses shut down to zero.

It couldn't be used in pure form against a human being. Total paralysis and death resulted instantly. But with Goddess diluted to acceptable proportions they had a mind-control device, that for approximately three hours before it wore off, brought on total obedience while leaving the prey in full control of cerebral function. Once you breathed Goddess in no more than a vaporous whiff, for the next several hours you were instantly obedient to the first words spoken to you.

Goddess would be the most tantalizing, barely discernible scent of perfume in the Church of the Ascension. In *all* the churches.

And it would be used with perfectly diluted amounts for key leaders of government and industry throughout the world.

Man would soon be started back to the moon.

And then to Mars.

They were all gone save Roberto Diaz and Al Templin. The two men secured the room and Diaz brought out a bottle of Suntory vodka, favored by these two. They drank straight, relishing the rare moment of easing down from razorsharp alertness to others about them.

"That was quite a session," Templin said with undisguised admiration to Diaz. Templin kicked off his shoes and raised his feet to the table. He looked over his glass at the man in janitor overalls.

"One of a bunch," Diaz acknowledged. "We've got four groups just like this one working day and night. None of them know about the others."

"Makes sense," Templin acknowledged. "Wipe out one or two and everything keeps marching."

"That's the idea." Diaz refilled his glass. "Funny thing, Al."

"What?"

"*I* don't even know that much about what's behind all this. I'm running the shop and I'm dealing with shadows."

"That a complaint?" Templin's eyes narrowed slightly.

"Hell, no. Stavers has made me a millionaire several

times over. I've got power, position, a great family, beautiful women in three cities, *and* a goal. No, it's not a complaint. It was a quirk of curiosity. If I didn't know Doug Stavers personally I wouldn't even mention his name."

"Well, it's no secret among the top people that you probably saved his life in South America."

"We saved each other's life several times," Diaz corrected. "Marden, also. It was one hell of a bloodbath down there. Out of every six people on both sides, maybe one came through."

Templin sipped his vodka slowly. "One thing's crazy, for sure."

Diaz waited.

"We're at some incredible crossroads of history. A fork in the road for the human race. The world's going through some wild social upheavals. Society is turning inside out. You, me, some other people, we're at the controls. But the man at the top of the heap couldn't care less about running the world."

"Well, shit," Diaz retorted, "look at the human race. They're not worth it. Not the masses, anyway. Stavers decided that a long time ago."

"But . . ." A note of protest sounded in that single word before he stopped.

Diaz laughed. "Maybe I should ask you the same question you asked me, Al. Did I hear a complaint get started and then get swallowed before it came out?"

Templin joined his laughter, but it was cautious and guarded. "No, not a complaint. You know me better than that. You know my relationship with Stavers. He gave me my life. Not just eating and pissing and breathing. He gave me meaning, pride—the whole goddamned ball of wax." He shook his head. "Forget it, Bob."

"So let me ask you another question," Diaz said, his sudden change of tone reflecting his inner concerns.

"Shoot."

"The woman."

"Ah, talk about a loaded question," Templin said softly.

"I'm *not* pushing, Al."

"I didn't think you were. The woman," he echoed. "The *doctor*. Beautiful, young, powerful, incredibly knowledgeable. Speaks more languages than I can count. A surgeon so capable she'd need a hundred years to learn what she knows. She looks maybe twenty-six, maybe twenty-eight. Probably in her forties. But even I can't figure it. A Jewish doctor who comes out of nowhere."

Templin leaned forward. "My job is to look after Doug Stavers. I do my job. This Jewish woman doctor shows up, she and Stavers are like two wildcats stuffed into a sack the way they tear after one another, and I figure she is *not* going to be alive very long. It doesn't figure. She's more than just a woman. Stavers has always had women clawing over hot coals just to get near him. So it's a hell of a lot more than that. They're at each other's throats. Nobody does that with Stavers and lives very long. One night I get a call to go to the emergency room; the infirmary. I get down there right away, and while I'm hotfooting it, I figure Doug has said screw it, and I've got a dead female body to get rid of. I couldn't believe it. I find Skip Marden unconscious, something hurting him so bad he's writhing even while he's out, and he looks like some devil's got *inside* him and just ripped him to shreds. We thought we'd lose him. But the doctor—Rebecca Weinstein—does things nobody understands, and then Marden is sleeping like a baby, and when he comes out of it the next day, he feels like a bulldozer ran over him a couple of times, but he's okay. Nobody says a word, *not one word*, about what happened, but from that day on everything changed."

They sat in silence for several minutes. Diaz spoke finally. "I know about the diamond, Al."

"I know you do."

"I was with him when we took that mountain apart down in South America. I didn't make the trip to India because I was all busted up and in the hospital. From what I heard it was a good thing I missed that trip. Only two people came out. Stavers and Marden."

"What do you know about the diamond?"

"Everything and nothing. Crazy stories. Wild stories. None of them made sense. Fairy tales, metaphysical crap. Nothing I could ever really understand. I overheard stuff, that's all."

"What kind of stuff? I'm not probing, Bob."

"The diamond of the messiah. Stuff like that. Hitler's name. Other names I don't even remember. I was busted up, on morphine to keep me from screaming. I needed both hands to keep my guts from spilling on the ground. I wasn't *that* interested in anything else. All I know is that there's a diamond like none other. I heard fire and ice. No sense to it. I'm repeating myself, damnit. I don't like to do that, but the whole thing is crazy." Diaz blinked several times. "When did Stavers get religion? *That* question I would love to get answered. The *Reverend* Douglas Stavers? From the man who'd spit in God's eye and kick him in the nuts?"

Templin laughed. "You've said it all. Nothing to add, my friend."

"Then one last question. Maybe you can answer it."

"I'll try. I really will."

"What the hell is all this stuff about going to Mars?"

Templin finished his drink, put down the glass slowly and held Diaz's eyes.

"I'll be fucked if I know," he said.

Chapter 16

"Now I know what they mean by Nordic music. It all comes true at a moment like this." Rebecca Weinstein gestured to take in the stunning and dangerous mountain terrain surrounding them on every side except directly above. "In the halls of the mountain king. The Valkyries. Asgard. I can see how the gods would have lived here." She gripped a handbar as the helicopter took a heavy blow from a downdraft. Massive peaks reared all about them, a thin reflected silvery trickle far below indicated a narrow stream drawing its life from melting snow. Mists and snow clouds blew across and down from the crags and abutments, while the blue sky high above mixed and churned with the white of rapidly passing clouds. "I never thought it would be this kind of *blue*," she went on. "Slate grey or coppery or black or white from snow, even green from forests, but not this kind of dark, brooding blue."

She offered a quick smile to Doug Stavers. "This is more beautiful than I'd expected. It's incredible. It's almost as if we were on a different planet—"

"Or thrown back in time on our own world," Stavers observed, in sharing the magnificent vistas through which they threaded, banking and turning to follow the narrowing walls of mountain-made gorge. He looked ahead and then to both sides of their helicopter, shaking from the steady throb of choppy air spilling down angry peaks. "National boundaries didn't mean anything in those days. It was all territorial and when winter came even that concept lay buried under thirty feet of snow. A better world, maybe."

"I should be surprised, but I'm not, really," she told him.

"Oh?"

"I expected you to sass me a bit," she said, squeezing his arm. "That old saw about not knowing I was so poetic; something like that. Now I discover that not only didn't you say that but you've been having the same kind of thoughts I have."

Stavers nodded. He appreciated beauty and above all he appreciated splendor on a grand scale. He grinned. "If you look hard enough, and the sun is just right, and it becomes a visible beam because of the snow dust clouds, you might even catch a glimpse of the old-timers. This is where Thor and his people hung out."

Her laugh was music. "Wonderful!" she cried aloud, clapping her hands. She turned to look at Skip Marden in the seat behind them. He sat wide-legged, body-braced against the turbulent flight, arms folded across his massive chest. What held her attention wasn't his physical presence but a sense of "faraway" in his eyes.

"What about you, Skip?" she asked gently.

She watched a man she had never met or even known existed. Sadness crossed his face, and in the changing reflections of sky and cloud and sudden mountain shadows she knew something deep had emerged. "I've never been here before," he said, so quietly and softly, his voice barely audible over the hammering punch of engines and rotors and wind that even Stavers turned to look at him. "Yet," he stopped his words, watching a sudden burst of sunlight cascading down tumbled slopes, and then it was gone with a rush of their speed, "I have the sensation, it's crazy, but it's so strong, that I've just come home. I've never felt such a . . . a," his eyes dimmed for an instant, "a sense of *belonging*."

"Crazy bastard," Stavers poked at him, then looked to Weinstein. "I think he's off on reincarnation. Patton was—"

"General Patton?" she interrupted.

"Right. General George S. He always believed he'd

once been a great general of the Roman Empire, and had come back to fight another war." Stavers jerked a thumb at Marden. "Now *he's* got the idea that he was probably a Viking warrior killed in battle and had his ass hauled to Asgard by some big-titted Valkyrie." Stavers shrugged. "Who knows? Maybe it was right in this same gorge. Maybe a rock fell on his head. Maybe," he chuckled, "*you're* Cleopatra. Maybe—"

He cut off his words as their pilot motioned for attention. "Straight ahead," he said, pointing. "The landing pad. They've got the strobe going, just as they said." He pointed again to a digital readout where glowing numbers flashed, blurred into motion, and stopped again. "That's the preset code, sir. Everything is exactly the way you wanted it."

"Take it down," Stavers ordered.

Their pilot was better than good. He *had* to be. Both Stavers and Marden were superb helicopter pilots and they knew what this man was fighting in wild updrafts and downdrafts, and winds that burst suddenly around crags. In this kind of crazy approach and landing, experience under these conditions was every bit as important as ordinary skill under normal conditions. They rocked wildly several times as the pilot fought the currents, lowering steadily, the jet engines shrieking, and then he put them down with a solid thump onto the landing grid. He signalled to several men standing at the edge of the platform. They ran forward and attached holding cables along the undercarriage and tiedown rings. The pilot got a thumbs-up signal, waited for a voice confirmation of the tiedowns, and killed the power. He turned back to Stavers.

"I'm supposed to reconfirm the moment we land and shut down. My orders are to remain here, keep the engines warm, be ready for takeoff whenever you say."

"That's right," Stavers told him. "What's your fuel status?"

"Plenty of fuel plus two hours reserve."

"Good. If you're not in this thing, where will you be?"

The pilot pointed to a solid door. "Transient crew

quarters right there, sir. Full communications to the installations inside this place."

"Very good. What's my name?"

"Sir?"

"I asked you what's my name?"

"Uh, it's on the manifest. Right here—" He started to look at his notes when Stavers' arm shot out to lock on his wrist.

"Use your memory, pilot. *Only* your memory."

The pilot's eyes were wide. "Uh yes, sir. You're Nelson, Shelly Nelson."

"And hers?"

"Quinn, sir. Dr. Roberta Quinn."

"And our Viking warrior back there?"

The pilot tried to smile but failed and settled for a grimace. "Alberto Degarmo."

"Great. We'll see you later."

They climbed from the helicopter. Three men in Swiss army uniforms, each carrying an automatic rifle, met them on the landing pad. Their ranking officer extended his hand. "Colonel Nelson, welcome to Transvale. I'm Major Johansen." They shook hands and Stavers introduced "Quinn" and "Degarmo." They walked through huge blast doors; as soon as they were through the doors they closed with a ground-rumbling thud behind them.

Stavers spent several moments looking about them, at the smoothly carved rock tunnels, the heavy cabling that ran along each side of the curving walls, the smooth floor beneath them. Overhead lights were more than sufficient, and he noted the heavy batterypowered backups spaced at regular intervals. The experienced eye works quickly and he knew Marden had picked out the same details. Loudspeakers. Telephones at regular intervals as well. Additional blast doors, three sets, almost invisible in their slots on each side of the descending tunnel.

"When was this built, Major?" Stavers asked.

"I wasn't even born yet," Johansen replied. "It was started in 1936. The king and his ministers knew even then we'd need some place like this for the royal family."

"To say nothing of a military command headquarters," Stavers added.

"Yes, sir. That, too."

"You have full orders about us, Major?"

Suddenly everything was tight, official, no-nonsense business. "I do, sir."

"Are there any restrictions?"

"None, sir. My orders are to cooperate fully with you in every way."

"What else, Major?"

"Colonel Quinn, those are my orders, period."

"Excellent. Let's go."

"Yes, sir. Stay close to me, please," Johansen directed. "We have a rather crooked path to traverse for a while. This way, please."

A hundred yards down the curving tunnel carved from solid rock they stopped before a large and open elevator platform. "We take this up for thirty meters," Johansen explained. "There are stairways on each side of this lift system, but we won't need to use them." They stepped onto the platform, Johansen worked a lever and they rose slowly. "The purpose of this lift is to continue the tunnel after the safety margin of these thirty meters, or, essentially one hundred feet. In this manner, if we were ever flooded through the main entrance, and all three barriers were breached, the water would still have to rise these thirty meters before it could continue into our system."

The lift stopped and they walked to a circular area. A single open car on rails stood before them. "I recommend we ride. We will go at least another quarter mile inside the mountain to the cryonics laboratory."

They took their seats and the rail car glided off silently with smooth electric power. Stavers studied the tunnel; a space ran between the rails. Neat and simple; he knew a cable stretched beneath the car to the power source well beneath them, and likely the main power source came from hydroelectric generators near this particular mountain. Whatever had been constructed here back in the 1930s had also been updated through the years. Stavers and Marden picked out the television scanners, infrared detectors and even the blast doors that could slam shut to close off this rail tunnel.

The car slid to a stop. They walked across another platform and entered a brightly lit, large room that was obviously a final checkpoint. All doors and walls were of thick glass, the kind that could take a direct hit from an artillery shell and remain unbroken. Stavers ran his fingers over the glass. "An excellent choice, Major," he said to Johansen. "The same material we use in the deep-diving submersibles. Better than carboloy steel. We've gone down to better than thirty thousand feet in the Marianas Trench with this stuff."

Johansen nodded slowly; he was surprised with this unexpected recognition of the armorglass in their security facility. "You will forgive me, I hope," he said, a bit more abruptly than he intended, "but we must confirm your identity patterns here with what is in the computer systems."

They'd expected this; Stavers had insisted on it. Paper identification in the form of passports, cards or other materials, even magnetized documents, would not suffice here. One by one they stood before a computer panel. "Please do not blink," Johansen told Weinstein. "We are running a match of your retinal pattern." They went from the retinal test to body mass and then the electromagnetic signature of their three visitors.

"Thank you," Johansen told them at the conclusion of the tests. "You have also been cleared for entry to the inner chamber."

They followed the major through several doors of massive armorglass and came to a dead stop before the final doors. No one had expected to see a great gold swastika over the entrance.

"Major, do you have any restrictions on information you may give to us?" Stavers asked suddenly.

"None, Colonel."

Stavers gestured to the doors. "Once we enter the cryonics system, are there any restrictions we may expect?"

"No, sir."

"Who pays the bill for this package, Major?"

"Sir?"

"This facility has been maintained at peak efficiency since 1944, Major Johansen. We're talking nearly a half century of very expensive systems. Who pays the bill?"

"It was all prepaid, sir."

"When?"

"The year you mentioned. 1944."

Weinstein moved forward slightly. "By the Third Reich, if my records are correct?"

"Yes, Doctor. They are correct."

"Who runs the operation?"

"Why, we do, Colonel. As you can see, all personnel here are from the Swedish army."

"I mean, *inside*."

"You will see for yourself, Colonel." Johansen turned and placed both hands, palms flat against a metal plate. Laser beams flashed briefly to study his retinal patterns. The last doors opened. They stepped into a gleaming chamber of fluorescent lighting, antiseptic cleanliness, masses of piping and strange equipment. They walked slowly through a strange and almost alien laboratory. At the end of the huge room, lined with steel and plastic, they saw what appeared to be a huge thermos bottle with armorglass along its upper surface. Dozens of cables and pipes ran to the cryonic capsule. Power hummed all about them; they could feel it through the floor, almost taste the electricity in the air.

A tall man came forward to meet them. Stavers, Marden and Weinstein kept their reactions under tight control at the sight of a Nazi field marshall in full uniform. The officer stopped, clicked his heels with a ringing *crack!* and extended his right arm. "Heil Hitler," he said quietly, immediately dropping his arm as if grateful to be rid of the necessary greeting.

"I am Field Marshall Heinrich Wolfson. I am in command of this facility. I have orders from my superiors to offer you absolutely full cooperation. You," he pointed to Stavers, "are Douglas Stavers. Your cover name is Shelly Nelson. You," he stabbed a finger at Marden, "are Steven Marden, known also as

Skip Marden. Alberto Degarmo is your cover name."

Wolfson looked long and hard at Rebecca Weinstein. "You are not Doctor Roberta Quinn. Your name is Rebecca Weinstein, and your fame as a surgeon is very well known to us. I had not expected a *Juden* name, but that has little concern to me. You are also known as Doctor Olga Gustafson, under which name you practiced medicine and surgery in Switzerland during the war years. Several of our leading officers owe their lives to your skill."

He looked at the stunned face of Major Johansen. "It is all right, Major. The use of the *non de plumes* was necessary and all prearranged. Gentlemen, Doctor, this way, please."

They walked to the cryonic capsule. Through the misty air of nearly three hundred degrees below zero, they stared at the face of a silent Adolf Hitler.

"Jesus fuc—" Marden shook his head. "General, is—"

"Field Marshall."

"Whatever, man. Is he really still alive?"

"He is."

"Since 1944 he has been here," Weinstein added.

Wolfson nodded. "Correct, doctor."

"Right after that attempt to kill him in July of that year," Stavers said. "That bomb at his headquarters meeting. It nearly killed him." Stavers moved closer to the armorglass to study the figure within. "So he must have been hurt a lot worse than we knew, and you've been keeping him on ice ever since to—"

Weinstein touched his arm. "Not a word of that is true. Hitler knew of the bomb attempt before it took place. He also knew his generals were plotting against him."

"And he knew the war was lost," Wolfson broke in, his face grim, hardened with anger at the memory.

"How old are you, Field Marshall?" Stavers asked.

"Eighty-four, Herr Colonel. And I am in excellent health. *And* I have been with my Fuehrer all these many, many years."

"If he wasn't hurt when he was placed in this capsule, then," Stavers said slowly, his mind rushing to piece it all together, "then biologically, physiologically, if that's correct, he is still—"

Weinstein finished the sentence for him. "He is fifty-four years old."

"Neat," Marden added. He was very clearly unimpressed with being this close to the German dictator. "He's screwed up the war, so he leaves a double to take the heat, and you people move him into this super icebox and put him in the cooler for forty or fifty years until you're ready to take your shot at a new takeover."

"Very crude, Mister Marden," Wolfson said, his voice as cold as the cryogenic systems about him. "Crude, unspeakably insubordinate, callous, even beyond redemption, and—"

"But accurate," Marden snapped. He was leaving nothing to the imagination. He didn't like Field Marshall Heinrich Wolfson and he didn't give a damn for all the Nazi trappings about him.

Marden turned to Stavers. "It's not tough to figure it. We're here because these people," he jerked a thumb at Wolfson, "have fucked up. They got their bully boy on ice but they're afraid to snap him out of his popsicle coma because all the experiments they've made with other subjects, with guinea pigs, if you like, have failed. They broke up into ice cubes or slush, whatever, and soldier boy, here, and his crowd, are convinced the same thing may happen to Shicklegruber and all their years of waiting go right down the crapper."

Wolfson's face was a dark red as he controlled his fury at the insufferable disrespect of the big American. Stavers loved it. "You win a cigar, Skip, old boy," he chortled.

Wolfson glared at Major Johansen. "I will not stand for this!" he shouted.

"Fuck you, asshole," Marden told him, not concealing his contempt.

"I have my orders, Field Marshall," Johansen said crisply, unabashed by the fury of the German officer. He seemed to draw strength from Marden's callous indifference to Wolfson. "And with all due respect, sir, I remind you that *you have your orders*. You will cooperate in every way, without hesitation, with these people." As an afterthought he threw in a final, "Sir!"

"But . . . but . . ." Wolfson spluttered through his anger. "Such disrespect! I have never—"

"Zip it, turdmouth," Marden barked. He studied Hitler from as close to the glass as he could get. Stavers and Weinstein joined him. Behind them Wolfson trembled with his rage.

Johansen gripped the old German officer's arm. "Listen to me, Heinrich," he hissed. "You are playing the fool! That woman, I do not know everything about her, but we have been told, beyond any question, she is the *only* doctor in the world who can bring back the Leader. *The only one*, you understand? If your temper turns them away then *you* will have lost the Fourth Reich its only real chance. *So shut up!*"

Johansen turned in silence to watch the three Americans (although there were strange and unanswered questions about the woman, whose past disppeared in a giant matrix of contradictions). Wolfson was well past his own time for death and he mattered little. He was here at this moment for facade value. Field Marshall, indeed! Field Marshall of a ghost army. The real *Wehrmacht* had decades before been chewed and strangled by the victorious armies on German soil, and millions more Germans had languished and many of them died in the Russian prison camps.

Yet, "they" had kept alive the dream of a Fourth Reich. The Germans, and many more from an international community, believed that Adolf Hitler brought back to life—miraculously, of course, and still at his "death age" of fifty-four years—would galvanize tens of millions of people fed to the teeth with the constant war bickering of the world since Germany collapsed in the late spring of 1945.

Strangely enough, they cared not a snit for Hitler personally. He was strictly a power figurehead, an emotional, religious figurehead combining magic with the touch of God by bringing him forth once again. If he could be imbued with his almost-satanic powers of captivating his audiences, there *would* be the opportunity to seize and hold a great power base in the world. The idea of another war was insane, of course. *But the threat of the war was not.*

Major Sven Johansen, commanding officer of the secret mountain redoubt known as Transvale, would have been shaken to his very core to know that the Americans studying the face of Adolf Hitler, agreed completely with him.

But for different reasons, of course.

"Can you do it?"

Weinstein turned from her professional study of the instrument readings of the cryonic capsule back to Doug Stavers. He caught the barely perceptible shake of her head; sudden disappointment fled as he realized she wasn't answering his question with a rejection of success, but wanted him to hold his questions until later.

Stavers shifted his conversation. "So we're running out of time, then, Doctor?"

"Time has become critical," she said tersely, all professional in her conversation. She motioned for the German general and the Swedish major to join them.

"I will be as brief as possible. Our special clinic in Canada is the best-equipped facility in the world to bring this man," she gestured to the capsule, "back to life. But returning him to a living, breathing being is child's play—"

"What?" Field Marshall Wolfson was stunned with her words and showed it physically by a sudden palsy; the helpless shuddering of emotional excitement. He had not heard such words for many, many years. The idea of actually talking to Adolf Hitler once again! *Mein Gott, I cannot believe—*

"Please. Allow me to finish without interruption," Weinstein said as coldly as the cryonic systems about her.

Wolfson exercised self-control, bowed briefly and clicked his heels. Marden could be heard murmuring in the background, "Fucking asshole." Weinstein ignored him.

"I repeat, reviving this man, and medically he is a

patient to me, no more and no less," Weinstein went on, "is not difficult. But revival and sustenance with a completely normal brain, now *that* is absolutely the key. Without success in this area we'd be kind to him to simply shut down all this machinery and let him lapse from cryonic coma to death in sleep."

Wolfson could not contain himself. "But you can do it? Restore him with that great mind intact? Functional? As brilliant as he was, uh, before . . ." His voice trailed away.

"Yes," Weinstein said brusquely, "I can. *I* can," she repeated with a sense of command that took the others unawares. She turned to Stavers. "We must remove him from this," she looked about her with distaste, "mausoleum. During that move there must not be any interruption with the power systems or the continuity and levels of temperature. They can't vary by more than one degree plus or minus or we'll take damage we can't handle."

"But where would you take him?" Wolfson called out, almost wringing his hands.

"Canada, I said."

"*Canada?*"

"You have either a brain disease or there is an unusual echo in here," Weinstein snapped. She looked directly to Stavers. "I want him flown as soon as possible to the Mannheim Institute."

"Good God," Johansen said to match Wolfson's sound of despair. "How could we hide such a move?"

"Major, your lack of imagination is stunning," Weinstein cut into the Swedish officer. "Mannheim is the world's leading center of hypothermia research. It is also the main school for arctic weather survival for the American and Canadian military. Cryogenic materials are delivered there on a regular basis. One more cryonic capsule means nothing out of the ordinary."

"But to bring a man back to life!" cried Wolfson. "Surely *that* would draw attention! It would—"

"Be quiet," Weinstein snapped. "We have restored life to at least a hundred people who were clinically dead. Science has come far since your stupid war so long ago."

She sighed with unconcealed exasperation and impatience. "*Mister* Stavers, if you please. I am not here to counsel frightened little people, *and* we are wasting valuable time."

Stavers picked up on her message and moved in closer to the others to wrap it up. He concentrated as hard as he could and could *feel* himself exuding a sudden flow of energy, a series of spasms as if a rock had been tossed into a silent pool and sent out spasms of ripples. He threw all his mental force into generating the aura that had mesmerized so many people before this moment, that had brought men to kill themselves for the love of Doug Stavers, that had twisted even Skip Marden into a jellied pretzel within his mind and turned his muscles into gnarly ropes. Stavers stood inches away from Wolfson and Johansen. They recoiled physically as if burned. Stavers concentrated on the diamond pressed against his chest and the two men before him felt a searing mental heat from this man who had suddenly become so frightening to them.

"Major Johansen, Sweden is party to an international arctic research program, is it not?"

"Y-yes, sir."

"Then you will arrange what Doctor Weinstein has just told you is required. There are two long-range Boeings with full cryonic controls. The aircraft are pressurized and equipped to maintain internal capsule temperatures down to only a few degrees above absolute zero. That emphasizes their range of control. You can bring in a heavy-lift helicopter with a cabin sufficiently large to accommodate the cryonic equipment, the capsule and liquid nitrogen supply source. You will fly that helicopter to the nearest field capable of taking the Boeing, and waste not a moment in transferring to the Boeing. The aircraft will have sufficient range to fly nonstop to the Mannheim Institute, which has a nine-thousand-foot runway. Our staff will meet the aircraft. Everything will be ready and waiting to set up the capsule, and we will then commence the steps necessary for, ah—"

"Rejuvenation," Weinstein broke in.

Field Marshall Heinrich Wolfson had never been given so many orders and commands in more than thirty years. Instinct and ego had him fairly bristling with anger. Several times he started to object, even to shout, and then a look into the eyes of Stavers sapped his energy, leaving him weak-kneed and fighting for breath.

It is almost like he was the Fuehrer . . . this is incredible. When I first met Adolf Hitler, this is exactly how I felt. I could hardly breathe, my heart pounded, my legs threatened to collapse . . .

Unbidden, responding to an overwhelming, surging joy that appeared through his heart and soul and his limbs as if by magic, Heinrich Wolfson brought his heels together and, shaking with his turbulent roil of emotion, thrust out his right arm—*not to Hitler, but to Stavers.*

He never again saw the face of the man to whom he had just given his loyalty, heart and soul.

Stavers, Weinstein and Marden were already at the far end of the cryogenic facility on their way out.

Major Johansen ran frantically after them.

Twenty minutes later their helicopter lifted from its mountain pad and swung down the twisting deep gorge. Kebnakaise Peak vanished in the mists closing the mountains behind them, and they fled in the Alouette to Kiruna Airport. The Bae 146 was off the ground in another fifteen minutes and heading south to Stockholm.

Three hours later they were in Amsterdam, boarding an Airbus for a direct flight to the island of Malta in the Mediterranean. The Airbus usually flew from Amsterdam to Rome on its route, but "arrangements" had been made for the unscheduled flight direct to Malta. They deplaned, the Airbus departed immediately, and the group walked into the cabin of their own Skua.

In Stockholm and Amsterdam, perfect doubles of Doug Stavers led teams of agents on long and tedious drives through the local countryside. In Rome, another surveillance team waited with growing frustration for the scheduled Airbus flight, until they confirmed the airliner would *not* land at that city.

In Malta, another surveillance group rushed to the island and watched through powerful telescopes as Doug Stavers, another man and a woman companion went deepsea fishing in a chartered yacht.

By that time, one Skua was flying nonstop from Malta for a scheduled landing at Lajes in the Azores, another Skua had departed for a long-range flight to Newfoundland.

In the third Skua to depart, Doug Stavers took his second martini slow and easy, enjoying his usual Portofino cigar.

The Skua flew at 61,000 feet, sharing airspace with the tri-weekly Concorde flights running north-south between Europe and South Africa. The Skua's destination was Bloemfontein, the judicial capital of South Africa, where Stavers had waiting for him a powerful but private military strike force.

He had plenty of time to ask Rebecca Weinstein for answers to hard questions. Her seesaw manipulation of Stavers' life was eroding his patience to the breaking point. His resolve to bring matters to a head dissolved with their initial exchange.

"Three hundred years old."

She nodded, a brandy in her hand. "Yes."

"I'd like to believe that."

"You don't?" She smiled at him in her damnable cat-and-mouse parrying.

"I'd like to believe it," he countered.

"You will."

"How many more like you?"

She studied him. She wasn't play-acting. He never missed in his judgement of others on *that* issue. "That's difficult to answer. The best I can tell you is that for a while—"

"Be specific."

"I can't," she said, shaking her head. "If I could, then I would *be* specific. I can't because I don't have all the answers to all the questions you're ready to throw at me."

He held his angry retort in check. "How old are . . . these others?"

"Older."

He raised a brow and sipped slowly. "Their health?"

Her laugh came easily and free. "Excellent. Like mine."

"You are bedeviling me, Rebecca."

"I do not intend to. In absolute honesty that's not my intention. But I *must* take everything step by step."

"Are you offering me this same . . . this same lifespan?"

A minute of silence held between them. Then, barely audible, she said, "Yes."

"When," he persisted, "will I know this will happen?"

No delay this time. "The moment you recognize a picture of my father."

"You're as crazy as a bedbug."

"It may seem that way, but what I just told you is true and absolutely accurate."

"When I recognize a picture of your father," he mused aloud.

"Yes," she repeated.

"That's insane."

"It is *not*."

"Can you revive Hitler? Like you promised that bunch of weirdos in the mountain? I mean," he stressed, "revive him with all his mental faculties?"

"He was already unbalanced when he was put into cryonic coma," she said, her tone flat and no-nonsense. "His mental state is speculation at this time."

"But you can bring him out of deep-freeze?"

"Oh, yes. But," she added quickly, "not by myself. I need one other element, one other person, who is still being prepared to make it all possible."

Her answer rankled him. "Who the hell is *that?*"

She squeezed his hand.

"You."

Chapter 17

Yuri Gagarin eased deeper into the frigid waters of the North Pacific. The 16,000-ton attack-and-strike submarine of the Soviet Naval Command rocked gently as its mass penetrated a shelf of colder water. The motion was barely discernible within the enormous vessel spanning thirty-eight feet from one side to the other of its hull and as great a distance from the top to the bottom of the hull. Despite its enormous weight and its size, more than 530 feet from rounded nose to almost-silent deep-running screws, *Yuri Gagarin* was virtually undetectable to the outside, above world. Yet the huge sub was not isolated. On the surface, twenty miles to her starboard, cruised a Japanese deep ocean fishing vessel, and a Soviet trawler. Both vessels were part of the "three-dollar-bill fleet," research ships and fishing trawlers to the observer, but in reality ships crammed from bow to stern with elaborate electronic and communications equipment. On this blustery night each ship knew the precise location of the other, as well as that of *Yuri Gagarin* far below. The surface vessels trailed deep lines with which they used maser beams for unbroken communication with the submarine.

The presence of the three vessels served but one purpose, and that was to provide total security for a meeting underway within the captain's spacious quarters of *Yuri Gagarin*. The submarine captain was not present. He was the captain and played no part in the meeting and was under the strictest orders never to know *anything* of this voyage other than routine patrol.

Admiral Bruno Zhukov chaired the meeting, although he held no more import or power than any of the others. Zhukov looked remarkably like his namesake from the Great Patriotic War, when his distant cousin led Soviet forces in their smashing victories over the invading Nazis. He had been entrusted with this mission by none other than the Secretary-General, and Gorbachev had spoken in his usual candid, if not sometimes harsh manner, with his instructions.

"Carry out this meeting. There will be six, and the American government is cooperating fully with us. No matter *what* may happen, except for your own survival you are not to take any aggressive action against *any* military move against you." The Secretary-General studied Zhukov. "You will be surprised with your contemporaries. Cameron Vanderhoff from the European Common Market, so we will have full interplay with western Europe. Cardinal Lodovici Tosca from the Vatican, and—"

Zhukov's words burst unbidden from his heavy-lipped mouth. "Vatican? *The Vatican?*"

Gorbachev smiled. "Do I next hear you ask the famous Stalin question as to how many divisions the Pope has?"

"No, no sir, of course not, but—"

"What, Bruno, *what?*"

"I hold the impression this meeting represents the leading power of the world, sir," Zhukov said quickly.

"It does. But divisions do not count in this matter, and the Vatican *does.*" The Secretary-General went on. "Harvey Schlemmel of Israel." Gorbachev paused. "That one doesn't seem to surprise you."

"No, sir, it does not," Zhukov said firmly. "I know Schlemmel. A general. A former commando, a fighter pilot, a brilliant strategist. *And* the man who has brought to his country's arsenal no less than four hundred atomic and hydrogen bombs."

"Including at least one such bomb," Gorbachev said drily in a mixture of annoyance and respect for an adversary, "in every Arab and Indo-European capital and major seaport." He sighed. "There will also be

Marsha Pardue—the only woman present—of the American government, and *do not* underestimate her. Finally, Chai Honwu of China."

"Yes, sir. I notice Japan is absent."

"Yes. Their power is brittle and bloat. A nation totally dependent on imports is not a lasting power. They are not needed."

"May I comment, sir?" Zhukov went on without interruption. "I am surprised there are no Arab representatives."

"Don't be so surprised. The Israelis, as we have just mentioned, hold them all hostage. Besides, they can't agree on anything among themselves anyway, and they are totally, impossibly incapable of keeping *anything* a secret."

"Yes, sir."

"When you are through, Bruno, report back to me immediately, and personally, and do not discuss anything with anybody until after you make your report to me. Good sailing, my friend."

Zhukov saluted and left.

And now he sat at the conference table 800 feet beneath the black Pacific Ocean. Cameron Vanderhoff, even wearing the comfortable jumpsuit ordered for them all, might have been ready to attend an evening banquet. Tall, silver-haired, masculine, smooth, and a master at negotiations, he was the perfect selection to represent the polyglot mixture of western Europe. Zhukov had been assured he spoke for them all.

The Cardinal baffled him. Fiery red hair remained in a shock atop a man sixty-eight years old; exuberant freckles and flashing eyes made him seem twenty years younger, and he was obviously unaccustomed to any authority save that of the Vatican. He wore the obligatory jumpsuit but he had placed atop that bright red growth a cardinal's skullcap. Ridiculous though it might be, it said much for the strength and some secret hand this man might play.

Harvey Schlemmel was no stranger. Through the Middle East he was known as the "Clint Eastwood of Israel," brilliant fighter, scientist, pilot, strategist and tactician, and recklessly contemptuous of those opposed to Israeli ambitions, *and* anxious to back up contentious exchanges with firepower. Yet, this tall and leathery man was a good friend of Zhukov. Years before, they had joined forces in secret missions within Iran and Iraq and formed a bond between true professionals and courageous men. Schlemmel's danger was that he was ready, even eager, to go to war at the drop of a fig.

Marsha Pardue was a mixture of blue-steel hair, angry dark eyes, a trim figure, clearly an athlete in excellent condition, and a computer and electronics genius. She had risen to the rank of major general in the Marine Corps of her country before being tapped for service directly from the White House. Zhukov appreciated women of such extraordinary talent and strength; she gave no quarter, asked for none, and spoke with the tongue of a clever viper.

Finally there remained only Chai Honwu. Zhukov disliked him intensely on first sight. He was the absolute antithesis of Pardue; he was soft, almost jellied in his flabby skin, a pasty white-yellow in hue, with slitted eyes that seemed closed from pus. His lips were always moist and he seemed to cringe if he stood or sat. Yet Honwu must not be held in less respect than his fierce reputation as a bloodspilling hardliner. This soft pillow of a man had swept Communist forces in spraying blood through the sudden burst of democratic nonsense that wracked China back in 1989. China's leaders had absolute faith in this man.

One other man commanded their attention. Unfortunately, this American, Douglas Stavers, was not present.

But he was the reason they had all gathered in so secretive and powerful a group.

Everyone knew before boarding *Yuri Gagarin* that no matter what they said, no matter what agreements were reached, their sole purpose was to muster all their strength and abilities to kill Douglas Stavers.

"We have killed him *three times!*" Cardinal Lodovici Tosca slammed his hand against the conference table, sending a sharp cracking sound through the room and turning his hand painfully red from the impact. His physical action and torrent of angry words demanded their attention, as ridiculous as was his statement of thrice sending Douglas Stavers to his maker.

"That is patently ridiculous," observed Cameron Vanderhoff. He was long accustomed to fiery outbursts and afforded them no more consequence than the thoughtless anal droppings of birds in public parks. "You do not kill *anyone* more than once. May I suggest you clarify this muddled remark?"

"You are a fool," Lodovici snapped. "Do you not believe I can separate childish fiction from actuality? On three separate occasions we tracked and we located this demon Stavers. He was twice killed, *individually*, by gunfire, and on the third occasion, strictly obeying *my* orders, he was held down, killed by knife blade, and his heart torn from his chest. I returned it personally to the Vatican in a steel box. Yet," and his face twisted in angry futility, "two weeks later Douglas Stavers was seen in Salt Lake City, giving a sermon to more than ten thousand people packed into that enormous glut of a sacrilegious church they—his group; whomever! —built in that city."

"He is no demon," Marsha Pardue observed. "He is a man, no more and no less, despite the tendency of your office to imbue anyone with demonic or satanic powers. Any fool would conclude there are many of these Douglas Stavers persons."

"It's not difficult," Zhukov said pleasantly, yet annoyed so much attention was being paid to the obvious. "There were at least eight absolute replicas of walking, talking Adolf Hitlers. Several times we were convinced we had killed off that maniac. Each time we were wrong. Not until we gathered his remains from the Berlin bunker were our pathologists convinced we had finally seen his end."

"Here in this gathering," Chai Honwu observed with a sibilant, wet-lipped hiss, "you give the ghost much substance. May we proceed with more pressing matters?"

"As soon as we are in agreement with what we face," Vanderhoff answered. "Obviously, this man Stavers has used plastic surgery, exquisite training and whatever other means necessary to create duplicates of himself. Each duplicate has a specific goal. There is only *one* Stavers. He has to date eluded us all." Vanderhoff turned to the Israeli. "General Schlemmel, am I correct in saying that you at one time encountered the original Stavers? The real article, so to speak?"

Schlemmel nodded, his gaunt features surrounding deepset eyes. He spoke in a gravelly voice, the result of an old injury. "Yes. In South America. We had a powerful combat force there to hunt down and destroy Stavers." Schlemmel laughed gently. "As did the military forces of our unhappy Catholic, here. *And* a Blue Light brigade of the Americans. We were there, it turned out, all for different reasons but seeking the same man."

"You did not succeed?" Honwu queried, knowing the answer in detail before asking his question.

"He tore us all to little pieces," Schlemmel replied, no apology in voice or expression. "He did not *escape* our combined forces. He devastated us and left at his leisure. If our combined intelligence proved correct, he next appeared in India, and, disappeared just as mysteriously."

"Stop, *stop!*" Zhukov broke in. "You are all avoiding *why* we are here!" He pointed a finger at Cardinal Tosca. "*Your* expertise is the church. Religion and God."

"About which you know nothing," Tosca replied in a half-snarl.

He failed to irritate the Russian. "Granted. I know nothing of statues, icons, mass wailing and ghosts. That is *your* province. Will you *please* report to us on the area you know the most?"

Tosca nodded, self-control again dominant. If he must speak with these heathens, at least it was at the express desire of the Pope himself. Tosca took a deep breath, considered referring to his notes and rejected them; better to keep it tight.

"This Church of the Ascension, as it is called, is a heathen possession of this man Stavers. Oh, not directly, but through the tremendous corporate structure he has throughout the world. There are, at the last examination, no less than one hundred and eighty-two such churches in the United States alone. They have spread like wildfire through Latin and South America. Much more dangerous, as Rome sees this issue, is their explosive outgrowth in the Asian areas. India seems stunned by the variation of this Ascension; the priests are regarded as true messengers of some gospel that guarantees their path to Heaven. I am not familiar completely with this diversity and management, but what *is* conclusive is that it is masterful in the psychological sense, it already has hundreds of millions of dedicated followers, it is supported by seemingly unlimited funds, and it brings together this disgusting religious prattle with the very hardline goal of flying to the moon and to the planet Mars." Tosca drummed his fingers on the table. "In short, Stavers' religious army is plentiful, powerful, growing explosively, it is now a great political and economic giant. Stavers seems to appear *everywhere*. The same man, physically identical, speaks flawlessly in at least two dozen languages."

Marsha Pardue slipped in a comment waiting to be dropped on the table like a cement overshoe. "*And* he is culling the best of the other religions, sweeping them up as if he has some enormous vacuum cleaner, from the other churches into his. One more thing," she gestured quickly to stave off an angry retort from Tosca, "his church promises no miracles. That is the strangest of all. He preaches—he or whoever appears to be Stavers—preaches the sanctity of the Spaceship Earth. He is against the odious outpourings of industry poisoning the planet. He and his minions preach that salvation lies in reaching other shores that lie across the sea of space."

She offered a rare smile to Tosca. "Forgive my outburst, Cardinal. I must add another point. There is now an overwhelming cry in the United States to divert many billions of dollars from our military programs to a renewed, day-and-night, no-holds-barred, hang-the-expense space program."

Harvey Schlemmel laughed. "Everything you say he

is doing has great merit. Less military spending. Less weapons. No sanctimonious bullshit from the established religions. Work for the safety and future of this world. Cleaning house from the false prophets. I find what he is doing admirable."

"I would expect that from a Jew," Cardinal Tosca said coldly.

"Bravo!" Schlemmel exclaimed. "Now we know where you stand. Protect the sanctity and the wealth and the power of Rome *at any cost*, even if this Stavers is a hundred percent right and Rome is a hundred percent wrong."

"Enough!" Zhukov bellowed. "Collect your thoughts and control your tempers, *please!* I talk now. You listen. To the devil with your competing desires. *Stavers counts. What Stavers does counts. Why he does what he does is critical for us to know.*"

"Answer is very simple," Chai Honwu slipped into the momentary silence. "Why you are so worried? This man, Stavers, he wants to go to the moon? Send him, then. He wants to go to Mars? Send him to Mars. He is taking control, as we understand, of rocket companies. He is taking control of those who build great motors and boosters. He is paying high wages. Perhaps he is mad. Perhaps," Honwu shrugged, "he is a genius. But if you help him and send him to Mars, he is no longer of any concern to us. He is goodbye and he is good riddance. What is your problem?"

"Our learned gentleman may have a point we have failed to consider," said Cameron Vanderhoff. "The French government, which has a powerful space capability, has signed contracts with Stavers' people. They have offered to launch whatever he wishes for him from the South American coast, from French Guiana. He is paying, as the Americans say, top dollar. The French are wildly enthusiastic for him. He has been invited to visit the country." Vanderhoff studied the group. "And I recommend to you that when and if that happens, absolutely no attempts should be made against his health or his life. We have been told as you are now being told," Vanderhoff stated with all the strength of his person and his office, "that if such a grave error were to occur, France will launch at least fifty-seven large missiles with thermonuclear warheads into the major cities of the world, without regard to friend or foe."

"The French are mad," Zhukov spat.

"They have always been mad," Vanderhoff admitted.

"And they can do just what we have been told," Pardue added.

"Admiral Zhukov," Schlemmel inquired, leaning forward to look directly at the Russian, "what is Moscow's position?"

"Assassination is idiotic," Zhukov rumbled. "As idiotic as what we have heard from our Cardinal here."

"Watch your mouth!" Tosca snapped.

"Be quiet," Zhukov replied quickly, determined to yield no more slack to the Catholic firebrand. "I tell you right out, my maniacal priest, that the French have included the Vatican high on their list for a one megaton warhead."

"Perhaps we should let him rave," suggested Chai Honwu. "The consequences are obvious. The firestorms of Sodom and Gomorrah in Rome. What a great moment," he lisped, "for history."

"Okay, that's enough for this Pompei Revisited," Schlemmel broke in. "Does Stavers present a threat to us with his call to arms for selected members of the human race to swim to Mars?"

His question unbalanced them. Nobody had an answer to that specific item. "He is creating a vast new religious movement—" began Cardinal Tosca, who was cut short at once by Vanderhoff.

"Cardinal, *please*," he said in tones clipped and diplomatic. "The question is valid."

"He threatens nothing," Zhukov tossed onto the table. "I believe Miss Pardue will agree. America and Russia are the leading space giants of the world. Stavers enhances our programs. He has offered even to add financing to them through his church. Cardinal, no offense is meant, but this Church of the Ascension promises more than one hundred *billion* dollars to advance our space stations, build the lunar base, and advance to Mars, *all at the same time.*" Zhukov gestured to Marsha Pardue. "If I have misrepresented, please correct me."

"You have spoken accurately," Pardue confirmed. "But I add to your remarks. Stavers' industrial groups have already bought up controlling stock interests in a dozen of our largest aerospace firms. What is baffling to us is that he hides nothing and has even invited in the government to see *everything* they are doing. And the more people he brings into his sphere of influence, the more support he gains, and the greater the effort exerted. It makes the old Apollo program look like a swim in the old fishing hole instead of crossing the Atlantic."

Lodovici Tosca sneered. "All this rush! This madness! God had shown us the way to outer space. *His* schedules do us well. We do not need this madman Stavers, and his sacrilege—"

Harvey Schlemmel burst into laughter. "*God* has given us a schedule from heaven? Cardinal, you're a fruitcake."

Zhukov chuckled. "The church always has *its* answer. *My* hero is Bruno Garabaldi."

Cardinal Tosca's lashback to the Israeli died unborn as he heard Zhukov's words. "Your hero is a great Catholic?"

"Of course. He lived about the year 1500. A learned man, a scientist, a brilliant man. He insisted that the earth revolved about the sun. The church cried sacrilege. It was the other way around. All the heavens orbited the earth. So they solved the problem with characteristic Catholic efficiency."

"Right," Schlemmel chuckled. "They burned him alive to rearrange the heavens."

"We will be in San Francisco before this meeting gets to the point," Vanderhoff said with a touch of contempt. "You babble like the Arabs. Smoke and fury and insults. Is nose-picking next? I propose we query this group one by one for an answer to the question raised earlier. Is the activity of Stavers to create a vast new space capability, and go on to the moon and Mars, of any danger to us individually or collectively?"

Silence. Several murmurs of "No." Mostly a slight shake of the head.

Vanderhoff saw that he had clamped his personal hold on the group. He snatched at the situation, caught Zhukov's eye and received a nod from the Russian to run with the ball.

"Stavers' group has gathered to itself an enormous industrial plant," Vanderhoff said, more solemnly than he intended. "Everything from steel to aircraft, appliances to vehicles, ships to—"

"Yes, yes, we know what comprises an industrial plant," Zhukov pushed him. "The point, sir, the point!"

Vanderhoff cruised slowly right through Zhukov's impatience. "Stavers has also gained control of an enormous share of the world media. This is far more dangerous than industrial or corporate stock control. I need not discuss all these elements. A list is available to you. Suffice to say his control of the media, worldwide and in many aspects, from print to television, also controls the thinking of literally several *billion* people. He is a hero without a political cause and the key ingredient to belief—overwhelming repetition *and* repetition through a variety of ways of saying the same thing—is handled with consummate mastery." Vanderhoff tapped his pen against the table. "So! Let us dismiss our muddling about Stavers' control of space boost capability being of any harm to us. Let us even admit that the rise to power of his Church of the Ascension is no threat save that to other religious groups." Vanderhoff looked directly at Lodovici Tosca. "The Catholic Church is, if nothing else, superbly equipped and experienced at surviving everything from famine to pestilence to world wars. They are hardly in danger of sinking from sight."

"May I? Briefly?" Marsha Pardue gestured for attention and the floor; Vanderhoff nodded.

"We are all treading on fragile eggshells in this meeting." She spoke quietly but with a sure grasp of her position that demanded attention. "I don't care, my government really doesn't care, what Stavers, or his many duplicates, does with their church. So far they function entirely within all laws applicable to religious institutions, including," and she looked meaningfully at Tosca, "paying their required taxes. But even *that* is not the issue. I could occupy you for hours with the manner in which paramilitary forces, obviously controlled through Stavers, have struck devastating blows against the most powerful international drug cartels. They have killed *hundreds* of these vermin. They have destroyed untold quantities of narcotics. Now, we, my government cannot *prove* this is the work of Stavers' forces, but when something walks, talks, waddles and looks like duck—"

"It's not a water buffalo," Schlemmel finished for her.

"Good enough. Permit me a few more moments, Mr. Vanderhoff, for I feel we must get to the hard nut of all this. We have plenty of staff subordinates who will compile for us all the data we need on the monopolistic activities of Stavers. Those are *numbers*, they comprise fiscal quantities, goods and services, and there is no secret to them. Even Stavers' dominance of the rocket launch capability is no secret and we can have all the numbers we wish at any time we wish. And the more we deal with these statistics," she stressed heavily, looking at each person in turn, "the more we avoid the *real* issue why we are here."

Silence trailed her remarks. Based on their expressions she knew she had struck home. They had all been skirting the issue no one wanted to introduce. It was so ridiculous it seemed part of some fantasy.

But it wasn't, as they all knew only too well.

"May I suggest—no; *I insist*—that we put aside the smokescreen our words have generated ever since this meeting began," she offered.

Lodovici Tosca bristled. "And what do you mean by *that?* Do you suggest I am here as a facade? That I play a role of deception?"

"You bet your sweet Catholic ass you do," Schlemmel snapped, catching the others by surprise. "Why don't you just shuck all this crap, anyway? You think that stupid little skullcap is a mystery shroud?" The Israeli looked at the others in a broad sweep of the room. "He may or may not be a cardinal, but he's no milksop for the Vatican. Oh, no," Schlemmel taunted Tosca. "That son of a bitch, and I call him that with respect he's earned, is the *leader* of the group known as the Second Six Hundred. It's one of the hottest, best-equipped fighting strike teams in the world."

"The *Second* Six Hundred?" queried Chai Honwu. "What was the First?"

Schlemmel grinned. "You *could* ask Puccini over there," he stabbed a finger at the cardinal, "but he'd lie to you. The first group was led by the damnedest woman you ever saw. Rosa Montini. Sworn to the Vatican to find and kill one Douglas Stavers and to get from him what the Vatican calls the Stone of God."

Cold seeped through the room. "There," Schlemmel went on, "it's out. It's on the table. Why we're really here. Because we're all scared shitless of something called The Messiah Stone, and Stavers has it, and the Vatican is having shitfits about *not* having it, and they've tried everything to get it. That First Six Hundred? Stavers took them apart, ate them for lunch, destroyed them. He had a hell of a love affair going with Rosa Montini and—"

"You son of a bitch, you lie!" Tosca shouted.

"—and when he was through with her, he killed her and tossed her ass out of a helicopter while flying in India," Schlemmel went on, unperturbed. "The Indians cremated her body, because she had cholera, courtesy of Stavers, and the church got the ashes back to Rome. They're in a crypt right now."

Honwu looked to Bruno Zhukov. "You know of this, what he has called The Messiah Stone?"

Zhukov clasped his fingers together, enjoying the scene. He nodded. "Yes. We know of it."

"And it is real?"

"It is," Zhukov answered tersely.

"What is this object that it could be given such veneration?"

Cameron Vanderhoff gestured easily, a deceptively casual move for a man recording everything in a superbly concealed recorder, most of the equipment *within* his body. "It is a mixture of myth and reality, fear and wonder. It is a kaleidoscope of dreams and terror. In its briefest measure, shorn of all save what may be the facts, the object is a diamond. Or," he added self-correction quickly, "it appears to be a diamond. Somewhat more than eighty carats, what the trade would call fancy yellow in color, but flawless even at a magnification of several hundred. Legend and reality together believe that two thousand years ago, at what is accepted as the birthtime of Jesus, or Jehoshua, as General Schlemmel might accept the name—"

Harvey Schlemmel nodded; he knew every word of Vanderhoff's before the man verbalized his memory.

"At any rate, the legends tell us that a meteor, or a comet, penetrated the atmosphere somewhere in the south of Africa and retained its shape until it struck the surface, when it exploded. The meteorite was to have impacted at the same instant as the birth of the Christ child. *So we are told, so many believe,*" he stressed. He took a deep breath before continuing.

"This stone, which became known to many as The Messiah Stone, to the churches as The Godstone, and by many other names, is reputed to endow its bearer with extraordinary powers over other people. Nothing so dramatic as you might see in a theatrical film, but the individual with the stone develops or generates an area that bends the will of other people to his—or her—own."

Chai Honwu smiled. "There have been other such objects with such powers believed to exist," he said.

Vanderhoff came back immediately. "You misunderstand. *I* make no claims. I reject no claims. I do not dispute the history of any other. I see directly ahead on this matter. Nowhere else. A native tribe in Africa, the Manturu, possessed the diamond. They ruled utterly without fear or danger until perhaps sixty or seventy years ago. A Romanian group led by Bibesco flew to the Manturu tribal lands. Remaining distant enough from the stone not to be affected, they devastated the tribe with modern weapons, seized the diamond, and fled. There is much more detail, but the gist of all that has transpired is that this diamond came into the possession of Adolf Hitler in the mid-thirties."

Vanderhoff went silent. He did not need to explain to anyone the strange powers attributed to Adolf Hitler, his ability to overwhelm through sheer force of mental energy the people about him, to mesmerize them, to literally bend them to his will, to instill a fierce loyalty and love for Hitler. He knew where their thoughts would take them in a brief travelogue of review of all they knew or had heard of regarding the messianic powers of Germany's "sainted" Hitler.

If this stone were real, or the powers linked to the stone were real, why . . . the world, the entire world, could be brought under its incredible . . .

Bruno Zhukov burst into laughter. Pragmatic Russian that he was, he found tremendously amusing what he knew transpired silently in their gathering. "So! Finally we have reached, albeit in silence, a complete agreement on at least *one* subject!" He laughed again, the sound carrying unmistakable ridicule for them all. "Are you through with your brief fantasies of unlimited power? Shall we get back to the business at hand?"

"Well, it damned well explains one thing," Schlemmel followed Zhukov's words. "I never did understand why almost every rocket scientist and physicist in the world was overnight a staunch and even a fierce follower of Douglas Stavers. *If* the powers of this diamond are real, it explains many things."

"I dislike emphasizing the crass against the metaphysical," Honwu broke in smoothly, "but may I attribute vast sums of money, and the means to play with their great rocket machinery, as also a source of great loyalty by these scientists for Stavers? After all, it is *his* checkbook that makes all this possible. If you marry dreams to the wealth to create your machines, then political boundaries and loyalties may be said to diminish in proportion to the sum of the money spent and the objects created."

"Is that straight from Confucious?" Marsha Purdue asked in a scathing tone.

"Perhaps," the Chinaman smiled.

"The French," Vanderhoff said. "Think of the French. We had reports that Stavers had spent time with the leaders of France. Upon his departure the French hurled their entire national energy into the huge booster rockets and advanced systems for deep space flight. Is this only from money? Is this diamond truly so possessed of these magical mind-bending powers that Stavers brought the French to their knees, to his will?"

"We agreed the French were mad," Zhukov reminded them.

"Mad, but not stupid," Schlemmel offered as correction. "No, there's a hell of a lot more here than we understand."

"And that is why," Zhukov thrust at them, "we had to meet as we do right now. That is why we must come to some understanding that to attempt to *kill* Douglas Stavers is insanity. His death could lose us, any of us or all of us, that stone. Forever. Along with what wonderful powers it may possess."

"The magic I see in this group," Chai Honwu spoke, as a teacher would address a schoolroom, "is belief in fantasy of an object no one has seen and has more chance of arising from an Arthurian Merlin than being regarded in the pragmatism of science. We Chinese are supposed to be steeped in tradition and metaphysics; not you Westerners. You amaze me. You babble like children. I do not believe what I have heard."

Zhukov leaned back heavily in his seat. "The eternal problem of the Chinese. If *they* cannot see, feel, touch, hear, bite, lick, squeeze or otherwise clasp an object, then they reject all that may be attached or ascribed to that object."

Honwu smiled. "Precisely. Your intended insult bites you in your own intestines. What you say is truth. At last," he appended.

Zhukov blinked as he studied the Chinese. "And I told the Secretary-General that to include your kind would be the height of folly."

"Why does he want to go to the moon? *Why* does he want to go to Mars?" They turned to Schlemmel. "Anybody here *know* why?"

Vanderhoff laughed. "We don't *know* any such things. Stavers publicly says these are his desires, his goals. Do you know if he speaks the truth?"

"No," Schlemmel answered.

Vanderhoff shifted in his seat to face Lodovici Tosca. "My friend from Rome, you have been uncharacteristically silent through all this. That disturbs me. Especially since we have learned your talents extend far beyond the stone walls of any particular church."

Tosca, relaxed now that this group knew of his military talents as well as his position as a Cardinal of Rome, regarded the group with a contempt he felt as strongly as he showed his feelings.

"My predecessor," he began slowly, "was Butto Giovanni. A Cardinal. The devout man who at the order of our Pope created the Six Hundred. He knew, this Giovanni, the unbreakable thread that runs through the history of man. He knew where the thread would twist and evil would arise. Every so often, when He deemed it necessary, God would speak through the sun. Through the shattering light of a million suns. Through Sodom and Gomorrah, Hiroshima and Nagasaki. Each moment of terror a warning, and each moment always a reminder, an arrow, to point the way."

They would have interrupted this impromptu Catholic sermon under the sea except that the man before them was now more soldier than cardinal, and he had through the sheer intensity of his eyes captured them all. "Two thousand years ago a million suns shone, but it was an inner light and our Lord was born unto man. The light that ignited in the hearts and souls of men blinded them to another sign. At the moment of our Lord's birth on this world there was sent to us an object of veneration, of holiness that would soar even higher than the chalice of the Last Supper. No chalice, no cassock, no crucifix could even approach what had been sent to men of the true faith. The great wars were coming. The atom would be unleashed to rage through mankind like the dogs of war. The only way to avoid Satan's triumph would be to bring men from the brink of destruction by turning their will from false glories to true faith. Men could not do this, so from On High we were sent the means of salvation. From the moment the hand of God lowered what you in this room call The Messiah Stone, it has been the mission of our Papacy to bring the Godstone to Rome, so that the Pope might bring this flow of power through his own mind to bend greedy men away from Satan. You smile, you patronize me, you mock me in your minds, and you are fools beyond redemption. You speak of this diamond as if it were some bauble from a jewelry store to be swung between the full breasts of a harlot! Diamond, indeed! You see only the shape and not the holiness within! *You!*" He stabbed a finger at Marsha Pardue. "You have already been soiled by Stavers!"

Her mouth fell open in utter astonishment. "Did we not hear you say you and your government did not even care what Stavers does with his church? With his unclean gatherings? *You do not care how God Himself is addressed? Or soiled? Those were your very own words!* And what else might we expect," he went on in a voice suddenly so hushed they strained to hear, "from someone under the control of Stavers so we must not interfere with Stavers' unholy mission?"

Tosca smiled coldly and directed his gaze to Zhukov. "And you, too, you miserable spawn of a succubus. Who would have expected Islam to have been so strangely accurate when they joined Russia and America as the claws and talons of Satan? But they saw! And it is *you* whose own words spoken to us were that it would be insanity even to think of killing Douglas Stavers, this unholy minion of the nether worlds. It is you who would leave him unfettered to spread his control of peoples and nations the world over, and sow like the teeth of foul-mouthed dragons his thugs and priests in their unspeakable orgy they call Ascension."

Lodovici Tosca's hand rose and fell, slapping gently against the table. "Not once have I heard what you all know. Not once even a mention of this miserable harlot who is always at Stavers' side."

"The doctor?" Zhukov asked, honestly puzzled. "This

woman, Doctor Rebecca Weinstein? A surgeon of great skill, and to you she is only a harlot?"

Tosca smiled. "She is no Jewess. Ah, but the Israeli general shows his surprise! He either lies well, or more likely, he is simply stupid or without knowledge. What do any of you know of this woman save that she is what you call a brilliant surgeon? She appears from nowhere. You can find little or nothing of her background. But we know because the records of the Church go back and back and back . . ."

His voice faded; he shook off some inner feeling of dread. "I talk too much already."

"Amen," Schlemmel said with dripping sarcasm.

"Jew, listen to me." Tosca shifted position so that their eyes locked. "This woman was a nurse in Switzerland during the war years of 1941 through 1945. That was a half-century ago, *but she is only some thirty years old.*"

His words fell like stones. "Have you seen her papers? Her records? *She was a nurse in Austria in the First World War, and she was then only some thirty years old.*" His voice hammered relentlessly. "She was a doctor, or a nurse, as she wished at any time, in the Franco-Russian War! She performed medical service through the great Persian wars! She was a brilliant surgeon in the Ottoman Empire! *And she is always some thirty years old!*"

"That's crazy," Zhukov said in a hoarse whisper.

"Nevertheless, it is true," Tosca said quietly. "Do not for one moment believe we have not exhausted every means possible to confirm what I have just said to you. Do not for a moment feel we act as we do from Rome because we seek to be triumphant over any opponent save evil. We do not know why she took this particular time to be with Stavers, but as powerful as is this man, and he has great and terrible powers, we believe hers is the greater. She is the serpent of Satan. He is the spawn of the devil. We intend to kill them both. We will, we shall, we must find the Godstone. If we are to be delayed in this holy mission because we must first cut away the Devil's hand by smashing these two, then so be it. We are sure of ourselves."

He sat back, head high, master of the moment.

"And you're as full of shit as a Christmas turkey," Harvey Schlemmel told him. The Israeli turned to Bruno Zhukov.

"This meeting is over. I have nothing more to say or to hear. I shall observe the rules of this vessel. I shall keep my word to you, Zhukov. But if you wish this maggot," he jerked a thumb at the white-faced and now-trembling Tosca, "to reach port alive, then I advise you to separate us. Because otherwise as my God and *his* God are my witness, I will kill that fanatical bastard with my own two hands."

Another voice followed his. It was the first time they'd ever heard a Chinaman say, "Amen." Chai Honwu chuckled. "Our Catholic has forgotten the promise of the French. The light of a million suns into the heart of the Vatican. I do not believe the Pope is so stupid as to risk the heart of the Holy See for the heart of a man."

Chapter 18

Skip Marden spread the photographs and topographic charts on the long table beneath intensely bright lights. He moved with an efficiency and silkiness never before observed by Dr. Rebecca Weinstein. This was, as she had suspected all along, a completely *different* man from the Marden she had come to know in the foregoing months. Hesitancy of any kind had vanished. The listlessness that plagued the man and made him as ornery and irritable as a flea-plagued hound dog had evaporated, as well. This was a man back in his own element, where *his* instinct, cunning and experience, and skills honed through a lifetime, were the primary factors in living and *continuing* to live.

After all, mused Weinstein, they were about to plunge into a hornet's nest. All the way inside, and when you're buzzing with the hornets in *their* home world, there's only one way to get along with the nasty creatures.

You kill them.

Skip Marden would have been astonished to know that Rebecca Weinstein gave no more thought to the mass slaughter they might ignite than she would hesitate in swatting a mosquito. Women were either fully aggressive against their opponents, or they wrung their hands and wailed piteously. Middle ground between these two extremes just didn't exist.

As far as Marden knew or understood, and he neither knew nor understood Rebecca Weinstein, who had planned for and waited a *very* long time—measured in multiples of lifetimes—for the event about to happen.

The lives about to be extinguished mattered not a whit to her. Through her own lifetime she had seen thousands of men, women and children perish within her own personal view, and she had been embroiled in events that in the vicinity immediate to her own, literally millions of human beings had perished. She felt no pity, no sense of loss, no empathy for any of them, for she knew the emotion was useless and therefore absolutely wasted. Her reaction was that of the indifferent observer until and unless she was involved personally.

She was returning, after an incredibly long wait, to the land of the Manturu. The original line of the warriors of the South African regions had long dissipated in broiling heat, disease and diluted genetics, and they had been replaced by groups of native warriors cemented into a force with singular purpose sustained by legend and myth and fearful superstitions. Whatever their reasons, Weinstein knew, these same warriors must defend and repel any invaders of their holy ground, a temple with a weed-overgrown facade as its exterior, and the greatest secret the world had ever held beneath the ground strewn with the droppings of animals and the native locals.

Only, these natives carried automatic weapons rather than spears and long knives.

"These are good." Doug Stavers tapped the sharp end of a Ghurka boot knife against photographs before him. To his left were high oblique pictures in ordinary light of an African plain with a single high mound, or more accurately a long low hill, covered with heavy undergrowth and trees. In the center, before Stavers, lay a photograph taken at night with infrared film. A glowing haze about the hill defined its parameters better than any daylight picture. But what held his interest the most, was a scene recorded in magnetic wavelengths.

He studied the presentation with as much unanswered intrigue as being able to define the readouts. Magnetic fields appear on film taken from high altitude in various ways; masses of ore or metal show with differing intensities of brightness. He looked up at

Weinstein. "This doesn't make much sense. The regular light photos are fine and so are the thermals. But this," he shook his head. "Look, if this were an underground installation we'd have linear or constant-curve definitions of *some* kind, and we don't have that at all. I've looked at plenty of these, Rebecca, and this is a mishmash. You got an answer?" He slipped the deadly blade back into a boot scabbard and took his time clipping off the end and lighting one of his favorite cigars. A glass of brandy lay untouched on a nearby table. Stavers, she had taken careful notice, never ingested anything that might interfere with thinking and cognition.

"I have an answer," she said finally.

Stavers didn't ask for it. Instead he turned slightly in his chair to study the woman. Once again she had shed an outer cocoon; the doctor was gone, the woman vanished, and in the stead of former personalities he looked at what might have been a dedicated, experienced, trained and deadly Sabra. A killer in Israeli desert garb, wearing combat boots, combat fatigues and jacket, and her body adorned with a variety of knives and other throwing weapons as well as for close-in defense. The heavy artillery, automatic weapons, grenades and the like, weren't needed for this moment.

"You know the answer, then," Stavers said after his long pause and slow undressing and redressing of the woman. He leaned forward. "I get the idea," he said slowly and deliberately, "that you've known all along what's under that hill."

Again her answer and her manner of response was maddening. "Yes," she said simply.

"Then why'd we go to all this trouble of getting these photos?"

"One, I might not be able to describe *in the terms you need* the amount of metallic substance under that hill. I might describe it with inaccuracy. I might not apply to certain elements the importance you and Skip might find so obvious." She glanced at the pictures, pushed them with one hand. "And there could have been any number of changes beneath that hill since the last time I had knowledge of its location and what it might contain. The reconnaissance coverage removes me from the uncertainties. This is *your* bag, not mine, my friend, and when it comes to assault operations, *I* take the *back* seat. In short, you run the operation. Skip runs it as your second-in-command and so on. My position is as advisor, and I would like to remain with that freedom so that in addition to being guide and advisor I can also cover your back."

He laughed. "That old bit of keeping me alive no matter what, right?"

"Yes."

"What's under the hill, Rebecca?"

"You will know soon enough. We launch in darkness? Within an hour after you open fire, you will know."

"And you insist that I wait until then," he added, repeating earlier conversation.

"I *must*. Anything else diminishes the effect."

"*What* effect?" He held up both hands to prevent her answer. "I know, I know. Wait." Abruptly he stood up. "All right, it's fun and games time. Skip!" he called to the giant who'd fought by him through so many past operations. "Final call. Get the team leaders in here."

Eight subordinate commanders gathered about the table. Eight men each with ten men under their direct platoon-force command. Every one a trained, battle-hardened, scarred veteran of wars small, large and rotten throughout the world, fought everywhere from ice-covered slopes to fetid garbagy ghettos.

Killers all.

"You already know the battle plan," Stavers told them. His mannerisms fascinated Rebecca Weinstein. He didn't need that stone resting against his chest to command these men. *They'd follow him right into Hell and tear the place apart because they believe in him. No wonder he commands and leads so naturally. And no one about him has ever understood that his genetic structure, different from all the others, is what makes this possible.* She laughed to herself, not a hint of that mirth showing on her face. *And it's why I need him.*

"No real changes. We've moved up the operation

precisely twelve minutes. A cloud cover will block out the moon, so night vision enhancers are important. No flares if at all possible; it blinds the IR and the enhancement systems. The flares give these black gooks a better crack at us." Three out of every ten men in Stavers' force were black. They took no umbrage with his *black gooks* remark. Those were natives. *These* men were the Stavers' team and they were second to none.

"No prisoners," Stavers went on as calmly and impersonally as if reading off the latest stock market report. "You see a man fall, make sure you put another round into his head before you go up to them. These loonies are like the ghurkas and the old Filipino soldiers. They'll take a half-dozen slugs and still keep twitching. Assign two men from every group to follow the other nine. They carry machetes. They lop off heads. Heads that roll around the ground without bodies don't talk. Don't let anyone break that rule. I do not want any identification of anybody when this is over, understood?"

He looked about him as they nodded. "Parker," Stavers cracked out the name and nodded to a burly, skull-scarred killer. "What's the other unbreakable rule?"

"Don't fuck up any of the rules," Parker answered in a sandpapered rumble of a voice. The men about him grinned.

"Specifics," Stavers pushed, unamused.

"Nobody ever works alone. There's always a team, two men or more. We bring out all our dead and wounded. *All.*"

Stavers shifted his gaze. "Stevens?"

"Anybody loses an arm or a hand, we bring it back with us. Nothing gets left behind that can be used later for identification."

"Garcia?"

"No exceptions. Men, women, kids. *Everybody* we find gets it."

"Sakamoto?"

"Marden runs the operation. You take us in. When we get there, Skip is top dog."

"Dallas?"

"If the woman gives orders," he nodded toward Weinstein, "we obey them."

"Not strong enough, Dallas."

"We obey them *no matter what.*"

Stavers nodded slowly, shifted again to another man. "O'Grady?"

"There's always the chance we may run into far more than we expect. If everything goes to hell, and the helicopters get greased, we all buy the farm. That's guaranteed."

"Hogan?"

"Three choppers. Each carries a tactical nuke. If it all comes unglued and we can't get out, any one of those nukes will blow. Everybody buys the farm. All of us, all of them."

Rebecca Weinstein turned white. She didn't know this! She'd never heard of it! And as quickly as she heard the words she knew it was too late to change anything. From this moment on, until they were beneath that hill—she and Stavers—she'd become a third wheel. It sent a chill running down her back. She hadn't been out of control of *anything* for a very, very long time. *But it could be fun*, she thought with a sudden surge of amusement.

"Question, sir."

Stavers looked up at George Sterling and nodded for him to continue. "Does the woman go in armed?"

"Yes. So that you know this isn't a babysitting operation she rates expert in every weapon we carry." Men nodded in appreciation of those words.

"Mitchum, your job is last-minute catchup. Anything?"

Jeb Mitchum moved forward and laid a package gently on the table. "These came in about two hours ago. One for everybody in our team. I've been testing them. They work. I want *everybody*, as soon as we leave here, to strip down and put theirs on."

"What'd you take?" Stavers asked.

Mitchum stripped off his battle jacket and shirt until he was bare-chested. Angry red welts and dark bruises covered his chest, stomach and arms. An angry welt ran along one side of his neck.

"Two spears and seven arrows. Direct strikes. I went back and down three times. These damn things really do the job." He opened the package and held up a shimmering metallic cloth. "Shark suits, gentlemen. Or rather, anti-shark suits. In the water you can have a blue or a mako or even a hammerhead clamp on an arm or a leg and bite down with all its strength. The teeth can't get through this stuff. It's a new kind of steelmesh. The only killer we haven't tried it on is the great white, and that mother can just about swallow you whole anyway." He looked at the team leaders with him. "You can take direct hits from spears, lances or arrows. They will *not* penetrate these suits. They'll knock you on your ass but they won't get through to your skin. Everybody wears one. It'll be hot as hell, but I'd rather be hot and alive than cold and dead. Now we know there'll be more than spears and arrows. Autorifles and small arms, for sure. These suits will stop a Colt forty-five or a police special. We don't know about magnum penetration, but my advice is not to worry about it. If the suit won't stop a forty-four magnum, your ass will be dead anyway."

"That's it," Stavers said suddenly, rising to his feet. "Get these suits to your men right away. Like Jeb said, everybody wears one. Then get your people into the choppers. *Into* them. Larson, after each chopper is loaded I want every flight crew, two men at least, to do a final weight-and-balance on each helicopter to be absolutely certain you're all in the ballpark. I don't want to have a machine go in because it wasn't loaded properly. Once they're in the choppers they stay in. Anybody needs to take a leak, he does it through a door or a window." Stavers glanced at his watch. "Coming up on zero four hundred. Marden, take over for time synch and get everybody into position."

He turned, nodded to Weinstein, and she left with him for the office he used as headquarters coordination. Outside, they were suddenly in the midst of a squalid native village with large round huts, a miserable page out of history. And a Potemkin village in reverse. Every "hut" was a solid building with full communications, weapons storage, and on wheels. They all stretched along a six-thousand-foot runway. Spread out at the far end of the runway, beneath the cover of huge "trees," three Antonov jet assault transport planes waited with their flight crews for these teams when—and if—they returned from the strike mission.

Stavers and Weinstein stripped to their underwear to don their steelmesh suits and replace their outer garments. "We've got one hour before we get into the second chopper," Stavers told Weinstein. "That means you've got just about thirty minutes to tell me why we didn't do the number on our Fuehrer icicle before now. And I want you to tell me why, and in language I'll understand, and for whatever reasons there were, or, are, that I'll understand."

She poured coffee from a thermos and sat on the floor with her back to a wall. She nodded to Stavers; he reached behind him to an electronic control panel. A gentle stinging sounded in their ears. Electronic interference; they couldn't be heard outside the hut and any recorders within the hut would record only hash.

"In that mountain cave," Weinstein began slowly, "we were in the midst of primitive equipment. Any medical facilities were strictly for emergency use of *normal*, or everyday, problems. Nothing in the cryonic systems were of any use to revive Hitler. What you saw there, despite all that cabling and tubing, was the most primitive and inadequate facilities. If we had made any attempt to thaw out that man he would have died in minutes. You see, he isn't in a true cryonic state; he's frozen, and at the time he was placed in storage, the people carrying out that procedure knew far less than your doctors know today, more than forty years later."

Stavers caught what Weinstein had never intended to say. She hadn't said "doctors." She'd said "*your* doctors." It was a slip that he'd have to mix with other data for its proper meaning. He nodded as she spoke, a silent request for her to continue.

"That capsule—like a thermos bottle—is basically a tank of liquid nitrogen. Its temperature is maintained at a constant minus 320 degrees. That's Fahrenheit scale. When Hitler went into cold storage the plans to bring him out of that storage were more dreams than medical science. Up until 1944, and it's one reason the Germans experimented with so many adults and children, they actually went through more than eight thousand people in freezing and retrieval. Most died, and very badly. The fortunate ones died quickly. The others went through agony because of clumsiness and stupidity on the part of the doctors, many of whom were veterinarians instead of fully trained medical doctors."

Weinstein reflected a moment, scanning her memories. "There was some success. The Germans seized on anything that held promise. The problem is that this method of freezing is archaic."

There it is again, as if she was on some higher plane, looking down on us . . .

"The freezing method with liquid nitrogen causes inescapable damage to the human system, to the physical body. For example, as it freezes, the body's water—"

"Expands," Stavers broke in. He wasn't uninformed on the procedures and he felt it advantageous for Weinstein to know this. "If I recall," he went on, saying less than he actually knew, "that expansion through freezing ruptures cells."

"Precisely," she said. "The expansion ruptures the cell membranes. That's just one of many problems. Sometimes the body water, despite its sodium content, expands between cells and crushes them. And then you have that chemical problem. As the body water freezes it separates many different kinds of salts. Normally they're not a problem. In rapid cryogenic treatment, however, these salts may gather in concentrations poisonous to the body. That killed thousands in the wartime experiments. I studied the system used with Hitler. They overcame this problem by freezing him under tremendous pressure, oh, at least fifteen to twenty atmospheres. That way the body liquids don't expand."

"Did it work with Hitler?"

She nodded. "There's every indication it did. Oh, he's alive, Doug. The problem we face is to bring him out of ice pickling so he'll be more than a zombie."

"I was going to ask you about that."

"The brain itself won't be a problem, as far as I can see. There were enough experiments run so that the Germans had at least one hundred revivals, and at the conclusion of those tests, they confirmed normal electroencephalographic activity. But those weren't longterm, so that remains a bit of an unknown.

"Most cryogenic storage cases today are with people who have already died. They pickle them so that their systems will remain unchanged in the hope that one day in an unknown future, medical science will have advanced enough that they can be revived and whatever killed them excised from their bodies. Organ transplants, whole blood replacement, genetic variation; that sort of thing. This isn't the case with good old Adolf. They had to freeze him *before* death, otherwise the odds were he'd come out of it more a cabbage than a human being. They were shooting in the dark, so to speak, and they did so because their war was lost, and the Germans always liked the touch of Valhalla in what they did."

She smiled at her own remarks, then continued. "They gave Hitler drugs that would block every possible sensation of pain. Then they opened the carotid artery, and the jugular, and they began to mix their chemicals with his circulatory system. Perfusion isn't that difficult, and if they could move the chemicals quickly enough through the system, and still keep the brain cells from expanding, then deepfreezing the brain and all its capabilities was within their grasp. They appear to have done very well with that."

"So the old boy will come out of it still convinced he's a world beater," Stavers said.

"He *should*. Something else is needed that will permeate the entire genetic system, give it a tremendous shock of viability."

"You—we—have that something?" he asked.

"We do. Or we *almost* do. I believe we can do it, but let me get to that point a little later."

"All right. I can guess that this same chemical substance went into his lungs?"

"Of course. Damaging the alveolar system for a continued exchange of gases after revival is absolutely necessary. It was *then*. Today we have the equipment to do it with machinery and electronics. Anyway, once these preparations were completed, they wrapped Hitler in a pouch, a body garment packed with finely crushed ice, and, I imagine they knew enough back then to include a kind of granular salt. This keeps the freezing process steady rather than sudden spurts or lunges. They appear to have done this to allow ice crystals to form slowly to prevent damage to the cutaneous surface. From then on it's like deepfreezing ice cream. They wrap the entire biological package in a type of foil—aluminum was the best material they had then—and slipped the foil wrapping into that cryonic capsule—that thermos bottle—that had been precooled with dry ice. They kept him that way for, oh, I'd guess six months or so."

"Why six months?"

"It gave them time to monitor everything that had happened and to correct any mistakes before they wrapped him up for good. Until attempted future revival, that is. After a few months of this kind of monitoring, they dump him into stasis for the promised land of future superscience. Until now the body temperature has been about 110 degrees below zero. That's not good enough for long storage."

"I saw liquid nitrogen in that lab. That's below 300 degrees, isn't it?"

"Yes; 320 degrees below zero. When they slide the body, which is already a big slab of meat, into the, let's call it the thermos bottle, then they administer the liquid nitrogen. But they don't seal the bottle. They leave it open so it can evaporate, or more accurately, so that it can boil. This drops the temperature rapidly and smoothly. It's a self-serving system. When the temperature reaches the intended levels, presto, the nitrogen no longer boils. Now the bottle is cold enough so it can be filled with more liquid nitrogen that remains in that liquid state. As they say in Hollywood, that's a wrap. The job is done. The years to come are spent in monitoring the system and making certain the temperature stays within a degree above or below the final freezing."

"You've hedged on a few points," Stavers said. Weinstein nodded.

"We don't have the medical facilities to awake Sleeping Beauty so that he's more than a walking toy, right?"

"The world doesn't," she said in a mild correction. "*We* do."

"Who's we?"

"Me. You. You'll find out how in a very short time now."

"Back to that bit about you can't tell me because I've got to see for myself?"

"Yes, Doug."

"While Adolf is in deep freeze," he spoke slowly, "the trillions of cells that make us the stuff we are remain alive?"

"I hope so. If everything works, yes."

"Can we expect organismic damage?"

"Most certainly. That's why we had to get him to Canada. I've already arranged for every possible replaceable organ to be available for transplant when we go into revival. I must say it again. The German medical science in the forties was crude. You see, you just can't stop a body from functioning. What you're really doing is slowing down tremendously the physiological processes. Like slowing down time so that a year is only a second; something like that. Normal life activity is a constant biochemical interreaction, a nonstop change. We are all aqueous and we all need molecular activity to remain alive. Few people realize that cryogenic storage doesn't stop time. That's fantasy, not reality. We are really slowing down time, but to a tremendous degree."

"Enough to preserve the integrity of the basic systems?" He held back a smile as he spoke. "There's digestive, cardiovascular, respiratory, just for starters. You've already answered my questions about replacing heart, liver, lungs, kidneys; whatever organs will be damaged. But what I haven't heard you answer yet are how this deepfreeze stuff keeps alive the cells that make up the organs."

"Nervous, connective, muscular and epithelial. Their tissue," she rattled off swiftly, "constructs from cells and

"*Cut 'em down!*" Marden roared.

called the organs' little cells. These are the nucleus, chromosomes, endoplasmic reticulum, the mitochondria. You keep right on descending to lower units into the enzymes and chemistry of submolecular makeup. In essence, we're dealing with well over a hundred different variations in cellular makeup. It's a marvelous heterogeneous composition, and it *can* be stored and, above all, with the application over and through the total body mass of a special energy at the time of revival, well, you can successfully wind up the tinkertoy human organism."

"I know," he said defensively, "wait a bit longer before I find out what your miracle energy is."

Again he heard that curt "yes" of agreement.

He rose to his feet. "All right, lady," he told her. "That's enough of revival. Now it's killing time." He grinned. "We're right in tune with nature. Only this time it's death before life."

Chapter 19

Skip Marden sat in the center seat of the lead Polotov helicopter, one of eleven powerful killer machines that were the best battlefield marauders produced by the Soviet aircraft industry. Each chopper, powered with three jet engines, could do better than 200 miles an hour. Each machine carried a strike team plus the flight crew, plus a murderous array of firepower including more than 400 minirockets, three Vulcan-type 30-mm cannon, and six hand-held .60 caliber machine guns with a firing rate of 1,700 rounds per minute. They enabled their pilots to fly in day or night with equal ease, and for long-distance damage each Polotov had slung beneath outrigger airfoils six homing rockets for use against other aircraft or particular ground targets. They had all been flown secretly from a Soviet base in Angola to a forward and remote staging area of the South African Air Force. That government accepted with quiet pleasure the transfer of ninety million dollars through French and Israeli banks to various accounts which eventually would enter the treasury of South Africa. For this fee the South Africans created a powerful defensive ring about the staging area, provided fuel for the helicopters and the three Soviet jet transports concealed beneath their camouflage, and the necessary food and other logistics for the Stavers strike force. The South Africans also provided an immediate loss of memory of what went on in their distant maneuvers area, which any sensible persons regarded as a promise of death. It was, all in all, an admirable arrangement, for which everything had been agreed upon verbally.

Marden looked to his left and right. Every Polotov ran its power levers to the same thrust; the machines were ready for flight. He checked his watch against the electronic timers of the flight crew, and pressed a button on a control panel directly between his pilots. In each helicopter digital counters snapped the number sixty into view. The final seconds were counting down.

Seconds fled, the counters all read zero, and eleven Polotovs lifted in perfect unison from the darkened earth and began a wide circling turn to the left before departure to the ancient land of the Manturu. The wide turn gave each crew sufficient time to check all engine and flight instruments. The precision-tuned machines operated flawlessly. Marden pressed another button and in each chopper a panel light read green and the cathode ray tube displays flashed PROCEED. The choppers moved out at 185 miles an hour 200 feet above the ground.

Their flight time to target point would be precisely fifty-one minutes and eighteen seconds.

The world beneath the mass formation of helicopters trembled and shook beneath the fury of its passage. Eleven helicopters, thirty-three jet engines and huge blades ripped the dewy, dark morning, flattening grass and bending trees and sending thousands of animals into terrified flight. The pilots flew with unerring precision in their formation so that from high above the helicopter formation seemed a single creature of many beating wings and dragon's torch cry. The weather gods smiled on the attack force; a heavy cloud cover blanketed the world only two thousand feet above the earth and continued on up to better than twelve thousand feet, providing a perfect two-miles-thick mass of water vapor and cloud to conceal from reconnaissance planes or satellites the blasting rush northward into Manturu country.

"Twenty miles," sang out the copilot of the lead Polotov.

"Kick out a probe," Marden ordered.

A safety catch was flipped away by a finger and a switch thrown. A dazzling flash appeared for an instant, then subdued to a deep steady red as a small winged missile tore ahead of the helicopter. Marden and the copilot studied a cathode screen. Far ahead of them the stub-winged missile scoured the earth ahead and below its passage, sending back signals in infrared television and radar.

The copilot's finger moved across the scope, tapping bright lights scattered across the countryside. "Cooking fires. Basic similar intensity. Some movement, mainly animals, horizontal readouts." A man would show up as a vertical mark on the scope. "Seems normal," the copilot added. Marden nodded in agreement.

"Fifteen miles," the pilot called.

"Notify the group," Marden snapped.

No radio messages; everything was electronically coded. The formation powered ahead. In each chopper another panel glowed in amber and the number fifteen appeared to signify distance remaining to the target, as well as groundspeed and time to target.

"Ten miles," sang out Marden's copilot. "No change in the pattern."

"Five miles."

The number five appeared in all the helicopters. That was the signal for everyone to lock and load, cock all weapons, arm all firing systems.

"Four miles."

Everyone looked forward from the cockpits. Marden felt a sudden unease. Whatever was going on down there, he knew a native system had flashed the word that all hell and fury was coming down through the darkened, clouded skies.

Fuck radio silence. Marden squeezed his transmit button. "Five, six, seven, move ahead, full release for static charge. All other birds, lift to eight hundred minimum, *now.* Stargazer, you read?"

Doug Stavers nodded to himself. Rebecca Weinstein watched him with alert, intense hawk eyes as he spoke. "Stargazer here. Go, Hammer."

"I got a funny feeling. You copy five, six and seven for static spray? Over."

"Three miles."

All the choppers save the three assigned to static charge release had zoomed to eight hundred feet. The other three Polotovs kept their original height above the ground, still whipping trees and foliage beneath them with sudden whirlwinds of passage.

"We're going to covered wagon," Marden radioed in the open to all his pilots. "The moment we get within one mile, slide into Indian formation around main target. Hold your altitude until you get the flash and the all-clear from the three cats down low. All copilots, get those goggles on and be prepared to take the controls."

"Two miles."

"On your toes, people, on your toes," Marden called.

A mile ahead of the main force, the three lead choppers slowed their headlong flight to fifty miles an hour. Beneath each Polotov in perfect line-abreast formation, spray booms released a heavy, cold flow of thickly ionized air and sodium-narkhov salts. A heavy ice fog descended in an enormous blanket over the low hill they had come to invest. It was almost time.

A bright orange color flashed ahead of the main force as they swung into a wide circling flight, like Indians on horseback surrounding a wagon train. Marden pressed his lips together. Too early for the fog to blow.

"You see what that was?" he pushed his pilot.

"Negative. That's fuel burning, but I—"

"Plowboy Three to Hammer. Heads up, heads up. I don't know how they got the word, but the people downstairs have fired hundreds, maybe thousands, of long spears. Catapults. Big stuff, high speed. We're like a pincushion. Plowboy One took a bunch in the cockpit and they went straight in." The bright orange flash mushroomed slowly to a savage glare as the Polotov's munitions let go.

Stavers turned to Weinstein. "They were expecting us."

"Not us," she said soberly. "Anyone. They've been expecting this for a long time."

He thought of a thousand long spears and lances hurled by catapult into the night sky. Weapons of ten thousand years ago snaring a multimillion-dollar, super-advanced, electronically-guided, jet-powered killing machine from the air and killing everyone aboard.

"Stargazer to Hammer. Don't wait. Light up *now.*"

Marden didn't bother to answer. "Plowboy, if you copy that last telegram, hit it."

"Choose your partner, it's dance time," a voice sang back.

A single long line of white light sped downward from a Polotov invisible to the eye. At the head of the light was a wire-guided electromag discharger. The wire laid down across the full length of the hill. The fog, hugging the ground, was unstable.

A blanket of viscous fog three-quarters of a mile long and a half-mile wide, *exploded.*

It was a very efficient explosion, hugging the ground, settled into every hut, every depression in the ground, within every bush and tree, in every ditch, *everywhere.* All the night world vanished before the spattering, coruscating, repeated flashes of explosions. In every chopper the copilots, having donned their night glasses to prevent temporary blindness, took over the controls and flew by instrument panels illuminated brightly for the moment. Ten seconds later the pilots' night vision returned. They didn't need it.

A great oval patch of earth more than two square miles in area burned fiercely. Everything above ground burned. Where the fog had settled into any crevices, the fires burned. Concussion had killed every living creature.

"Hit it!" Marden shouted.

The choppers went down hard and fast, bristling firepower ready. Two landed on the fire periphery. The flames would die out quickly and the men, running in heavy asbestos-lined combat boots and fire-retardent fatigues, ran onto the burning ground, weapons at the ready.

The other choppers hovered, rocking from side to side, instruments and eyeballs searching for moving forms. "Plowboy Six, far left side. Three openings in the hill. Holy shit, they're coming out like ants. Hundreds of them. *And they ain't throwing spears.*"

No one needed further orders. Two helicopters slid sideways, began rippling fire. Each salvo sent out a hundred concussion and shrapnel rockets into the cave openings from which natives rushed by the hundreds. No one needed to be told their automatic weapons could rip into the Polotovs, kill pilots, bring down the deadly but vulnerable machines. So the key to all this was immediate, overwhelming slaughter.

The rockets ripped through native ranks. Chunks of bodies and constant bursts of exploding blood and body fluids filled the air. Still more natives rushed from the hill.

"They must have fifty openings," Stavers snarled, verbalizing his thoughts rather than talking to Weinstein.

Marden's voice came into each Polotov. "Watch your eyes! I want blinders out immediately! As soon as they light off, work 'em with the Vulcans!"

Shattering light split the sky, blinding white, intense, eye-stabbing, vision-killing. More than a thousand armed natives reeled about, stunned, blinded, in pain, momentarily helpless.

"*Cut 'em down!*" Marden roared.

Each Polotov cut loose with the Vulcans, modern descendants of the Magic Dragons that had sown such terrible firefight death in Vietnam. More than twenty-seven heavy cannon with a firing rate of seven thousand rounds per minute ripped into the moving figures on the ground. Fury and hell erupted from the devastating impact.

"That got most of them!" Marden shouted. "Okay, Six, Nine and Eleven, stay upstairs and keep circling. Everybody else, get down there and take them direct. Use those knives! Roll heads, you bastards!"

The choppers swooped, mushroomed on heavy air currents, settled fast and hard. Marden's killer teams raced away, machine guns and flame-throwers at the ready. No more than a hundred natives remained alive, burned, broken, wounded hideously.

The raiders cut them to pieces with pointblank fire. Within three minutes the only movement was the slashing attack of the raiders, machetes rising and falling, chopping into necks and heads, making wet sloppy killing sounds, a ghastly singsong of horror.

Stavers hit the ground, ran to the side of the helicopter, Weinstein right behind and to his side. Six picked men fanned out behind and alongside them for cover. Their orders were simple. Stay with Stavers and Weinstein. Cover them. No distractions. Stay out of the other fight.

Stavers turned to Weinstein. "Okay, girl, it's your show. You know where to go. *Move!*"

They ran quickly, crouching, dodging twisted bodies and pulverized chunks of flesh, slipping on gore, wincing as their cover team rattled off quick bursts at anything that couldn't be recognized and so much as twitched. Over the sound of *blatting* helicopter blades and shrieking jet engines, strangely loud, came the macabre sound of steel slicing through necks, adding to the grisly pile of severed heads, confirming the newly formed adage that heads that roll around the ground without bodies don't talk. *Snick*, *slash*; strange sounds, and every now and then a clanging of metal as a downward slicing blade missed soft flesh and whacked into resisting bone.

"There! See that third entrance to the left?" Weinstein called. "That's the one we want!"

"You people get that?" Stavers shouted. A chorus of calls confirmed his team of six men had the word.

"Doug! Once we go in have a force cover that entrance while we're down below! I know these people," Weinstein sang out. "They'll try to trap us underneath and we've *got* to have the way clear to emerge. We—"

She staggered back as three arrows tore into—*against*—her body. Stavers whirled around as a spear crunched into his hip, hurling him off balance. *But no puncture wounds; the sharkskin suits were holding. They'd already saved their lives.* But where the hell had they come from? Stavers heard a man's scream drop to a bloody gurgle. Simms; one of his men, an arrow into his mouth and back through his throat and emerging from the back of his neck. Goddamn sharksuit didn't mean shit from that kind of hit. Another man took an arrow from a second fusilade, directly into his eye and he tumbled screaming to the ground. Stavers hurled himself sideways and fell atop Weinstein. "Stay down," he snapped. He thumbed his radio. "Cowboys, you got Stargazer in view?"

"Gotcha, Stargazer. Looks like you need some help."

"Hit those motherfuckers with everything we've got—"

"On the way," came the confirmation before he said another word. "Keep your heads and asses down, folks. Here comes Big Poppa."

Two Polotovs rushed up to them, swaying wildly as the pilots slammed on rotor brakes. Hovering, they launched a terrifying barrage of minirockets into the side of the hill. The rectangular entrance Weinstein had pointed out disappeared in blinding explosions.

That was only the beginning of two minutes of unprecedented fury. Salvos of Vulcan cannon stuttered in ear-hammering bursts; the hill itself was being shredded, being blown away from the shattering firepower.

"No movement, Stargazer. Looks clear," the helicopter leader called.

"Bullshit on that!" They couldn't miss Marden's roar on the radio frequency. "One of you choppers, get in tighter, and I want liquid flamethrower into all three openings! Now! Fire, you sons of bitches! *Fire!*"

Stavers and Weinstein and the four men still able to move and fight pressed themselves against and into the blood-soaked earth as a Polotov glided up and over them, and erupted as might a huge dragon of myth. A sheet of intense flame, no thicker than a firehose, sped ahead of the Polotov, and suddenly widened in all directions, becoming a barrel-thick lance of liquid fire ripping into the openings. The earth beneath them rumbled; the flames were racing far below ground, cooking alive—instantly—anything with life to it.

Stavers leaped to his feet, body-dragging Weinstein

to a standing position. "Skip!" he called, "Cover us! We're going in now!"

"The hell you are!" Marden shouted back. "Hold your position! I want a squad in there first. Team Charlie, get the hell in there ahead of Stargazer. Get down that opening on the left. No matter what moves, kill it!"

"Skip, goddamnit it, I said *we're* going in first!" Stavers yelled.

"Skip! We've got to go in first!" Weinstein shouted, desperation in her voice. "We must go in—"

"Fuck you, lady. Get off this frequency, goddamnit! Boss-man, you cool your jets. I run this show and *you* follow orders, got it!"

Stavers laughed aloud. Marden was absolutely right; that's how they'd stayed alive through all their battles and wars. "Got it. Make it fast, man. We're on a schedule down here."

"Yeah, I gotcha, Stargazer. I'll pass your complaint on to the chaplain. Charlie Team, where the hell are you?"

"Inside, Hammer. Charlie's inside and around a turn. You were right. At least fifty of them in here, and they had it all. Assault pieces, even bazookas. We got fifty pairs of fried frog's legs now. We're making chopped heads."

"What's ahead of you, Charlie?" Stavers broke into the frequency.

"Big door. Logs, crisscrossed, don't know how deep. Looks like a trap. We blow in the door, something comes busting out and chews us up. Give us a minute or two, Stargazer, and we'll tend to business."

"Go, baby," Stavers called back. He pushed Weinstein down to one knee. "Just cool it, babe," he said, turning back to look at the entrance they also needed to penetrate.

The ground shook wildly beneath them. Voices coughed on the radio frequency. "Charlie Team here. Just like we thought. Log barricade went down before a charge, and about a hundred long spears came flying out. But that looks like it. Just beyond there's some kind of a tunnel. We tossed a biodetector down. No sounds, no signs of life, no infrared signs coming back. My money is that it's empty."

"Go on in," Marden commanded.

"No!" Stavers roared. "Charlie Team, stay the hell out of that tunnel! *That's an order*! Hold your position, secure everything else around you. I'm coming in with the woman, and when we get there she and I are going through and you cover our backs. Hammer, you read that? Confirm it to the teams, goddamnit!"

No more than a moment's hesitation as Marden listened, weighed all the issues of the moment, and yielded to the urgency in Stavers' voice. "Hammer here. Go with what you just heard. Stargazer runs the show downstairs. Follow his orders. Everybody topside, you play the game with my rules."

Stavers and Weinstein dashed up and ran directly for the opening. Several men waved them on. They slipped, cursing, on the bloody froth mixing with mud and grass, and then they were at the entrance, digging in their heels as they descended along a steep slope, the powerful arms of fighting men extended to assist them. They went through the open area with broken spears and heaps of bodies and a jumble of severed heads piled in one area. A thick wall of double-hatched logs had been blown to charred splinters, and everything stank of burning wood and flesh and earth. A man directly ahead of them held a dazzling hand light; he turned it from their eyes and held it to the tunnel.

They stopped in the midst of the smashed logs, their feet slipping on smashed wood and blood.

It was different a few feet farther on.

The floor of the tunnel was gleaming metal, and then it curved from sight, beginning another descent.

Stavers moved forward slowly, taking the light from the man by his side. Another figure moved up and handed a light to Weinstein. Then, following orders, the fighting men withdrew to the opposite side of the opening they'd blasted.

Stavers moved cautiously, playing the light about him. Metal everywhere. A cold and impossible echoing of their footsteps, their voices gaining a ringing sound.

They moved through a long circle and stopped before a massive metal doorway. "It operates like a camera shutter," Rebecca Weinstein said. Stavers stared at her. *She knows all about this place. She knows how it works. What in the name of God—*

"How . . . how do we get through?" he asked in a hoarse whisper. He didn't dare ask aloud what lay beyond.

She smiled; joyous, radiant. "Slip off your jacket. Here, let me help. Now, the shirt. Remove the top half of the sharksuit."

Moments later he stood barechested except for the steelmesh strapping about his body.

She pointed to the steel casing about the diamond. "Open it, Doug."

He started to protest, to ask questions, to do *anything* save obeying her orders with such immediate precision. Something told him not to waste his time or his effort. She knew what was happening and he didn't. Yet caution moved him several feet from Weinstein as he opened the steel casing to reveal the great yellow diamond.

It blazed at him, flashing, sparkling, hurling out needles of light, turning everything about them an intense, marvelous yellow.

She smiled at him. "Don't you understand yet, Doug? *It's alive.*"

"Alive?" he echoed.

"Look at the door. *Think it open.* It won't work for anyone except you."

He blinkd. Stupidly he thought, "Open, Sesame!" It was an idiotic feeling.

He was wrong.

The door sections revolved and yawned wide.

He stared beyond, stunned and speechless.

Chapter 20

All the disbelief he had ever known in his life swarmed over Stavers, a swirling fog of living denial, of refusal to accept what lay before him. Shock—culture, personal, scientific, common sense, technological—struck him with physical force. He found himself sucking in air in great painful gulps; he couldn't recall the last time his heart had beat so pounding-hard within his chest.

He saw it all, and he believed it and he refused to believe it, all in the same cerebral gulp. It's too much of a jump for the man who hasn't encountered it before to bring together in a single glance thousands of years of the past into the present and a leap untold thousands of years into the future. His mind raced at full throttle, howling with furious mental speed, and then slammed on the brakes, squealing and refusing the adrenalin surging through his system like water through a fire hose.

It was huge. Wide and broad and high and deep, God knew only how deep, for what he saw was enormous, and it had the solidity and massiveness of a great battleship of thick armor and enormous sweep of steel and monster guns, and the battleship was a pitiful anachronism against what now invited him to come forward. Technology speared its visible reality at him. Science so overpowering it humbled him and made him feel as primitive as he really was before this incredible machine of somewhere-sometime. Seats, controls, strange metals and plastics and glass and materials he had never seen or dreamed about and couldn't even imagine played away before him, the splendor and shine dimmed by time and the dust of the ages. He stared at the great ports and the huge sheets of transparent material, and he knew that men, men and women, perhaps human, perhaps not, but bipedal, like himself, had looked through those ports and sheets and gazed upon stars and galaxies and nebulae, at moons and planets and comets and stars birthing and others dying.

And this was only the flight deck.

This was that tiny portion of machine that housed the flight crew, like the small space allotted the two men high up forward in the nose of a 747, and behind them stretched an enormous machine with nearly six hundred people, riding the high top of a world's air ocean.

He reminded himself again that *this is only the flight deck, and it is gorgeous and magnificent and wonderful . . .*

He failed to handle it all, to accept the devastating mental punch that staggered him so. It was too much, and yet a part of his mind told him that was nonsense, that he knew that *somewhere* the enormous vessels of science in a far future ghosted a thousand times faster than the speed of light through unimaginable fields and plains of the cosmos, where passing stars flickered weak and yellow or bright and ice-blue as they swept by. He knew this could happen, that it likely had happened, somewhere, *but this was here and now, not somewhere without focus.*

He drew on memory to bridge the gap, to steady his reeling mind. Pictures flashed through his memory, snatches and moments from paintings and photographs and films. He saw the huge vessels from *Alien* and *Aliens*, the utterly incredible spaceliners of *Close Encounters of the Third Kind*, and there was *2001* and *2010*, and *Black Hole*, and as much as they helped they were still flat and distant and distressingly two-dimensional. But there were the other ships, the *real* ships. He forced himself to think of Vostok and Mercury and Gemini and Voskhod and Soyuz and Apollo and Skylab and Salyut and Mir and the Shuttles, and pictures from the robots flashed in his mind to show him the reality of the sands of Mars and the thickly invested savage heat and ocean-like atmosphere of Venus, the scarred hell of lifeless Mercury and the turbulent magnificence of Jupiter, and its rings, and the huge sweep splendor of Saturnian rings and dozens and dozens of moons, the thickened atmosphere of Uranus and the deep blue gaseous ocean of Neptune; he thought of Io smashing fire into vacuum and fractured worlds and frozen worlds and ice volcanoes, and it helped. It carried him, just barely, over the edge.

Doug Stavers had always been exceptionally self-disciplined and at this moment he called into play every ounce of mental strength he could muster. His brain felt like a thousand clattering and whirling dishes settling down, dissipating the discordant outcry, settling his brittled vision, easing his mind and lending linear substance to his thoughts.

He turned to Doctor Rebecca Weinstein. Her face remained calm but with a deep, even a mighty assurance that *she was at home here*. That stopped his first planned words before they could be formed by his tongue and lips. *This woman is at home here. Until this instant she's been the stranger, in a world not so strange but utterly primitive and alien.* Her calm was fresh cold water rushing over an alien bridge and it diminished the heat of his furious astonishment.

It all begins to fit. Damn, she was right! I would never have believed. I could never have absorbed it all. A single glance here is more than all the conversation ever spoken. This is the true reality; not verbalized description. And this is the same woman I was so prepared to k—to end her life so many times. Of course she dodged and twisted and led me down one primrose path after another! She had to!

He mustered all his self-control to this instant. *Stop gawking. Quit the ohs and ahs and the awed bullshit. This is as much a test as anything else. Make the jump, Stavers. Make it or you'll be tossed aside like useless garbage. So start with something closer to home than this stellar battlewagon.*

The diamond . . .

He reached down and held the flashing yellow diamond—or whatever it was—so he could look into its incredible icy fire. *It's like looking into my own mind. I don't understand—*

"You said this . . . diamond . . . is alive," he forced out, turning to Weinstein.

"It is. It is an *arbatik*. It is *not* a diamond. That is strictly coincidental. Nature produces diamonds under awesome pressure. So was the *arbatik* formed, but by man." She smiled. "*Man* will do. The term is quite acceptable."

His head began again to swim and he snatched at the brass ring of stiffening resolve within himself.

"*Arbatik*," he echoed.

"It's the best I can do in translation to English," she offered. "Think of it as an energy focus. The universe is a violent maelstrom of energy, Doug. Forces that could vaporize this entire planet in an instant are quite commonplace, but they destroy only when interference is created. Those forces aren't intelligent, but they are all about us. Like radio waves," she suggested. "We didn't *invent* radio waves. No one ever did that. We learned how to harness the waves, tune in to them, match their vibration. Think of microwave parabolic transmitters, a million of them, a billion, a trillion of these transmitters out in space, all attuned to the frequency of the *arbatik*, pouring their energy into, and being received by, what you call the diamond. That's a very crude description but it'll have to do for now. The real key is not receiving the energy, but releasing it specifically and deliberately and under control."

He held the flashing miracle in his hand. "But how did this thing work with, I mean, how did *I* link up with it?"

"You'll hate me for this," she said, unsmiling and her eyes penetrating into his mind, "but it was not an accident or a series of incidents. As much as it was possible to do so, it was *directed*."

That he refused. "Bullshit," he answered immediately, and a sense of himself emerged with his retort.

"I needed you," she said. "It's that simple. You see,

the energy system—the *arbatik*—doesn't run machinery. It doesn't propel anything or operate anything. It is not simple or even pressured carbon. It's composed of an incredibly complex genetic code, a DNA control a thousand years into your future. Which, and I do not intend to be superior in tone or words, is still archaic to my science. When the main *arbatiks* are—were—created, they were fashioned after a genetic code. A mind that must be, well, call it human. Yours; mine. The trillions of neuronic subsystems that constitute your mind are matched by what you now hold in your hand."

"How could it be *my* mind?" he shouted. "This is thousands of years old!"

"You, Douglas Stavers, are of a very specific type of mindset. Brilliant, headstrong, domineering, totally beyond ego where ego is replaced with absolute conviction; it's rather a long list. You fit them all." She sighed. "Look, our people have been into the use of what you'd call superadvanced science for a longer time than you can imagine. Yet, if we were able to do so, we could have brought Albert Einstein into one of our, what you would call think tanks, and he would be just as much at home with our science and mathematics as any of our own scientists. Oh, certainly, there'd be catchup, but that would be simple to someone like Albert. His mind was quite capable of super quantum leaps of this sort."

He waved a hand in protest. "You told me your family, you, your father, were related to Einstein. That can't be true, can it?"

She smiled and shook her head. "No, it's not. But the official records of birth, marriages, communities, licenses, that sort of thing, were all created so that to anyone investigating the matter, it *would* be true. I knew Albert quite well. Not my father." She hesitated and a frown moved quickly across her face. "He's not here."

He let that remark pass. "You mean that my mind—you said *mindset*," and he watched her nod, "is linked to this . . . this super engine? I wish I knew what the hell to call it besides your cosmic Hungarian, because that's what it sounds like."

She laughed. "God, you're incredible. You've made the jump so quickly! That's marvelous. Your own form of quantum leap into another reality that not too long ago was impossible to you, and already you're arguing with me!"

"How does this doodad work? I mean, what happens? From what you've been saying, my mind operates on, let's say, a wavelength, right?"

"Broadband rather than tight; yes," she confirmed.

"And it matches a *neuronic* pattern in this thing?"

"Yes."

"*This* is a mind? A brain?"

"No; *no*. It's a link between your mind and a power control. Think of yourself in the cockpit of your plane. You grasp the throttles and you move them forward. What happens? You suddenly create more than a hundred thousand pounds thrust behind you, and your machine comes alive with all that wonderful power and it leaps forward and does all the things super airplanes are supposed to do. But your hand didn't move until your mind bade that move. Understand? It's a physiological-mechanical link. Very crude, but very effective."

"You mean, if the airplane system was set up to use this doodad—"

"*Arbatik*," she said firmly.

"This camel whip," he went on, deliberately irreverent because he needed to be to keep that grip on himself. "If the airplane system was set up with this thing, then all I need to do is sit back with my hands in my lap and *think* those throttles going forward?"

"A clumsy analogy, but it will do."

"I don't understand something. As powerful as this thing is supposed to be, and it *does* work, it's still low-key, lady. I mean, it will get someone to shove a thirty-eight muzzle in his ear and squeeze off a round to bye-bye land, but a shot of LSD or etorphin will do the same. This thing is more efficient, that's all."

"This thing, as you call it, functions at about a billionth of its normal cruising level of energy."

He stared at her. "What?"

"To function properly it must be *within* your body."

"Oh, for Christ's sake, Rebecca, *it was* inside my body!"

"Let me use the airplane analogy again," she said patiently. "Your jet runs on fuel. If you poured that fuel into the cabin, on the seats and along the floor, could it enable your machine to fly?"

"Of course not," he said with annoyance. "You know that. The fuel's got to be in the tanks, with the right pumps and pressure—"

"And with controls for proper and varying flow, through heating systems, into spray systems and burn chambers and igniters and the rest of that sort of thing, *and* it needs power to function, and it's got to accommodate inverted or weightless flight, and—"

"I get your point," he said, chagrined.

"The analogy applies to the *arbatik*. It must be within your body but it must also be close to your heart, behind the heart, in fact, with neuronic connections to the heart and the spine and the brainstem. The surgery for this is intricate, dangerous, and also quite necessary."

He studied her carefully. "I get the idea I'm being led down a primrose path to a surgical ward."

She didn't answer immediately. "Under those conditions, with proper implantation and connection, you could think about this vessel and it would lift from this planet, quite silently, slowly, under absolute control and when you were above atmosphere, you could accelerate to . . ." she smiled again, "to unimaginable speeds."

"Just by thinking about it," he echoed.

"Please eliminate the word 'just' from your description."

"This neuronic surgery; you said it was intricate—"

"Dangerous," she finished. "But well worth it."

"Damn few things are worth it if you're dead," he said sourly. "Or alive and a cabbage for a brain. Or alive and paralyzed because someone screwed around with the spinal nerve system."

"True. But there's more."

"I'm already way over my head, Rebecca, so don't quit now."

"When two or more people have *arbitak* implantation they gain a form of telepathic communication. I do *not* mean you hold conversation telepathically. But the impressions, ideas, visualizations, that sort of thing, are strikingly sharp and understandable. You had that basic ability before what you call The Messiah Stone ever came into your possession. The *arbatik* enhanced it."

"Wait a moment," he said slowly. "You; a doctor. *A surgeon.* Have you performed this sort of operation?"

"Yes."

"What's your success ratio?"

"Perfect."

"You said that when two people have this thing they can communicate without verbalizing?"

"Yes. And you have an overwhelming effect upon ordinary minds. *Normal* minds. You've mentioned etorphin. Ten thousand times more powerful than morphine, you said. *Arbatik* control is far greater than that because you can use it and release it or, to use what you're thinking of right now, you can tweak the power output and performance like a vernier control."

"You just read my mind?"

"*No,*" she said immediately. "*You cannot read minds.* But when you ran a review in your mind about power systems I received a strong visual impression of the equipment about which you thought. That's how I knew what you were thinking. You see, you were also broadcasting in the blind, so to speak. In other words, you weren't trying to hide or disguise or protect your thoughts."

"Let me go back to the *arbatiks.*" He used her crazy language phrasing because it was easier to communicate that way. She smiled at him; so she'd picked up on that, too! He pushed aside the thoughts to concentrate on what he needed to know. "Your reference seems to indicate that your crew, or the people aboard this ship, or all your people who go cruising around the galaxy, whatever, I mean, that a whole bunch of your people have these things inside them?"

"Yes. But I must repeat that those with the genetic code to generate high levels of power, either to operate the systems for these craft, or to affect other and many minds at great distances, are extremely rare. Again, and forgive the repetition, the throw of the cosmic dice, Doug, picked you."

He rubbed his chin. "Jumping way ahead of what you're saying, I get the idea that if I wanted to rule the world, then having the *arbatik* properly—surgically—implanted, would give me that power."

"It would. But you won't."

"Won't what?"

"Want to rule the world."

"Why the hell not?"

"It's a boring thing to do," she said easily.

"A hell of a lot of people don't think so," he retorted.

"A hell of a lot of people believe the way to nirvana," she snapped back, using his own syntax, "is to inject poisonous substances by needle into their bodies."

"Checkmate," he grinned.

"It takes *time* to learn such things," she added.

"It's *really* that boring?"

"God, yes." She laughed. "Just imagine the paperwork."

"I've got a million questions, Rebecca."

"Start with one at a time."

"Too late for that," he admitted. He looked about him. "This is the flight deck."

"You said that as a statement and not a question and you're right."

"How big is this monster?"

"It's not a monster and it's not that big. Um, think of a 747 expanding in size to about five times its width, length and height."

"Goddamned big bird."

"That, then, is this ship," she explained. "Only this was a scout."

"A *scout?*" He shook his head. "Goddamnit, forgive me, Rebecca. I must sound like a parrot repeating everything it hears."

"It's a scout," she repeated. She looked about her, a haze of sadness seeming to appear about her. "One of sixteen the main ship held."

"How bloody big is the *main* ship?"

"Think of a small city. That's how big."

"Damn . . . can we see the rest of this ship?"

Sadness increased; she shook her head slowly. "No, we can't. It was destroyed. An impossible, one-in-a-trillion sort of accident."

"An accident destroyed this ship?"

"This flight deck is all that remains. Oh, the rest of the ship is here. Mangled, crushed, mostly melted." She drifted back in time. "It was our first landing here. In the scout. We drifted low across the countryside. Gods to the natives; obviously. We drifted across some low hills. We didn't know one of them was a volcano. It exploded directly beneath us. Our pilot, he . . . he was killed instantly. I suppose it was molten magma, but it came upward at some insane speed and it speared into the ship. Our ventilators were open. We'd tested the air and it was acceptable. We'd bring in local air, move it through the purifiers, and then let it into the ship. But the ventilators were open and that left us exposed. Normally, when the ship is sealed, even an atomic bomb can't hurt us. Force fields; that sort of thing."

"Uh huh," he said.

"The flight deck took a direct hit. I was just aft of the deck. Wearing an armored pressure suit—full environmental control screens—preparing to lower to the surface. When the volcano ripped into us, it sent the magma—burning lava—*into* the ship. Everyone in the flight deck died. The ship went out of control just as I left beneath and to the right. The ship went down, very hard, and everything aft of the flight deck exploded or was crushed and melted. Really, all of that sort of thing happened."

He held his silence for a while. He heard dim sounds of machinery above them. He'd forgotten completely about the battle. It didn't matter. The Manturu were dead. The choppers would be in the air hunting down any survivors. How insane; he walked through the flight deck of a master scientific race and right over their heads his men were decapitating the locals. *Terrific.*

"What about the natives?"

"The Manturu were the lead group. The ship exploded in their midst. A great many of them died. But it was obvious this was a great sailing vessel of the gods and they considered their casualties a guarantee of their ticket to heaven."

I bet they don't think that way anymore, he thought of the grisly events above them.

"They made the crash *the* religious event of their history," she went on.

"What happened to you?"

"I was in shock. Everyone aboard this vessel was closer than family or lovers to me. We all had that kind of empathy. The loss was devastating."

"How old are you, Rebecca?"

"In your years, Doug?"

"They're the only years I have, lover."

"I hate to say this . . ."

"I'm a big boy now, lady."

"I was a thousand of your years old when we reached this planet," she said, barely audible.

His head reeled. "But . . . but that was two thousand years ago!"

"Doug, the longevity of the human race not so long ago was perhaps thirty years. Neanderthal era, before and just after. It's three times that now. Ninety years. Your next real jump will be like so many others. Your medical science will learn the body's *controls* for aging. You'll triple lifespans again. I don't know why but that's how it happens. It triples. You've already gone from thirty to ninety. The next jump will keep people alive from two hundred to three hundred years. And the jump after that will bring them close to a thousand."

"The planet will tip over, for Christ's sake," he told her.

"Nature abhors more than a vacuum," she answered. "It also abhors and eliminates a glut."

"Okay, okay. Let me get back to you. What happened?"

"The suit . . . I stayed in the suit. I was fully protected. I had regenerative systems, full sanitary facilities, temperature control, unlimited power, food and drink. I could live in that suit for more than a year. I couldn't leave. Imagine, Doug, *try* to imagine, all those people aboard this ship who expected a normal life span of—never mind; it was much longer than mine—and in an instant they died horribly. *All that life*, snuffed out."

"There's a whole bunch of life just got snuffed upstairs," he reminded her.

"Do you mourn the butterfly that has a lifespan of one day?" she asked, a chill in her words.

"No."

"Then don't concern yourself with butterflies that don't have wings," she told him, dismissing the carnage as incidental.

"You stayed. Would you tell me," he asked gently, "what happened then?"

"By the time I regained my senses—I suppose I was in very deep shock for a long time—the Manturu had already begun their new religion. To me it was ghastly, disgusting beyond belief."

"I don't understand—"

"Our pilot was dead. But he was a god to these people. They dissected him, very carefully and with veneration. They *ate* him to gain his godly strength." She swallowed. "They feasted on him piece by piece. Heart, eyeballs, ears, nose, all his organs, every last bit and substance, and then they melted down his bones in some incredible, choking porridge, and they ate *that*. They believe what they did was right. When they finished, only the *arbatik* remained."

"Wait; wait a moment," he broke in, as the ancient drama began to reveal itself from ordinary, expectable extrapolation. And he didn't know how much he was receiving from this woman himself.

"The Messiah Stone . . . it *was* their Godstone. It was real to them! It became their god!"

"It glowed. It shouldn't have glowed, but it did. And it gave them strange powers. Natives who came to learn what had happened came within reach of the *arbatik* and fell under their power. The legend," she added slowly, "had begun and it was real."

"But . . . but it glowed, you said. And you two were the only . . . I mean, *you* were the only survivor. How could it glow? What gave it its life? It needed a neuronic system with a living form, with intelligence, to . . . oh, holy Jesus . . ."

She had slipped off her combat tunic, her sharksuit and the clothing beneath. Her bra came away next, her full breasts heaving free. "Turn out your light, Doug," she said softly. "Close your eyes for a few moments so you can acclimate better to the dark."

He did as she asked. "All right, Doug."

He opened his eyes. *The room wasn't dark.*

Almost, but not quite. He stared at a soft orange glow, reflecting on globular shapes to each side of the glow, and a dim reflected light above and then he realized he looked at her breasts, and her face bathed in the soft glow *that came from within her chest.*

"You . . . you have one . . . of these . . ." he stammered.

"Think hard at me, Doug. Think *very* hard."

He squeezed shut mental eyes and tried to transmit, although he hadn't even the remotest idea of *how* to transmit, to send out his feelings on this kind of basis, and then, suddenly, he relaxed, and he felt as one with the great "diamond" in his hand, and light flickered, then brightened and grew steady, and the *arbatik* glowed a magnificent yellow.

"You had questions," she said.

"A thousand. A million," he responded.

"But you had a specific question."

"Yes. For this moment."

"The answer is also yes. I'll do the surgical implantation."

He thought long and heavy on that one. No matter how good she was, no matter how incredible all that was happening, surgery would necessarily be performed with instruments that to her science would be as crude and clumsy as a stone axe. And the idea of leaving himself helpless on *any* table, surgical or otherwise, cut deeply and wrongly to the bone. Instinctively he thought of his time-honored protection: *I die and you die, very slowly and very painfully.* A fat lot of good that would do against *this* woman who had managed to survive here for more than two thousand years!

Again the enormity of his own thoughts streaked in with skull-smashing impact. The realization of what had just run through his mind was so staggering he'd failed to grasp its true worth.

More than two thousand years old! Impossible, incredible, crazy, impossible . . . yet absolutely plausible, and the flight deck of this ship, well, it blew away any defenses he had that it *wasn't* not only possible, but real, actual, literal. A burst of sardonic laughter whipped through his mind, mocking him; he recognized himself ridiculing himself.

You're so fucking smart! So know-it-all! You kill with ease, you rule the minds and bodies of men and women, you're a splendid savage with your weapons, a king of technocracy and suddenly you find yourself a poor, simple babe!

That wasn't *all* true, and his own psyche had gone overboard in its sharp-bladed self-immolation. Put the average man in today's world naked, in a jungle or a desert, and you had lunch for insects and animals just waiting to be served up. Put a skilled survivalist in the same situation and you had a survivor. All men for all things in all places and at all times; was that it? No. *Adaptation*, swift and certain, was the key.

And it's the smart man who knows when it's time to run away so you can fight another day. What was that line for all fighter pilots? *And I'm a goddamned great fighter pilot* . . . You *never* fight the other man's fight or you get your ass waxed.

"Do we need to stay here any longer?" he asked her suddenly, caught by surprise that she had dressed and stood by him fully clothed.

"No. Not really," she said with that sweet sadness of hers. "This ship is a buried monument. I told you I couldn't explain it before in words. You had to be *here* to see, feel, touch, drink it in."

"Okay," he said, forcing strength back into his mind. "I've seen, felt, touched and drank it in and my head's spinning. Besides, we've got the reality of right now still going on above us. We set off enough explosives to carry sound for fifty miles. These fires have been seen for a hundred or more. Right now this place is the center of attention for enough people so that a small army is on its way here, and that means we've got to clear out *now.* I've got a million questions for you, Rebecca, but we're in the wrong place at the wrong time."

"Agreed."

He looked about him. "I don't want this found like this. Let this cat out of the bag, lady, and every top government and military power in the world will be after us day and night." He thought furiously. "We could use one of those small nukes—"

"A hundred kilotons? That's crazy," she rebuked him. "With radioactivity drifting downwind and—never mind, Doug. That's out."

He grabbed his radio. "Hammer, this is Stargazer."

"Where the hell you been, you crazy son of a bitch?" Marden's voice burst through the speaker. "What's going on down there? That woman with you? What—"

"Shut up, Skip, and listen. Get every magnesium and thermite flare from every chopper through that entrance we used to come down here. I want them brought to where my cover team is waiting. They are *not* to come any farther than that, got it? Anything that will burn on that scale I want. I want it *now.* Don't question me. Just do it."

"Okay. We've still got three tanks of that electric gas. You want that?"

"Yes. Immediately. Move it, babe."

"It's on its way."

Twenty minutes later the combat teams were in the helicopters, the wounded were aboard and the dead were stacked neatly with the living. Stavers and Weinstein looked behind them, through the splintered log entrance, to the splendorous flight deck of an entombed, shattered starship. Spread across the deck and against the bulkheads were ninety-two violently-explosive incendiary flares. Three tanks spilled cold gas through the deck and began to reach upwards. Doug Stavers knelt down and set a timer. He looked up at Weinstein.

"Fifteen minutes."

Her face was unreadable. "Set it and let us go," she said.

He set the timer and activated the system. Digital numbers began to flash. They turned and ran along the tunnel, upward to the entrance. They ran to the helicopter with its door open waiting for them. Marden's hand reached out and he swept Weinstein into the Polotov, Stavers right behind her. Stavers motioned to Marden.

"Move out," Marden called, and the message went to all the choppers. They rose like giant locusts in the light of early dawn and raced away at top speed.

Stravers and Weinstein looked back, waiting, silent.

Along the horizon a yellow-orange glow appeared, an inverted bowl of light, silently growing and then fading.

Rebecca sat in a corner of the helicopter cabin, knees drawn together, arms crisscrossed on her knees, her face buried in her arms.

Doug Stavers didn't need to look at her to know she wept.

He felt her tears in his mind.

It was like hearing angels crying.

Chapter 21

Stavers looked out across the peaks and valleys of the mountains that formed the spinal backbone of Colorado. He leaned back in an easy chair, his favorite cigar in one hand and a snifter of brandy in the other. His room lay within granite walls. Behind the balconies and viewing windows of the "Colorado ski resort" spread the most modern and best-equipped surgical center in the world. Most of its equipment bore familiarity to surgeons. Not all; some had been modified to the orders of Rebecca Weinstein. *Or whatever the hell her name is.*

He turned at the sound of a door opening and closing. Before he turned he knew it was Rebecca. She took the seat by his side, sharing the view with him. "It's lovely," she said finally. "Lovely and native and quite rare. This planet is remarkable *and* also quite rare."

"Sure," he agreed without much caring to share her tourist's view of the world. "But right now it's going bananas. I had no idea this church gimmick would take off like it has." He shifted in his seat to turn more directly to her. "The Vatican's declared a great moral crisis, the baptists are screaming about demons, the Jews—"

"That's the negative side," she broke in. "The positive side of all this is that the Church of the Ascension now has more than a billion members. They support Ascension heart and soul. Much more to the point," she smiled, "your people are *very* effective. Many of the church members are rocket scientists and engineers, politicians in the right places. To say nothing of statesmen and generals. It has been an extraordinarily effective campaign. A religion with its heavenly lights visible to us in the night sky. Pale moon and orange Mars. I haven't seen anything like it since the message of Christ spread like wildfire. Of course," she added with a hint of amusement, "it took him a great deal longer than your campaign to reach so many people."

"There weren't a billion people alive on the whole planet when he was around," Stavers offered a criticism.

"He preached love. Douglas Stavers preaches the same message but with different words. Love for the planet. Love for all mankind. Love for the future. Hope and longevity for the race. It's what your advertising people would call the best of the soft and the hard sell."

"You amaze me. You come down out of the stars and you've got your finger on the public." He snorted. "In thirty languages, to boot."

"What matters is that it's working," she stressed. "They're building the great boosters. They're already in the new orbiting stations. It was really quite helpful, almost amusing," she offered the afterthought, "that the United States had always secretly planned on a manned station at fourteen hundred miles. The Russians saved time by bringing together six of their Mir stations, but those are clumsy and they're only three hundred miles up. Nevertheless, despite variations, *it's working*. Ships for the moon, ships for Mars."

"Yeah," he grunted.

"Why so mournful, Doug?"

"I'm always this way when the woman I've bedded down is going to slice open my chest and separate spinal nerves like strands of spaghetti. That sort of thing."

She leveled her gaze at him. "Why did you say that?" Her voice was feathery soft.

"Say what?"

"Ah, so quickly forgotten," she said, rolling her eyes in mock despair. "Bedding me down. Why the sudden emphasis on *that* when we're involved with ships for

Mars? Why is the single most common mutual act of mankind, outside of eating, perhaps, of such importance you needed to intrude it right now?"

"What the hell are you doing? Spoiling for a fight?" he demanded.

"I'm better than that and you know it. If I wanted a fight we'd have been tearing at each other's throats long before now," she retorted.

He shifted his position, mildly uncomfortable. "I don't know *why* I said it," he said abruptly.

"You're certain of that?"

"I'm *not* sure," he answered. His eyes narrowed. "But I am damned sure I'm keeping a tight lid on my words right now."

"God, you never fail to amaze me. Here is the adult male, the macho stud, the powerhouse, still wrestling with sophomoric sex zits. Psychological, of course." She paused only a moment. "Are you asking me to apologize for what happened back in that room with our zonked out human mattress beneath us? Does my being specific cause you any pain? *Do you need to be reassured?*"

"You *are* pushing," he snapped.

"Of course I am! I want this nonsense out of the way once and for all! You lost a hard on; big damned deal. We've made love ever since then, *but you weren't attacking me.* You weren't quite sharing, I'll admit—"

"Then what the hell was I?" he shouted.

"Making certain you were on neutral ground," she said sweetly.

"Neutral ground?" he echoed.

"Of course. What else? It wasn't worth assaulting me because inside me I simply turned you off. You weren't a lover, or a rapist or a human. An alley cat, perhaps, but that's all. Do you think your forcibly ramming sperm into me was going to *impress* me? You don't need to answer that because we both know you don't believe that. So you quit the caveman routine, but you couldn't yield yourself completely, because you were still smarting about not performing. And, so again, you chose neutral ground. That's been us. Great sex, because you are good, and you're big, and I enjoy that, but the bottom line is that what we have between us is really platonic fucking."

She laughed at his expression. "You're staring at me, Doug."

"I can understand *why*. You're really spoiling for a confrontation between us."

"No, *I'm not*. You brought it up. Subconsciously, perhaps, but it's always gnawed at you inside. *Get rid of it, Doug*. It's like a cancer. It'll grow and eat you alive." She went on quickly. "Do you think I *always* orgasm with you?"

"Yes, I think you *always* come with me."

"You're wrong."

"More of the needle?"

"No, *no*. So many things can interrupt— Look, just accept this, will you? Orgasm is *not* the ultimate result of lovemaking. It's the end of the trip but it's only the shortest part of the sexual journey." She sighed. "You'll have to fight this battle on your own turf inside your own head. We need to get on with more serious business. Can we leave your testicles and get to your brain, *please?*"

He couldn't believe all this. Once again she had seized on a few words of his and turned it into a screw she kept turning inside his head, and then, swiftly and expertly, she shifted to a different subject they both knew *was* much more important in its overall context and, as well was impelled by a time constraint.

"Doug, listen to me," she said, resting her hand on his arm. "If you're bedeviled with doubts or uncertainties or fears about this surgery, *you should be*. We're not just paring toenails."

"That's not it. When I commit I go all the way," he said, relieved deep within himself they were free of this miserable twittering about sex. "If I go under your knife it's without reservations, *and* I *am* going under your knife."

She smiled. "Your people *do* consider you fearless. I've always felt you were."

"There's fearless and there's dumbshit. For the first descriptive I stay in control of what I'm doing and whatever comes down. For the second descriptive I've got to put *all* my trust, to say nothing of my ass, in the hands of someone else. The kind of trust that will leave me totally helpless."

"Then *do it*," she said. "I've waited twenty *centuries* for this moment."

"Sure, sure. You ever hiccup when you're slicing and dicing?"

She laughed. "Not yet."

He didn't care for her hollow humor. He had too many questions left. "Let's take the time right now," he said slowly, "to fill in the blanks."

"Excellent," she said brightly. "The fewer questions you have the less resistance your mind and body will offer to the, ah, implant."

"Why'd you need *me* for this global religious caper? You have the *arbatik*. Why not handle it yourself?"

"Because I can't. My implant is of far lesser energy than what you will have. Remember; the man in whose body it lay was a pilot. What you would call a space jockey. He was also a master engineer; you're both of these. He also had tremendous organizational capabilities. So do you. Genetically you two could have been twins."

"You never use a name for him."

"You have no name that fits."

"Aim for the target, anyway. What comes the closest?"

"Wolfram."

"*That* fits."

"I'm glad to hear you say that. It brings you closer."

"What the hell does that mean? He was served up as the main course two thousand years ago, remember?"

"The *arbatik*. The resonance, or wavelength, or neuronic vibrations, whatever it really is, was a living part of Wolfram. So it will be for you."

"Wait a minute. You said this boyfriend of yours—"

"*Please*, Doug. That's a crude and weak reference to—"

"Skip it. You said Wolfram had the moxie for organization and so do I, right?" She nodded. "You're hardly a slouch in the department of running things, Rebecca."

"I couldn't touch his control and I can't come close to yours. This world, its people, will accept a woman as a leader only within specific guidelines."

"Don't believe it. We've had women running countries—"

"And within specified guidelines. The men never really relinquish final control." There was that touch of sadness again. "The male is necessary for what you're doing. And there's more to it than that. I've had to wait so terribly long because I had to let technology and engineering and science catch up to my needs. I couldn't build—or lead others to build—great rockets and control systems and spacecraft until the technological levels reached the point where they are now. Remember, Doug, the Romans were masterful engineers but they couldn't even build a radio, or a crude combustion engine, or—" She stopped in midsentence. "Doug, your people haven't even been flying for *a single century.*"

He nodded slowly, licked his thumb and held it upright before him. "You got me there. Score another point for the lady."

"Are you bitter about something, Doug?"

"You haven't said it but I know we're going to Mars together."

She clapped her hands with a burst of pleasure. "Wonderful!"

"But I'm goddamned if I know *why.*"

"I promised that you would. That you'd understand. That you'd want to more than anything else in the world."

"Promises, promises. You've got some strange schedules in that beautiful head of yours. The mystery woman herself. *Everything* has to be on this crazy guideline of yours."

"Not crazy. Have I failed you yet?"

"Not yet."

"You fear I will?"

"All things on God's good earth, like roses and scorpions, are possible."

He poured himself another brandy. "History lesson, if you please."

"As you say, shoot."

"We never got into this before," he said cautiously. "But everything I know about this . . . *arbatik*, is, well, contrary to just about everything I know about that thing as; shit, the Messiah Stone will do."

"No accident there, Doug."

"How do you mean that?"

"The story about the *arbatik* has always been the story about a great yellow diamond. I had to do that."

"*You* had to do that?"

"The truth could never have been told. It would never have been believed. That is just for, well, just for starters. And there had to be a cover story. The explosion that destroyed the scout ship and killed everyone save myself was easy enough to describe as a meteorite impact, or the crash of a comet. Communications were slow in those days. It took months for news to travel from one place to another. And by the time any news did move from one land to another, it was usually so twisted it hardly resembled the truth. So the story was safe. The diamond was either formed in the tremendous heat and compression of impact, or, as many chose to believe, it fell from heaven. It was really convenient this way."

"I suppose," he said slowly, "that having a messiah pop up in Bethlehem or Palestine—wherever—was pretty damned convenient, too. Did you also arrange *that?*"

Again that musical peal of laughter. "Of course not! But in those days, Doug, a new messiah *did*, as you put it, pop up. Every week. Messiahs and prophets were a dime a dozen in the so-called holy land. They were found on street corners hawking their heavenly wares, to be crass about it. Do keep in mind there were no Christians in the world then. No sons of Islam, either. There were the Jews, who were constantly slaughtered by ruling empires and wild tribes, and the non-Jews. And they were *all* panting for the messiah. So, as usually happens when supply and demand are in sharp focus, there is always a messiah available."

"How'd you pick Jesus?"

"*I* didn't pick Jesus! Of course, there *wasn't* any Jesus

then. You need to remember that to keep it all in perspective. Jews kept tearing their hair and muttering parables and claiming to be the only true sons of God. They were everywhere."

"But Jesus—"

"Jehoshua, if you please." She smiled. "It is really all so simple. The world loves and cherishes its myths and fables. That whom you call Jesus was in reality Jehoshua. When the Greeks compiled and wrote the gospels, oh, some eighty years after his supposed death on the cross—"

"Supposed?" he broke in.

"One thing at a time, please." He nodded and she went on. "When the gospels were written they were written *in Greek*. Later they were again translated. But Jehoshua the Anointed, which is what *this* prophet proclaimed himself to be, was translated and translated again, he became Jesus the Christ. *Christos*. It's a title. *The* Christ. Jehoshua becomes Jesus. The languages spoken then about the Sea of Galilee were Hebraic, the language of the wise men and elders of the Jewish communities; and, Arabic, of course. But the language of widest usage and choice, shared by all, was Aramaic. Let me get through this moment of history quickly. In none of these languages will you find such a name as Jesus, but you will find Joshua and Jehoshua, so there could never have been a Jesus during his lifetime."

Stavers stared at her. She laughed at his seeming discomfiture. "And his mother's name follows the same pattern. She was Miriam, who became Mary through the repeated translations."

"You knew him?" He was almost afraid to ask the question.

"I did. I traveled by sea from the coastline nearest the Manturu, northward to the holy land. As a woman I was always in peril. But I had the *arbatik*, which gave me not messianic powers—that would have been unthinkable for a woman in those days—but the powers of a priestess, one with great friends among the gods. In what was Egypt, I gained power swiftly. Power, money, and a devoted cult following. I made certain not to become so large in size that it would hinder my movement. I arrived in the holy land, oh, some fourteen years after our crash. Which, I must add, was an event simultaneous with the birth of that little Jewish boy."

"It's incredible to think you actually *knew* him."

"Why is it so incredible? You seem to have accepted most admirably the fact that years have nothing to do with aging, once you achieve meaningful genetic control."

"Not your age, Rebecca, but *who* he was."

"He was a self-proclaimed prophet, Doug!" she said with sudden impatience. "That was as common as an evangelist today preaching in some small town, or a wandering hellfire-and-brimstone minister selling religion on the hoof. Understand this; he was brilliant. He was gifted. He had psychokinetic powers that were very real. And as a teenager he was a nasty little fellow, using those same powers to hurt and even to kill."

"I don't think," Stavers said slowly, "I'd advertise that where the Catholic church could hear it."

"Bosh! They've always known it. They were no fools! Those who created the church and gathered its strength were great political leaders. Emotionalism fills a vacuum, but it runs out just as quickly. It takes political smarts to build a church *power*." She laughed. "You of all people, leader of the Church of the Ascension, should know *that!*"

Stavers hewed to his original thoughts. "You . . . did you ever speak with him?"

"Playing my role as an inferior member of the human species, the female, yes, I did. I spoke with him and with three of his five brothers, including Judas."

"What the hell are you trying to tell me?" Stavers demanded.

"Simple truth. Need I tell you about his three sisters as well?"

"Who the hell can believe you *now?*"

"Careful, my friend. You should be more diligent in reading the bibles of your own people. King James, Scofield Reference; many others. Right in those books you will find his true Aramaic name, *and* the names of his brothers. But you will find no reference, because these gospels were struck from the so-called good book, to his time as a youth. In *your* jargon, in the language of your lexicon, he was a nasty little shit. Then," she shrugged, "everyone lost touch with him for a while. When he reappeared, he had the burning eyes of a zealot. He radiated power, immense energy. The devotion people felt for him was real. As a young adult he was truly an amazing, incredible human being. But most of what you and everyone else knows of him is fiction. As usual," she sighed, "the unknown is greater than the popular fable."

He stared at her in silence. "Were you there when, I mean, when—"

"I never expected you to struggle through fables, Doug."

"You keep turning worlds upside down, woman."

"I'll make it easier for you. So much of it is myth! There was never a Barabbas. Nor a Barsabbas, as this mythical creature was known at that time. There was no choice by screaming Hebrews to release Barsabbas and crucify Jehoshua. That's nonsense. Jehoshua, or we'll use the name Jesus because it's obviously less confusing to you, broke Roman law. The Romans would *never* have listened to a howling mob. The Jews were rabble to them. You broke Roman law, they didn't haggle, they nailed hands and feet and ass to wooden stakes. The Appian Way was littered with the bones of crucified criminals. And *anybody* who broke Roman law was a criminal. Period," she concluded with emphasis.

"What about the miracles attributed to him?" Stavers asked, frowning, angry.

"He was a master magician, a brilliant politician, and a genius with semantics and psychology, as well as having a powerful psyche. So powerful he could get people to believe just about anything he wished them to believe. Mass hypnotism, induced hallucination; he was a master at it all. Look, Doug, just think of the expression, Jesus of Nazareth. *He* had nothing to do with that phrase, but it's bandied about within the church like soda pop at a teenage party. The *first* building went up in Nazareth maybe eighty or ninety years *after* his reputed death on the cross. *Damnit, Doug, I was there in Nazareth! I know.*"

She rose from her seat to pace the room. "Jesus planned just about everything he ever did. He was, as I said, a true master in that respect. He had a program. A plan. He was brilliant and tireless and dedicated and he could play a crowd like an orchestra leader creating music with his baton. *That's* what you've got to understand. And he had to do all this while weaving a precarious pathway through oppressive Roman law, which looked upon Jesus as just one more of thousands of Jews in rags and babbling nonsense."

She turned again, suddenly, as memory struck a chord. "Let me give you another example that cuts a straighter line than the crooked pathway of biblical, as you call it, bullshit. This business of the name of *Christ*, or, *Christos*. Did you ever study the history of the Jews? No? Well, few people have. But if you had, you would have learned that when David, as written in the Old Testament, was anointed—listen to the word, Doug; *anointed*—when he was anointed king, then David became known as the Christ, or, with equal usage, as the Messiah. The words were equal in value and import and were used quite interchangeably. And after David's reign, *every* Jew of his lineage who became king was also known, at that time, by his own people, as the Messiah, or as the Christ."

She laughed at his blank expression. "I will put the lid on this issue, friend Doug," she said with that awesome quiet confidence of someone who has lived through the issue instead of only hearing of it centuries later. "If you have the time, Doug, read the books that describe the Roman occupation of Judaea. Every high priest appointed by the Roman conquerers was known as the *Priest Christ*."

She let a long period of silence follow. It was a big swallow all at once. Not that Doug Stavers hewed to any discipline of Christianity but it was always something of a shock to learn that you had believed all your life the same nonsense heaped upon untold generations of wide-eyed followers of a religion that in reality was a magnificently crafted political force. The divinity of the term Messiah had no more substance than the glass slipper of Cinderella, and perhaps even less.

"Why," Stavers asked abruptly, "is all this so important? What do I have to do with Christ, or you, for that matter, or whatever is your reasoning for pushing this flight to Mars? What the hell are we going through all this for?"

Rebecca offered him that all-knowing smile again, but there came no tease or delay with her reaction.

"We're going to bring him back," she said quietly.

"We're going to do *what?*"

"Bring him back."

"Jesus Christ—"

"Is that an epithet or a question?"

"Both. It's a neat trick to resurrect old Adolf. I mean, we're working with cryonics and that sort of thing, but someone who was crucified nearly two thousand years ago? I don't believe you, Rebecca, and I don't believe you believe yourself."

"We're not going to resurrect Jesus." She shook her head, only a trace of the smile remaining. "This can get complicated but I can wrap it up neatly for you."

"By all means," he said acidly.

"It involves a series of events, a series of hard data, and correcting a few critical misconceptions."

"Don't lecture me, goddamnit. Just get to the point."

"All right. First, Christ never died on the cross. In fact, he wasn't crucified on the Appian Way. Nor was he hung on the cross as the Gospels describe what happened, at Golgotha. In their own translation, that would be what they called the site of the skull. The Gospels relate he was crucified on Golgotha, which was a hill northwest of Jerusalem. It's not true."

"But he *was* crucified?"

"Local parlor magic. Pretty common in those days, and as the decades and then the centuries went by, local trickery became legend and then became accepted as fact. You've got to find the lines hidden in the bulk of the text and you'll find the key in the Fourth Gospel. The exact quote is, 'Now in the place where he was crucified there was a garden; and in the garden a new sepulchre, wherein was never man yet laid.' That's in John 19:41. The crucjfixion was a very private ceremony, agreed to by Pilate for a very handsome sum of gold. You can find another key line in Matthew 27:60, where the reference is to the garden with the private tomb. And this was the personal property of Joseph of Arimathea, who was a powerful man in his time, very wealthy, and very cozy with the Roman rulers."

Stavers didn't need the entire picture painted in detail for him. "You're saying the crucifixion was a setup, then."

"Absolutely. It met the need to sustain the heavy hand of Roman law, Pilate got a bagful of gold, and Joseph of Arimathea, who was *very* close with Jesus, went through the whole ritual and then got Jesus off the hook—sorry, I didn't intend that as a pun. Anyway, the rich get richer, the agitator *appears* to be dead, Roman law is upheld, and Joseph follows whatever incentive led him to do whatever he did. My personal belief, and secret sects of the church appear to agree, Jesus and Joseph, the Joseph of Arimathea, were actually relatives. My personal belief has a bit more to sustain what happened than the mumbo-jumbo of the church that came into existence long after all this happened."

"Relatives? Jesus and Joseph of—who?"

"Arimathea."

"How were they connected?"

"Jesus was his brother-in-law. Specifically, Jesus long before the crucifixion had secretly married Joseph's sister."

Stavers shook his head. "You're asking me to swallow a hell of a lot, woman."

"I'm not asking you to swallow anything. I don't know how well you know ancient Jewish law—"

"I know it as well as I can read Sanskrit, which is zero."

"Then you aren't aware that in Jesus' time, and never forget that he was Jewish, it was absolute Judaic law that a healthy man be wed. To be celibate was to violate the law of God and to invite terrible punishment. This went for *all* Jews. Jesus at an earlier age hadn't yet claimed to be messianic, and remaining unmarried could have caused his death by stoning. In fact, his own father would have been attacked by the locals if he hadn't worked day and night to be certain his son tied the knot and contributed to the population."

She returned to her seat, close to Stavers, and gripped his arm. "Don't—absolutely do not think of Jesus as some starry-eyed, glazed-over missionary stumbling in thongs across the desert. He was a powerful man in physique and in mind; extremely powerful, healthy, and incredibly aware of whatever traps might snare him before he declared himself the son of God. That meant not violating whatever his own people considered sancrosanct. His *not* being married would have had the same effect as painting himself green and wandering naked through the local towns. Remember, Doug, he was dedicated, brilliant, disciplined and extremely crafty. He was as tough as nails. He *had* to be in order to survive his times. The bible—that bag of fables and legends rearranged to lend power to the aristocracy of the church—pictured Jesus as mumbling parables as he drifted about the countryside. The church wasn't able to extinguish *everything*, and I assure you the church would like to have excised a great deal more from the historical records and the bibles than they have." She thought of her own history, of all the time in the world for her own thorough research, and a smile came unbidden to her lips.

"What the Gospels dared not say *was* written, but in a series of biblical texts that had been hidden for some fifteen hundred years. They weren't discovered until, um, either December of 1945 or January of 1946."

Stavers wasn't entirely unaware of Middle East history. "That would be the Nag Hammadi scrolls."

"Exactly!" she said, obviously pleased with his own thrust of memory. "What do you remember of them?"

"Basically that they contradict much of . . ." He hesitated as he realized what he was about to say. "Much of what is believed about Jesus as a saintly, gentle creature."

"Someone who was in that garden where Jesus spent

a few hours on the cross before he was taken down, recorded, apparently word for word, or close enough to it, what Jesus told his family and friends after that little tempest in the garden. It's in a document known as the Second Treatise of the Great Seth, and he lays it right on the line."

"I can guess what comes next. How he spooked the Romans."

"*And* whatever part of the world interfaced with the Roman Empire. I know that passage perfectly."

"How the hell do you remember all this? I mean, memorizing passages, that sort of thing?"

She laughed. "The next time you have twenty centuries to hang around waiting to get something done, you'll be able to answer that question yourself."

He couldn't help it; he grinned. She was so right. "Let's hear it," he said.

"All right. This is supposedly a first-person quote from Jesus as this scribe wrote it down. 'I did not succumb to them as they planned, and I did not die in reality but only in appearance, so I would not be shamed by them. For my death which they believe actually happened, for in their error and blindness, they believed they had nailed this man unto his death. But it was another who drank the gall and the vinegar; not I. They struck me, but this was meaningless, for it was another, Simon, it was he who bore the cross. It was another on whose brow they placed their crown of thorns, and through it all, I was laughing at their ignorance.' "

"I'll be damned. That fits a biblical passage that I'll bet the church wishes had been excised," he offered in reply to her quotation.

"I can guess what it is."

"I'll bet you do," he said. "It's in Luke. He tells his followers, and I guess anyone else who was listening, that he's no patsy, to use the modern idiom. The quote is that he came among them, and this is the quote, 'not to bring peace, but a sword.' There's more; his followers are to buy swords, and he's going to set father against son and brother against brother, and so on. In fact, according to the Gospels, wasn't Peter wearing a sword, or carrying one, when the Roman soldiers arrested Jesus?"

"You have an apt word for this moment," she told him. "Bingo!"

"I can do without priestly learning," he said suddenly. "Let's cut the mustard, Rebecca."

"Everything I've told you is true," she said, not defensive but untouched by his remark.

"I've been putting two and two together," he said, and she was just as suddenly aware that this man already knew much of what she had been saying, that he had let her run with her story, and that he was *not* completely unacquainted with the writhing distortions of biblical history.

"There's the story of the Fisher King," Stavers said. "It's mixed in with Arthurian legends. With long poems. With stories of the Green Knight. But above all with this Fisher King. The man who wrote of the Fisher King wrote of the Holy Grail, which you have conveniently left out of everything you've said."

"Is that an accusation?"

"Statement. Fact. Because you triggered something in me with a name you used. *Wolfram*. That's the name of the writer who described not only the Fisher King and his realm, but also the Holy Grail. Which," he said carefully, "is *not* a cup or a chalice."

Her eyes gleamed. "Marvelous," she said, her voice a whisper. "How much do you remember?"

"Wolfram wrote about knights. A lot about the Templars, but he gave them special powers. Magical. I don't know if Merlin figured in any of this—"

Her eyes seemed to mist over. "I will quote again, my friend, and it will be exact." She breathed deeply and seemed to float away as she spoke. "Wolfram told us of the knights and how their lives were completely affected by the Holy Grail. 'I will tell you how they are sustained. They live from a stone of the purest kind . . . It is called *lapsit exillis*. By the power of that stone the phoenix burns to ashes, but the ashes give him life again.' Then Wolfram wrote of a promise of immortality. He said that the man who saw the Grail, this stone, 'cannot die . . . And in looks he will not fade. His appearance will stay the same, be it maid or man, as on the day he saw the stone, the same as when the best years of his life began, and though he should see the stone for two hundred years, it will never change . . . such power does the stone give a man that flesh and bones are at once made young again. The stone is called the Grail.' "

No smile accompanied her words this time. "In its broadest terms *lapsit exillis*—"

"Means a stone from heaven," he broke in. "I know Wolfram's poem. He also says the Grail, the stone, can bring all manner of men to serve that man who is in possession of the stone, to serve him even to their deaths."

"Have you yet made the connection, Doug?"

He stared at her, his eyes widening, as the full impact struck him. She voiced his thoughts.

"The Holy Grail is that stone, the *arbatik*, that is in your possession—and that I will bring to its full power by making a living part of you."

He had to force himself to talk. He was drowning in the impact of heady realization.

"Why is it so important for me to go to Mars with you? Obviously," he continued before she could answer, "the main ship of your people is on that planet."

"Obviously?" she taunted him.

"It sure as hell fits the bill," he said quickly. "Let it go for the moment. *Where* that ship is. What I'm asking you is *why* you need me with that ship, but only *after* this crazy surgery you're setting up. What happens then? Do I *think* a ship to lift? Some sort of super psychokinesis?"

She shook her head. "No. Your presence on that vessel, just as you described with the *arbatik* a living organism again, is a key. It is *the* Holy Grail of our vessel. We, a physiological organism, cannot operate so enormous and complex a ship. Computers that are as alive as we *are* the ship. They take us through vast maelstroms and dimensions infinitely beyond our capacity to comprehend, let alone navigate. But those computers, and that is a very rough analogy, require a genetic system and the *arbatik* as one, to function."

She leaned back in her seat, her face unreadable, but her words powerful and inescapable. "To that vessel, Doug, *you* become the Holy Grail. The keystone to renewed passage through time and dimensions beyond all description. *That* is why I told you that ruling a world was boring. I referenced a comparison that at the time you could not understand."

"I don't know," he said wearily. "Running a whole planet seems like child's play compared to what you've got going."

He rose and stood before the view of mountains glowing golden beneath a setting sun. "Tell me, Rebecca, how we can possibly bring Christ back to us. And, second, *why* would we even want to do that?"

She moved to his side. "The answer to your first question is that we use magic. Christ is dead, entombed outside a village in France. It is called Arques, and it is several miles, three miles, to be precise, from the Chateau of Blanchefort, and twice that distance from Rennes-le-Chateau. The tomb once had an inscription carved in its stone. It is no longer there, but a very long time ago I stood there and read its words. *Et In Acradia Ego*. That is unintelligible Latin, but it may be transcribed, and then it would read, in English, '*Begone! I conceal the secrets of God*.' "

Stavers faced the woman. "That is nearly two thousand years ago. And not all the magic in the world can change the fact that in that tomb is dust and bones. *You*, Rebecca, are the living result of thousands of years of super science, of far-future biology. Christ was one of us. Born and died, buried and dissipated. You're not going to bring *that* back."

"But that is where Christ went after he left the crucifix. That is where Joseph of Arimathea carried Jesus, his wife, and his children. That is where the direct lineal descendants of Christ live *now*. And there is one of these descendants, whose genetic code has been sustained all this time, who would be recognized by the Jews of two thousand years ago as the original Jesus. *That* is who we will resurrect. A touch of sleight-of-hand, so to speak, but it will serve our purpose."

"Which is what, Rebecca?"

"You will have your surgery. When you emerge from that moment, the *arbatik*, and yourself, will be a single entity of dominance. This new Christ—his name is James and he is thirty-seven years old, which also fits our needs—will love you, be dedicated and utterly slavish to you. And it is then we will add your own touch to our purposes, so that when he is, let us say, out of range of your direct influence, he will perform as desired."

It all came together. *Etorphin.* The ultimate mind-control drug, diluted to exactly the dosage they would need. A scant touch of etorphin to reassemble the brains of James, the influence of Stavers, the instructions they would give to this remote descendant of Jesus Christ, and they'd have a messiah that would turn the Christian world upside down.

"It will work," Stavers said aloud finally. "By God, it *will* work! *He* won't do it, except through us, and we won't even have to be there."

He turned to grip Rebecca's arms. She saw Stavers coming alive with his old grasp of the moment and of the future. "You never knew Joey No-Name," he said suddenly.

"Who?"

"We called him Joey No-Name. A crazy, absurd, absolute lunatic and pure genius. Joey was an old friend. I really believed he didn't *have* a second name, but oh, that smart son of a bitch, he did." Stavers slipped into memory with obvious pleasure of his recollection. "Joey grew up with me. We spent time together as kids and we learned together how to survive the streets and alleys. What I never knew was that in reality he had become a most successful career man, and he was Colonel Joseph Mitchell of our air force and the CIA. No one knew that." Stavers grinned at the mental picture of Joey No-Name. "That crazy bastard walked around in a skin-ripping toga and sandals. He'd grown a long beard and was an expert at acting and speaking as a lunatic. His voice carried for miles. He was always preaching some silly gospel but he could have had half the country carrying his bags for him. Joey joined our group that hunted down Patschke in India, where the old Nazi had gone to hide. When he still had the diamond—oops, the *arbatik*."

Stavers relit his cigar, his hands making swift motions as he raced along with recollection and its telling. "Joey predicted where we'd find Patschke, even *how* to find him. As Joey told us, in between his raving and ranting, so that you had to pay careful attention to what he said as he buried it in his lunacy, was that *all* messiahs plan *because they must plan, in order to control.* While the aspiring messiah is alive he becomes a religious cultist, and the religions form only *after* the messiah or the prophet has gone to the happy heavenly hunting grounds."

Stavers laughed, striding rapidly about the room with his excitement. "Christ, Mohammed, well, the intended messiahs had to be elevated to godhead status because they had the smarts to know that the other would-be messiahs would be out to cut their throats so *they* could take over. Maybe that's the true chorus of angels; all the bibles drip with murder, slaughter, assassination, torture, rape and pillaging, plotting, scheming, cheating, all of it a grasp for power, and then they spend centuries watering down the reality of their whole bunch so the gullible will flock to them for their ticket to the promised land."

"Neatly spoken," Rebecca told him.

"Hell, *I* didn't come up with those answers. I could have but I didn't pay attention to them the way Joey did. He could sniff out beatific shit like a starving fly on the wing. Joey told us not to look at the good books; they're protective lies because they hide the real man for us. One of his favorite sayings was that we tend to forget that a man is pretty vulnerable when he's holding his dick in his hand and leaning against a cactus to take a piss."

Stavers downed his drink. "Joey gave himself the

name of Akim Asid for the trip to India. Rosa Montini was with me then. Joey drove her mad. He used to prattle on about Christ being alive and well and a prisoner in the Vatican—" His voice stopped with a silent crash. "I *will* be damned. Joey was prophetic as hell. Without his ever knowing you or this moment, he actually predicted that Jesus would be in the Vatican and alive and well!"

"What did you say before? Under God's mantle all things are possible, even roses and scorpions?"

"Close enough. Joey, you see, didn't *guess* about where I'd find Patschke. It rose from knowledge and extrapolation. There's more cults and religions in India than anywhere else in the world. Patschke had the Godstone, and he had the power to sway people, but he was old and he was swiftly running out of time. So he had to whip up the religious fervor he needed as quickly as he could. Bingo," he smiled, "as you said. Drop your nickel in the slot and pull the handle, and all the bells and cherries and plums go round and round and round, and when they stop, look carefully to your left and you'll see a temple and inside that temple will be Patschke and his stone from God. You had to look carefully. As Joey explained it, India's a vast force of cults that overnight can assume frenzied proportions. It's a theological swamp so vast and so thick, and with such ravenous religious hunger, that even a successful new cultist could hide from the outside world in those thickets."

"Until that leader was ready to emerge and make his move," Rebecca added.

"Joey said that was like an atomic bomb going off underwater. You don't even see the fireball until it punches out its shock wave and vaporizes everything about it and comes roaring and screaming from everywhere."

"Just as we're doing with you right now," she said quietly.

"Okay," he snapped, whirling about, standing inches from her and glaring into her eyes, "it's time to fish or cut bait, lady. One, I get the medical trip and the stone ends up inside me and wired to brain and balls. Two, as soon as I'm recovered—"

"Which will be swift because of the—"

"Shut up, Rebecca, unless I ask for something. Two, as soon as I'm cruising again on all eight cylinders, we go pick up James in France. Or does number three come first?"

"Hitler?"

"Yes."

"We revive him before we go for James the Christ." She laughed. "I like that. James the Christ," she repeated herself.

"Save the fun and games, lover. *Why* do we deliver James to Catholic City?"

"Because we'll have the world on its toes waiting to see if it *is* Christ. The Second Coming, Doug. The Vatican is losing ground steadily to your Church of the Ascension. You're pouring a fortune in money, people and political power into your message, and you've got fifty mirror images of Doug Stavers driving them straight up a wall. Now with all the pomp and circumstance we can deliver, so the whole world knows what we're doing, we deliver to them James, whom we'll obviously call Jesus. We prepare James with exquisite care. We make certain that we cleanse his body externally and internally as well so that all trace of any modern drugs is *gone*. Nothing artificial save his clothing, which will be of modern materials, which makes good common sense, but of the shape of antiquity. If James has dental fillings we'll make certain they aren't too modern. If he has any false teeth I'll make certain they hearken back a long time. In short, we'll dazzle and baffle the Vatican. The world will want to know if there really *is* a Second Coming. The powers that be in the Vatican won't believe it for a moment *but they'll have to go along with it as long as they can.*"

He snapped his fingers. "Of course. They'll use messianic Jimmy boy as a counter to the good Reverend Stavers and his upstart merry band of theological dandies. Counter-propaganda. They'll convene special boards, special groups. They'll investigate. They'll question the poor bastard until his eyes roll."

"And they'll get answers that will drive them mad. Because James *is* of a direct, unbroken genetic lineage, his skin, its texture, everything about him, will be descended directly from those of Galilee. And what will he say? Ah, it fits so well, Doug! Under *your* power with the *arbatik* he'll think he's been talking with God. With enough etorphin to totally command his mind, and yet leave not even a chemical drop to be detected, *he will remember everything we tell him as truth.* He will believe everything he says, he will relate the marvelous stories of the bible and of his times because that is what he knows and believes and will say, *even to his death.*"

"But they can't kill him," Stavers said slowly, "because it looks too suspicious."

"Not while you're around, they can't," she affirmed.

"And they need to get rid of me."

"In your own jargon, Reverend Stavers, now you're cooking," she said, thoroughly enjoying this moment.

"Which means," he said slowly as it all fell into place, "that they must also get rid of me without killing me, because if they succeed in knocking me off, our control of the world press will lay all the blame and guilt on them, and the walls of the Vatican are damned well going to crack and crumble—"

"Ah, religion is *so* convenient," she laughed, "just like the walls of Jericho, and with your control of the global media, that's a mighty fine trumpet you have there, Reverend Stavers, to blow down the walls."

"So the Vatican boosts my—your, our—all-out drive to get the ships into earth orbit so we can light the fires and launch toward Mars."

"And they'll pray fervently you'll never return."

"But what if I *do* return?"

"You won't want to."

"Why not? I really *could* take over leadership of the world then!"

"Would you be king of a small backyard, forever trapped there, or be a voyager who can live for thousands of years and know the wonders of a thousand worlds?"

"I get your meaning, Rebecca."

"Then you're ready for surgery."

"Hell, yes. *Let's do it.*"

Chapter 22

The needle went in, smooth yet with its own stinging bite and was blessedly forgotten with the rush of thiopental through the circulatory system of Doug Stavers. He paid no attention to the battery of surgeons, technicians, and doctors, the multiple teams of anesthetists, the monitoring systems beeping and chirping and making physiological-musical sounds. He knew nothing of the shining scopes and the digital numbers, the snakelike dance and sine waves of robot caretakers, the touch of yet other sensors and their tunnel vision of heartbeat, pulse, respiration, temperature, pressures and levels of consciousness and unconsciousness. Oxygen went with the thiopental and he heard Rebecca's voice, warm and trusting. "Count down from a hundred, Doug. Nice and easy, count down, follow the numbers . . ."

Her voice drifted, swirling gently in the warm fog enveloping him, tolling sweetly one hundred, ninety-nine, ninety-eight, ninety-six, ninety-one, eighty-two, ninety-four, sixty-two . . .

"He's under. He's doing just fine." Voices rising and falling, the surgical team that had run through this procedure at least twenty times, the backups and standbys ready to move in at no more than a hand signal. Emergency equipment at the ready, serving its best purpose by never being needed. Steel blades, needlepoints, shimmering lasers, superfast saws of the finest alloys; adrenalin, oxygen, glucose, the liquids and gases of life.

Skip Marden shuddered. He stood on a raised platform in green gown and cap and mask, no part of the surgery of the man he loved, whose well-being was more important than his own life. He stood in the operating theater because he refused to be anywhere else. Because of, well, *anything*. He saw gleaming metal open the chest of the man for whom he had fought and protected so many years and his own skin went cold. The chest cavity opened. Instruments and probes and gloved fingers went within. He watched Stavers' beating, pumping, jumping heart and his own heart shrank and beat madly and all life became unreality. He was so vulnerable! So he stood frozen, his alertness masked by cloth and fear and helplessness and love, and he felt mad that all this was going on with such purpose and deliberation. And Doug's last words to him pounded in his brain. "Watch. Don't touch. *Don't interfere.*"

Watch, hell. His eyes raced across and back and forth and from every side and corner of the room to the other. The heart monitors mesmerized them, signalling as they did the flow of life in this man who was more god to him than any creature sculpted from history or myth or legend. Here in this room were all the Christs and the Gods and the Creators, encapsuled in this one man, and now . . . the heart beating nakedly, the spurts and flows of blood, the waiting blood and plasma ready for that instant when an excess of life-giving fluid might drain or bulge away from Stavers. To think of that heart no longer beating was unthinkable; to imagine the brain monitor showing a flat line was unimaginable. To lose Doug Stavers was the end of all purpose in life.

So he watched, and he itched and ached and pained and his surgical attire became dark with the soak of his own sweat, and inside he raged against all that was happening, and yet he stood mute, muscles twisted and agonizing, because Doug said this was what he must do.

He watched the glittering facets of the great yellow diamond as it slowly sank into that opened chest of pink flesh and white meat and leaping heart, pulsations and throbs and rise and fall, heaving and sinking. He failed to understand why Stavers and the woman had only hours before subjected the Godstone to lances of hellish fire so thin they could be seen only by their glowing; the hair-thin lines of laser fire through the Godstone. Marden did not understand that neuronic fibers and nerves and other parts of Stavers would be slid through the laser-lanced lines; he did not need to understand and so he was never told.

"Don't interfere."

Marden knew he was torn with love-fear-hate of this woman whose hands moved deep within Doug, moved muscle and fiber, heart and veins and arteries, kneaded sinew and muscle and tendon, touched against the exquisite symmetry of spinal column and the fibers of life. Time melted to unmeasurable something. Time was measured in the knots and spasms of his own body.

The *arbatik* rested precisely where Rebecca Weinstein wished. It fed through the cranial and spinal system. It felt the pulses and heaves of the heart. It gained the life it had not known for two thousand years. It was no stone, no diamond; it was genetic tissue of some science so far across galactic sweeps its orbs of origin were invisible from this planet they called Earth.

Man and *arbatik* became as one. Unconscious, unknowing, unheeding, Stavers—the *new*, different Stavers—fed energy into the space of the operating theater. Energy unwilled but present; energy somnolent yet felt by those about him; energy ancient yet sentient.

Rebecca Weinstein took a deep breath. She had made her agreement with Doug Stavers. She had fought against this coming moment, had argued and pleaded, cursed and cajoled, using every desperate wile of which she was capable. All to no avail.

Rebecca Weinstein looked at her surgical team. "Step back from this man. Do not touch anything. Do not *do* anything unless I order you to do so. Is that absolutely clear?"

Their eyes showed puzzlement and confusion and no small alarm. Unexpected digression at such a moment is always dangerous, undeserved, violently *wrong*.

Rebecca waited. They were clear.

She reached forward and shut down the oxygen supply to the unconscious form of Doug Stavers.

Monitors pinged, melodious tones sounded, oscilloscopes showed silent screams. Rebecca Weinstein shut down other systems.

The leaping, jumping heart fell still.

The EEG line went flat.

A steady tone issued like a cry of ultimate finality.

"He's dead!" a nurse screamed.

"Stay back!" Rebecca snapped, her eyes blazing furious above her mask.

"Goddamnit, bring him back!" Marden roared. His head whirled, he felt hurled into some surrounding, impossible maw of death. Everything was unreal, impossible. His own brain reeling, he stumbled forward. "Bring him back, goddamnit!" he bellowed. No thought moved his arm; instinct and fear and reflex and hate as his hand slammed against the side of Weinstein's head, splitting ear and scalp, hurling her against a table. She fought for her balance, retained her feet.

"He's dead, you fucking whore! Bring him back to me!"

Marden's hands jerked, a robot circuitry gone crazy, moving frenziedly, wanting to do *something*. Weinstein, the side of her face dripping blood, faced him. He *felt* her fury, he knew how helpless he was.

"If you want this man to live, get the hell out of my way," she hissed.

"W-what?"

"Get back, damn you! *You're killing him, Skip!"*

A shaking hand pointed. "But . . . but . . ."

"Get out of my way!"

He stumbled backwards, tears within his mask, terrified, gone mad, crying, his only ability left to kill, and he knew he could not do this.

Rebecca moved forward to Doug Stavers, silent, still, the clock of his life winding down.

This is what you wanted, you beautiful son of a bitch. The ultimate trip, you said. To know you are going to die and must die and then to live again. The touch of the gods, the joining, the perfect transforma-

tion of self. Jehovah and Zeus and Shiva and Allah, hello there, all of you!

She leaned forward, one hand against his forehead, the other against his silent heart. She watched the *arbatik* deep in his body, and she energized herself. She had done so before. For three thousand years she had done so in that marvelous gestalt of her own people; it was as real and automatic a reflex as breathing harder during exertion.

She knew that behind her gown and within her own body the genetic wonder of a galaxy pulsed and glowed, *and the light within Doug brightened, orange and amber and then fierce, brilliant yellow.*

Mystery and wonder surged in the surgical ampitheater. Energy flowed from Rebecca to Doug Stavers; two tiny but enormous engines of power, sucking in the bands of force that invisibly threaded through all the universe. Waves of gravity and quantum particles and vast rushes of radiation, space-time bent and twisted, drawn into the *arbatiks*, the homing antennas and transmitters that Rebecca's people had used for uncounted centuries to open starfields for their pleasure, to give them godlike powers of life and regeneration.

Magic for man, mystery for the human race.

Describe a fission-fusion-fission device to a Neanderthal.

Tell the aborigine how beams of light will cut and reshape an eyeball and give to a man the cunning sight of the eagle.

It is not simply impossible; *it is inconceivable.*

Fusion, laser and *arbatik*. All a matter of time and scale.

One person only in that room knew what transpired. Rebecca fed energy as a transceiver and conduit to the dead man before her, because he had desired this moment. The ultimate trip. And to come back from the dead through manipulation rather than miracle, ah! There was the *true* resurrection!

Move over, Jesus! Get the hell out of my way!

The heart quivered, accepted electrical impulses, jerked, beat faster and returned to its normal, powerful, heaving, beating rhythm. Blood flowed, pressures rose and stabilized, liquid coursed through the system, electrical synapses flashed and glittered in the limitless orchestration of the mind. Skip Marden stared at Rebecca Weinstein. She returned his look without a twitch of emotion. Skip sank slowly to his knees, thunderstruck, overwhelmed, joyous yet crushed, and in the face of the impossible and the inconceivable, the human killing machine gripped his face in his great hands, and wept.

Rebecca turned to her team of doctors and nurses, staring, stupefied, awed to muscle rigidity. "Let us get with it, people," she said calmly. "Doctors, do your jobs. Close him up." She stepped back, observing, permitting the trained teams to do with the human body what they had done so many times before.

They could hardly believe what took place beneath their hands. That strange glowing light . . . the swift closure of opened vessels, and flesh and muscle and fiber. The patient seemed to be healing before their eyes and beneath their hands.

Rebecca Weinstein smiled. That is precisely what Doug Stavers was doing. After all, it was hardly unusual for a medical science with a hundred thousand years behind it to perform such a simple task.

Stavers swam upward through a warm, grey sea. Colors shifted gently about him as he ascended, from grey to warm pink, a swirl of gauze and foam, of sparkling spray beneath the surface so far above him. Recollection came slowly as his body forced away the effects of thiopental, as his tissues eagerly sucked in the oxygen pushing into him under pressure. He felt more discomfort than pain, and it mattered not at all. He was swimming, yet not swimming. Was he levitating? Floating? Drifting weightlessly? His limbs felt weightless, unencumbered; no, that wasn't it. They weren't free-floating. He still lacked sufficient feeling in arms and legs for proper feedback for the mind to acknowledge.

He heard his own voice telling him, not in speech or words but imaging in some manner he couldn't comprehend, to *go with it; go with the flow . . . Stop fighting, relax, it's okay, okay.*

Hey, there's a light above me. Do I have tunnel vision? I'm going along a tunnel of light, and this ocean is a womb of birth and I think maybe I'm dead. Really? Dead? Me? No way, Jose, a voice chuckled within him. *Why am I giggling? What the hell's so funny about being dead? And why did I die? The surgery . . . I remember now . . . the arbatik . . . surgically implanted. Can't be. Must have failed. But if it failed, how come I'm talking between me and myself? So I'm not dead. Limbo? Maybe; maybe I'm floating in the pea soup of limbo, neither here nor there or anywhere, but I'm everywhere.*

The light. Go for the light. Push, heave yourself to the light. Don't use your body! Use your mind, push yourself upward through the amniotic fluid—what? Never mind, just do it! Go, go, go! Holy shit, I've read about this death experience . . . floating, drifting, and that bright light and you move toward it and God's waiting on the other side of the tunnel. You're not in a tunnel, you idiot, you're ascending, you're powerful, hey, the light's getting brighter and brighter . . . now I'm supposed to see angels. Those beautiful, beautiful angels with white-pink hair and gorgeous wings and lovely full, round breasts and no navels, didja' know that angels don't have navels, but I knew a few that had navels, really, and there's one of them above me, holy shit, she's gorgeous and she's looking at me and smiling and I'm getting closer to her and—

He blinked. Once. Again. Several times. The blinding light stabbed into his eyes.

He saw faces. *The angel. Rebecca the angel. Is Weinstein also an angel? There are two of them. Twins. Look; they're merging! Now there's only one. Beautiful, beautiful . . .*

That goddamned light. Blinding. Hurts.

The medical staff edged closer, breathless, awed, stunned. This man had died. Right before their eyes. Zero line on the brain waves. Zero line for cardiac output. BP and pulse and—hell, *all* of it went to zero, and here he was, emerging from death prolonged for several minutes and the instruments and monitors sang and chirped and whistled and toned, they rang and gonged and hummed in a song of life.

They'd done it all now. He was closed and sewed, stitched and sealed, his systems monitored, the thiopental flushing its last remnants from his body. He was still a very long way off, he still saw through gauze and haze, but the voices, disembodied and floating, reached him. A babble from a gaggle; he giggled to himself.

"He's almost out of it. We should keep him sedated. There's going to be a lot of pain."

A voice very close to him. Physically close? He wasn't sure, but the sound of the voice and the connections he made, it was *everything*. "No drugs. He won't need them."

"Let's keep the IV going. He'll—"

"Disconnect the IV. I'm *ordering* you." Sweet angel. You *tell 'em, baby. Get me unhooked from all this shit. I feel something surging upward from within me!* "You're not going to disconnect the monitors! My God, doctor, if anything fails or—"

"*I'm* not your God. Disconnect the monitors. *Now!*"

He lay free of connections except to himself and that marvelous glowing engine deep within him, an integral part of him now, against his spinal column, twisted within his nerves, connected to his heart. Did *arbatiks* carry memories with their genetic structure? *Hello, Wolfram!*

He didn't laugh as loudly, or as long as before. He was becoming himself now. *All* himself. His eyes remained closed, but there was an inaudible *snap!* inside him, all about him, and he knew he was back.

He opened his eyes. The angel's face hovered close above his. Her smile . . . golden light.

"Hello, bitch," he said. He managed a weak grin.

"Ah, a soul saved from hell." She smiled again, but her eyes studied him carefully, looking for any sign of a problem. None. This was a newer, better, more powerful Doug Stavers. "Not too many people shake hands with Lucifer and come back to talk about it."

He took long, deep breaths. "You lose. No Lucifer, babe. Swimming . . . not water. Pink and gold and bright lights. Always coming . . . up. Ascending."

"I understand, Father." Her laugh infected him. "Or is it Padre?"

"Up yours, sweetheart." He closed his eyes, sucking in strength from the invisible forces of the true reality about him.

"Still ascending, Doug?"

"Yeah. Better every minute."

"Want to sit up?"

"Yes."

She motioned to the medical team. "*No!*" The voice burst from across the room. Stavers didn't need to turn. He knew the anguished cry of Skip Marden. Skip was there suddenly, enormous arms cradling Stavers. "I'll lift him," he said, leaving no room for argument.

Stavers looked with quiet surprise at his closest friend. The professional killer was still crying.

"You died, you motherfucker," Marden grated. "*You died!* I saw . . . I was here. I, I wanted to die *for* you."

Stavers reached out. It took great effort so quickly from emergence, but he had to do it. His hand touched Marden's cheek, brushed away wetness.

"It's okay, fella. It's okay." Stavers turned to Rebecca. "Get me the hell out of here. Get me where I can see the mountains. Then I'll *know* I'm back."

She looked to Marden. "You move him. No one else. You and me."

"You're goddamn right," he agreed.

Chapter 23

Al Templin stopped in the doorway, his face a turbulence of mixed emotions. Surprise, wonder, disbelief, relief; they raced like rivulets across the small lake of his features.

"Holy shit," he said.

"What the hell's the matter with you?" Stavers asked, knowing full well what Templin fought within his head. His security chief had never played games with trying to conceal his feelings and reactions.

"You know what I was told!" Templin half-shouted. He came fully into the room, studying Stavers, looking to Marden and then to Rebecca Weinstein. He nodded to Marden. "Skip?" was his only greeting; these two had never needed more. Professional mercenaries rarely need words. Templin looked fully at Weinstein. "Lady doctor, it's good to see you. Although," he appended, "a lot of people were trying to give me some heavy doubts."

"Sit down, Al," Stavers said, gesturing to an easy chair directly across from himself. A small low coffee table separated them. Templin took the seat gratefully.

"I came here straight from Chicago," he said quickly. He gestured with one hand. "Full precautions, but you already know that." Stavers nodded, Skip Marden sat like a cement giant, Rebecca Weinstein sat back, observing, studying, measuring, calculating.

"You know something, Doug? In all the years we've been together, I've never had a drink. I need one now."

Stavers nodded and pressed a button on the arm of his chair. He knew what Templin drank long before this moment. "Wild Turkey," he said to the microphone concealed within the arm. "Bring the bottle. And bring Suntory vodka and fresh orange juice." He switched off.

"What's the beef, Al?"

Templin leaned back but he remained hair-trigger. "I had been told," he said slowly, "that you were dead." He waited for a reaction, found none and knew he should go on. "I was told, and by very reputable sources, that surgery was performed on you," he glanced at Rebecca, "by one Dr. Weinstein, and that you died."

Stavers held out both arms. "Here I am, Al."

"Jesus Christ, I can see that!" Templin burst out. "What I want to know is how and why I got the story I did!"

A waiter tapped at the door, Marden studied the security video monitor and went to the door personally to escort in the waiter with the drink order. The man placed his tray on the low table and without a word or a sideways glance left the room.

"That's not so important," Stavers said, obviously the old professional again. He leaned forward. "What I want you to find out, Al, is *who*, not how and why. *Who* told *who*."

"I found out." He poured Wild Turkey into a large shot glass but waited to drink. "A nurse from here. Sue Banks. She told it to Dr. Chester Stanfield. Chicago Academy of Medical Science."

"He's very high up," Weinstein interjected, her face showing concern.

"How's his mouth?" Stavers asked quickly.

"He's one of those holier-than-thou administrators. He'd keep it within a very tight group," Weinstein replied. "He's not given to equal conversations with subordinates and almost everybody is subordinate to his ego."

"Kill him," Stavers said.

"Agreed," Templin replied, acknowledging the order with a gesture with his drink. "I figured you might want that. The machinery is set. Your phone?"

Marden came forward with a radiophone. They waited in silence as Templin dialed in his codes. When he spoke it was with a thick Spanish accent. "Juan here. My office, they call me. You assholes, you hold up construction work. Make the delivery *immediately* or I cancel your contract. Pig!" He switched off.

"Before the day is over," he said directly to Stavers.

"I imagine it will be a very large cement truck," Stavers smiled.

"Here's how," Templin replied, sipping his drink. Dr. Chester Stanfield would be driven in his limo from the medical academy to his home outside Chicago. On the way there would be a terrible accident and a huge cement truck would crush the limo. *Finis.*

"Anybody else talking?" Marden queried Templin.

"A few. You can forget them," Templin told him.

Rebecca Weinstein moved forward and took a chair slowly. "Obviously, the medical team here talks too much," she said.

"Send them all to the Mannheim Institute in Canada," Stavers said quietly. "We're ready to warm up Hitler."

"*Who?*" Templin's eyes were wide.

"Listen. Just listen. You're my top watchdog so you should know. But whatever you need to know you'll hear," Stavers said quietly, "without a need for questions."

"Yes, sir."

"Skip, you handle it. Use Colorado Leasing. A DC-9 or a Fokker 28. It goes boom at cruise altitude."

"Got it. I'll be back soon."

Marden left the room. It was just another job. The medical staff that had made up Weinstein's team had been informed they had a major surgery in Canada. No secret there; Mannheim was second knowledge to them all. Marden would lease a commercial jet from Air Colorado. It would climb to 34,000 feet. And then it would blow up. One loose mouth in the group had guaranteed the death of the entire medteam.

"Adolf Hitler is alive," Stavers told Templin. "He's still biologically fifty-four years old. He's been on ice since 1944. We brought him out of Sweden in a thermos bottle; he's still on ice at Mannheim. We're going to pop him out. Then we deliver him. Where he's going he won't be a hero."

Templin nodded, and Stavers and Weinstein knew he'd already drawn a wrong conclusion. Templin took Stavers' words too literally and figured the Fuehrer was destined for delivery straight to Moscow. Stavers contained a smile. That was too simple. He had better plans. Stavers didn't say anything about James Christ. *Not yet.*

"I need to recommend a move," Templin said.

"Shoot."

"There's too many rumors around not to rock the company boat," Templin concentrated on his direct problems. "We still haven't eased out of the investigations from that scene at LaGuardia Airport. It's the insurance companies. They let loose a whole passel of dogs to sniff out everything they could."

"A detail," Stavers said indifferently.

"That's true. But it adds to the package. Look, three of you have been killed at various religious hoorahs around the country. The fanatics; that sort of thing. I know, *we* know, they were stand-ins. And you predicted it would happen, and you were also right in that it would broaden the mystery and draw in bigger crowds."

Stavers laughed. "Just look back to the original Roman coliseum for technique. Go on, Al."

"We need to display you."

"You *what?*"

"Display you. Get you out in front for a grand look-see by the public, by certain people in industry and government. Put the bullshit to rest."

"Are you out of your fucking mind?" Marden burst into their exchange. "Why don't you just paint a bullseye in the middle of his forehead?"

Stavers motioned for Marden to stay out of it. "What's your pitch?"

"We could do it on television but that won't work as well as I'd like. Small-screen scenes don't make it. We need a personal appearance and the best place would be a bangup job in one of the bigger churches."

"And they could all see Doug and sing *Nearer My God To Thee*," Rebecca Weinstein commented, her sarcasm not lost on the others.

Templin turned to her. "You're right, Doctor. That's exactly *why*. We need zeal and fervor. We're starting to stumble in the drive to get the spacecraft ready for the big mission. First the moon and then off to the red planet."

"In your own terms, Mr. Templin, screw the moon. That's a billboard project only."

Templin blinked. "What?" he said, feeling stupid even as he did so.

"I thought you were faster than that," Weinstein snapped at him. "The moon's a billboard. Satisfaction for the lunar station crowd. We're interested in the Mars ship. Assembly in high orbit from the American station, Grissom, and launch direct. The lunar flights can be made from the Russian station. So I don't care how many problems you have with Armstrong Base. We—myself and that gentleman over there—are flying nonstop to Mars."

Templin absorbed what he'd heard. "All right, I'll accept whatever you say. It only reinforces my point. You cannot, you simply cannot, have an operation of this magnitude without negatives, without rumors, without the usual bullshit. He's dead, he's hurt, he's alive, he's mad *a la* Howard Hughes. If we're going to keep on schedule it means putting all the bad stuff away and reinforcing the good."

"My God, you sound like an ad for vitamins," Weinstein said with disdain.

"Unfortunately, he's right," Stavers added. He polished off his drink. "Okay, Al, here's what we do. First, I'm leaving here with the doctor and Skip."

"When?"

"Tonight. No use wasting time."

"Where?"

"The air force has a secret planetary training facility at Westover, at the edge of the great salt flats in Utah.

The whole damn thing has been kept under wraps. We know the air force would like to start a full-blown United States Space Command and push NASA back into donkey trips with commercial space stuff. None of that matters. What counts is that Stavers Industries has footed most of the bill for that place because Congress wouldn't pony up the long green. That also means we have complete access. Rebecca, Skip and myself are scheduled for full astronaut training there. Accelerated schedule; it's a piece of cake. The Mars ship will be almost fully robotic; computer-run, that sort of thing. Anyway, I can put a few things together. As soon as we're settled in there, you bring my top team to Westover. You'll be met by military people who'll take you all to the training facilities. We'll let *my* team see me in full training, and there won't be any doubt in *their* minds as to whether or not I'm hale and hearty. In fact, you can take all the video you want while you're there and make the most of it later."

"Excellent," Templin said, clearly pleased with what he'd heard. "What about the press?"

"Sorry," Stavers said. "I don't do scumbags."

"They could be important—"

"*That* conversation's ended."

"Yes, sir."

"But I want another group. As soon as we finish with our own team."

Templin nodded. "Yes, sir. You have the names?"

"Yes. They'll be tough to get. But I have a hunch they'll also be so fascinated with the chance to get close to me they'll buy their ticket. I'll go into it with you later."

"Got it. When do you want the—your group at Westover?"

"Three days from now. It's good to see you again, Al. Stay tight with the people."

"Yes, sir, I sure will."

Stavers had thought of bending Templin's will even more strongly to his own. It was ridiculously easy with that Godstone—he disliked the name *arbatik*; it sounded like he was talking Zulu—alive and energizing within his body and linked to his mind. But he had no reason to bring the hammer down between Templin's ears. He didn't own Al Templin like so many others. He didn't need to. Al had dedicated himself through his own code of loyalty. He'd kill anyone Stavers selected.

Including himself. *That*, of course, Stavers smiled to himself, just *might* take a bit of squeezing the other man between the ears.

They watched with a sense of awe. Doug Stavers, to his industrial and professional team, had always been regarded in just those modes. Industrialist. Super executive. Manager. Former mercenary. Icy blood and super-efficient. Brilliant, tough, fast, fair, brutal if he thought it necessary. A man never to be crossed. But still in that professional mode of the CEO. But now, in a giant centrifuge.

Roberto Diaz, director of his industrial might throughout the world. Ed Carson with the wide blanket of director of field operations. Doctor Hammad Al-Binn who ran the hospitals, clinics and medical facilities absorbed or controlled by Stavers Industries. Mark Baxter, computer genius and a raging zealot for wielding power on his own. Maxine Stark, ostensibly in charge of all research for the full team, but concentrating on overseeing the program to get the Mars ship assembled in orbit and on time for a flight within the proper planetary conjunction. *That* moment, when Earth and Mars were in the best positions for the most effective and least time-consuming flight, rushed closer and closer and was only two months away. And Dwight Grayson, "cosmetics kingpin" who ran global operations for cosmetics and just about every kind of drug ever invented.

Stavers didn't care for reports from his team. He had the best, and Al Templin was more than his security chief. He ran a tight ship through what he called his "killer CPAs," a computerized team that kept all the company books and activities on a constant, always-updated level. This gathering was for the show Al Templin had felt was needed in the psychological sense.

Stavers rode the centrifuge to the expected 4G levels

of liftoff acceleration when his moment of actual earth departure would be on hand. The enclosed flight control deck, in a huge clamshell egg at the end of a long counterbalanced swingarm, spun so rapidly that it reproducccd the forces of liftoff acceleration. At 4G, Doug Stavers weighed nearly five hundred pounds. His key staff watched the clamshell whirling around with locomotive energy, and then on the closed circuit television monitors studied Stavers as he manipulated controls and ran through his actual mission profile.

"Take it up higher," he instructed the centrifuge operator.

The air force technician glanced at Dr. Rebecca Weinstein, and she nodded her assent. She wasn't that pleased with the centrifuge run. This quickly after his surgery, despite the awesome powers of the *arbatik*, Doug would truly be pushing his body's limits.

Power whined at a higher pitch and the *whooshing* sound of the clamshell rose to a swiftly pounding surf of energy that could be heard and felt within the observation room.

"We've got six G's," Weinstein told the assembled group. "Mr. Stavers has a basic body weight of 220 pounds. At this moment he has a weight equal to some *nine hundred* pounds."

Maxine Stark's hand pressed tightly against her lips. "But . . . that could *kill* him!"

"The average, healthy adult male can stand a load of six G's for some two minutes before grey out and loss of peripheral vision, then blackout, followed by death as blood drains completely from the brain. Death occurs in three to four minutes."

"But it's longer than that!" Stark exclaimed.

Dr. Hammad Al-Binn leaned forward, quiet excitement evident in his reactions. Without taking his eyes from the monitors he responded to Stark's outcry. "Trained astronauts have endured ten G's without problem. Some men have gone higher. Do you remember the first Mercury suborbital flights? Shepard and Grissom each went to fourteen G's. And several Russians in a high abort went to seventeen."

"But they were *trained* astronauts," Stark protested. "Mr. Stavers, he's—"

"He's tougher than any astronaut who ever went into space," Weinstein broke in. She wasn't enjoying this. She knew Doug could take twelve or even sixteen times the force of gravity. But there wasn't any reason to go that high. This was stupid. "Doug, this is Weinstein. I'm bringing you down." She reached past the air force technician and began to slow the centrifuge.

"Hey, I want a run at twelve," Stavers grunted through the enormous loads on his system.

"Six is enough," Weinstein said coolly. "Doctor's *orders*," she added.

Al-Binn shook his head as he studied the physiological readouts. "He's amazing. He shows no more physical strain than a man jogging around the block."

"I intend to keep it that way," Weinstein told him. The clamshell eased to a stop in the main pit.

Ed Carson watched technicians unstrap Stavers. "I don't think it's that tough," he said, obviously unimpressed with what he'd seen and heard. "Fighter pilots do this all the time."

"Not for *sustained* periods," Weinstein corrected him.

"Hell, I could do what I just saw, standing on my head," Carson retorted. Weinstein studied the man; beefy, strong, clearly a body builder. He'd been a steelworker, a lumberjack. He *was* tough. She smiled to herself and waited until Stavers joined them in the observation room. She passed on Carson's remarks.

"Also, Mr. Carson has asked to make the centrifuge run," she told him. Stavers was soaked in perspiration, but he grinned with her words. He clapped Carson lightly on his shoulder. "Good enough, Ed. I like my people to stand behind what they say. However, you don't need to stand on your head. Get into the pit. I'll have them hook you up and we'll give you a ride."

No one said a word. Carson hesitated only a moment, tightened his lips and left the room for the clamshell pit. You did not shoot off your mouth to Stavers without backing it up. They watched through the window as he was hooked into the monitors in the clamshell. The doors closed and they now watched Carson on the TV monitors. "I'll work the controls," Stavers told the air force technician, and took his seat.

He accelerated the centrifuge at full speed. The load on Carson went from two on up to four. "Christ, he's grunting like a pig," Diaz laughed at the sound of Carson's voice through the speakers.

"Coming up on six," Stavers said.

"He's starting to take some real pain," Weinstein noted.

"Yeah, that he is," Stavers answered. "We'll hold him at six for three minutes."

Roger Sabbai moved forward. "But—"

Stavers turned. His eyes burned into those of the other man. Sabbai seemed to stagger slightly. He paled. "Sorry," he blurted. "I didn't mean—"

Stavers had already turned back to the centrifuge controls. He heard Weinstein's voice behind him. "Rapid cardiac rate, circulation impaired. We're getting breakdown of lesser blood vessels. He's into greyout and loss of peripheral vision."

On the monitors Carson's face looked as if an invisible elephant sat on him. His cheeks pulled far back, opening his mouth in an animal grimace. His breath came in gasps.

"We're losing him," Al-Binn said, frightened.

"Nah," Stavers smiled. "He's not even standing on his head." He pushed the control to nine G's. No one spoke. No one questioned that Stavers made every move deliberately. *A lesson to them all for a loudmouth.*

The air force technician moved to Stavers' side. "Sir, you're going to kill that man."

Stavers shut his eyes for a moment. Inside his head he squeezed, opened his eyes and smiled at the technician. "Sorry, sir," the man stammered. "I don't know what made me say that."

But they *were* losing him. Weinstein said but one word, "Doug," and sent him a wave of alarm. Stavers nodded in response to the soundless message, smiled again, and eased off the whirling speed of the centrifuge. He'd timed it perfectly. Ed Carson was still alive, but unconscious, with blood dribbling from his nose, eyes, mouth and ears. *And from his ass*, Stavers smiled to himself. *And when he pisses it will be crimson.*

He killed the power. Carson had been virtually without brain oxygen for five minutes. His circulatory system was in shambles. Medical technicians swarmed to him, rushed him away to the infirmary. "Is . . . is he dead?" Maxine Stark asked in a quavering voice.

"He's *brain* dead," Stavers answered her coldly. "His body is alive but Mr. Carson has left us. Permanently, I might add. You can file his name between cabbages and cowshit for all the good he's to us now. Of course, he won't be shooting off any smartmouth remarks any more, either."

The remainder of the demonstrations went quickly, smoothly, and thoroughly. No one made any wiseass remarks. When his top team departed Westover, they were more convinced than ever that Doug Stavers was in phenomenal physical shape and that he had become a more powerful force than ever before. Their "loyalty quotient" would never again be questioned.

"We get them all?"

Al Templin shook his head. "Almost. Cameron Vanderhoff from the European econoplex was almost dancing a jig when he found out he'd have a face-to-face with you. Lodovici Tosca balked; he didn't tell us but we've got a line in the Vatican that he got into a shouting match with the Pope. Claimed you were the Antichrist himself and he might lose his soul to you."

Stavers grinned. "It gets better all the time. I assume the Pope changed his mind."

"Threatened to toss Tosca out of the church on his ass."

"Schlemmel coming?"

"Yes, sir," Templin confirmed. "He's an old friend of yours, isn't he?"

Stavers nodded. "He worked with me and Skip. A very tough customer, and even more brilliant than tough."

"Very good. Bruno Zhukov agreed immediately. The

same with Marsha Pardue. We had doubts about her but she's on the slate for a real shot at the vice presidency. She figures that with all the media attention you're getting she can use this meeting with you to good advantage." Templin put away his notes. "We didn't get Chai Honwu. He pissed off somebody higher up in his government and he ate some bad food. Killed him. Big state funeral. Tom Kai-Shek is his replacement."

"Location?"

"This one was ticklish. We could have used the United Nations building in New York, but I don't want you even near that state until the LaGuardia episode is put to bed once and for all. Then, security at the UN is for shit. Plus about another hundred reasons for staying away from that septic tank of a city."

Stavers nodded, waiting. "I won't bother you with the entire list, but we narrowed it down to why there'd be so much in the way of heavyweight people gathering from around the world. We passed the word that it's a very hush-hush economic conference, that Stavers Industries is prepared to invest sixteen billion in a new world conservation and reforestation program. We can't keep the lid on that tight about you, Doug. So the best bet is to tell them something instead of rumors flying like migrating geese. The economy stuff is real, sounds real and meets all questions. We promised an announcement afterward, but no one knows *where* the meeting takes place."

"Who does know?"

"Right now, two people. Me and Marden."

"Make it three people."

"You're the third to know. Florida State University in Tallahassee. The people come in under the guise of professors and scientists. Normal, routine, everyday stuff. Enough high politics in the Florida capital for additional cover. You'll meet in the university where no one will ever expect you to gather."

"Can I guess?"

"I doubt it," Templin said confidently.

"Nuclear reactor research building sounds good," Stavers said. "High security, shielding, that sort of thing."

"Nope," Al Templin smiled.

"Okay, you've got feathers all around your mouth. Where?"

"Locker room of the girls' gymnasium. And *that* is *real* security!"

"When?"

"Tomorrow night. Seven o'clock. Big doings at the university so there's plenty of cover. You'll all be lost in the mobs."

"Who briefs them?"

"Me," Templin said. He hesitated a moment. "The lady doctor going to be there?"

"The lady doctor is *always* with me, Al."

"Yes, sir. You have anything special in mind?"

"Yep. When the session is over I want to be the first one out."

"No, sir."

"What the hell does that mean?"

"Anything big and fast leaving Tallahassee that same night attracts attention. I got bad vibes about that. You leave first, but no one recognizes you. Or Weinstein. After your meeting you become fat, grow a thick grey beard, you're an assistant football coach, and you're going fishing at Wakulla Springs, just south of the city, for two days. I've got half the rooms rented as well as half their boats, all in different names. After two days no one would ever believe you'd still be around. You'll go by chopper from Wakulla to a target field in Eglin's weapons test grounds. Security there is *real* grim, and you jet away from there." He frowned. "*I* don't even know where you're going."

"You're not supposed to yet."

"Yes, sir."

Stavers needed only a glance to see just how thorough Templin and his team had prepared the meeting. The lockers had been moved from their orderly rows against the walls and windows to provide a metal barrier against outside intrusion. To enter the room you walked through an S-curve of lockers, and well into the center you reached a large worktable with hard wooden chairs. There were plastic cups and several bottles of spring water and ashtrays. Nothing else. It wouldn't be a long meeting. Several men stood guard at the entrance to the toilets. If Marsha Pardue or Rebecca Weinstein went in, two security women went with them. If any of the men used the facilities, two security men accompanied them.

Stavers suffered a sudden, unexplained headache twenty minutes prior to the scheduled start of the meeting. Immediately, Weinstein was at his side. "What is it?" she asked quietly.

"Headache. Came on without warning. A real bitch. Feels like a wire around my forehead."

She studied him carefully "I've got one also."

He raised eyebrows. "Tell me you've also got a premonition. Something bad. *Real* bad."

"I have it."

"Get Al in here." As she left, he gestured to Marden. "Stop every one of those people coming in for the conference before they get more than ten feet inside this building. Separate them. Take no shit from anyone, Skip. Separate them and strip-search every one of them. Right down to bare skin. Then get jogging suits or sweatsuits for them. They do *not* put on their own clothing until we're well separated from them. *Go.*"

Templin brushed by Skip as he came running in answer to Weinstein's message. "There's a ringer in the crowd."

Templin didn't waste time asking questions that went nowhere. "Marden took off fast. I assume he's blocking entry."

"Yes. Separate everybody, strip search, take their clothes and anything they've got with them, bring them in here in sweatsuits provided by us."

"What's your *feeling*, Doug?"

"Bad; very bad, man. Heavy, black—" He shook his head.

"That's enough," Templin said, and he was gone on the run.

Weinstein came back with coffee in a thermos. "I brought our own." She poured for them both. "If we share the same dark feelings, that means someone's prepared to do you in at this meeting. I think we ought to call it off. Get us the hell out of here."

He shook his head. "Rebecca, you may have hung out around here for a couple of centuries, and star-hopped through a bunch of galaxies, and you've got heavy poundage for brains, but you don't know shit about handling people at this level. If I split now because we *feel*, even if we *know*, we've got trouble, it's running for cover. Rabbit time. And in no time at all you'll hear the hounds getting closer and closer."

"But—"

"No buts. Back off, woman. This is my kind of ball game. In another few moments we'll know who and what is coming down."

"But how can you—"

Templin appeared in the doorway. "We got him."

Rebecca Weinstein was surprised and in a rare moment she revealed her feelings. "You see, Doug? Why I *waited* all this time for you? You're right. I don't know how to handle this."

"Let's go. I'll show you."

They followed Templin to the shower room. Templin stopped just short of the entrance. "You read the specs on the people coming here, Doug?"

Stavers nodded. "The Chink. How much does he weigh?" he asked.

"One hundred sixty-two even," Templin said.

"What kind of physical shape?"

"Excellent. Martial arts black belts. Bunch of them. *And* a new doughnut," Templin answered, smiling.

"New doughnuts are bad news." Stavers *wasn't* smiling.

"Right. A Chinaman weighing 162 pounds, athletic, martial arts, excellent shape. All of a sudden he's got flab."

"Al, get to the point," Weinstein fretted.

"I did. You missed it," he chided her, and looked to Stavers. "You know what we got in here? An athletic, slender Chinaman with a doughnut he didn't have eight days ago."

Stavers grinned. "Very good, Al."

"What the devil are you two saying?" Weinstein demanded to know.

Templin half-bowed and extended his arm. "Exhibit A, my lady. Look for yourself." He pointed through the doorway.

Marden stood before the naked Tom Kai-Shek, his back pressed hard against a tile wall, legs wide apart, his arms spread wide, each wrist grasped by a burly security man and held against the wall. He might as well have been pinned like a giant bug.

"See?" Templin said to Weinstein. "A slender Chink with an ersatz doughnut." He laughed but there wasn't any humor in his voice.

"I still don't understand," Weinstein said.

"The doughnut," Templin repeated.

"False stomach," Stavers said.

"Bet a buck to a jelly roll," Templin said slowly, "it's flat strips overlaid, one atop the other, with masinex. My bet is type three. About ten times nitro yield."

"He'd have taken out *everybody* . . . killed every one of us," Weinstein said slowly.

"That's the general idea," Stavers told her. He might have been discussing a football game play for all the concern or excitement he showed.

"You'll pardon me," Templin said. He moved quickly to Kai-Shek. Abruptly he squeezed the Chinaman's nose, cutting off his breathing. Kai-Shek gasped and opened his mouth to suck in air. Instantly Marden moved in from the side and jammed a wooden block between the man's front teeth. It forced his mouth wider.

"Tape his hands behind him," Templin ordered. "Tape *and* wire." Two men moved in quickly, bent Kai-Shek forward and bound his wrists and fingers together.

Templin turned to another man. "You got that spreader bar? Over here." The man handed Templin a steel bar four feet long; at each end was a steel clamp, still open. Templin bent down, snapped a clamp about each ankle, locking the naked man's legs wide apart.

Templin returned to Stavers and Weinstein. "Here's the story. He's got the masinex under that false skin. I know how these people work. It's a suicide run; means if he does his job his family lives top dog the rest of their lives for his service to home and country. He doesn't do his job, they all die very slowly." Templin looked directly at Kai-Shek. "They're going to die very slowly."

He pointed to Kai-Shek's stomach bulge. "They always have two ways to set it off. He can reach hard against his stomach and squeeze and set off the detonator. He'll also have a molar trigger. If he bites down real hard, he'll compress an aluminum tooth and that will close the contact. A hearing-aid battery, something like that, in another tooth, gives enough juice to detonate the masinex. But right now, he can't squeeze anything with his hands secured. He can't bite down. And he can't belly flop or throw himself against the sharp end of a table or chair because he can't move with his legs apart and his hands behind him. So we're safe."

"Kill him," Weinstein said abruptly.

Stavers laughed. "The tigress extends her claws. Nah, that's a dumb move, Rebecca. He's just one of two they set up."

"*What?*"

"You'll see. Al, put a piece on that table, there. Revolver. Good. Remove two rounds. It's double-action, right?" Templin nodded, *yes*. "Right. Okay. I want the hammer to fall on empty chambers the first two times the trigger's pulled. The third time is fun and games."

Stavers waited until Templin set up the .38 Special. "Okay, bring in the rest of them," Stavers ordered.

They came in, each flanked by a muscular escort, moving to the table in the locker room center. They stared at the naked Chinaman spread-eagled and splayed against the wall.

Marden grinned. "They sure look different when you take away their fancy duds. Sweatsuits must be democratic. Everyone's the same as everyone else."

Marden laughed alone. Tension hung heavy in the room. Cameron Vanderhoff was an old master at politics and a survivor of diplomatic convolutions. There's a time for the fancy and a time for the plain, and this was clearly the latter.

"This is a strange meeting, Mr. Stavers," he said calmly.

"Stranger than you might believe, Vanderhoff," Stavers said easily. "It was *supposed* to be a meeting. Cards on the table, that sort of old tradition. But we discovered it was really a bushwhacking party."

"I don't know what the hell you're talking about!" Marsha Pardue's voice was shrill, her face white with anger. Stavers and Weinstein glanced at one another. Their eyes told them what words were needed for others. *Vanderhoff's clean. This Pardue woman is clean. She's too wild with anger to be faking it.*

"Answer me, damnit!" Pardue shouted to Stavers. "Why were we put through this . . . this indignity! I came here openly and honestly and—"

"So did we, Miss Pardue," Stavers told her. "But not everybody did. You see our Chinese friend there?"

She glanced again at the naked man. Her voice toned down as she turned back to Stavers. "That's not Chai Honwu," she said. "I don't understand—"

"Last-minute replacement, really," Stavers answered. "He's an assassin. And I should add for the benefit of all of you, all of us, everyone here, he showed up to kill us *all*." Stavers pointed. "See that belly bulge? There's enough explosives in there to level this building. With us in it, I might add."

Harvey Schlemmel stood relaxed between his guards. Stavers smiled to himself. Harv was of the same breed as himself or Skip Marden. Good as these guards were, Harv Schlemmel could take them both in less than three seconds. *But he's not even tensed up. It's not Harv. So that leaves Zhukov or the Pope's bully boy.*

"Interesting." They looked at Zhukov, arms folded across his chest. "I would have expected a Japanese," the Russian went on. "You understand, kamikazes and that sort of nationalistic rubbish. But not a Chinese. Not enough, how would they say it in London? Not enough pomp and circumstance. The Chinese just love to die when there's a lot of ceremony going on."

"*Kill him!*" Lodovici Tosca shouted. The Italian's face was dark red from anger and frustration. "Kill him, I say! He's put all our lives at stake, so why does he still live? Kill him!"

"Hell, kill him yourself," Stavers said, his words strangely calm.

Tosca glared wildly at Stavers; then, in a swift and agile motion, he ducked away from his guards and threw himself at the table; clutching the revolver left there by Templin. He only glanced at Kai-Shek for an instant, then spun about to face Stavers, the gun aimed at Stavers' heart.

"You waited too long!" he shouted. "For the glory of God, for—"

He pulled the trigger, his face a mixture of stunned surprise and outrage as the hammer clicked on the empty chamber. He squeezed again, and once more the metallic click sounded. Tosca let out an animal cry, whirled about and pulled the trigger rapidly three times, and each time a shot boomed in the enclosed room.

Each time a lead slug ripped directly into the midriff of Tom Kai-Shek, *directly through the plastic explosives.*

Tosca lifted the gun, staring in disbelief at the gun and then at Kai-Shek, blood spurting from his body. He fell forward, his legs held rigidly wide by the spreader bar.

"Get him!" Templin called out. Two men had already moved in, catching the body and lowering it gently to the floor.

"You blew it, Cardinal," Stavers told the shaking Italian. "That gun's no good for setting off plastique like masinex. You need an electrical charge, asshole."

"I'll kill you!" Tosca shrieked, eyes wild. He leveled the shaking gun at Stavers. "There's one more bullet left!"

Stavers walked slowly toward the screaming man. "You can't do it," he said quietly. "You can't kill me. You're unclean, Tosca. The demon rides in you. You're filth. You know that. You're a pawn of Lucifer. Filth." Stavers stood directly before Lodovici Tosca, and in his mind he squeezed, hard, driving the pressure at the man before him. Tosca blinked repeatedly, pale, shaking worse than before. "Cleanse yourself, Lodovici. You must cleanse yourself to save your soul from hell. Do it, Lodovici. For Christ and the Father, *do it now!*"

"Yes, *yes!*" Tosca howled. He jammed the muzzle into his mouth and squeezed the trigger.

Brains, bones, flesh and blood sprayed across the room.

Stavers turned to his "guests."

"I don't take kindly to someone trying to murder me. That Chinaman was a professional assassin. He and that filth from Rome were in this deal from the word go. That they would also have killed *you* doesn't matter to me. I want you to go back to your governments. Tell them anything you want, but above all, tell them never to fuck with me again, is that clear? Because if you mess with me or my plans again, if anyone pulls this bullshit, I make you a promise. The big birds will fly. Oh, not all. But enough of the missiles with thermonukes, in enough right places, so you won't be able to keep from firing back. And that's the third world war and a nuclear party for *everybody*. Got it?" He nodded to Templin. "Get them the hell out of my sight."

"Wait a minute," a voice called out. Stavers knew before he looked that it would be Harv Schlemmel. The Israeli wasn't upset or even piqued. "How'd you do that, old friend?" he asked Stavers.

They all knew his reference was to Tosca blowing away the top and back of his head when he could have killed Stavers.

"Interesting, wasn't it, Harv?" Stavers said.

"You were always good," Schlemmel said, smiling, "but this one, wow."

"Got any guesses, Harv?"

"Damn right."

"Do me a favor. For old time's sake."

"Name it. I owe you."

"Take a detour on the way home, Harv. Stop off in Rome. See the Pope. Have a friendly chat with the old man. Tell him what happened here. Tell him *how* it all came down. Tell him anything you want, but most of all, tell the old buzzard that if he fucks with me ever again, there's a one-megatonner in his front yard that turns the Vatican and the local countryside into good old radioactive steam."

"I'll do that, Doug."

"I figured you might. I appreciate it, Harv."

"*Hals und beinbruch*, buddy."

"The fishing trip is off, Al. Send some doubles for us," Stavers said. "Do whatever you must to fill out the plan you had. I've got a hunch someone knows it, and Wakulla Springs has some company in waiting."

They walked rapidly through an underground tunnel beneath the FSU campus; Stavers, Weinstein, Marden and Templin.

Templin nodded. He was still wild with anger at himself for not picking up sooner on the assassination attempt that had come so incredibly close to succeeding. And it kept getting worse; more and more the fanatics in power roles were taking dead aim at Douglas Stavers. He was gaining too much power, too much strength. He'd become a world figure and apple carts were already toppling in high places.

"I'll take care of it," he said quickly. "Look, I'm *pleading* with you, Doug. Call off this crazy showtime gig you're planning for the church scene. Goddamnit, you're setting yourself up for—"

"Hey, it was *your* idea, asshole," Marden broke into his words. "Remember? You wanted him to be *visible*, for Christ's sake."

"There's no time now to argue. We're going through with our plans. I'm making some changes. You'll find out about them in due time, Al. Right now, I want the hell out of here. It's great to be on campus and all that crap but—" He shook his head. "Never mind. What's the transport?"

"End of the tunnel. Party bus."

"Party bus?" Weinstein queried.

"Uh huh. There's the big game. Half the campus is stoned or drunk out of their minds," Templin replied. "Parties everywhere. A lot of the kids hire buses and motor homes with drivers. That way they carouse on the run and don't get hit for drunk driving. I've got a bus, special job, armored and armorglass, and a group of people who work for us. They'll be singing and drunk, but not really. They'll head for Pensacola. Big party jam there. On the way, when it's clear—and I'll have a chopper upstairs to be sure—the bus cuts off the interstate and takes a road through the restricted area in the Eglin complex. A Skua's waiting for you there."

They reached the stairway that would take them to the bus. Templin stopped Stavers at the last moment. "If I don't ask you I'll go crazy. What that Israeli said to you. It was German, wasn't it?"

"Sure was, Al."

"But what did it mean?"

"*Hals und beinbruch.* Break your neck and a leg. It's an old pilot's way of wishing a friend good luck, and come home safe. So long, Al."

"Don't take any wooden nickels, Doug," Templin called out. He watched the bus roar off into the night.

Three hours later they were in the Skua, the nose-wheel coming off the long Eglin runway smoothly. They boomed into the night sky, two F-15 fighters sailing with them into the high dark. At fifty-four thousand feet, following Stavers' last-minute change in plans and schedules, the F-15s held course as the Skua eased off to the right, heading northwest.

"No more waiting," Stavers told Weinstein. "I want a good steak and a beer, and a couple of hours sleep, and when we get to Mannheim we kick Adolf in the ass and twist his mind a couple of times. Right after we deliver him, all hell will be breaking loose."

"And that," Weinstein smiled, "is just the beginning."

Chapter 24

"He's coming out of it."

"He's steaming like a barbecued porker. Jesus, it's like a storm sewer grating on a cold night."

"That's not him, dummy. It's the heat exchange, and—"

"I know what it is. It just seemed like the right thing to say."

"You think," Stavers said slowly to Rebecca Weinstein, "anybody will ever thank us for bringing *the* Adolf Hitler back to real, breathing, living, talking, walking life?"

"To paraphrase one of your great writers, Doug," she answered, smiling, "all the world loves a madman."

Skip Marden, face hidden beneath his surgical mask and cap, leaned down for a better look at the human form within whom life forces beat and swirled faster and faster. Oxygen enriched cells long on a starvation diet. Molecules stirred, organs trembled, fluids burbled; thousands and then millions of processes, most of them invisible to the human eye, extracted from "frozen life/death" the man who had launched the best of the civilized world on its path of savage immolation.

"It's hard to believe," Marden said abruptly, then lapsed into unexpected silence.

"What's hard to believe?" Stavers queried.

"All the things I've read about Adolf Hitler," Marden said. "The incredible way he took a country broke and bleeding and dragged it out of the mud. Built it up. Whipped people left and right to do what he wanted.

Crawled into their minds. That aura of Hitler I've heard so much about. I've talked to former German soldiers, pilots; even their generals. They said his aura was *real.* You walked into a room where Hitler was waiting and he slammed into your mind like a wet towel snapping at your ass."

"He's eloquent enough," Weinstein said admiringly to Stavers.

"What's your first impression now?" Stavers asked Marden.

Marden didn't answer for the moment. The figure in the medical chrysalis for the past several hours had twitched; muscles achingly returning to life and miniscule movement, all functions arising from autonomic systems "coming back on line." There had been the agonizingly dreadful moments of learning whether the sensitive nudibranches of the alveolar system would still function after being so long in deep freeze. That supersensitive miracle of the exchange of gases, of oxygen highly enriched pouring into the system, stirring exquisite leaves and filaments to accept life-giving oxygen while yielding up for exhalation and throwaway gases clouded with the debris collected throughout the body from returning streams and rivulets of blood. A single glop of phlegm could kill this man.

And yet it was working. Tissues, nerves, muscles, neuronic connections, electrical impulses, pressure changes, enzymes, proteins, sodium and potassium and hundreds of other elements so critical to functioning had never really been dead but "on hold." Weinstein, drawing on long-established practices unknown to doctors anywhere else on the planet, had sent a constant trickle of electrical spasms through the entire body, a feathery stimulation to which the tissues and all their components responded. It was much like trying to revive an ancient river and its thousands of tiny tributaries. The human body is in reality an oblongated bag of liquids, but they've all got to flow in synchronous and coordinated movement so their many parts and pieces can march to the same tune of life.

Fingers twitched, then curled. Eyelids fluttered in

the safety of unconsciousness. Toes moved, muscles throbbed gently.

Hitler's eyes opened, closed; they opened again, but he was still unseeing. Too early yet for the optic system to function. "It's like starting a car on a morning when the temperature's below zero and the battery's dead," Marden said with simple but unerring accuracy.

"The lady's got the battery charged," Stavers chided him.

"So I see." He peered closer. "Doc, how long before he climbs the ice mountain back to knowing what's going on?"

"I presume you mean brain function?"

"I mean he'll know enough to piss into a urinal instead of all over himself," Marden cracked.

"What we're doing either works or it won't," she said in a flat tone. "There's no halfway margin as best as I can tell."

"So if he comes out of it he'll be as sharp as he ever was?"

She nodded. "Yes."

"And if he doesn't?"

"Then he'll die. Let me put it another way. It's a full black or white and no grey areas. He won't come partially out of brain stasis. Then we'd have a walking vegetable on our hands. But," she stressed, "that won't happen. If he *doesn't* emerge, then his brain will . . ." she sought the proper wording, "well, it will have the equivalent of a complete short-circuit."

"All lights out for good, huh?" Marden asked again.

"Lights out; yes," Weinstein confirmed.

"How much longer does he go through this routine? I mean, is there a performance envelope for the body and the brain?" Weinstein looked with a new touch of respect at Marden.

"There is. We'll know any moment, and—"

"It's playtime," Stavers broke in as Adolf Hitler opened his eyes.

Weinstein bent closer. *Perfect! Eyes clear. He's focusing on me. There; he's moving his eyes. Dilation and contraction, good movement. He's studying Doug. Now*

Marden. Excellent! Questions and negative responses.

She stood erect. "We owe ourselves a bottle of champagne."

"Bingo," Marden said with admiration for Weinstein.

"Rebecca, you're fluent in his lingo. You better do the talking," Stavers suggested.

She leaned slightly closer to Hitler, now fully alert, trying to remember. His memory had to span back to 1944 but in terms of brain function there was no conscious time between when he was "iced" and this moment of emergence.

"*Mein Fuehrer*," she said softly.

The corner of his mouth twitched in the hint of a smile. She knew memories were flooding back. "*Fraulein* . . ." he said weakly.

"Fuck you," Marden said, his face mask removed. He grinned broadly.

Weinstein shot him an angry look. Marden smiled at her and held up his middle finger. "Don't push it, Doc. He may be a great medical triumph to you but he's still what he always was to *me*."

Stavers had his mask off as well. He turned to Marden and spoke in an angry stream of Japanese. Weinstein listened; she nodded in agreement. They all three understood and spoke Japanese. Hitler didn't. He knew enough English to recognize words and phrases, but not the Oriental language. And if the Nazi leader's memory still put out on all eight cylinders, the Japanese would at least represent the language of a wartime ally.

Not that it would matter for very long. Marden followed Stavers' instructions and flipped on the music. Hidden speakers sent classical Wagner softly through the room as a backdrop. *More conditioning*, Weinstein smiled.

Hitler was asking questions. Not getting his replies, he began demanding answers. *Excellent. He's still the absolute master of all about him, so he thinks.*

She turned to Stavers and Marden, shouting at them in German, gesturing angrily. All part of the setup. Stavers and Marden turned to leave. As they exited through one door, several men and women entered through another. Two wore hospital outfits. The others wore various German military uniforms. They all spoke perfect German, and they brought with them food and drinks, carefully researched to duplicate Hitler's favorite during the peak of his power.

There's nothing like fawning over a man to let him believe he's still top dog.

Weinstein smiled to herself. The howling would come soon enough.

Stavers and Marden dropped heavily into padded lounge chairs overlooking a sea of Canadian hills and forests. The fourth floor of the Mannheim center was reserved for living quarters and the relaxation of its working staff and frequent visitors. It had been a long time since the two friends had this kind of a quiet moment together, and they willingly eschewed fine whiskey and gourmet food. They chowed down on hamburgers and onions, drank beer straight from Budweiser cans, and followed with Stavers' favorite Portofino cigars, their shoes kicked off and feet resting high on ottomans before them.

"The lady doctor handles it from now on?" Marden asked the other man.

"Yep. She'll razzle-dazzle the old boy. Bow and scrape like a good Nazi broad; that sort of shit. Flatter his ego, but at the same time let him know he's an alien stumbling through a very scary and strange forest."

"You mean the time jump. From 1944 to now."

"Hell, yes. It's been a half-century, Skip. Adolf's boys in boots and shiny caps not only lost the war, and our Fuehrer expected that, but he's coming into a world he won't believe. It's a *real* time jump when you think about it." Stavers laughed. "Rebecca's got some great film and video from Israel. When Adolf sees a *Jewish* army and air force strong enough to take on *all* the Arab nations combined, and kick ass from Africa to Asia, he's going to wonder what the hell *really* happened."

Marden crumpled a beer can and popped another. "How about the Fourth Reich shit?"

Stavers shrugged and smiled. "Hitler will believe Rebecca is part of the secret Nazi movement that's been underground all this time, and now it's their chance to take over again. All they've been waiting for is for dear old Adolf to bubble up from deepfreeze. First," Stavers began ticking off the programming to which Hitler was even then being subjected, "she'll let him see how the war ended. Germany in ruins, Russian soldiers tearing the heart out of Berlin. We've got some good footage of Russian soldiers gang-raping German women. It's real enough. The Russians rounded up a whole mob of Germany's top ace fighter pilots, along with their wives and daughters, and then they gang-raped every female in the group, from little kids to their mothers, and made the pilots watch it all."

"*Der Fuehrer* should get a kick out of that," Marden grinned. "A kick, but not too much pleasure."

Stavers nodded. "Rebecca really knows how to handle this stuff. After she shows him a Germany demolished and a communist sweep of half the world, she hits him with the atomic bombings of Japan. Some wild footage inside those cities right after the bombs went off. She'll do the run right on up through the big ICBM's. It's cut back and forth. She'll show him films of himself watching V-2 rockets being launched, then she'll cut to the big ICBM's and show him hydrogen bombs being tested, and tell the crazy son of a bitch how brilliant he was in laying the groundwork for the future he's in right now. Because it was Hitler who finally gave the full support for the Peenemunde crowd to develop the V-2. That's what's critical about this. To establish the link in Hitler's mind that what's happening today is a direct result of what *he* did a long time ago. He won't feel so completely separated."

"I wonder," Marden mused aloud, "how he'll react to watching men walking on the moon."

"Shit, he'll believe *he* was responsible," Stavers answered quickly. "After all, it was Hitler's V-2 that started the whole rocket program, remember? The crazy bastard will end up taking all the credit, which is what we want."

"How long do we keep him?"

"Not very long," Stavers said with a grimace. "There's a kind of stink about him you can *feel*—"

"I got my own feeling," Marden broke in. He sat up abruptly, leaning forward, his expression suddenly serious. "You know something? This ain't no joke either, Doug. I had to restrain myself before. When we watched that fucker coming out of his bad dreams. He looked at me and I could almost feel worms crawling around inside my head. Like he judged me as some lowlife scum, an insect, and he was on the same level as God."

Stavers studied his friend. "He's had that effect on a lot of people. They were scared shitless of him."

"I wasn't *scared* of him, goddamnit. I had to hold myself *back*. I've heard so much of his aura, how he dominates people through his psyche, and I could feel that, too. But I had this picture in my mind, holy shit, but it was real, of two fingers of one hand stuck as far up his nose as I could reach and with my other hand I was slowly twisting his head until I busted his whole neck. I could almost feel it happening."

"You're a nasty fucker," Stavers grinned.

"I'm serious," Marden insisted.

"No, I know what you mean," Stavers said, becoming serious for the moment. "It was a hell of a temptation."

Marden studied Stavers. "You felt it, too?"

"Wouldn't *you* like to be the man who personally tore out the heart of Adolf Hitler?" Stavers asked.

"Yeah." Marden leaned back and smiled. "And I'd cook his fucking heart on a stick over a fire and I'd eat it, too."

Stavers didn't answer for a few moments. He watched a round orange moon dragging itself higher than the horizon, and he thought of that moon growing larger in the sky as one day, soon, he would be leaving the world of this horizon and heading out toward that lifeless orb. He pushed himself back to the moment.

"I guess you would," Stavers responded finally to Marden's remarks. "Probably paint your face like some fucking aborigine, too."

"You bet," Marden chuckled.

"Well, we'll do better than that. Rebecca winds him up like a tinker toy for three days and nights. By the time she's through he'll be raging again that traitors undercut his shot at running the world. The same old shit, but he'll believe it. The whole time he's getting caught up on current events one-oh-one, he's getting just enough of that ersatz etorphin to cement his beliefs and make him a bit wilder than he already is."

"You've never told me what we do with him," Marden said.

"You'll see soon enough. We've got to be sure that Russia and communism are Hitler's proof of Satan taking control of the world. That sort of stuff. And only Hitler and the might of the Fourth Reich can save the world and the innocent Germans from the communists and their power tool, the Jewish missile mob in Israel. We want Hitler absolutely to believe that there's a few million Germans ready to rise up, this time with hydrogen bombs instead of just panzers and Stukas."

Stavers motioned for another beer and received the toss from Marden. "Then we wrap it up. Our own team is already spreading the word that an incredible event is about to take place. We'll drop all kinds of rumors around—"

"You're going to tell them about giving back their loonie?"

Stavers laughed. "We'll hint at it. And when everybody is hanging by their fingernails to know just what's *really* going on, we let them know that the big surprise is on its way. It's delivery time."

"Damn, I'd love to be there in Moscow when you deliver that son of a bitch to the Russians!"

Stavers smiled. He didn't answer or respond to Marden's last remark. Moscow, hell.

Roberto Diaz and Al Templin handled the job personally. They controlled enough media in the newspapers, television satellite nets and other press to let the world know something *very* big was coming down. They told the world to start looking to Frankfurt. Especially the airport at Frankfurt, headquarters for Germany's internationally-reaching airlines, Lufthansa. A big field. A hub for the world. Then they flew in top newsmen. Half the city began to crowd in toward the airport on the selected night. The Germans grew restless, upset, ill at ease as loudspeakers atop trucks driven to the field without any advance notice began to play, at ear-hammering volume, the favorite martial music of wartime Germany. Barely discernible, and mostly on a subliminal basis, was the voice of Adolf Hitler in his shrill calls to the German people to overcome all their enemies.

It had to be timed *just* right. Diaz and Templin had shelled out money freely. As the crowds pressed into the airport the roads behind them began to close. Trees and power poles fell across the roadways. Abandoned trucks, unable to run, littered the highways. Those who were in would remain until the last moment.

Then it was time to lower the boom.

The telephone rang in the control tower of Frankfurt airport. "In a few minutes you will hear from the captain of a 747 inbound to Frankfurt. His call sign will be One Niner Four Four. That machine will make a straight-in approach to your main runway. The pilot will not respond to any orders from you. He will come straight in and land no matter what other aircraft you are working. Please understand I mean what I say." The speaker ignored the protests and interruptions. "Be quiet. Any moment now you will see that aircraft's lights and the pilot will call you. After landing he will taxi directly before the terminal. Your ground control frequency will be hearing from several drivers who are setting up a welcoming committee. They will have a platform and a public address system waiting for the 747's passenger. That is all."

In the background, Heinrich Koenig, tower manager for the first night shift, heard the first call from the speakers. "Frankfurt Approach, 747 One Niner Four Four with you, transmitting on both Approach and Tower frequencies. We are on a straight-in for your main runway. Herr Koenig has already been informed of our approach and landing and our taxi position when we are on the ground. Please confirm. Over."

Dozens of pilots in other aircraft looked quizzically at one another. What the hell was this? In the distance they saw the lights of a dozen airliners approaching Frankfurt, but one carried additional lights, a huge twinkling torch approaching in a steady descent.

Koenig shouted into his phone. "Wait a moment! Just a moment! Who is this passenger? You have no right to do this! Tell your pilot to turn away!"

A calm voice responded to his near-hysteria. "Herr Koenig, I will not say this again. The 747 *will* make its approach as stated. It will *not* turn. After it lands, and taxis to the terminal, it will shut down. You may do anything you wish then. The passenger will leave the aircraft and he will go to the public-address podium."

"But who is this passenger?" Koenig yelled.

He heard a low chuckle in his earpiece. "Why, the Fuehrer, of course, my dear Koenig. He has come home at last."

The phone went dead. Koenig looked at the useless set in his hand. "Crazy bastard . . ."

A controller appeared in his doorway. "Sir! We've got a 747 coming straight in and he refuses to veer from his approach! We have a problem!"

"Clear all aircraft from landing! Have them break away!" Koenig shouted. "And get all other aircraft off the runways and clear the taxiway to the terminal. *And call security!*" He gestured wildly. "*Nein, nein!* Attend to the aircraft. I will call security myself!"

Stavers, Marden and Weinstein watched the satellite feed from Frankfurt. It went off beautifully. The 747 drilled straight down final approach, lights and strobes blazing furiously as it landed feather-light. It rolled to the end of the runway, turned off to the main taxiway and taxied to a stop before the center of the terminal building. Dozens of security vehicles and crash trucks, red and blue and amber lights flashing, mixed with and surrounded a long flatbed trailer on which stood a speaker's podium and microphones.

A ramp lowered from the aft belly of the 747. Lights played immediately on the ramp. An escalator began moving. Cameras located within and atop the terminal building, and from newstrucks, zeroed in with zoom lenses on the moving stairway. The boots of a man appeared, and then he came into full view, standing straight, erect in military posture, head held high, in gleaming uniform and a swastika armband. He stepped away from the escalator and walked without wavering to the flatbed truck. Security guards rushing to apprehend the stranger stopped in their tracks, staring in disbelief, shocked and stunned as Hitler's eyes struck them with physical force. They melted back, speechless.

Adolf Hitler, Reichsfuehrer, took the speaker's stand. He looked left and right and then straight ahead. The thousands of people seemed unable to move. Disbelief cemented their feet and their thoughts.

And then Hitler began to speak, his voice low at first, his gestures tentative, and his right arm, half-circled before him, began to move up and down in a manner most Germans had seen only in the old films of a war many decades before.

Then the riot began . . .

"So you see it now, don't you?" Stavers asked Marden. "All this time you figured we'd deliver him to Moscow. Offer him up to the Russians so *they* could put him on trial."

"I never figured you'd send him to *Germany*," Marden answered, still amazed at what he'd seen.

"Sure, because it seemed the craziest thing to do. But look at it this way. The whole world has seen Adolf Hitler *in Germany*. The Germans have him. They'll have to verify that he's real. And that will tie up that country and all of Europe in the biggest damn knot you ever saw, and *then* the German government will have to put him on trial for crimes committed against his own country. In the meantime, the Russians will be raising every kind of hell that *they* want him, and the Israelis are liable to do *anything* to get him . . ."

"Jesus," Marden said.

"Well, almost, but not quite," Stavers laughed.

"You two all through?" Weinstein broke in. They turned to look at her. She tapped her wristwatch.

"The clock runs, my friends. We've got a schedule to keep and a lot of traveling ahead of us."

"Where to, Doc?" Marden asked.

"First, France. Then, South Carolina. And from there, straight south to the Kennedy Space Center."

"And then?" Marden asked again.

For answer, Rebecca Weinstein pointed.

Straight up.

Chapter 25

Karldan Tai.

Through the years—*through the decades and the centuries*—she had taken many names, some ordinary, others befitting regal standing, still others dictated by ethnic cloaks or even periods of conquest enveloping whatever land on which she stood at any particular time. She had been married more times than she recalled, and on more than one occasion she had used her secret, futuristic medical knowledge to bring on "accidents" or "illnesses" that made her a widow and possessed of considerable wealth. From her first moments of being stranded on a planet that only sporadically and remotely had advanced beyond the aborigine stage, she understood the meaning and the necessity that "money spells power."

Now it was all coming together. Now it had reached that peak where the aborigines had thrown away their spears and clubs and advanced to computers, jets, rockets, electronics and hydrogen bombs. The natives of this world they called Earth were constantly a brawling, snarling, aggressive, abrasive and combative lot, and that was all to her advantage. It is not the cow grinding grass in its molars that changes the world; one needs hungry, angry, jealous, possessive savages to break free and begin the climb upward to a world of technological prowess.

It served her best from the beginning of this final century to become and to remain Doctor Rebecca Weinstein. *Karldan Tai* had been pushed far back into the recesses of her mind, to be recalled only within the privacy of her own thoughts and *never* to be spoken aloud, unless that momentary slip led to questions she could not easily answer. For there were too many periods in this turbulent history when these people fought witches, demons, trolls and other creatures their psychotic fears brought to reality—and horribly oppressive times when torture and mass killing became their overwhelming occupation.

She threaded her way through these perilous moments by dint of her superb medical knowledge. Medical miracles applied to a ruling despot's family is a marvelous guarantee of despotic protection. Then came the current century and she made her decision to "become" a brilliant Jewess surgeon, with a history crafted artfully and beyond suspicion. Her skills at modifying records and ancient books guaranteed the protective lineage of parentage; those she found unable to control suffered maladies that quickly claimed their lives.

She knew from past experience that the many elements necessary for her to leave this planet and voyage to the biting winds and rockstrewn dunes of Mars would all come together in a headlong, even a dizzying rush, a tremendous implosion of technology and timing. As the world emerged from that last great war that spawned what she had waited for all this time, the great machines and the computers that sped man beyond his atmosphere, she concentrated her search for the specific type of human required to bring the *arbatik* to the genetic-triggered generation of power.

The search was dreary, wearing and seemingly endless—and she had no control over whom to select. That element lay entirely beyond her control. *Who* was a gods' throw of the dice, a slim genetic needle in the vast human pool. Then she began to notice the signs for which she had searched so long, the elements of one man who performed in so many different ways against what should have been insurmountable odds against his survival. Daring, skill, even genius; incredible adaptability. A mind so powerful he generated his own natural aura of domination over people about him. The more she studied Doug Stavers, the more she learned, the more she rushed headlong into a dichotomy of selection *and— well, there's no way around it. The word is revulsion.*

Strange, the way the genetic dice came together with positive and negative in this one human. In many ways Douglas Stavers was amazingly akin to many of her own kind. The similarities abounded the deeper she studied Stavers from afar, delved into his records, used all her wiles and cunning to obtain his medical histories. She knew more about this man than he knew about himself, for she had the knowledge of where and how to pry into what he truly was; a study of *self* he could never have known, let alone conducted.

If she had *her* choice in the matter she would have dismissed Stavers from even the slightest relationship to her future. She admired his survivability. Her own people needed that very same talent when confronted with lethal, unpredictable situations on different planets. But they followed an unbreakable rule: do what is necessary to survive and *only* what is necessary to sustain survival.

Killing was the law of the animal universe, but in all races, in all fauna, there existed a natural law. Killing for the sake of killing was so disgustingly wasteful it went against the grain of the *future*. Killing for the pleasure of the kill, especially against the helpless, vanished from the social mores of every advanced race they ever encountered. And they were *all* advanced races that did *not* permit wanton brutality or killing, for those that permitted such conduct inevitably destroyed themselves.

This world might do the same. It was a planet of unbridled savagery, of lustful killing, torture, hate, treachery, mass murder, and above all, conscienceless administration of death to meet selfish means.

She sighed. She had just described Doug Stavers. Oh, there had been those moments when he became human, when a woman had penetrated that leathery exterior and gentled him. But when he had been hurt through the loss of that woman, he adjudged all the world responsible for his pain and he left nothing undone to assuage his own misery through a noncaring, utterly indifferent destruction of other advanced life forms. *People.*

Doug Stavers had the fire. But not the warmth. Yet, she had no choice. He was the only lifeboat aboard the sinking ship and she must immerse herself in human garbage in order to render the aid her own people needed. She would, she *had*, done everything needed to meet her goals. Doug Stavers was simply a tool; a walking, talking, performing instrument.

And yet, she knew that when her mission was accomplished, she could not kill this man, no matter how great her own conviction this world, and others, might benefit from his non-existence. The moral grain of her people dictated that rule. *But there was work to do and her people to save.*

So Dr. Rebecca Weinstein began her moves to slip within the tight, suspicious and dangerously defended confines of the "inner circle of Doug Stavers." She accomplished her goal through several means, chief among them her ability to have her name and records brought before Stavers and his lead staff, and, her unquestioned record as a brilliant, innovative doctor and surgeon. To all the world she was still in her thirties, with vast experience, capable of speaking every major language of the planet, *and* free to join the Stavers' inner sanctum.

Rebecca Weinstein now initiated the most complex and the most dangerous part of her program. Long before this moment she had altered records in several cities about the world relevant to the "great yellow diamond," spoken of with reverence as The Messiah Stone. During the years prior to the Second World War she had moved with speed, daring and great skills in arranging the records of the diamond cutters in Europe, of bringing to the table an actual great yellow diamond to be sliced and shaped into the world's first radiant cut, when all along she only was aware the diamond was to be cut into the exact same shape as the *arbatik* that she knew had been created in that shape and size, thousands of years before. There are times when events shoulder aside and ride roughshod on the best of plans, and Weinstein knew she could not keep the diamond—the *arbatik*—from the possession of the Roumanians who finally brought the incredible stone as a gift to none other than Adolf Hitler. There, at least, its possession was secure.

Mystery, confusion and manipulation; Rebecca Weinstein wove her incredibly delicate balancing act to bring together powerful forces and events so they would create what she needed so desperately—a flight to Mars, where a huge starship and its remaining crew had waited two thousand years for her return.

Doug Stavers must be raised from relative obscurity to the public and the political officials of worldwide governments to an individual recognizable instantly by such individuals and groups. This carried with it the danger that he would be perceived as a threat to many of these same power groups, but the danger could not be avoided and must be met head-on, a skill that required the ingenious abilities of Stavers. To say nothing of his miraculous survival skills!

Concurrently with this program, Weinstein began to orchestrate his recognition as a figure of enormous theological power. Thus was created the Church of the Ascension, masterminded from its beginnings by Weinstein. For she needed to raise Stavers to unprecedented heights where hundreds of millions of people would accept him as having some sort of divine connection with God—and whatever God was involved mattered little; this planet had an overabundance of such deities. Ernst Patschke had long before fled Hitler's bunker in the savage pyre of devastation wrought by invading Russians, but he had done so with possession of that same *arbatik*, still regarded as a meteoric godstone with divine powers. Patschke had initiated an enormous religious movement in India, and his Asian sweep was well underway to overflowing proportions when *his* skills smashed headlong into those of Doug Stavers.

The result, as Weinstein had predicted as well as helped, was inevitable. The stronger must survive and

Stavers was the ultimate survivor. Patschke tumbled ignominously into death. The Vatican with a powerful military strike team of do-or-die zealots ended with the latter; they died. And other powerful forces of other nations also fell headless and shattered before the enormous momentum of Stavers in pursuit of whatever goal he cherished the most at any particular time.

Now, *now* must come the ultimate, the exquisite, the perfect orchestration of men, power, governments *and time*; now Rebecca Weinstein must weave a brain-blinding tapestry of moving a vast chessboard of power-plays to a single final moment with a countdown running to zero and *all* the players in their proper places.

The Church of the Ascension was rattling theological cages the world over. More specifically, it shook to the cellars and the rafters the powerful religious organizations from the Vatican to the Asian temples. It threatened their political power, their sociological control of their masses, their continued accumulation of land, property and liquid assets. That must draw to its inevitable conclusion. The theological powers-that-be must eliminate Doug Stavers.

That, however, wasn't enough. Weinstein knew they must tip their hand openly rather than continued covert assaults of murder against Stavers. To commit openly was an act so drastic they must be accepted in the most drastic manner: might is right.

Her first step was to create and build Ascension. That came about through power plays of political, financial and diplomatic avenues. Almost all peoples await eagerly the arrival in their midst of some new messiah, supposed or real. Weinstein knew from her experience on this world, and others, that a planetary population faced with extinction from the horrific attention of atomic and hydrogen bombs, biological weapons, chemical savagery, controlled starvation and famine, will always seek its shield in the form of some new spiritual salvation. *Wouldst thou protect us from the savageries of Satan?*

Weinstein smiled with the question that came in many languages and in many wordforms. To use the spirit of this world, the answer came clearly: *You bet your sweet ass I will. Just get on your knees and pay loud homage to me.*

A few world-shaking events must appear in rapid succession concurrently with the great engineering machinery Weinstein needed. The Church of the Ascension was *in*. Not even the most powerful religious factions in the world could ignore its potential for soaking up membership by the millions and, in so doing, deprive the established fountainheads of the various Gods of *their* dues-paying faithful. But assassination and destruction are handmaidens to proper timing, and Rebecca Weinstein was long an expert in throwing dice with the moving hands of the clock.

She needed, next, a world-grabbing *goal*. No mistake that the most explosive servants of the Lord carried with them the message that Spaceship Earth was decaying, rotting, disintegrating, moldering, burning and otherwise being poisoned with industrial wastes and gases, with nuclear flotsam, toxic horrors piled one atop the other, and with a planet's forests, its very sources of fresh oxygen, being hacked, sawed, cut, smashed, burned and raped day after day. Enter the Church of the Ascension and its leader with a direct line to the Lord to tell *you* how to avoid churning the planet into a cinder. Look up. Look *out*. Reach for other worlds, for *this* one is tumbling backwards and becoming a celestial sewer. Listen to the Reverend Douglas Stavers! Listen, and do his bidding!

Okay, that one was well on its way. The "murder" of Doug Stavers once, twice and then thrice—after which Stavers continued to appear—fed juicy controversy and anger onto the global pool-table of religious conflict, with each controlling force smashing one into the other like idiot numbered spheres, clanging and banging from one side of the table to another.

Then the need to snatch *all* the world's attention to, of all things, the one man accepted as the worst mass murderer of all time. Little matter that he might *not* be that archfiend of death and destruction (the manipulators of the world's food supply and medicines had killed far more than ever succumbed to the deformed dreams of the Fuehrer); the planet recognized Adolf Hitler as the worst of the worst. That Stavers' group controlled a vast percentage of the world media was no accident, and with Hitler's pending delivery to the German government in Frankfurt, under the inescapable glare of floodlights, radio and instant globalwide satellite television, the explosive uproar was pure guarantee.

Every former enemy screamed for Hitler's head; no, for the full living, breathing, shouting, eye-glaring body of the bloodlust figure of Nazi Germany. And the West German government dared not and would never yield up this ultimate symbol of national disgust and depravity. For if the Germans put this creature on public trial, and ran *all* his crimes before the world, and *then* executed the madman, *then*, oh, sweet opportunity! all the Germans, individuals and nation, could cleanse their souls, one and all, and put behind them once and forever the stigma of the Third Reich that had endured not its promised One Thousand Years, but the turbulent nightmare of only twelve years.

Weinstein smiled; that pot would be kept boiling until the play was carried out to its last scene, its final word, its ultimate act of hanging the beloved Adolf by the neck until dead—with an audience of billions.

There must now take place three additional events in succession so short-coupled in time they must occur with rapid-fire sequence.

First, the appearance of the Reverend Doug Stavers before a live audience of hundreds of thousands of the devout; weeping, screaming, praying, hair-tearing, breast-beating faithful, who would be fired up and hurled into loving adulation beyond their ability to control. It must be an emotional onslaught so overwhelming that its very existence could and would be felt psychically and physically beyond that immediate area where it would take place.

Weinstein met with Roberto Diaz and Al Templin. "Are you familiar with that abandoned nuclear powerplant in South Carolina? The huge bowl they used to film the movie, *The Abyss*? As an idea of its size they poured seventy-five million gallons of water into the bowl. They made a movie ocean miles deep. It's got good access and yet it's remote. It's got excellent power facilities brought in for the film. It's perfect for assembling a half-million people. It's ideal for satellite feed throughout the world."

"They're getting ready to shoot another movie there," Diaz said. "We won't be able to interfere."

"Buy them out."

"No deal. They really want to make this new film."

Weinstein looked at Diaz with contempt. "Buy the goddamned movie company, you idiot. Buy all the rights."

Diaz stared at the woman. He'd seen her for a long time and, Jesus, she was a *doctor*! What the hell was she doing running this show? Talking for Stavers? Diaz turned to Templin to complain.

Templin cut him off before he could say a word. "She speaks for Stavers. When she tells you what to do from now on, it's Doug Stavers talking to you. I have this from the man himself. Don't take anything personally, Bob. That would be a terrible mistake."

Diaz looked back to Weinstein. "All right, lady, you—"

"Doctor Weinstein," she said, her words coated with ice.

"Yes, ma'am, Doctor Weinstein," Diaz complied immediately. "You'll have it as soon as I can—"

"Tomorrow. Leave *now*."

"Holy—yes, ma'am." He was gone.

Al Templin grinned at Weinstein. "That was beautiful."

She ignored the compliment. "You're hung up on something, Al. Spell it out," she ordered.

"Security in that bowl area is lousy," he said curtly.

"Yes, I know. Your ideas?"

"You just told me about the place. Anything I say right now would be a vacuum. Meaningless," Templin answered.

Weinstein turned to a computer, her fingers flying about the keys. The great nuclear bowl appeared on the screen. Templin watched, fascinated, as Weinstein ran through changing angles one after the other. The screen stopped with a long oblique angle of the bowl. "Ideas, Al?"

He nodded slowly. "Yeah. Now I can see a way in and out."

"I want absolute security, Al."

He smiled at her. "Doc, there ain't no such animal. That's like asking a sawbones for an absolute guarantee every operation he does comes out perfect."

"Admitted."

He was still taken aback, surprised, his favorable reactions mixed with wild curiosity. He seemed to be talking to a familiar face behind which a total and incredibly strong stranger had emerged.

"It's going to be a doozy—"

"Tell me about it, Al."

He worked it out through the computer, made certain there were only two copies. "Destroy them," she ordered.

He knew the difference between argument and question. "Why?" he asked.

"Then only you and I know all the details. Everybody else need only take their orders, and perform. They won't have time to ask questions."

"Stavers said you're the boss on this," he said, shrugging.

"Yes," she said again. This woman could knock down buildings with that simple *Yes* of hers, he thought with a flare of anger.

"There's more," she said suddenly. "When this show is over, and I'll expect you to run it several times for repeats with comments on the overwhelming adoration for the Reverend," she said, smiling, and then the smile vanished, "then we must move, very fast, and in absolute secrecy. You're not going to get much sleep, Al."

He shrugged again and stood up. "You through?" he asked.

"Yes," she told him.

This time the one word wasn't quite so heavy. "Then I'm gone," he told her. He left without another word.

* * *

They'd need three days to prepare the huge bowl in South Carolina. Rebecca Weinstein started bringing together all the pieces. Al Templin, despite his position of security chief for Stavers, knew nothing of the swift movement, destinations, or the people involved.

One hour after Templin's departure, Doug Stavers and Rebecca Weinstein, with four large men moving loosely about them, stepped inside a Concorde II in Los Angeles. Forty-three other passengers bound for a high-priced whirlwind tour of France completed the passenger manifest. None of them knew Stavers or Weinstein, who traveled under the names of Walter and Ina Quinn. They "melted" into the tempo of the pleasure flight as the supersonic airliner raced nonstop for Paris.

If everything came off on schedule, two powerful jet helicopters would await them in Paris. Skip Marden had gone on ahead and true to form, everything *was* on schedule. Customs and State performed flawlessly; the French officials waived inspection. They rode a small private bus across the airport. The two swift helicopters, one primary and one backup, waited with engines idling and rotors turning lazily.

Four minutes later they were in the air and flying southward from Paris. Rebecca Weinstein adopted a low profile for what came next. It would be a swift hit-snatch-run and this was their ball game.

Skip Marden reveled in his moment of glory. Glory appeared whenever he was given an assignment calling for speed, covert movement, swift death or incapacitation, and success in his mission. At precisely two o'clock in the morning, as scheduled, his teams rose from their places of concealment in the countryside about the French village of Arques. Telephone lines sang in the night as they were cut and tumbled to the ground. Power lines went down with short, sharp blasts from plastic explosives. Bridges tumbled, rock slides covered roads. Even the microwave transmitters for radio, telephone, television and computer lines were churned to scrap metal and torn plastic.

Arques and everything for twenty miles around went electrically dead, save for isolated generators and the lights from automobiles and trucks. Communications-wise, Arques was a blinded oasis.

Four powerful jet helicopters dropped from the skies onto the grounds of the Chateau of Blanchefort; a fifth remained airborne as aerial shotgun and command center for the operation. Marden and forty hardened special forces veterans punctured the isolation and simple defenses of the Chateau. The twelve powerful dogs patrolling the grounds died within a minute of each other, as did their handlers. Heavy doors flew away from the blasts of plastique. Every man with Marden had memorized every corridor, level and room in the Chateau.

They took the ancient stone stairways at full speed. Marden pointed to a huge double door at the end of the hall. "Full cover," he snapped, and his men formed a cordon immediately about him. They went through the unlocked doors in a fury of power.

Two monks faced them, trembling with fear and hate. Marden shot them both, his silencer-equipped magnum blowing away most of their heads.

A man sat up in the large, heavy wood bed.

James Christ looked back at Skip Marden. His eyes radiated an incredible pale blue. For a moment Marden felt he was falling down into pale blue waters. He shook off the sudden, devastating effect by hurling a jumpsuit at the man. "Put it on," he snapped.

James Christ, direct descendant of a line unbroken from the days of his ancestor, known to the world as Jesus, said simply, "No."

Marden expected the refusal. Two men rushed in from each side of the bed to grasp James' arms. Marden stepped forward, a small aerosol can in his left hand. He sprayed the knockout drug directly into the face of James; the man with the straw-blond hair shuddered, his eyes rolled, and he collapsed. "Get rid of his nightshirt," Marden snapped. "Get that suit on him. And the boots. Throw a hat over his head. MacReady; take him."

Bull MacReady slung James Christ over his shoulder as he might carry a child. Surrounded by the others with automatic weapons at the ready, they ran down the three flights of stairs to ground level, through the outside garden, and dashed into the big Alouette helicopter waiting for them.

Marden was the last in. He threw himself through the open door and shouted, "*Go!*"

The chopper lifted, the others slid into escort formation and they raced toward a long runway of an abandoned French air force station ninety miles distant.

The helicopter with James Christ aboard touched down only yards from a long-range Skua waiting with engines running. Doug Stavers looked back from the cockpit as MacReady eased the unconscious James into a seat and secured his straps. Rebecca Weinstein, in a doctor's white uniform, immediately began an emergency study of her "patient." She looked up at Stavers and nodded.

The crew closed the doors, the helicopter lifted away to vanish into the night. Stavers taxied to the runway, swung the Skua and eased power as he turned. Nineteen seconds later they roared into the night sky and began the long nonstop flight to South Carolina.

A couple with the names, passports and other identification of Walter and Ina Quinn had already joined the tour group that had flown nonstop aboard the Concorde II from Los Angeles to Paris.

Dr. Frank Everest Harlow waited in the aft compartment of the Skua for his "patient." He glanced at his watch; the machine should be at cruising altitude now. His timing proved impeccable. A door slid aside and Dr. Rebecca Weinstein entered the compartment, followed by a huge man carrying an unconscious figure in his arms. Skip Marden placed James Christ gently on a couch and turned to a third man to come into the compartment.

"Watch his eyes," Marden told Doug Stavers. "The

son of a bitch can draw you in like you're diving into a lake." Marden shook his head with remembered wonder. He'd encountered some heavy psyche before with eye contact. He'd watched for years as Stavers' steely-eyed, penetrating look unnerved other men to the point of abject fear. And he'd even seen Adolf Hitler at pointblank range. But *never* had he felt such incredible depth. It *was* like tumbling into water.

Weinstein looked with a sense of wonder at Marden, then back to James Christ. *This man has been isolated,* she pondered. *Generation after generation removed from that bearded, sandaled Jew. And yet, now, after all the centuries, that look is still there. His forebearer mesmerized thousands with his eyes. From what I have just seen and heard, this James Christ could be just as compelling. How this is possible is beyond me . . .*

She studied the other "doctor," and as she did so and thought of why he was here, on this airplane, she shook the cobwebs from her head. *So we have a Jew who once talked to God, and this descendant of his perhaps can do the same. It doesn't matter. This idiot race has taken this marvelous jewel of a world to turn it into a cesspool. God's been gone a very long time. . . .*

"Time is critical," Weinstein said sharply to Dr. Harlow. "Begin your program."

Frank Harlow leaned forward to study the face of the bearded man stirring back to consciousness. A strange and forbidding sense of familiarity shuddered through him, a sensation of needles pricking his body and his mind. He *knew* this man, he knew this face, and he also knew he had never before faced "James," the only name Weinstein had instructed him to use.

James' eyes opened. Harlow looked into deep blue waters. He felt a brush of dizziness. He shook his head to clear his senses.

"What's wrong?" Weinstein demanded harshly.

"I—I don't know," Harlow stammered.

Instantly he felt a steel vise clamp about his arm as Doug Stavers spun him about as he might swing a rag doll. "You're supposed to be the best," Stavers said coldly. "The world-renowned hypnotist himself. The man who can mesmerize a brass statue. Who's put an audience of thousands into deep trance. What the fuck's wrong with you? You're almost drooling like an idiot!"

Harlow nodded mutely and turned back to "James." He felt the presence of enormous power. A sense of foreboding warned him not to hold direct eye contact with this man. Yet he knew as well that *not* to carry out his contract with Stavers could mean his life. That was the deal. Put the "patient" into deep hypnotic state, open him up for suggestions and instructions so they would become "his own thoughts and beliefs."

"Do you hear my voice?" he asked "James."

The man smiled. Harlow felt as if he were a child once again. He squeezed his eyes tightly shut, railed at himself to stop this nonsense, opened his eyes again and stared into the blue pools before him.

And "fell" into the waiting waters. Harlow turned with a wet-lipped mindless grin to Stavers.

Stavers knew then, despite the silence of the moment, that all hell was breaking loose about him. He backhanded Harlow with a terrible impact, splitting open the side of his face and his lips. Blood spurted; Harlow was hurled back from the blow against the side of the cabin. Still grinning, drooling blood, he slumped to the floor.

"Cover him!" Stavers shouted to Marden. Instantly Marden went forward, one hand clamping down on "James' " eyes, the other squeezing his skull with a crushing vise of powerful fingers.

"Goddamnit, I didn't want to use the etorphin—"

Weinstein was pale. "You'll *have* to. Immediately." She grasped his arm. "Doug, I've never seen such *power*. He's dangerous. Terribly dangerous. More than I ever dreamed. I—"

"*Do it!*" Stavers shook off her hand. "Do it *now* or *I'll kill him!*"

Weinstein moved smoothly, quickly. The needle slipped into James' jugular. A carefully prepared mixture of etorphin. Enough to make a slave out of any man. "He'll be under in a moment," she said, straightening.

"The hell he will," Stavers snarled. "Give him another dose. He's too goddamned strong." Stavers felt a sixth sense of dread he hadn't known in years. "Hit him again," he repeated. "I want him out cold, understand? And before he comes around I want blinders on his eyes until we can get to him. And *you're* going to do it."

"Me?" she echoed.

"You've used hypnotism in surgery, remember, Doc?" Stavers said coldly, his impatience rising as swiftly as his dissatisfaction with the moment. "You've used mesmerism right on down through the ages, *remember?* Now, goddamnit, there's no one else strong enough, who we can get quickly enough, or who we can trust. From this moment on you stick like glue to this blue-eyed shaman or whatever the hell he is."

Stavers moved to within inches of Weinstein. "You don't let him out of this fog he's in. I don't give a damn if you pump etorphin and daffodils up his ass until they come out of his ears. And you start *now* with the routine. He's not James. *He's Jesus.* Fuck what's wrong or right with the bible. We're not talking to the historians any more. We're going to be dealing with the public. You read me, Rebecca? The big, dewy-eyed, fanatical, crazy, suck-ass public; that's who we're after. *And* you talk to him in Italian. I know you speak all the languages and I know *he* does. He's been in that fucking rockpile all his life and he's brilliant, but I want him talking in Italian when he talks. Or Latin. I don't *care* just as long as it's one or the other."

Stavers gripped both her wrists. "But when he comes back to the world of reality he's still *under our control.* Not even God or the Devil himself can fight off etorphin, and Little Boy Blue, here, isn't nearly up in that league. When he comes out of it, Rebecca, I want him believing, I want him *knowing* that *he is Jesus Christ.* The original article, the one-and-only just stumbled in from the desert and all full of parables and homilies and the rest of that crap. *He is Jesus. This is the Second Coming.* I want him wearing sandals and that flour sack or toga or whatever the fuck it is he wore when he rambled around Jerusalem, *and I want him preaching.*"

Stavers took a deep breath. "When we get to South Carolina everything's supposed to be ready for the big show. Skip," Stavers turned to Marden, "you stick with the doc and old blue eyes. You get them anything and everything they want and you don't let anybody or anything interefere with them. You have the routine of how we move when showtime is over?"

Marden nodded. "I have it here," he tapped the side of his head, "and I have it down on paper, and before we leave Carolina I want you to confirm what's on the paper."

"Good," Stavers said. "Don't worry about that Concorde. I'll make sure Diaz has it set up as a charter flight and with a light load aboard and extra fuel we'll make it direct from Carolina to Rome."

"What about bubble-mouth, here?" Marden asked, looking with disgust at the whining figure of Dr. Harlow.

"That piss-ant," Stavers grunted. "Use the jettison tube. In fact, do it now. I'll wait here."

Several minutes later they felt and heard a distant, muffled thump as air pressure changed drastically in an airlock chute. Marden came back, grinning. "It's twelve miles straight down. He ought to be hitting the water just about now."

Stavers nodded, turning back to Weinstein. "You got it all, Rebecca?"

"Yes."

That's what he loved about this woman. No bullshit. She did wonders with that one *Yes*. "Good. We don't have the room or the time for fuckups."

Stavers went forward alone. Rebecca Weinstein smiled with pleasure. Doug Stavers was in full control again. He ran the whole operation with all the power for which he was known. Hard, tough, mighty, unstoppable. Everything his own way.

Precisely as Dr. Rebecca Weinstein had so carefully planned.

Chapter 26

"I thought I'd seen it all," Al Templin said slowly, shaking his head with disbelief at the sights displayed on the multiscreen video monitors of the control room of the Grail. Even the name was a stroke of genius. They'd tossed names about like feathers in a verbal windstorm. The Bowl. The Crater. The Cup of God; those and a hundred others. And then Stavers snapped his fingers as remembered thoughts reached him. "Grail," he told Templin and the others with him. "Call it the Grail. The crowd will flesh it out and this whole thing will become the Holy Grail."

He was right, Templin mused, as his eyes ran from one monitor to another to give him full coverage of the incredible massing of the devout in the South Carolina countryside. What had been a perfect setting to film a movie about man's undersea encounter with an alien race, *not* necessarily extraterrestrial, had become even more suited to this holy (*holy shit* is more like it, Templin chuckled to himself) assemblage.

More than one million men, women and children had gathered and still more were pouring in. Cars, motorcycles, bicycles, trailers, trucks, motor homes, buses; anything that could roll, lay scattered amidst the packed throngs. The promised "deliverance" would take place soon after dark. They needed nightfall for the event. Templin checked the weather. Terrific; a low and solid cloud deck at twelve hundred feet. Sounds would bounce back and light would reflect gloriously and there'd be virtually no way for aerial interference except through mechanical-electronic means such as radar imagery or extremely sensitive infra-red. And why would anyone bother to do that, when they were televising the whole thing?

The appearance of the Reverend Doug Stavers, already being acclaimed as the only true new messiah—*here we go again*, Templin laughed to himself—was a marvel of coordination, orchestration and exquisite timing to bend minds and stun brains, and sunder normal caution on the part of the true believers. If all went as planned a million people—perhaps twice that number—would leave here finally to disperse to their homes throughout the country, and even to other lands, to carry the message of the faithful.

This couldn't be your old-fashioned and melodramatic evangelistic bullshit. This time they needed more than organs and loudspeakers, pretty girls, flowers and a man condemning the sinners in the crowd and exhorting them to some dalliance with either God or his true son. *This* time their belief had to be down, down deep and rock-solid. This time these people must be brought to the point of yielding their lives if that was what the Reverend Stavers ordained. If he pointed his hand and a steel finger, turning in a slow circle from the center of The Grail, and commanded his faithful to surge forward and immerse themselves in the baptismal waters (all seventy-five million gallons worth) of The Grail, then the crowd must do so, even if a half-baked idiot realized that such a move would quickly drown most of the blindly-obeying faithful.

They didn't need a lemming-inspired crush to drown hundreds of thousands of people. The faithful dead were useless. So, for that matter, was this mob when the show ended. Because by the time the show was over, and it *was* a *show*, Templin reminded himself, they would have served their purpose.

Hold their attention while the Concorde II raced for the Eternal City, while the enormous sleek jet sliced at supersonic speeds for a rendezvous with the Vatican. And an emotional, hate-frenzied orgy that would ensue.

No; Templin corrected himself. That would explode in its fury.

Templin laughed aloud. So many of the world's religions, small or great, had emerged from deliberate, careful hokum. The crowd is always anxious *to be pleased*, and to be pleased they'll snatch at anything that smacks of a message "from the beyond." In the middle 1850s, he recalled a bitter religious war sending blood cascading down Mexican hills and slopes. The infamous Caste War, vicious, murderous, brutal and a slaughterhouse of women and children as much as fighting men, erupted when the Maya assaulted Europeans and mixed castes alike. For eight years they savaged one another, often obliterating entire towns and villages. Then came the "wonder" of the times. The new Mexican Republic hatefully rejected and tried to oust every element of the Catholic Church from the land. They failed to reckon with the Maya, so long before converted to the fiercely devout. But something new was needed, and in a stroke of genius Jose Maria Barrera convinced one of the Mayas that his special talent was needed to bring together the fighting men of all the Maya. Manuel Nahuat was an accomplished ventriloquist. Together, Barrera and Nahuat traveled the countryside with a "talking cross." And to the superstitious natives, the cross talked. It talked on and on and from its flowery speech rose the cult of the Cruzob. They were tough and they were mean and they carved out their own Empire of the Cross, and not until 1901 when a powerful new Mexican army descended against them with modern weapons did the Cruzob finally fall before steel and shot.

But for nearly half a century they endured because they *knew* the cross of Christ "talked" to them, courtesy of a very clever ventriloquist.

Now it was time for a modern edition of the Empire of the Cross, and their messiah was the Reverend Doug Stavers.

"It's the ultimate circus," Stavers observed. "Al, you've done a hell of a job."

"Don't count out Diaz," Templin added quickly. "That

son of a bitch is pure genius when it comes to handling crowds."

"Well, it's pure genius. And if we keep the timing just right we'll pull it off."

"Let's do a run-through," Roger Sabbai insisted. "Any time you put more than a million of the devout in one church, indoor *or* outside, I get clammy skin."

Stavers laughed. "You're orchestrating the greatest religious gathering of all time and you feel like a lizard?"

"You bet," Sabbai confirmed. "I got lizards in my belly and they're all biting. I'm a wreck. When this is over I'm going to be drunk for a month."

Stavers clapped him on the shoulder. He didn't care what would be going on *here* a month from now, but that was none of Sabbai's affair. "You got it. Put it up on the computer."

"Better than that," Sabbai said. "I've run it through so we can get a three-dimensional look at what we've got here. We'll need those special glasses for the big screen. In effect, we've choreographed the whole routine."

They donned the glasses, Sabbai worked the computer controls, and before them on a large curving screen the great Grail shimmered into three-dimensional reality.

"The cables are in place," Sabbai began. "See how they run crossways along and above the water? They have a maximum stretch of two point one percent and we've already compensated for that. All the cables intersect at dead center of the bowl, twenty feet above the water surface."

"Got it," Stavers said. It *was* a terrific setup. The bowl stretched more than 400 feet from one side to the other and in dead center there rose a silvered podium of glassite with lights that flowed and shimmered from within.

"That platform is thirty feet across," Templin broke in. "The glassite is a real eye-twister. It's all mirrored and the angles are wild. We use laser reflections so that you'll appear to be facing everybody, no matter where they're at when they watch you."

Stavers nodded slowly. "I didn't think you could work that out," he said candidly.

"Neither did we," Templin told him. "But it was good old serendipity at work. See here? We went the mirrors and lasers route to increase your security. You could be anywhere within this circle of thirty feet, but you'll still *appear* to be in deadcenter. Anyone taking a long-range shot at you, if he's dead-on to target, has less than one chance in a hundred of actually hitting you."

"Good odds," Stavers grunted.

"Better than that. If someone has a long gun to use, it means they have to bring it through the crowd that adores you, and then lift it up and sight the damn thing—still with that crowd about them, and, well, uh uh. I don't buy that routine. If it's a handgun it better be a .357 mag or better, with damned good sights, and the user's got to be goddamned good at that kind of range, and that's without—"

"I know," Stavers grimaced. "All those loving, adoring people."

"Yessir, by golly," Templin laughed.

"What about sound?"

"Well, first, the pickups. Supersen mikes are in your clothing and we use tight radio freq. No wires. The pickups are in the glassite but we'll also be using microwave antenna long-range pickup—that stuff they call the bionic ear. It can hear you whisper from a thousand feet and it zeros right in. We're using eight of them. Any one will do, and no matter what means we use for transmission, we're going to hear everything you've got to say, and we microwave transmit to the speakers arrayed about and through the crowd. The best omnidirectional output, by the way. The reproduction of voice is so good it sounds like you're talking to them directly. Besides, we've made sure there'll be some extra attention."

Stavers raised an eyebrow. "You up to your old tricks, Al?"

"Uh huh. I worked this one out with Baxter and Stark. Them is sharp apples, Boss-man. Anyway, when you're talking we want the adoring ones to feel uncomfortable. So we're piping in a very thin ultrasonic frequency. It's too high for them to hear but it will do two other things. It'll drive a dog mad, which doesn't matter, but it also impinges on the bony system of the ear and sends, well, a wire-thin needle into the ear canals of your adoring and faithful. I guarantee it holds their attention."

"That's for the high stuff," Stavers acknowledged. "And the low?"

Templin gestured in an offhanded manner to show just how easy all this had been handled. "There's the usual bass output and the woofers and all that bullshit. It works. It moves a lot of air through the speakers, but we're not using the humongous boom-bangers from the rock music concert crowd. We've got to do better and we are with our Volkman systems. They're magic. But I'm going to send an infrasound rumble through them when you're talking. That way they get a needle in the ear and an eggbeater in the ass and it's all going to happen because you're talking."

"The old system," Stavers admitted. "Grab 'em by the balls and they'll follow you anywhere."

"That, too," Templin said happily. He paused a moment. "This is a big church deal. Who you got on the organ?"

Stavers smiled. "No organ. No player. You have that computer system set up? The Ballard-Timkens equipment?"

"Yessir. Linked in to the pickup, transmit, broadcast systems. But *I* still don't know what the hell it does."

"You'll find out very soon," Stavers said mysteriously. "You'll get a kick out of it." The pleasantries disappeared of a moment. "Update me on Weinstein and our guest."

Templin picked up on the sharper, more serious tone of Stavers and responded in like manner. "The airfield's exactly thirty-seven miles from here. Military base; Godfrey. We have permission for the Concorde II to land there, get refueling, and standby with startup equipment whenever you're ready to go."

"The woman, I said."

"I was coming to that, sir. The base has a top security area for alert crews. It's blastproof, underground; the works. The old crews on standby alert used it. We have it for now. The, ah, doctor and patient are there along with Skip. Plus his own crew that he selected personally. You can't get near the place without tripping a dozen alarms and autofire systems. So the blue suiters are playing along with us. Washington gave it full authority; the locals are convinced we're part of some special Blue Light team, and they're trained to *not* ask questions."

Stavers nodded. "And the, uh, patient? Did you see him *personally?*"

Templin answered carefully. Stavers was on some kind of hair-trigger spring and that could be extremely dangerous to anyone in his immediate vicinity if he ever cut loose. "Yes, sir, I did. I stood as close to him as I am to you right now."

"He's conscious?"

"Hell, yes, sir!"

"Why the reaction, Al?"

"His eyes. Damndest thing I ever saw. Skip warned me that to look into his eyes is like falling down a hole to nowhere. And he's right. It's crazy, sir. The man's tanked out on the eto stuff, and yet *something* really extraordinary comes through. There's another thing I don't get."

"Tell me, Al," Stavers said softly.

"He thinks he's Jesus Christ."

Stavers didn't answer but nodded for Templin to go on.

"I mean, he looks like Christ, or what most paintings I've seen of Christ look like," Templin said, disturbed with his own report. "He looks like him in that weird sort of toga and sandals and that beard, and those blue eyes of his, they're like neon signs, and the things he says, well, I've heard them before, and they're word for word—"

"Where'd you hear them, Al?"

"Maybe not hear all of them, but I've read them. The

bible, of course. New Testament. I remember a lot of it when I was studying for the priesthood—"

"You what?"

"I know, I know," Templin said, annoyed because his secret was out. "It was for a couple of years—"

"Another story, another time," Stavers broke in.

"Anyway, this man looks like and talks *exactly* like the Christ I know from the Bible. It's like turning back the clock two thousand years."

Stavers rose to his feet and clapped Templin on the shoulder. "It's not like going back two thousand years, Al. It is exactly what we have done."

Templin went white. He pointed a shaking hand in the direction of the distant airfield. "Are you telling me that he *really* is . . ."

"I sure am. The original article."

"But that's impossible!" Templin shouted.

"Who was Jesus Christ?" Stavers asked.

"Why, the messiah . . . the son of God."

"So why do *you* find anything impossible for God to do?"

"I . . . I mean . . . well . . . "

Stavers was all professional again. "That's enough. It's getting late. It's showtime, Al. Let's go do it."

Roger Sabbai thrilled to the sight. For too long he'd been bedeviled (*no pun intended, thank you,* he told himself) with the hardware logistics of coordinating the multifarious needs and growth of the Church of the Ascension. At first it had been a blast, this pulling so massive a wool blanket over so many millions of eyes. Then it decayed into hard logistical supply and demand and became a thorough pain in the ass. *Then* Doug Stavers had given him the ultimate assignment for the ultimate appearance.

"Short of my floating down from heaven in a chariot of fire, Roger, which I believe is just a mite beyond your capabilities, I want you to go all-out on this one," Stavers told him as he gave him *carte blanche* for the "messianic triumphal appearance."

Roger Sabbai sat within the mobile control room deep underground in what had been a monitoring cubicle for radiation output from a huge nuclear generator-reactor that had never been built; from this same cubicle two movie companies had already churned out their great celluloid adventures, including *The Abyss*, in the monstrous bowl of water. Sabbai was almost a many-tentacled controller of the night, monitoring fully twenty-eight separate TV scanners, with twenty-eight separate video controllers working for him, as well as technicians for lights, sound, chemical dispersants, ground control, airborne activities and the like.

All lighting save that controlled by Sabbai and his team was strictly forbidden among the crowd now estimated at nearly two million people. Along the central and outer fringes of the huge throng there rose giant television screens, so that those who could not see Stavers directly, or saw him only as a tiny figure in the far distance, would at least be able to gaze with adoring eyes on their leader.

Suddenly *all* the lighting snapped off. Bright floodlights from high towers snapped and cracked as they went dead, groaning and crackling as heat dissipated. First an alarmed cry, then a hush, then a growing murmur rose from the now-frightened human mass. Before their own sound could become a throaty uproar, a deep bass thunder swelled in their midst, growing into a sound of absolute purity, rising higher and higher. A blue glow appeared from within the great bowl, became red, and then yellow and on through the spectrum as Sabbai released the computer to run through the programmed light show. The water exploded in light; laser beams stabbing upward and bursting into the sky, knifing through and also reflecting from the low cloud layer, an ethereal and eye-stunning display of an artificial aurora borealis, color and sound sweeping the adoring faithful.

The lights faded. Sweet scents floated through the air; computer-programmed valves releasing the synthetic fragrances, all with the barest, faintest trace of massively diluted etorphin. *What they see and hear tonight they will believe absolutely*, Sabbai mused. He punched in the computer control for Stavers' appearance.

A single sourcepoint of light grew in the sky directly above the platform in dead center of the great water bowl. It was too intense to make out any detail, and then another light appeared and yet another, and another, until the aerial illuminating stabbing downward was too bright to be looked at directly. "Bring in the sound," Sabbai directed his team. Ethereal music flowed from the heavens, from the water, from ground-embedded speakers and from balloons far to the outer spread of the crowd, balloons holding massive speakers on cables so that all the world was a volcano of musical thunder.

Which mixed with the same frequencies of several huge Sikorsky Skycrane helicopters, invisible from the ground because of the huge and powerful lights they held beneath their long bodies, spraying glare against the human eyes below. At the exact moment of synchronizing sound and light, Sabbai flashed the signal.

"Start him down."

A battery of multicolored laser lights began to play into a selected point in the air well above the water. A gasp from nearly two million throats arose to mix with the music and thunder. A figure floated magically in the air, the lasers flicking back and forth about his body, reflecting painfully from the form as it lowered slowly toward the platform in the center of the water. Streams of sparks showered upward, laser beams flashed like magical knives of light, and in a play of lighting that paled the wildest sets of any rock concert, Doug—*oops; the Reverend Douglas Stavers*, Sabbai corrected himself—drifted downward, a magical slow levitating descent. Against those lights, laser beams, sparkling showers, the cable attached to his body invisible, as was the helicopter concealed above the blinding lights above. The cascade of sparks and lights grew to intense fury, and suddenly, music faded, sparks ebbed, the lights dimmed and Stavers stood magically on the glassite platform.

Those goddamned laser mirrors are pure genius, Sabbai thought with immense satisfaction. *You can't tell where he is except that he seems to be dead center of the glassite.* And to every person who saw Stavers directly or watched him on the giant video screens, the man stared *directly* into their eyes.

Stavers began to speak, slowly, powerfully, his voice carried from the glassite platform microphones through a computer that washed away irregularities, adding a deep crispness to every sound, and giving his voice a stentorian strength reduced to a commanding yet friendly tone. Those who listened to his words and his voice stared at his eyes, unaware they were subjected now to the same effect Stavers had seen Ernst Patschke use with such tremendous power in India.

Stavers' eyes *glowed.* They glowed with a marvelous lavender shade, and the color twisted and roiled within itself. Color grown from contact lenses and an invisible laser beam in ultraviolet light that had no effect on Stavers but brought his eyes to worshipful light. Stavers spoke of Spaceship Earth. He stood before his entranced audience in a white hooded cape, his arms folded within, a living statue of wonder. He spoke of the moon and of Mars, proclaiming that the Lord was calling His People to reach out from Earth, to colonize other worlds so they might also be fruitful with mankind and animals and new growth. He told the enthralled he was answering The Call, that soon he would depart this world for another.

A cry of near-desperation and anguished loss met his last words.

Then, suddenly, he threw back the hood and they saw a white space helmet, glittering and gleaming (*can't beat those lasers*, Sabbai grunted with satisfaction). The cape fell away from his shoulders and they saw the white spacesuit, fitted out with marvelous gadgets and tubes and hoses and more of those laser-pumped jewels and stones.

Then Stavers went for the real kicker. A glowing halo appeared in thin air before him. It literally floated (*magnetic levitation's not that tough*, Sabbai thought pleasantly, *it's been around for decades*) in midair. Stavers gestured, and the halo rolled slowly from a position horizontal to the platform to remain suspended in the vertical. Stavers moved his hand so that it entered the space within the halo, between the three feet of open space, and his hand twisted slightly.

Music erupted from the heavens, the air, the water, the skies, the ground; music ethereal, powerful, soothing, bringing tears flowing from the astonished, wondering faithful. Stavers' hand twisted again, and the music rose and fell, soaring crystal, crashing mountains, rushing waters, the clarion trump calls of the gods. As his hand moved Stavers was creating his own symphony—*and it was all true*. The halo was for show, but not the space within the glowing circle, where an electromagnetic field responded to the power gloves and wristband worn by Stavers beneath his spacesuit. The theremin, the electromagnetic field, *was* a complete orchestra. Each move of hand or fingers twisted the field and sent it back continuously to the computer-run Ballard-Timkens synthesizer. This was the creation of music by interaction, and added to the music were the notes and tones that knifed into the listening brains directly affecting the alpha, beta, and theta frequencies.

The combined effect of all the input of music, sight, sound, fragrance, infrasound and manipulated biofeedback reached a devastating crescendo and then, with a flick of Stavers' hand, *silence*.

"Tonight," Stavers spoke. "Tonight is *the* time. Our church has the power, the right and the might. We are the true children of God. We need only the truth and *we* are the truth. We answer the call from the heavens by preparing to go to the heavens. But not all the people believe us. They need a—" He paused, his hand moved through the theremin, a single note as if ripped from a thousand violins tore through his listeners, and then he continued.

"They need a . . . *gift*," he said finally, adding a trumpet blast this time, a brass-echoing cry of angels. "And tonight we give to all Christendom their gift, so that they might truly know the wonder and the power and the glory of who we are. Let my voice be heard through this land! Let it be carried to all the world! Tonight!" Another shattering cry of sound; breaking crystals falling forever and raising hackles on skin, then:

"Tonight we bring to the heart of Christendom, at the Eternal City, in Rome, in the Vatican itself, tonight we resurrect The Christ! Tonight we will deliver Jesus to the Vatican!" Another musical eruption, a roll of drums, thunder and glory and a bass rumble that shook earth and heavens.

"Tonight, it will be done!" Stavers cried, and all the lights exploded into being, savage white and blue, laser beams crisscrossing, sparks and embers whirling through the air. Music so loud it hammered at the senses, and the light, mixing and glorious and so intense it concealed completely the cable lowered from the hovering helicopter. Stavers was held aloft, one hand grasping the invisible glass cable, and his foot rested on an equally invisible glass step, and he rose wonderfully and spiritually and magnificently into the heavens, and when the lights dimmed and the music ebbed to a soothing cry, he was gone, *vanished*.

Chapter 27

"I'm sorry I missed it," said Doug Stavers. He hunkered down in his plush viewing seat, an unlit cigar clenched in his teeth, a steaming coffee mug in one hand. By his side, more uptight than he'd seen her in months, Dr. Rebecca Weinstein sat straight-backed, legs neatly together, feet flat on the carpeted floor. The theater that could seat 800 people was empty except for themselves, and a technician in the projection control room. Before Stavers and Weinstein rose a motion-picture screen three stories high, the fabled IMAX theater screen at the Kennedy Space Center on Florida's mideast Atlantic coast.

"I imagine it was interesting," Weinstein replied after a long pause. "I caught a few minutes of the CNN newscast live from Rome. The place is a madhouse—"

"Everything go as planned?" he interrupted.

"Perfectly. When you did your vanishing act and hoisted into the helicopter, the Concorde was already starting engines. Our guest, ah, James, was perfect. He believed, he *knows*, he's the original article. The original Jehoshua about to proclaim himself as the long-promised *true* messiah. Your double, and whoever you got to take my place, fitted in perfectly. Everyone expects Doug Stavers to have his personal shotgun with him at all times, so sending Marden to the Vatican with blue-eyes was a marvelous move. At this moment they believe it's the real Doug Stavers with the resurrected Christ in the Vatican. Nobody except a very few chosen people have any idea you're *here.*" Weinstein smiled. "Or what's about to happen."

She pressed a microphone button on the arm of her seat. "Can you hear me?" she asked.

"Yes'm," a voice replied, coming from speakers through the theater.

"Do you have the count for the shuttle?"

"Yes'm. The bird is fully fueled, most of the crew is aboard, and they're into the simulated countdown drill right now."

"Thank you," Weinstein said. "Give me a brief drifting series on the station, please. Music only; no dialogue."

"Coming right up, ma'am."

The lights began to dim and music drifted gently about them in the theater. Several seconds later they had a vertiginous view of the Grissom space station, looking down at the station and at the curving limb of the Earth, huge and blue and white, beyond. The camera view continued slowly at the beginning of what would be a filmed drifting survey of the American space station. Just beyond the station was what Stavers wanted to see: the great gathering into a single jumbled mass of *Gulliver*, the ship that had been assembled in orbit of huge cylindrical fuel tanks, engine clusters, and separate quarters for crew accommodation and scientific research. It was a monstrous vehicle, ungainly and awkward, but it would float through the space ocean with the smoothness of a feather in silent air.

Stavers forced his attention back to Weinstein's report on the Vatican. "You said few people have an idea of what's about to happen," he said. "Did you mean here, where we are, or Puccini land?"

"Both. Let me give you a prediction of what happens in Rome. The Vatican," she said carefully, "can't afford to ignore what you did. They don't believe it's a resurrection, of course, they know Christ died when he was just beyond eighty years old, and that his line continued and was kept secluded in France. They'll put the numbers together and figure what you did. It may take them a while to work out the details of James talking with the exact words we read in the Bible, but that was a pretty neat turn. They can't reject the possibilities until they have time to regroup, and when they tell the world it's *not* Christ resurrected, that's the same as signing your death warrant."

Stavers raised an eyebrow. "Oh?" He chuckled. "Nothing's changed, then. They signed that a long time ago."

"This time they'll *have* to carry it out. Most likely they'll link you with a Moslem movement."

"Buddy-buddy with Mohammed, huh?"

"In effect. Of course," Weinstein smiled, "we *could* be on the edge of a holy war." She laughed aloud. "Like the one the Catholic church must absolutely launch against Ascension."

"I will admit," Stavers said lazily, "last night was a doozy." He sat up straighter to study her face. "What about Skip? We're here and he's in Rome and you're talking a holy war."

"Skip's a survivor," she answered carefully.

"And you just avoided my question."

"He'll have to come out of it by himself and his own team. You can't help him now."

"Are you telling me," he asked with disbelief, "that I've abandoned my closest friend?"

She shook her head. "Not yet. But in a few hours, yes."

"Ladybones, there'd better be a damned good reason for all this," he said icily.

"You can't go back," she repeated. "*Not now, not ever*. You said it yourself. A holy war. You're too dangerous now to *everybody*. Your past record. That incredible move with chunking Hitler right into the arms of the Germans. Your new church and its spectacular spread. Among many other things. Now stuffing Christ down the Vatican's throat and invoking the anger of the Moslem world. That brings in governments. You've upset the apple cart, and badly. You're a threat to power, finances, politics, diplomacy, treaties, religions—"

"I get your point. Peck's bady boy."

"This time it will be suicide teams after you. Even you can't hold that off. You're not the only one with etorphin or its equals. To say nothing of the kamikaze spirit that will be invoked." She held his eyes. "In short, Doug, *Earth is no longer safe for you.*"

He looked up at the huge IMAX screen and the huge, clustered form of *Gulliver*.

"So up is now out," he said a bit more grimly than he intended.

"Yes."

"But that shuttle doesn't fly for a few more weeks," he noted.

Instinctively she leaned closer. "It flies in three hours. Only the launch team and flight crew is aware of that. They don't even know it in Grissom. It flies in three hours and we're aboard."

He took a deep breath. "What about *Gulliver*? It's not ready to boost. And if we're stuck up there for a few weeks, *and* the world is after my ass, well, lady, it's not that tough to take out an entire space station. One small nuke does the job."

"That won't happen. Look, I've got to change the subject. We have less than thirty minutes in here before we leave for the launch pad."

"*That* tight?"

"Doug, I've worked harder on this than I ever did on anything in my entire life," she stressed. "Will you *please* let me use that screen to tell you what I've held back for so long?"

"Your timing is something else, Rebecca. I finally get to meet Daddy, is that it? You wait until I'm on the edge and it doesn't matter what I *know*, just so long as I can't go anywhere except with you."

She surprised him. No argument. "That sums it up well. Now, do I have your attention?"

"Sure. As long as you keep me laughing, Doc, you live, I live, we—" He shook his head. "Let it go. Shoot."

She pressed her microphone button. "Control, pull the Grissom film. Let me have NASA Viking Frame three five Alpha Seven Two, please. Be sure it's the enhancement frame from Carlotto."

The technician's voice came through the speakers. "Right away, ma'am." The screen went dark, they waited several seconds, and then Frame 35A72 flashed thirty feet high before them.

Stavers leaned forward, staring, absorbing every detail. He knew this picture! The "Face" of Cydonia on Mars . . . a huge monolithic structure of a humanoid face with what was obviously a spacesuit-type helmet. He heard Weinstein's voice. "This photograph was taken by a Viking orbiter *back in 1976*. The Viking Orbiter was at the time passing over the Martian region of Cydonia—"

"From what height?" Stavers snapped.

"One thousand miles. That face is, as I'm sure you gathered by now—"

"Your father."

"*Yes.* What you see is a surface feature carved by lasers and lifter beams. It measures more than a mile from the chin all the way to the crown. And it *is* a sculpture of my father. I had to wait from the time I arrived on this planet until 1980 to see the original of this photograph." She leaned back in her seat and sighed. "When the NASA project team first saw this picture they became terribly excited. Then they decided it was impossible, that they were seeing a mixture of lights and shadows. I nearly went mad with frustration because they ignored the picture for more than three years. Then someone in Jet Propulsion Laboratory decided to go for computer enhancement, and the lights and shadows disappeared as this picture, what they called the Face of Cydonia, appeared. Finally they published it and I knew that the members of my ship on Mars were still alive, still waiting for that combination of genetic code and the *arbatik* that we lost when Wolfram died. My father knows me well; we tend to think in highly logical terms. If the terrestrials managed to reach Mars with equipment like the Viking, they would take pictures—"

"But *one* monolithic structure?" Stavers protested. "That doesn't make that much logic, Rebecca. It could have been obscured by a Martian sandstorm, or cirrus clouds, or they could have missed it altogether."

She smiled. "You're right, of course. So they left

other signs. They could have communicated by radio, for example. Or transmitted video pictures. But that also could have meant a barbaric race with technological ability—*your* race—might have come to Mars with thermonuclear weapons. Your people are, in your own terms, trigger-happy. Shoot first and ask questions later. Kill them all and let God sort them out. This planet is covered with blood and horror. No; direct contact was too dangerous. So they set up these features, because all races tend to believe that what they may see is not evidence of a superior race. That's begging for a battle and we didn't want that." She laughed lightly, but with barely a touch of humor. "We are long-lived. The two thousand years, I'm certain, has been an incredible bore, and I imagine most of the people from our ship spent most of that time in stasis sleep. For them, going to sleep for a thousand years or more is the same as you sleeping one night *here*."

"Jesus . . ."

"Look at the crossbanding on the forehead, Doug. That's the mark of a pressure helmet, although it's really far more complex and intricate than that."

"Was this the only sign, or monolith?"

"Not at all. They probably built, and I tried to imagine myself in their place, living structures on the planet. A sort of field expedition to see how they could adapt, genetically and physiologically, to the particular conditions on Mars. So somewhere in the sixty thousand photos the original Vikings took I expected to find more."

"And?"

She pressed the talk button again. "Control, you have the preselected series from the Viking orbiters. Please start the sequence."

The three-story-high image vanished and another took its place. "This is six miles southwest of the Face. You can clearly see the pyramid-like structures and squares, a form of agora design. Every one of these features was a message for me to see. If I stood directly in the center of that square, right there, I would see in profile the face of my father. Look carefully, Doug. You'll see that those pyramids are actually pentagonal in shape and they're also at least one earth-mile in length. The other pyramid-like structures are the same as we built on other planets; they're the mark we leave wherever we decide to stay awhile and build. That way, wherever we have been, those who come behind us know immediately of our past presence. And if we had the time, which we don't right now, you'd be able to measure everything at perfect separations to these structures. The measurements always double, see? One, two, four, eight, and so on."

"What about the Russian probes that went to Mars in, um, 1989, wasn't it?"

She nodded.

"They were going to photograph the planet in great detail, oh, camera resolutions down to two feet or so. And land on the Martian moons. If I remember right, both mother ships went into orbit about Mars—"

"No. Only one. Our people disabled the first one before it reached the planet."

"Disabled? Deliberately?"

"Yes. The second ship went into Martian orbit. We were almost too late. Understand that even though I wasn't there, I knew what they *would* do. The presence of orbiters and landers on Mars, their ability to tell that terrestrial ships were orbiting Earth with men, that they landed on the moon—"

"How would they know that?"

"Doug, television transmission from this planet is wavelength garbage. There's no avoiding it."

"Okay, okay. But why knock out the Russian ships in Martian orbit?"

"Because my father, our people, can extrapolate timetables. First your moon, and then, Mars. Your government won't say anything publicly, but the Face at Cydonia, the Crater Pyramid two hundred miles distant, and the long features in Utopia, on the other side of Mars—well, more than those, but they'll do for the moment. So our people have been expecting a manned expedition, but they had to be careful and make these features appear to be ancient. And the last thing they wanted photographed, to be recognized by any government on this planet, was our ship. I'm certain that by now it's been uncovered, all its systems checked, and it's waiting only for me, and you, to descend to the Martian surface."

She let out a long, shuddering breath. "Then and only then will we be free to return to the other worlds, to renew our journey from one star to another." She gripped his hand tightly. "You and I, Doug. We're the keys to unlock the gravity chains of Mars and bring our ship back to life."

She glanced at her watch. "It is time," she said soberly. She pressed the armchair button again. "Control, thank you."

She started along the aisle to the exit. "Let us go, Doug. There's a vehicle waiting for us outside. But we may have trouble. We're breaking a long-established schedule being followed by many people. The shuttle on the pad is going through a full-dress rehearsal for launch. Everything right now is ready for that launch. When we get aboard that ship, you're going to need all the strength you have to push that crew through the launch sequence."

"And what about the people in launch control?"

"They'll go along. They believe this is a secret military move to get the shuttle up to the Grissom station weeks ahead of the schedule the Russians are watching."

He walked with her to the exit. "Something still bothers me. So we get aboard Grissom. So what? The station isn't going anywhere and we're like bugs on flypaper, stuck *in* orbit."

She stopped just before they went outside. "We're not going to the station. We're going to dock with *Gulliver*. The planetary alignment isn't perfect but it meets our velocity requirements. And *Gulliver* is ready to boost."

"I'll be damned," he said.

She took his hand as they walked into the night. *Not yet, not quite yet*, she thought in response to his words.

Chapter 28

Doug Stavers paid little attention to the complexities and wonders of the countdown for *Athena*, the first of the second-generation shuttles. Normally his finely-honed pilot's expertise would have brought him to watch every movement, listen to every sound, note every detail. Not now. On the brink of the most stupendous flight of his life he was far removed from the technological spilling away of minutes and seconds. Entering the craft with their jumpsuits, which they'd donned in the van taking them from the IMAX theater to the launch pad, they aroused sudden interest, and then the interest subsided among the launch pilots and scientists to a nondescript acceptance of their presence. Stavers performed as Rebecca bid; used all his mental strength, Stavers and that glowing *arbatik* stitched to his heart and nervous system, and the crew found itself intensely occupied with the countdown and other immediate-prelaunch details. At virtually any other time the appearance of two unknowns in a shuttle manifest would have generated more than interest; a direct probing of who, what, why, and when would certainly have been forthcoming from the ship's commander and its pilot.

But this wasn't virtually "any other time." The crew had been briefed secretly. No more than three people in the launch control and flight pattern complex knew the launch would actually take place. It had happened before in the space program, even as far back as the first Atlas to put a payload into orbit, a tape recorder tucked in its innards so that once orbiting the planet it could broadcast that taped message from President Dwight Eisenhower. That old Atlas, which few people believed capable of doing the job, became a hallmark in the advancing space program. Even the range safety officer, uninformed of the actual mission, stabbed his destruct button when the Atlas veered from its *ballistic* flight path. And stabbed it again and again in futile desperation and anger until someone pulled him firmly but gently from his control panel, stained by blood from the torn skin of his hand.

And *Athena* was no experimental craft, but the long-term development of the earlier shuttles. Add to these elements the fact that the flight crew was all military, that seven other engineers and technicians were in the "passenger manifest," that the ship carried secret equipment for a secret program, and that the passengers were in a pressure compartment within the cargo bay itself and never seen directly by the pilots, and there wasn't *that* much out of the ordinary for the last-minute arrival of two passengers.

They settled into their seats in semi-supine position, donned their lightweight suits and helmets that would be pressured up only in the event of loss of cabin pressurization, checked their restraint systems, and, like all such moments, waited. At least they were able to listen to the two-way communications between the flight crew and launch control, accompanied by satisfying bumps, thuds and clangs accompanying the ticking off of the countdown items.

Then Rebecca heard the words for which she'd waited. She squeezed Stavers' arm and with her other hand tapped her helmet to signify him to pay close attention to the voice exchange. "Ah, *Athena*, we're in a five-minute hold for catchup, everything's on the mark, and would you take a moment to study your flight plan, ah, Seven Six Able? Please check. Readback is not required, but we'd like you to verify you have that complete flight plan."

"Roger that, Flight. *Athena* confirms Seven Six Able."

"Very good, *Athena*. Please run a scan check and update on the flight computers."

A pause of fifteen seconds, then: "Flight, *Athena* here. Confirm Seven Six Able update primary, backup and standby computer and flight logic. We are go for Seven Six Able."

"Thank you, *Athena* . . ."

Rebecca lifted her helmet and motioned for Stavers to do the same so she could talk directly without using their radio intercom systems; the conversation remained private to them only. "Seven Six Able is the flight plan modified for ascent direct to *Gulliver* instead of the station. We're going straight to the Mars ship. It has all but four of the crew aboard. That four includes us and two technicians aboard this shuttle. We—"

"*T minus ten minutes and counting* . . ."

She left her sentence unfinished and immediately closed and sealed her helmet. Stavers did the same, so that the onboard check systems would indicate full suit integrity for them.

They felt power surging through the ship, pumps kicking in and accelerating, the countdown calls proceeding like familiar clockwork ticking, the call for onboard engine start and vibrations rattled the cavernous hold, metal straining and groaning and then the three main liquid-propellant engines of *Athena* lit off and rammed them back in their seats, and then they sat, the engines screaming as they built up power, and they heard the final call that *Athena* was at one hundred three percent power, and the automatic countdown computer lit off the solid boosters and this time the pressure shoving them down into their seats remained.

Stavers felt cheated instead of elated. He couldn't see a damn thing! They had no windows in the cargo compartment passenger capsule, and they were just so much cargo at this point and nothing more. He felt the ship rotating as it began the turn to orbital climb, and the g forces built steadily, but he'd lived most of his life under punishing high-g pounding, so that didn't mean much to him. They went through maximum aerodynamic pressure as he expected; the call to throttle back the liquid engines, the bumpy rattling ride through the sonic spread, and then power back up to one hundred five percent. He felt some discomfort from the knowledge that they were still tied to those solid boosters that in an instant could transform them all into a single boiling mass of blazing fire, and a small knot deep inside him untied itself as they came to 146 seconds for the Mark II solids, then a terrific bang went through the compartment as the pyrotechnics blew to sever the connections with the solids, and the flight crew in laconic terms confirmed solid sep and they continued upwards on their own engines.

They waited for the first power shutdown; it came smoothly and they floated upward into their seat restraints. They'd coast just short of orbital insertion for eighteen minutes. Keeping suit integrity was called for—Stavers hated his "trussed like a gagged pig" status and twisted uncomfortably in the suit—but the time passed. He riveted his attention to the radio calls between *Athena* and the ground stations over which they passed with speed that made a rifle bullet a bumbling slug in comparison. Then the engines powered up again, shoved them once more into their seats, and he counted down the minutes in his mind, forcing away all other thoughts.

Shutdown.

Zero gravity.

Some more waiting as the maneuvering engines fired on and off with their dull thuds and bangs, listening to the calls between *Athena* and *Gulliver*. He felt the sudden stop, the impact of airlock clutches catching and securing, and that was it.

"Okay, people, we've got confirmed solid airlock status. Everybody ashore that's going ashore," came the easy comments from the flight deck.

The movements were like a high-tech tourist trip. No one aboard *Athena* or *Gulliver* had any idea who the two latecomers were. Doug Stavers and Dr. Rebecca Weinstein were strangers whose duties had only been hinted at in a distant and inconclusive manner. Weinstein attended to that problem in short order when they floated to the main crew quarters of the Mars vessel.

"Dr. Rebecca Weinstein," she said of herself. "I'm a

specialist in environmental systems, trained specifically for Martian conditions. My job will be to search for life spores and elements of life systems in the underground water, frozen, of course, of the planet. This is Dr. Kurt Stevens," she gestured to Stavers. "His field is planetary geology, and we'll be working together on surface explorations and deep sampling programs."

As ordinary as tap water in a kitchen. There wasn't time to do much more than this brief greeting ritual of those already aboard *Gulliver* and the newcomers. Stavers spent his time studying the ship and its control systems and especially the computers. He had the shadowy feeling he'd need to know them as well as he did the controls of a familiar Skua.

Weinstein spent her time with two other women of the crew, who shared her intense interest in onboard systems and controls.

They never understood that they were writing their own death sentence.

Weinstein moved slowly, drifting in zero gravity to one of the landing vessels tucked securely within an aft cylinder of the *Gulliver* cluster. She closed the hatch to guarantee their silence from the crew. She turned slowly to face Stavers.

"You understand the control systems to your satisfaction?"

"Yeah. This whole thing is going to fly on autopilot anyway," he confirmed. "The people aboard are just along for the ride. If something goes wrong we're supposed to fix it. But the human crew is superfluous to the trip. This might just as well—no, that's wrong. This is a fully automatic flight. The computers do it all."

"Could you run this thing, clumsy and antiquated as it is," she pressed, "if the flight crew weren't aboard?"

"I think I know what you're getting at," he said slowly. She was tougher than he had imagined. But she was so close to rejoining her people. The massive weight of two thousand years crossed his mind and his understanding deepened. He nodded to her. "Yes, I can run it. *You* could probably run it better than me. Hell,

Rebecca, we're not *flying*. This whole trip is just boosting from one velocity level to another and the course is all computer-run, anyway."

"I had to be certain you understood that. Absolutely."

"I understand. Now get to the meat of all this."

"You know what we have to do."

"I get the picture. All of them?"

"All of them. One wild card, one emotional reaction at the controls, *anything*, could destroy everything we've done to this moment."

"You brought the stuff with you?"

"Yes. Enough to do the job."

"When and where?"

"There's a crew briefing starting one hour from now. In the flight afterdeck. We have enough time to go forward, leave the aerosol on timer, and return here. We wear fully pressurized suits the moment we get back here. We can hook up to the ship intercom so we'll know when it happens."

He felt he was on a dizzying plunge.

He also knew there was no other way.

"Let's go," he told her, and pushed hard to float back to the flight afterdeck.

It went ridiculously easy. Since they were still in Earth parking orbit and *Gulliver* was on standby status, largely powered down, the great ship cluster was monitored by automatic systems, leaving the crew free to attend to their own duties, relax, or start the repetitive checking of equipment for the long eight-month flight to Mars. But . . . *not yet*, and a better moment would not come.

They went together to the flight afterdeck, floating through the passageways, pulling themselves along on the cable guides. Twice they encountered other crew members, but by unspoken agreement, little was spoken during such encounters. Because the outbound flight was scheduled for eight long months, everyone aboard *Gulliver* intended to squeeze every new aspect of their lives small bite by bite, so as to lessen the feeling of interminable flight aboard a tin-can craft that would become balkier and more smelly with every passing month.

In the flight afterdeck, floating above the conference table and computer control monitors, alone in the cubicle, Rebecca Weinstein found just what she wanted. A large console against a bulkhead with at least six inches of open space behind. She slipped the aerosol container she had hidden in her jumpsuit behind the panel, adjusted the timer release, and floated away. Without a word they drifted back to the landing vessel where they had placed their pressure suits.

"Suit up now," Stavers ordered her. "If anyone comes along we won't be pressurized, and it's a normal equipment checkout."

Forty-five minutes later the ship intercom speakers came alive. "All hands, conference in the flight afterdeck fifteen minutes from now. Punch in from wherever you are so we can get a count." Stavers tapped a crew call button twice, others did the same from throughout the ship, and the first officer's voice came on again. "All hands accounted for. Thank you, people. See you in just fourteen minutes."

"Pressure up," Stavers instructed. "*No radio, and no intercom.* If we need to talk, press our helmets together. The vibration will pass our words through."

She nodded. There wasn't any need to talk. Weinstein checked the intercom speaker. It was accepted practice to leave the transmit sets open during any conference, so they would know when the meeting started and could confirm that everyone else was in that afterdeck.

She had worked out the rest well before this moment. Weinstein had lived for centuries with starship computer systems against which *Gulliver*'s computers were drooling idiots. She had accessed the main computer line; she opened the connection relay console in the passageway by the landing vessels. They waited; voices came from the afterdeck and then they heard the words they needed to begin the sequences already planned.

She pointed to her suit wrist timer. Stavers nodded. The aerosol was opening at that very moment, and a thin mixture of etorphin sprayed into the afterdeck. With no instructions to go with inhalation of the gas, the flight crew simply went mute, remaining where they had been the moment the gas reached their brains, living but dumb rag dolls weaving for several moments in weightlessness as they continued to breathe.

"Let's go," Stavers said. They floated forward into the afterdeck, moving among the crew, releasing velcro and other holddown straps and floating the men and women by the door to Airlock Two. They closed off the afterdeck pressure hatch to the rest of the ship from the opposite side of the afterdeck, opened the hatch between the afterdeck and the airlock, and then—

The airlock hatches opened. Instantly the air in the airlock and the afterdeck exploded outward into vacuum. As their own bodies sprayed boiling blood and liquids from the violent decompression, the dead and dying men and women were flung by air rushing into vacuum away from the ship.

"Close deck hatch," Stavers instructed. Weinstein tapped the buttons and computer panels confirmed the proper operation of the hatch. "Okay. The fan systems will have carried traces of that gas through the ship. Let's open her up. *Everything* opens."

Every hatch and panel leading to vacuum yawned wide. Every last trace of air and gases vanished into space. Red lights played everywhere on the panel.

"Close her up," Stavers added. Weinstein worked the controls. They heard and felt dull thuds as *Gulliver* resealed itself. Hatch lights glowed green. "Pressure up, all air systems full functional," Stavers went on. Twenty minutes later *Gulliver*, sealed and working perfectly, had normal spacecraft atmosphere content and pressure.

Weinstein opened her faceplate. "There's no time to lose. The telemetry systems will have reported a massive failure aboard this ship, and they'll be sending people over to investigate."

"How long before you can fire the engines?" Stavers asked.

Weinstein moved forward to the control room, Stavers

directly behind her. "As soon as we get there. I'd already programmed the computers to respond to immediate countdown. We take our seats, kick in the autosequence, and go. I've got manual override on the propulsion system and the ship will adjust automatically with the thrusters to the new flight profile."

"I was going to ask you about that," Stavers said. "I've pretty well figured out what you planned to do and even how you'd do it, but you're the space jockey around here, not me."

"Let it hold until we're on our way." They eased into the flight deck, Weinstein took the commander's seat, Stavers the pilot seat to her right. Weinstein studied the control panels for several minutes, then nodded to herself. She lifted a safety cover, moved a lever forward and twisted it to the left, opened another panel, and pressed the control marked FULL SEQUENCE, AUTOCOUNT, AUTOFIRE.

She smiled at Stavers. "Twenty-eight seconds to go. Hang on to your seat, lover."

Far behind them *Gulliver* pressured up, groaning and heaving within its innards, turbines spinning, pressure lines trembling, and then without any more thunder than a distant muted roar, the engines ignited, a great plasma sheath erupted with violet plumes behind them, and *Gulliver* moved away from the Grissom station.

It was a sight the crew members of Grissom would never forget. In that spreading plasma sheath little flickers of fire danced and twinkled as the bodies of the *Gulliver* crew flew in spaceflame.

Chapter 29

Flying to Mars on an outward-from-the-sun swing of centrifugal force is a journey the duration of which is related directly to the cost of the ticket. *Gulliver's* computer was programmed originally for a "Hohmann Ellipse" orbit which slings the spacecraft on a long and tedious journey halfway around the sun. To answer the question of "how far is it between Earth and Mars" pinches reality in a painful fashion because the answer depends upon the relative positions of the two planets at any one time. If Mars is on one side of the sun from the Earth then it's a hell of a distance measured in a couple hundred million miles. If you use the celestial tape measure when the two planets are closest then the distance is thirty-five million miles. But you can't race for Mars at the closest distance because on the celestial merry-go-round Mars is farther than is Earth from the sun and Mars moves with slower speed. It's back to celestial duck-hunting with proper aiming lead for the hunter and the target.

Rebecca Weinstein was more than overly tired of all the mathematics of such planetary flight. To the vessel within which rode her race the greatest rockets of Earth were the clumsiest and most archaic of all possible machines; hand-carved metallic dugouts of questionable reliability and terrible performance. Yet Weinstein, with Stavers, remained imprisoned within the greatest possible speeds of which *Gulliver* was capable—all matters that Stavers had brought to her with almost harsh demands for answers.

"This trip is programmed for eight months," she told him. "That's the *original* trip. We're not going to spend eight months in this bilious clanking ark; we don't need to."

"From everything I know about launch geometry," he protested mildly, "the most efficient flight is from 220 to 300 days."

"I know that very well," she said with great patience. It was extraordinarily difficult for her not to talk *down* to a man with the incredible versatility of Doug Stavers, but his skills and even his brilliance in flight were with winged aircraft within an atmosphere. You didn't "fly" a spacecraft. You selected velocity, angle, timing and other intricate factors dictated by the celestial gods of gravity and positioning and relative velocities, all of which were dealt with by *her* ships as posing no more problem than an airplane turning left or right, but for humankind's ships these were towering and angry problems demanding constant attention and maximum effort.

"Look," she said with immense patience, "the most efficient trip calls for absolutely minimum use of fuel and maximum use of trajectory and planet gravity. But why are you so hung up on that? We're not after an efficient flight, Doug. We're after a wasteful, fuel-consuming trip that will cut the 271 days programmed for *Gulliver* down to less than a hundred."

"How? *Why?*"

"Because, first of all, *this is a one-way flight.*"

"Hot damn," he grinned. "The most obvious to see is the wart on the end of your own nose."

"Aptly put," she laughed with him. "You see it clearly, then."

"Sure. We don't need to arrive at Mars with enough fuel to deorbit and then, with our main engines, boost out of Martian orbit for the return trip, have enough fuel for trajectory changes, and then deboost into Earth orbit."

"Bingo," she sang, using an expression she knew she'd carry to the stars in the future. "So I've reprogrammed the computer to give us the fastest possible course to Mars, while leaving enough fuel to slow us down when we get there, and place us into a highly elliptical orbit."

"Which at perigee will be as close to Mars as possible," he went on, the obvious rushing to him now. "And at low point we'll be in the best position possible for a landing at Cydonia."

"Another bingo. And even then we can be as wasteful as we want with the fuel in the landing craft. We're not planning for taking off from Mars in that clunker. In short, we've got fuel up the gazoo to burn."

He nearly broke up with her response. "There are times, lady, when you floor me. A woman of the stars with bingo and gazoo for tech talk."

"It makes it much less painful."

"How long do you figure from here to Mars?"

"Ninety-one days on the nose. En route the computer will update constantly our position relative to Mars, the usual navigational garbage, and we may have a midcourse correction, but it won't be much of a Delta-V. When the engines cut off after the first burn we were right down the slot."

"The numbers?"

"Well, if we were using an aircraft LORAN it would tell us forty one point zero degrees north and nine point four degrees west. That pinpoints Cydonia."

Stavers drifted to a viewport to watch the curve of the earth growing more sharply defined. "I understand now how Borman and the others felt."

She drifted to his side and slid her arm through his, pulling him close. "I'll tell you this, my terrestrial friend," she said softly. "As many times as you see this sight, watching a world, yours or another, recede in the distance until it's only a marble, and then a glowing dot, the wonder, the incredible wonder, never goes away. For a race so barbaric as yours, your people still produce marvelous word pictures. What best fits this moment would *the music of the spheres*."

He nodded, and they drifted from the window to a large soft couch. Strips of velcro held them down as she moved within his arms.

"What do you do when you have three months of from here to there?" he asked her.

"What else, silly. You make love."

"Makes sense, too."

"But the best of all is that we're in zero gravity and you've never made love under these conditions."

"True."

"So I guess I'll have to educate you."

"Uh huh."

Having a flight-programming computer with a synthetic larynx was like having a third crewman aboard.

Ninety one days, three hours and fourteen minutes after propulsion cutoff, *Gulliver* deboosted into its stark elliptical orbit about Mars, and the engines fell silent as the spaceship swung in its wide circling rush about the planet. At its lowest point it was barely forty miles above the Martian surface.

Rebecca spoke torrents of words with her ship's complement on the planet in a language hopelessly beyond anything Stavers could comprehend. His feelings of wonder had abated during the three-month journey. Now, hearing this alien language—a language from deep space—he felt a growing sense of wonder again, an exultation that he would join this very same race. And there was so much more!

"We can modify you genetically," Rebecca told him in a quiet embrace after a long and slow session of making love. "We have those facilities aboard our ship. Even if your genome background lacks the preparation our people have, there's no reason why you can't live at least a thousand years."

"It sounds too real, too good, to be true," he said cautiously. "What the hell, Rebecca, why would your people bother to drag me along? I'm primal, remember?"

"God, yes," she said, squeezing him gently between the legs. "Damned good primal, too. But to answer your question, once the combination of you, your genetic makeup and the *arbatik* energize the ship, you'll have become a part of us. You'll *be* one of us."

His dreams were wild for weeks afterward . . .

* * *

The computer spoke in clipped phrases. They were in the main landing craft, resembling an oversized Apollo but with landing legs jutting out widely, thrusters about the ship, and three main engines beneath them. *Gulliver* was already on its way up along the elliptical orbit; they'd separated from the ship to deboost and dropped into a lower orbit, their highest point above Mars now only seventeen miles, and they kept their hands ready at the controls for an emergency situation while the computer ran through its program to bring them safely to the surface.

"*High gate coming up. Through high gate now with eight-three percent available. Prepare for repeat deboost and deceleration to two g load.*"

Engines fired immediately after the computer warning and they sagged in their couches; after three months in weightlessness the 2g load was punishment. "*Descent track nominal, trajectory nominal. We are in the keyhole slot for anticipated main engines burn. Manned crew suits will inflate for anti-g resistance.*" At those words their suit bladders squeezed hard against their legs and lower torso to prevent blood from pooling in their lower extremities.

The ship fell like a great stone, balanced by a small drogue parachute whipping in the thin wisps of atmosphere.

"*Main engines ignition in fifteen seconds. Manned crew take brace positions. Ignition in ten seconds. Nine, eight, seven . . .*"

SMASH! Cruel deceleration; the computer ignored their personal distress. "*Three engines ignition, full chamber pressure, nine nine point eight seven nominal in the burn. Radar ranging functioning properly. We are GO for continued descent. We are approaching low gate entry. All systems GO.*"

"Hurry up and get it over with, you son of a bitch!" Stavers cursed the computer.

"*Low gate, low gate. Beginning pitchover from oblique trajectory. Curve is GO, radar ranging tracking. We have an acceptable landing surface. Engine operation nominal. Coming up through low gate to vertical descent. Decelerating. Raising dust. Seven seconds, six, five, four, prepare for stop, two, one, impac—"*

CRUNCH!

"Engine cutoff. Pressures nominal. Bio systems fully functional. Congratulations, congratulations, congratu—"

Rebecca reached out to kill the computer voice system.

"Jesus Christ," Stavers said in an awed whisper, "we made it. We *really* did it!"

He raised himself from his couch to look through the viewport. The face of Cydonia rose huge in the near distance.

Massive.

Unfriendly.

Alien.

Between the face mountain and their ship he saw a trail of dust moving towards them. He knew his words would sound ridiculous but he couldn't help himself.

"Here comes daddy," he said.

Chapter 30

Glorious *glorious, GLORIOUS!*

He felt the power surging through him. Incredible energy beyond anything he had ever known, anything he had ever *imagined.* Power surged within him with the fury of a blazing star. His mind, his body, his very essence of being had become a conduit for the energy that permeated all the universe. It was the energy of space-time and massive gravitational warps, the energy streaming at speeds incomprehensibly faster than light to bind even the mighty quasars in their positioning of one to the other.

They had explained that to him. As best they could, anyway, for not even all of Doug Stavers' knowledge could prepare him for the depths of understanding necessary to *know* the meaning of interstellar energy streams. Karlden Tai—Dr. Rebecca Weinstein's persona had been banished forever—knew him best and also understood how Stavers' thinking and perception worked. As best she could she described to him the almost-magical energy that enabled their huge vessel to *transfer*—not simply to travel—in hours, distances measured in thousands of light years.

They walked through the energy drive system of the huge vessel that had been their home for thousands of years. He found it beyond his grasp to comprehend a ship several miles in length and almost as large from side to side and from top to bottom. "Let the comprehension wait," Karlden Tai told him. "That comes with time. It's much more important for you to understand how the drive functions. You're going to be an integral part of it."

He nodded. He also noticed that the other members of this race met him in regal and warm fashion, an unspoken gratitude that he would be able to function as had the long-departed Wolfram. He *knew* he was critical, he knew he was actually life-giving, to this almost-inconceivable machine. That strange, even mysterious combination of genetic coding and the *arbatik* was a combination that tapped what Karlden Tai called the *masstime stream*.

"But it's something you need almost three brains to visualize," she told him. "We can all envisage a stream, whether it's liquid or a plasma jet or a laser beam. It's a stream of quanta or wave energy; which one doesn't matter. If that stream has enormous gravity, it folds space all about the stream into itself. It changes the fabric of space through its mass, which means it also warps, or bends, time, and the resistance you'd expect to encounter in, well, call it highspeed flight, simply isn't there."

"It sounds as if you're driving a wedge before you so that the ship moves into a vacuum—"

"But a vacuum of *everything*," she stressed, breaking in. "That's what you've got to grasp. A vacuum of particles down to the smallest subatomic muon or charmed particle. A vacuum of anything molecular, of course. But also a vacuum, a total absence, of space and time. So you don't have any mass and *any* kind of limitation no longer exists."

"Wait a moment," he said, standing before machinery that distorted his vision. Machinery that seemed to have no actual shape, that shimmered and pulsed constantly, glowing from within. A monster waiting to be brought to full life from a slumber of two thousand years. "Let all that go for a moment. How do you tie into what you call this interstellar stream? How do you use it to get from here to there?"

She smiled. "You've never heard of *chrentsua*, of course."

"Of course," he said drily. "What the hell is that?"

"It's our word for what your science calls a quasar."

"That's quasi-stellar. It's hardly new to us," he added.

"*Chrentsua* is a particular category of pulsar. In English the best translation would be a Pulsar Z, only your science hasn't given it that name yet. Back in 1989, not so long ago, of course, your astronomers discovered the first of these ever known to your world. A quasar more than eighteen billion light years from your sun. Do you remember that?"

He nodded. "Yes; yes, I do. I, yeah, they said it was a single star that generated more energy, more light, from just this *one* star, than the light and energy from a thousand galaxies, each galaxy made up of more than a hundred billion stars."

"You can't conceive of those numbers," she said quickly, "and neither can I. But we're talking about a single stellar object more than eight billion miles—your miles—in diameter. However, you don't need to understand all the numbers. It's important, however, that you understand such quasars of this magnitude are the waypoints of the universe."

He was actually getting ahead of her explanation. "If I read you right, Rebecca—damnit, sorry about the name—if I read you right, these quasars are like energy stations located throughout the universe, like power transformers."

"Very, very crude," she said with faint praise, "but accurate enough." She studied him carefully, then went on.

"You understand that the more you're at ease with this entire system the more efficiently you'll be able to function in providing the power required for our vessel?"

He nodded. "Machinery is machinery," he said, sincere in his statement. "It's all complicated until you *know* it. Then it becomes second-nature to function *with* the machinery."

"Excellent! Now, the most critical aspect of all this is that every *chrentsua* has its own energy signature—"

"In the band of the usual spectrum?"

"No. Or, only partially. The power of one of these quasars in some ways is even greater than a black hole.

They function differently. That's a crude yardstick, but it's real."

"Okay. Go on about the energy signature."

"It matches the combination of your genetic structure, combined with the *arbatik*. You and the *arbatik* for a transceiver. You tune in to the energy stream of the *chrentsua*—that's something the computers will do, of course—and, when you're in the precise position for our drive system *also* to become part of the, well, of the system, then the energy flows to you, Stavers and *arbatik*, and *through* you to our drive."

He thought for several moments. "Roughly, it's like a microwave transceiver-transformer."

"Roughly, yes." She took his arm and they started down a long curving corridor, plastimetal yielding beneath their feet as might a luxurious carpet. "We're going to the observation rotunda first, so you can see from there the view we'll have among the stars. Then we'll go to the propulsion system. I want you to look, touch, *feel* the system, stand within it. Do you notice, even as we get closer to the drive, that you can actually *feel* the energy flowing through you?"

"God, yes," he said, his sense of exultation growing slowly. "It's . . . I never felt anything like it. I could move a mountain, wrestle with a damned dinosaur, I could—" Words failed him and she laughed. She squeezed his hand. "It gets much, much better," she promised him. "Wolfram often said you didn't feel you had the power of the gods; you *were* a god."

She smiled at the entrance to the observation deck. "I promise you, Doug, a feeling and an actuality of *power* beyond even your wildest dreams."

She led him into the luxurious trappings of the great observation rotunda, strewn carefully with deep, welcoming softness. He stood before the great bulbous dome of a material absolutely transparent but which was immensely stronger than any metal ever developed on his own world. The view was sensational, and he recalled their assurance that the observation material was not only so strong, but also provided full protection against the unfiltered ultraviolet radiation of a smaller, more distant sun than he'd known all his life. He looked out across the boulder—strewn surface of Mars, orange and dusty, cratered in the distance, the sand billions of years ancient, lying beneath an atmosphere only a faint whisper of Earth. Yet this ghostly remnant of an air ocean was alive in its own phantom sort of way. Looking beyond the mile-long face of Cydonia he spied a tall and sinuous dust devil dancing along the Martian boulders and sand dunes. He shook his head; this was only a taste of what was to come on worlds he couldn't yet imagine.

Again she took his hand. "The drive room. I've been asked to have you study the equipment. As I said before, not simply to understand, but to *feel.*"

"Let's do it," he said, revealing his own eagerness.

He walked around the drive that towered a hundred feet over his head, multilayered and multileveled and that seemed to extend outward in constantly shifting angles. He climbed transparent steps to the midlevel of the drive. "We go in here," Karlden Tai said, motioning him to follow her. Now they moved through an incredible structure of layered transmitters, glowing areas his eyes failed to penetrate, what appeared to be enormous cabled columns, all of it intertwined and part of a single system.

They stopped before a space hollowed out within what looked like ice, or some form of clear plastic, its exterior studded with glowing ovals. "Those are the energy transfer points," she explained. "You and the *arbatik*, in this space, bring us fully to life. Notice that the space is perfect for your body."

"It sure seems to be."

"The computers have already taken every measurement of you they need," she explained. "You'll fit in here with no physical discomfort—"

"What about hookups?" he asked warily. He had a sudden vision of being laced with wires and needles.

"None," she said to reassure him.

"None?"

"Doug, we don't need *wires* to carry this level of

energy. Any wire made would melt instantly, be turned to gas."

"Then how do you contain or channel the energy?"

"Um, think of it as an enormous magnetic field, a flux that *guides* the energy. Just like," she brought up memory, "the magnetic field bottles your people are using for fusion energy research."

He nodded. "Got it."

"We need to confirm the measurements and sizing, Doug. Your clothes. Remove them, please."

"*All* of them?"

"Buck naked, lover."

He grinned. "Jewelry also?"

"Everything. Then just ease into the space, feel it, make sure you're comfortable. But I warn you, you're going to sense just the gentle edges of the energy you can control. It's, well, like a super cocktail. It's wild, marvelous—"

"I get the idea," he said, cutting her off. Moments later he was stripped to his skin. He moved into the body space waiting for him. He expected it to be cold, or at least cool, but learned quickly the material, whatever it was, matched his own body temperature.

And she was right. He felt a tingling about, on, *through* him, as if the first strikes of thunderbolts had just reached his skin. A feeling of power—he could be Thor of Asgard. He could be anything, anyone!

"Relax where you are, Doug. We're going to close the system and test the energy field flow. Any questions?"

"If it gets better than this, I can't wait," he said, grinning broadly at her, already forgetting her, even forgetting thinking, the urge to sense and feel and be part of this enormous energy, a hunger exploding within him.

A mist formed before him, within seconds solidified so that he was now in dead center of the block of material, which in turn was in dead center of the great propulsion system.

Energy—

Glorious, *glorious*, *GLORIOUS!*

* * *

Bitch!

He railed with the overpowering urge to *kill*.

Rotten, scummy, filthy fucking bitch!

He railed at himself with a near-insane fury. *I could have killed her! I could have, I should have skinned her alive! I should have torn out her heart and eaten it myself, I—*

His thoughts stuttered like a dying truck on a badly rutted road, bumping and slamming up and down and sideways and going nowhere.

"*Bitch!*" he shouted. "*Rotten, conniving filthy whore—*"

The thoughts shouted thunderlike in his head. His lips didn't move. The only sounds he created came from within his mind and remained there, echoing and crashing off the inner walls of his own thoughts. He cursed himself for his myopia, for his stupidity, for *trusting* this woman who'd led him about like a child with a ring through his nose. How the hell had she pulled it off? He had the *real* power, the aura, the overwhelming psyche; *he* had the energy to drive a million-ton vessel at a thousand times the speed of light, and this woman, this Weinstein-Tai bitch and her people—

"Fuck all of you!" he howled. His words punched back at him, swirling around and around, and he lapsed into a bottomless bowl of dejection, for he *knew* that his thick steely exterior had been no more than dust to Rebecca, to this woman Tai, that he had been controlled with magnificent psychology—

A tone sounded in his head, gentle, warm; a notice of entry, and then her voice, clear and woman-husky as well, crisp and yet musical, through pulsing coils of soft and sensate energy, he heard that voice, and as he did so *they* manipulated his own mind so that *she was there before him*, a mental hologram realer than life.

Her voice whispered in his mind.

Hello, lover.

She paused to let her words and presence sink in.

This is hello and goodbye, Doug.

She was so real, so . . . *so human*! But, *no! Alien; she's alien! Much more than human.*

He struggled to move. So foolish; he couldn't even do that. Not a muscle twitched.

He couldn't even blink his eyes.

And he wasn't breathing. He had no feeling of respiration, yet he breathed. He could not move, yet trillions of movements functioned within his body.

I don't know how much you have determined by now, Doug. But you're intelligent. More than that, you're cunning, and you figure things out quickly. But to be certain, because this is the only time I will ever speak to you, because this is the last time you will ever hear the voice of anyone, we wanted you to be certain you know how well you will serve us.

You are an intelligent dinosaur. A creature frozen in the violent past of a planet but with an intelligent mind. An incredible, inexplicable quirk of nature. A savage beast capable of warmth, love, devotion, fealty, sympathy, dedication, honesty, compassion. A beast capable of such emotions, but you chose to put those aside.

Animals that kill for pleasure when they have the choice of not doing so are throwbacks. The universe has no use for them, except where and how they may serve others. We do not harm others. We do others no injury. We kill only for survival and when there is no other choice. We protect our enemies whenever and wherever possible. This is madness to you. We know that, but it is you who truly are mad, your mind so twisted you exceed the hatred and ferocity of any mindless beast I have ever encountered.

Yet, within this unbridled savagery and joy of pain of others, nature has created you as a rare, rare mutation. Your genetic code, by the miracle and wonder of chance, matches the arbatik connected to your heart. They both beat within your chest. And because this is so, we fling ourselves with casual energy through all of space and we prepare to enter new dimensions and realities.

We do this now because of you, and in our strange and wonderful measure of the ironic, we both despise what you are, and are yet grateful for what you have become and what you do for us now.

You power this vessel.

You will live for thousands of years, Doug Stavers. The computers and our medical science will feed you energy, keep your systems and organs functioning. But you will not move. Electrical energy will keep your muscles fit and trim. Nutrients will keep you well. Your eyes will see but they will not move. You will never again hear a voice. You will never again speak.

Above all, Doug, you will remain sane. We will not permit you to crawl back into the depths of your primitive mind and escape through your own induced insanity. We are capable enough to prevent that exit. You will be with us, in your own terms, forever.

Know, again, we are grateful to you.

Know, also, that we give you life far beyond what your own feeble physiology could ever grant to you. You have become the stuff of dreams of your race, the first man to live for thousands of years.

When you last hear my voice you will have all that time to think. To meditate. To learn from your own self. No one knows what you will or may find. Perhaps you will find God.

Or you may become God in a universe where you alone live.

You are to be tested as never before. We will not give you pain, but we know you will inflict it upon yourself. You will never know hunger, but you will hunger to end what you are.

So be it. You are both Worshipper and God. You are all the good and especially the evil that permeates your world.

But you will never again hurt another living thing.

Goodbye, forever.

HE'S OPINIONATED

HE'S DYNAMIC

HE'S LARGER THAN LIFE

MARTIN CAIDIN

Martin Caidin is a bestselling novelist, pilot *extraordinaire,* and expert on America's space program. *He's also a prophet of technological change.* His ability to predict future trends verges on the psychic, as when he wrote *Cyborg* (the novel which became "The Six Million Dollar Man") and *Marooned* (which precipitated the American-Soviet Apollo-Soyuz linkup mission). His tense, action-filled stories are based on personal experience in fields such as astronautics, aviation, oceanography and the military.

Caidin's characters also know their stuff. And they take on real life, because they're based on real people. Martin Caidin spent a stint as a merchant seaman in Europe and Africa, worked for Air Force Intelligence in the U.S. and Asia, and has flown his own planes to many parts of the world. His adventures can be yours in these novels from Baen Books.

— — — — — — — — — — — — — — —

EXIT EARTH—Just as the US and the USSR have finally settled their differences, American scientists discover that the solar system is about to pass through a cloud of cosmic dust that will incite the Sun to a paroxysm of fury. All will die. There can be no escape—except, possibly, for a very few. *This is their story.* 656 pp. • 65630-9 • $4.50 ______

KILLER STATION—Earth's first space station *Pleiades* is a scientific boon—until one brief moment of sabotage changes it into a terrible Sword of Damocles. 55996-6 • 384 pp. • $3.50 ______

THE MESSIAH STONE—"An unusual thriller . . . not only in subject matter, but in the fact that the author claims that the basic idea behind the book is real! [THE MESSIAH STONE] concerns the possession of a stone; the person who controls the stone rules the world. The last such person is rumored to be Adolf Hitler. . . . Harrowing adventure and nonstop action."—*Science Fiction Review*. 65562-0 • 416 pp. • $3.95 ______

ZOBOA—It started with the hijacking of four atomic bombs, and ended with the Space Shuttle atop a pillar of fire. . . . "From the marvelous, cinematic opening pages, Caidin sweeps the reader along in a raucous, exciting thriller."—*Publishers Weekly* 65588-4 • 448 pp. • $3.50 ______

To order these Baen Books, check each title selected and return with a check or money order for the combined cover price. Send to Baen Books, 260 Fifth Avenue, New York, N.Y. 10001.

Distributed by Simon & Schuster
1230 Avenue of the Americas • New York, N.Y. 10020